"Full of sexy vampires, stro...

—*Fresh Fiction*

"The chemistry is electric . . . Kate Baxter has done her job, and masterfully." —*San Francisco Book Reviews*

"A jackpot read for vampire lovers who like sizzle . . . brimming with heat!" —*Romance Junkies*

"Mikhail and Claire's love story ha[s] that combination of romance, steam, and suspense."

—*Book-a-holics Anonymous*

"If you like the Black Dagger Brotherhood . . . pick up *The Last True Vampire*, you won't be disappointed."

—*Parajunkee Reviews*

"Kate Baxter has done a remarkable job of building this paranormal world." —*Scandalous Book Reviews*

ALSO BY KATE BAXTER

The Last True Vampire

The Warrior Vampire

The Dark Vampire

THE UNTAMED VAMPIRE

KATE BAXTER

St. Martin's Paperbacks

This is a work of fiction. All of the characters, organizations, and events portrayed in this novel are either products of the author's imagination or are used fictitiously.

THE UNTAMED VAMPIRE

For information address St. Martin's Press, 175 Fifth Avenue, New York, NY 10010.

ISBN: 978-1-250-12539-2

Our books may be purchased in bulk for promotional, educational, or business use. Please contact your local bookseller or the Macmillan Corporate and Premium Sales Department at 1-800-221-7945, ext. 5442, or by e-mail at MacmillanSpecialMarkets@macmillan.com.

Printed in the United States of America

St. Martin's Paperbacks edition / May 2017

St. Martin's Paperbacks are published by St. Martin's Press, 175 Fifth Avenue, New York, NY 10010.

10 9 8 7 6 5 4 3 2 1

ACKNOWLEDGMENTS

Thanks so much to the readers for continuing on this wild ride with me! You guys are why I do this!

Thanks also to my awesome agent, Natanya Wheeler, who is my ultimate cheerleader, and my amazing editor, Monique Patterson, for continuing to make me a better writer with every book/novella/story I write. Huge thanks as well to everyone at NYLA and Alexandra Sehulster. I so appreciate everything you guys do for me! I want to give a shout-out as well to the killer copy editors, marketing team, and amazing cover artists at SMP. You're the best book family and I'm so happy to be a part of it!

Believe it or not, I owe this book to a couple of firefighters. Kevin Courtney and Juan Bonilla, thank you for sitting in a hotel room with me in Sun Valley, cell phones in hand, as you eagerly researched Viking culture, provided me with backstory, and even a fair amount of conflict. Kevin, these Viking werewolves are all you—beards and all!

As always, I take full credit for any and all mistakes. With a world this vast, I'm bound to slip up, but luckily I'm surrounded by people who keep me on my toes. To anyone I might have missed in my ramblings, you know who you are and what you mean to me!

CHAPTER
1

"I want to see Siobhan."

Chelle Daly waited as Mikhail Aristov, the vampire king, studied her. The unnerving quiet, the penetrating intensity of his cool blue gaze sent a ripple over her skin. Mikhail was powerful. But did his power rival hers? That was the point of today's meeting. Chelle needed answers and the first step to getting them was a face-to-face with a dhampir she'd been forbidden to visit. It had been months since Chelle had seen Siobhan and the female had something she needed.

"Why?"

The one word hung in the air. No inflection gave away Mikhail's mood. *Figures.* He loved to keep people guessing. Chelle was no exception. In fact, he kept her more in the dark than most. Chelle wasn't a member of Mikhail's coven. She wasn't connected to the Collective. The memories of vampires long since dead didn't float around in her noggin like they did Mikhail's. Chelle was different. Other. Made a vampire through magic and not by the bite and blood of another vampire. Chelle was a dangerous variable and Mikhail knew it.

"She has something I want." Giving Mikhail too much information was sure to end with him shutting Chelle down completely. But not giving him enough would cause him to be suspicious. It rubbed Chelle the wrong way that she had to ask for permission at all. The words *You're not my dad!* came to mind and Chelle swallowed down a snort.

"What?"

Apparently Mikhail was only capable of uttering monosyllabic words today.

"A key."

He leaned back in his chair and regarded her. "To what?"

Jeez Louise! One more clipped response from him and she was going to tear her hair out. "Nothing." As far as Chelle was concerned, Mikhail was on a need-to-know basis. "It's just a useless relic. But I stole it and gave it to her for safekeeping. I want it back."

Mikhail's gaze sparked with silver and his eyes narrowed. "A key that unlocks nothing? Why do you want it, then?"

That silver stare might have been intimidating to some, but Chelle wasn't fazed. She flashed him a feral grin. "Sentimental value."

Mikhail's lips thinned.

Chelle let out a sigh. "Look, it seriously doesn't even unlock anything. It's completely useless." That part wasn't exactly a lie. The relic was one part of three. Without the other two pieces, the key was essentially useless. "I'd think you'd want me to get whatever relics I could out from under her." Using Mikhail's rivalry with Siobhan might be dirty pool, but Chelle was grasping at straws at this point. The vampire king's expression remained inscrutable. Her voice dropped a couple of decibels. "You can't keep me a secret forever, Mikhail."

Mikhail looked away. Finally an emotional response from the stoic vampire. His guilt pricked her skin. He'd kept her a virtual prisoner for months. He'd forced her into a state of solitude so unbearable that Chelle had accidentally turned a dhampir with her overzealous bite. Lucas was the only member of her dysfunctional little coven and she was grateful for his company. Without him, she would have gone mad a long damned time ago.

"Siobhan has been asking about you." The admission took Chelle aback. "For a few weeks now. She has the chest."

Set's Chest. That fucking box was the very magical relic that'd made Chelle a vampire. A power-hungry panther shifter had shoved her inside, and when Chelle emerged, she'd been changed. The memory of her time in that dank, dark basement twisted her stomach into knots. She could still smell the moist earth, the mildew. Could still feel the cloying touch of magic as it crawled over her skin. A chill slithered down her spine. She'd known her twin, Ronan, had given Siobhan the chest after they'd recovered it from the shifter. She'd failed to consider the dhampir would connect the chest to Chelle's continued absence.

"I have no loyalty to Siobhan," she told Mikhail. "Not anymore."

She might have been a member of Siobhan's coven at one point, but her allegiance ended the day Chelle became a vampire. She was the mistress of her own coven now—small as it may be—and her loyalty was to Lucas.

"I'm not concerned about your loyalty." Mikhail was careful to mask his emotions, as well as his thoughts.

Chelle couldn't help but wonder how much he knew about her unusual powers to take such precautions. "I'm concerned about Siobhan's agenda."

Siobhan desired one thing above all others: to be independent of the vampires. And that would *never* happen. Dhampirs needed vampires to exist. No matter how much Siobhan wanted it otherwise.

"A magic coffin isn't going to give Siobhan what she wants."

Mikhail gave Chelle a dubious glance. "No? You're separate from the Collective, therefore separate from every other vampire and dhampir in existence. How can that not be attractive to Siobhan?"

Mikhail had a point. Damn. Siobhan might not even realize it yet, but that damned coffin might just be the answer to her prayers.

"I'm not separate from Lucas," Chelle pointed out.

Mikhail gave a swipe of his hand as though that little tidbit of information were inconsequential. "Ronan thinks the chest is safe in her care. I'm not so sure."

Of course Ronan would. Chelle couldn't help but roll her eyes. "I'm not as trusting as Ronan," Chelle said. "But I do know the last thing Siobhan will do is climb inside the chest to see what it does."

Mikhail cocked a brow. "What about after she sees you?"

"Siobhan hates vampires," Chelle replied. "*All* vampires. She'd die before she'd allow herself to be turned. By anyone or anything."

Mikhail rested his elbows on the armrest of his chair and steepled his fingers in front of him. "You've been incredibly cooperative considering your situation. You've been patient despite your restless nature. Thank you for that."

Chelle hiked a shoulder. "I haven't been *that* well behaved." She'd turned Lucas after all. And no one needed to know about her secret late-evening Starbucks runs. She might've agreed to a temporary life of captivity, but she'd never agreed to go without caramel macchiatos.

A corner of Mikhail's mouth hitched in a half smile. "Have you met you?"

When the haughty king let his guard down he could actually be quite charming. She supposed that considering her track record before her turning, Chelle had been pretty damned well behaved lately. "How are Claire and the baby?"

Mikhail's mate had given birth to their son about a month ago. Mikhail had kept close to home during that time, not letting either one of them out of his sight. Chelle couldn't blame him. Not as long as the Sortiari and their lapdogs still ran rampant across the city. The secret society had waged war against the vampires centuries ago, nearly eradicating the race. Over the past year, they'd abandoned their cause, but the rumor was that their berserker foot soldiers hadn't gotten the memo. Either way, Mikhail wasn't taking any chances.

"They're well." His bright smile conveyed every ounce of love he felt for his mate and son. "Both are healthy and happy."

"That's good." A twinge of emotion tugged at Chelle's chest. Would she ever know that sort of love? Would her soul ever be tethered and returned to her? "I'm glad to hear it."

Mikhail's gaze burned through her and a few quiet moments passed. Chelle tried not to squirm, but damn, the male had a way of making someone feel downright uncomfortable in their own skin.

"Siobhan is a variable I can't afford to turn my back on, but neither do I have the time to keep an eye on her." Mikhail swiveled in his chair and his brow furrowed in thought. "Go see her. Get whatever relic it is you want. Gauge her mood and the climate of her coven. But Chelle"—a sizzle of power sparked the air—"don't make me regret the decision to cut your strings."

The prospect of getting her hands on the relic far outweighed her annoyance at being treated like a child who'd been given permission to cross the street alone for the first time. She gave Mikhail what she hoped was a reassuring smile. Besides, it's not like he wasn't getting anything out of the deal. In so many words, he'd requested that Chelle spy on Siobhan for him. A bold request considering she'd been a loyal member of Siobhan's coven for over a century. Ronan's alliances had shifted easily enough; perhaps Mikhail assumed that Chelle's would as well.

Mikhail wasn't far off in his assumptions. In truth, Chelle was on only one side: her own.

"I'll get a read on her." What Mikhail didn't know was that Siobhan's thoughts would be bare to Chelle if she wasn't careful. Chelle's powers were unlike those of any of the vampires in Mikhail's coven. The scope of her abilities frightened Chelle. Distracted her focus. And drove her to find answers to the mysteries of her newfound vampiric existence. Siobhan was formidable, but the dhampir's strength was nothing compared to Chelle's. "If she's up to anything, I'll let you know."

Mikhail smiled, showing the tips of his dual sets of fangs. "Good."

Hopefully her visit with Siobhan would prove to be good for Chelle, too.

"Gunnar, we need to talk."

Gunnar Falk looked up to find his second standing in the doorway to his office. Aren's stern countenance and the set of his jaw was a clear indicator that whatever Aren was about to tell him, Gunnar wasn't going to like it. No surprise. With the reemergence of the vampire race, the supernatural political climate was rapidly changing. And Los Angeles—a mere thirty minutes from their compound—had become the epicenter for all of it.

"What is it?" As the Alpha of the Forkbeard pack, Gunnar dealt with petty squabbles and disagreements all the time. Werewolves were volatile by nature. Living in close quarters didn't do anything to tame that. The pack functioned more like a monarchy, with Gunnar playing judge, jury, and executioner to the petitioners who laid their grievances at his feet.

Aren walked into the office and closed the door behind him. He took a seat opposite Gunnar and fixed him with a serious stare. Gunnar massaged his temple, already feeling the onset of a tension headache. *What is it now?*

"Rumors are beginning to circulate about an uprising."

In the three hundred years he'd been Alpha, Gunnar had yet to be challenged by a member of the pack. One brow arched curiously as he regarded Aren. "Who?" In the recess of his psyche, a low, territorial growl resonated. Any male who sought to challenge him would meet a swift end.

Aren's brow furrowed. "No. It's not within the pack. Ian Gregor is planning a coup against the Sortiari."

Gunnar settled back in his chair as he regarded Aren. The berserker warlord's infamy spanned continents and centuries. He'd been the Sortiari's right hand for as long as Gunnar could remember. The berserkers' history with the guardians of fate was a tangled mess of treachery and dysfunction. It served to reason that Gregor would turn on the ones who held his leash eventually. In truth, Gunnar was surprised it hadn't happened sooner.

"The berserkers' quarrels with the Sortiari are none of our concern," he replied after a long moment. "It's not pack business."

Aren's lips thinned. "Don't be so sure."

Gunnar's wolf scratched at the back of his psyche, agitated. With the full moon only a couple of weeks away, that animal part of his nature had been quiet while the moon was on the wane. But now that the lunar cycle brought the waxing moon, the wolf became restless, anxious to be let out to play. And something about Aren's demeanor agitated the animal.

Aren's dark brows came down sharply over his light golden eyes. Gunnar scrubbed a hand over his shaved head and blew out a breath. Apparently his wolf wasn't the only one on edge. "It might not be pack business now," Aren began. "But how long do you think we'll be able to stay out of it?"

Gunnar pushed out his chair and rounded the desk. His wolf wanted to pace and Gunnar shared in the animal's restlessness. His muscles were taut and twitched with every step. They needed the full moon and to be free to run and hunt. Over the next fourteen days, that need would only intensify.

"As long as I can manage." Gunnar fixed Aren with a stern expression. "The last thing I want is to incur the wrath of either Gregor or the Sortiari."

The Sortiari were as old as recorded time. A secret society that infiltrated every aspect of civilization, the self-proclaimed guardians of fate took it upon themselves to guide the course of history as they saw fit. Two hundred years ago, they'd attempted to eradicate the vampire race. As evidenced by the race's resurgence, that particular directive hadn't gone as planned. Some considered it a sign that their power and influence had begun to flag. Still, Gunnar had no intention of drawing their attention.

"Why not strike while they're weak?" Aren shrugged a casual shoulder. For a moment Gunnar remembered his friend as he'd been centuries ago: a warrior clad in leather and fur. Unapologetic. Fierce. Viking. A feral grin lit his sharp features. "And reap the spoils of war."

Gunnar let out a snort. Modern warfare was a far cry from the time and world he'd been a warrior in. "What spoils do you think we'll reap?"

Aren's eyes flashed with a golden light as his wolf rose to the surface of his psyche. "Power for starters."

Aren was an ambitious fool if he thought it would be so easy. "What do you think, Aren? That Ian Gregor would simply bite the hand that feeds him and walk away?"

"I think Gregor is interested in vengeance and little else."

It was true that vengeance motivated every move that Gregor made, but Gunnar wasn't convinced. "If Gregor manages to depose Trenton McAlister, may the gods help us all."

A growl rumbled in Aren's chest. "You overestimate the berserker."

Gunnar fixed Aren with an icy stare and held it until the male was forced to look away. "And you underestimate him."

Aren shifted in his seat, slumping down. He knew better than to be at eye level with his Alpha. "The Highlanders are hotheaded and rash. There's no way they could run McAlister's empire. It was our legends that gave those beasts a name. All they're good for is fighting."

It was true that the Norse legends had given a name to the Highland beasts: berserkers. And Aren was right that their talent lay in violence and little else. Still, it would be stupid to discount Gregor's calculating mind. The male was much smarter than anyone—Trenton McAlister included—gave him credit for.

"What do you suggest, Aren? Side with the berserkers to overthrow the Sortiari and then turn on them as well?"

Aren smiled and his gaze shone with bloodlust. "Why not?" The male didn't lack for ambition, that much was certain. "Think of it, Gunnar. You'd be the most powerful male in the country. Hell, the world. The legacy of Sweyn Forkbeard would live on in a new kingdom and you would be its king."

Grandiose plans to be sure. Gunnar's great-great-uncle, Sweyn Forkbeard, had indeed been a king worthy of fear and respect. He'd usurped his own father's throne and ruled Sweden with an iron fist for almost thirty-three years before his death.

"The king of Pasadena?" Gunnar asked with a sardonic chuckle. "Or better yet, high king of California? I think the local governments would have something to say about that."

Aren brushed the quip aside. "You know what I mean. We're not subject to the laws of mankind. There would be no supernatural power in the country that would rival yours. Especially if you managed to knock McAlister off his metaphorical throne. The pack's supremacy would never be called into question."

Gunnar leveled his gaze. "It isn't now."

The wolf growled in Gunnar's psyche and the sound echoed in his chest. Aren's suggestion that his power would be called into question even now further stirred his annoyance.

"There's no need for that sort of reaction." Aren relaxed his posture and let his gaze drop once again. "I'm only saying you should consider the possibilities."

Gunnar stroked his fingers along his bearded jaw. "With the berserkers and Sortiari engaged in battle, the vampires will have a prime opportunity to come into power."

It was rumored that their numbers were still small but that didn't mean their population wouldn't quickly grow. Gunnar didn't admit to know much about the vampire race, but like werewolves, a bite was all it took to make one. A few vampires could easily become a few hundred in a single lunar cycle.

"Do you really think Gregor doesn't have his sights set on them as well?" Aren met Gunnar's gaze for the barest moment to drive his point home. "If he can manage it, he'll take out all of his enemies in one fell swoop."

On that they could agree. There was no way, after centuries of strife, Gregor wouldn't finish what he'd started and wipe every vampire—and dhampir—from the face of the earth. "None of this matters." Gunnar rounded his desk and settled into his chair. "All of this is nothing but conjecture."

"Possibly." Aren moved to stand but waited for a nod of permission from Gunnar. Only with his consent could a member of the pack stand taller than the Alpha. "But every rumor is founded in truth."

Could be. Gunnar wouldn't discount what Aren had told him today, but neither would he jump to action or side with any party. Gunnar's only responsibility was to serve the best interests of the pack. So far, Aren had told him nothing to convince him that taking sides in a centuries-long war would benefit the Forkbeard pack in any way.

"Keep your ear to the ground," Gunnar said. "And notify me if there are any more rumblings of uprising on the wind."

Aren gave a sharp nod of his head and said, "Of course," before taking his leave.

Gunnar let out a slow breath and relaxed back into his chair. His wolf continued to fret just under the surface of his psyche, disrupting Gunnar's thoughts. The animal was on edge. Antsy. It didn't bode well for what was to come.

Change was on the wind and Gunnar feared it wouldn't be for the better.

CHAPTER
2

"Siobhan will see you now."

One thing was certain, Siobhan's coven had become more formal since Chelle belonged to it. She followed Carrig, Siobhan's most trusted confidant and protector, through the ruins of the dilapidated building that served as the coven's home. Security seemed to be more of a concern than it had been in the past, with dhampirs standing guard at various points throughout the building, most of them armed in one fashion or another. Had the coven's numbers grown? Chelle certainly couldn't remember there being so many dhampirs in Siobhan's fold, even though hers had already been the largest coven in the city.

It was possible another coven had merged with Siobhan's. Los Angeles was home to thirteen dhampir covens. It served to reason that with the vampire race's rebirth, there would be those who would side with Siobhan in seeing that rebirth as a threat.

She's turned . . .

Two sets of fangs. The better to tear out the throats of her prey.

Dangerous.

She doesn't smell like the other vampires. Not like Ronan at all. What is she?

Chelle turned her head as she caught wind of that last thought and her gaze met that of a dhampir thirty or so feet away who studied her with intense curiosity. The female's dark brown gaze locked with Chelle's and her lips curled into a wan smile. That the dhampir recognized the difference in Chelle's scent piqued her curiosity. She committed the female's face to memory. One to keep an eye on for sure . . .

Chelle turned forward and kept her gaze focused straight ahead as she did her best to block out the thoughts of the dhampirs who didn't know any better than to project them right at her. Her skin pricked as their curious gazes followed her, the scent of their fear both repelled her and ignited her thirst. Chelle was a predator and they were her prey. She swallowed against the dry fire in her throat and focused instead on the sound of the thick soles of her boots as they made contact with the cracked industrial flooring.

It wouldn't do to lose control on her first official outing. Especially when there was so much at stake.

Siobhan looked very much like a queen holding court, perched atop an elaborate chair on a high dais. She waited for Chelle to approach, a pleasant but not altogether friendly expression affixed to her beautiful face. Her emerald-green gaze narrowed as Chelle came to a halt a few feet away. A hiss issued from between Siobhan's teeth.

"Vampire."

The one word was spoken with open hostility and disgust. Chelle bristled and a warning growl gathered in her chest. One dark brow arched over Siobhan's eye, a silent challenge, daring Chelle to become hostile.

Chill out, Chelle. Play her game, get what you need and GTFO.

She'd never minded playing to Siobhan's ego in the past. But now, it caused Chelle's hackles to rise. Chelle answered the dhampir's hostility with a pleasant smile. Not too wide, though. She didn't want to appear antagonistic by revealing her new set of fangs.

"I am a vampire," Chelle replied. "But that's the only thing that's changed."

Siobhan let out a soft snort. "You treat the absence of your soul with such triviality, Chelle. Your physiology isn't the only thing that's changed."

The reminder of her untethered state might have caused Chelle pain if not for the absence of her soul. Siobhan thought to rattle her, but Chelle was too numb for deep emotion. Too empty to be anything but indifferent. Upon her turning, her soul had been sent into oblivion. The only way it would be returned to her was the moment her soul tethered itself to her mate's. Fat chance of that happening anytime soon. "Oh, come on, Siobhan." The formality between them was beginning to make Chelle twitch. "We've known each other for too long to play the whole frenemy angle."

Siobhan's haughty façade dropped for the barest moment and a corner of her mouth hitched into a half smile. "Frenemies. Is that what we are, Chelle?"

Chelle laughed. "Not by a long shot."

Siobhan's gaze once again became serious and shrewd. "Mikhail is not your maker."

A statement of fact. Chelle knew what Siobhan suspected. She couldn't find any point in trying to deceive her. Siobhan was much too cunning for that. "No."

"Then the legends are true."

Chelle gave a slow nod of her head.

Fear chased across Siobhan's expression. "I should take

an axe to that coffin. Chop it into a million pieces and burn it to ash."

Chelle hiked a shoulder. To be honest, she wouldn't mourn its loss. Anything with the power to transform dhampirs to vampires and humans into demons probably wouldn't be so easy to get rid of, however. "You won't, though." Siobhan would no more destroy a relic than she would cut off her own arm. She might have reviled the vampire race, but she recognized her heritage and sought to preserve their history just like Chelle. It was one thing they'd always had in common. History was meant to be remembered. The second you allowed yourself to forget, you were doomed to repeat the mistakes of those who came before you. Besides, knowledge was power. Siobhan collected relics and studied their history for exactly that reason.

"No," Siobhan said as a matter of fact. Storm clouds gathered behind her eyes. "I won't destroy it."

And I'll probably live to regret it.

The thought rang loud and clear from Siobhan's mind as she pushed herself from her makeshift throne and approached Chelle. Chelle sensed the dhampir's unease. The slightest bit of fear that soured her scent. Chelle did her best to remain calm and unassuming. Nonthreatening. It wasn't easy. Her very nature urged her to capitalize on Siobhan's unease. To make her prey. To sink her fangs into the creamy flesh of the female's throat. The fire of thirst ignited in Chelle's throat and she willed the flames to die. She'd feed from Lucas when she got back to the cottage. Until then, she could keep her shit together.

She had to.

Siobhan's eyes lit with mischief. "I suppose Mikhail will think that allowing me to see you proves he's a magnanimous king?"

Chelle let out a gentle chuff of breath. "You really think he's responsible for me being here today? He hasn't wanted me to leave the house, let alone come and see you. He doesn't want me here. I insisted."

Siobhan studied Chelle for a brief moment and took a measured breath. Scenting the air for any sign of a lie. She must have been satisfied by what she smelled because she smirked. "I knew you wouldn't fall to your knees and pledge allegiance as easily as Ronan did."

It was true that Chelle hadn't exactly pledged loyalty to Mikhail. But only because her agenda didn't run parallel to his. She had more important business than the fate of the race to weigh on her. There were other, more pressing mysteries that needed to be solved before Chelle could pledge her loyalty to anyone or anything other than herself and Lucas.

"I came for the Alexandria key." She didn't see any point in beating around the bush. Time to get down to business.

Siobhan's eyes widened a fraction as realization dawned. *She's found the other two thirds.* Chelle forced away the amusement that threatened. No one could ever say Siobhan wasn't sharp as a tack.

"I'd forgotten about that . . ." Siobhan purred. Chelle could practically hear the gears cranking away in the female's brain. "You wouldn't be asking for it if you didn't already know where the other two pieces are."

Siobhan had in her safekeeping only one third of the key. If the legends were correct, the key wouldn't work unless all three pieces were joined.

Chelle allowed a wide smile this time. She leveled her gaze on Siobhan. "Exactly."

Siobhan's own expression became hungry. No doubt Chelle would have to strike a deal to get the key back even though it was technically hers to begin with. Whatever the price, it would be worth it.

Siobhan's smile grew as well. "Tell me more."

The clean scent of freshly cut grass invaded Gunnar's nostrils as he filled his lungs with the cool night air. His bare feet moved silently over the immaculate lawn that stretched out beyond the mansion that housed the pack. Pasadena was far enough from L.A. to offer him respite from the political turmoil stirred up by the vampires and Sortiari, and his estate was close enough to national forest land to allow the pack a place to run and hunt when the moon was full.

Apparently, though, Pasadena wasn't far enough to avoid being drawn into a war he wanted no part of. Despite Aren's advice that they choose a side, Gunnar knew that forming any alliance would only lead to disaster. He didn't trust Ian Gregor. But neither did he harbor any love for the guardians of fate. It seemed only logical that the vampires would be forced to side with their enemies and fight alongside the Sortiari if the berserkers declared war. Whatever happened would have a ripple effect that would spread throughout the supernatural community. In the end, would any creature be left standing?

What a clusterfuck.

A blur of movement caught Gunnar's eye. Almost too quick to track. The breeze shifted and he brought his nose up to sniff. A delicious scent wafted over him, waking the wolf that slept in his psyche. The animal tugged at Gunner's consciousness, anxious and on edge. It urged him to investigate, damn near howling with impatience.

His cell buzzed in his pocket and he pulled it out to find a text from Aren.

Motion detectors tripped. North end of the property. Nothing on the cameras, want me to investigate?

Gunnar's fingers moved over the screen as he typed a quick response. **I'm outside. I'll look into it**. For some reason, instinct urged him to go it alone. It could have been his wolf's arrogance. The pack Alpha shouldn't need backup. But he sensed there was another reason for exercising caution and not alerting the pack to the possibility of an outsider being on the property. Gunnar only wished he knew what that reason was.

His phone vibrated again. **I'll join you.**

A warning tremor raced down Gunnar's spine. **No need.** He fired the text off quickly. **I'll call you**.

Aren replied, **10–4**. Gunnar rolled his eyes. Did his second have to channel his inner long-haul driver?

With silent steps, Gunnar stalked across the vast lawn toward the north end of the property and the mysterious streak of movement that had caught his eye. His heart picked up its pace, pounding against his rib cage. The scent that drove his wolf wild intensified, clouding Gunnar's thoughts. The full moon was still two weeks away and yet he found himself give way to the animal in a way that shouldn't have been possible.

He suspected magic might be in play. In which case, he'd need Aren and the entire pack to combat it. A witch or mage powerful enough to sway his wolf was to be treated with a certain amount of caution. And yet, Gunnar exercised none. He let his senses guide him as he tracked the intruder, past the south-side patio, the pond, and the garden. Gunnar whipped around as another flash of movement drew his attention and he looked up at the towering, three-story main house looming above him. The place was downright ominous in the low moonlight, its windows gazing over the property like watchful eyes. Whoever was brave enough to break into this fortress must've had a death wish as well. Because there was no way the intruder would make it out of here alive.

A warning growl gathered in Gunnar's chest. But that cautionary sound wasn't meant for any potential threat. No, Gunnar's wolf was warning *him*. The suspicion that foul magic was at play grew within him and a chill raced down his spine. In all the centuries he'd walked the earth, Gunnar had never encountered a force that could create such divisiveness in his dual nature. He and the wolf lived in synchronicity. And yet he felt like an outsider in his own skin. As though he were the usurper of his form, and not the wolf.

Quiet the fuck down.

As though the command would carry any weight at all with the animal. Gunnar needed to get his shit together. Someone was on the property and not by any stretch of the imagination was the intruder friendly. Berserkers were fast. Faster than a werewolf. As fast as a vampire. And a single berserker in full battle rage could easily take out several foes without expending an ounce of effort.

Gunnar's phone buzzed. He glanced down at the screen to see another text from Aren. **Motion sensors, attic.**

"Shit." The word escaped from between clenched teeth. The only thing on the attic level was the safe. Someone thought to steal from him? Gunnar would rip the thief's arms out of their sockets.

Gunnar didn't bother with the front door. He scaled the trellis to the second story in a single leap and propelled himself onto the balcony. From there, he jumped up and grabbed the wrought-iron ladder on the third-story fire escape. His body swung in a graceful arc as he propelled himself onto the wide ledge of the bay window. The damn thing was latched but Gunnar didn't waste any time putting his fist through the pane. The alarms on the property were programmed at a frequency that only a werewolf would hear. Pack members would be alerted to a forcible entry, but their thief would assume no one was the wiser.

Until Gunnar showed up to tear the fucker's throat out.

Steal from him? Another growl rose in his throat. Gunnar willed his wolf to the back of his mind. He'd show the son of a bitch how he dealt with those who tried to take what belonged to the Forkbeard pack.

Gunnar climbed through the broken window. A jagged edge of broken glass caught his biceps and slashed the skin open. The pain barely registered through the haze of anger that washed over him. He'd heal. One of the benefits of being a werewolf. A warm trickle of blood ran down his upper arm and dripped from his elbow, marring the ancient tattoos that marked his skin to his forearms.

Gunnar's bare feet padded with silent grace over the hardwood floors as he made his way to the safe room. The door was cracked, a sliver of light cut through the darkness like the slash of a well-honed blade. That delicious scent he'd tried to ignore slammed into him and Gunnar's wolf howled in his psyche. The damned animal practically ran circles in his subconscious, eager as a pup on its first hunt.

Gunnar didn't know what annoyed him more, that someone had the audacity to steal from him, or that his damned wolf refused to settle down.

Adrenaline dumped into his bloodstream as he neared the room. He eased open the door, and his anger flared as he noticed the thief had already managed to crack the safe door. Gods damn it. First thing tomorrow, he was replacing the entire unit. The pack owned too many invaluable assets to lose one because a crafty burglar could crack the safe. Fort Knox would have nothing on this place by the time he was done with it.

The safe door had been left wide open. Stupid mistake. The slender form of his thief, clad from head to toe in black, searched through the drawers, discarding one treasure after another. A frustrated sigh rent the quiet and

Gunnar used the momentary distraction to pounce. He took the thief to the floor, slamming the bastard's beanie-clad head to the floor. A grunt of pain answered the blow but it didn't faze the asshole. No. This one was damned strong.

He lifted the bastard up again, prepared to put his dome through the gods-damned floor. His wolf rose up with a snarl and Gunnar froze. His nostrils filled with the sweetest aroma, like a summer meadow after the rain. He snatched the beanie from the thief's head to reveal long flowing locks of tawny hair. Deep green eyes that swirled with cold silver stared back at him.

Her eyes went wide and her jaw slack before she replaced her expression of awe with one of aggression. "Get off me, werewolf. I haven't eaten today and it won't take much to convince me to drink you dry."

By the gods. A vampire. And female.

His wolf yipped in his psyche and a single word resonated in Gunnar's mind: *Mine.* A worse omen, he couldn't conceive of.

CHAPTER
3

Shock froze Chelle in place. She stilled beneath the werewolf's hulking form, her back arched as her soul slammed back into her body, filling her full to bursting. She sucked in a gasp of breath and choked on the exhale. Power flooded her, made her dizzy and giddy. Her throat burned as though she'd chugged a fifth of bourbon. The scent of the werewolf's blood called to her. Overrode any sense of reason. Her secondary fangs punched down from her gums and Chelle began to struggle beneath him, prepared to put the werewolf on his back so she could sink her fangs into the tender flesh of his throat and glut herself on his blood.

He'd tethered her. *How?*

The werewolf pinned Chelle's wrists high above her head. He bent over her, a snarl building in his chest. The intensity of his icy blue stare sent a chill over Chelle's skin. He made a show of sniffing her and she cocked her head to one side, curious. In the recess of his mind, she heard the contented purr of an animal followed by a low growl. She'd never heard a werewolf's thoughts before and it fascinated her to learn that it seemed the animal lived within the male's psyche. Another low, pleasant rumble sounded, followed by a single thought:

Quiet.

His command to that part of his mind was as clear as if he'd spoken it out loud. The animal quieted, but that low, pleasant purr continued in the background of his thoughts.

Chelle met his gaze to find that the werewolf studied her with the same intense curiosity. She bucked her chin up a notch, unwilling to show anything but strength. "Let me go."

A feral grin split his full lips. "Not a chance, vampire. Who are you and what are you after?"

The slightest accent flavored his words. Hinting at a language that hadn't been spoken in a long while. Whoever he was, the werewolf was old.

Power emanated from him in a vibration that danced over Chelle's flesh. Her gaze roamed from his head, shaved on either side of his scalp with a wide swath of golden hair left long down the center. Her gaze traced his strong jaw, covered partially by a longish but well-kept beard. Chelle wanted to laugh. A hipster, lumber-sexual werewolf. The funny thing was, he probably hadn't changed his look in about ten centuries. Ancient tattoos decorated his head, his neck, and disappeared under his T-shirt before reappearing on his heavily muscled arms. Her gaze fixed on the trail of crimson that marred his left arm and her thirst intensified a hundredfold. She'd never thirsted for anyone as she did this male. The urge to pierce his vein and glut herself stole Chelle's focus and she lost her train of thought.

"Answer me!"

The werewolf gave her a gentle shake and Chelle snapped out of her reverie. She'd tell him what she'd come to steal when hell froze over. Tethered or not, he'd get nothing out of her. Chelle locked her jaw down tight and returned his stare with open defiance.

"Go to hell, furbag."

The male's smile grew arrogant as he leaned in closer. His grip tightened, though not painfully so, and she realized there was no way she'd be able to overpower the male. Chelle had never gone toe to toe with a werewolf before. Stronger than she'd anticipated. Or maybe it was just this particular one who seemed to overpower her with ease. Either way, it didn't sit well with her. She'd be damned if she let him get the upper hand. She had a reputation as a badass to uphold, damn it!

His voice dropped to a menacing murmur. "You knew what you were looking for."

A low growl echoed in his chest. In the back of his mind, Chelle sensed a conflict between the male and his inner animal. He conducted what sounded to Chelle like a one-sided conversation, giving the animal orders to stand down. What had the beast wanted to do? she wondered. A smile threatened to surface but she swallowed it down.

A golden light shone behind his irises and he ran his nose along her jaw as he inhaled deeply. His beard tickled her neck and it made her stomach do a pleasant flip. Did a werewolf recognize its mate in the same way a vampire felt the tether? If so, did this male know what he'd done to Chelle? Maybe that's what he argued with his inner animal about. She wanted to kick him in the nuts for the distraction. She couldn't worry about a tether—or a mate—or anything else right now. She needed answers to the mysteries of her turning. This was a complication she couldn't afford.

A complication for sure. But . . . could she use it to her advantage?

Guilt tugged at her chest but she forced the sensation away. The sudden return of her soul brought with it a flood of emotion she wasn't quite ready to deal with. She couldn't let a conscience stand in the way of what she wanted. Not when she was so close to getting it. When life handed you lemons . . .

"Do you know what I am, werewolf?" Chelle let her voice go soft and breathy.

"Vampire," the werewolf replied from between clenched teeth.

"No." His eyelids drooped a fraction at her softly spoken word. Chelle almost felt sorry for him. He was no different than any other male. So easy to manipulate. "I'm *yours*."

The male stilled. A tremor of anxious energy coursed through Chelle's veins. His grip on her wrists tightened yet again and she forced herself not to show any outward discomfort. Maybe her celebration had been a little premature. Damn it.

"You're mine, all right," the werewolf growled. "Do you know what I do to thieves, vampire?"

Chelle opted not to answer.

"I rip out their arms and leave them to bleed out."

Charming.

Diplomacy obviously wasn't the male's strong suit. Chelle focused her attention on his thoughts. The animal had begun to growl and yip, as though in warning. The golden light behind the male's eyes grew brighter, nearly swallowing every bit of blue. It transformed his face, turning him into something wild, and a hot rush of excitement coursed through Chelle's body.

The male paused. His eyes grew wide, pupils dilated. He lunged toward Chelle as though about to capture her mouth with his when a voice shouted from somewhere in the lower levels of the enormous house.

"Gunnar!"

Gunnar. Definitely Scandinavian. A Viking werewolf? This time, Chelle's lips curled before she could stop herself. She'd always been fascinated with Norse legends and myths and it seemed the male who'd tethered her stepped right out of one of those stories.

Focus, Chelle. This isn't the time to geek out.

In an instant, the gold drained from his eyes and once again reflected icy blue. He released his grip on her wrists and pushed himself up to stand. "Go." The command rang with authority that brooked no argument. "Now."

A warning? Chelle might have been a virtual treasure trove of knowledge, but she didn't know everything. Obviously. She hadn't studied anything about werewolves or pack mentality, but from Gunnar's tone, she sensed if his pack caught her there, she'd be as good as dead. Though it pained her to escape without the prize, in this case Chelle surmised that tonight, caution would be the better part of valor.

Chelle propelled herself up in a flash of movement. She headed for the open door but Gunnar caught her by the wrist. He hauled her against his wide chest, cupped the back of her neck. His mouth met hers in a hot, wet, crushing kiss that left Chelle's knees weak and her brain buzzing.

He broke the contact and gave her a none-too-gentle shove. "Go!"

Shell-shocked, she raced out the door and down the hallway. She searched for the broken window she'd heard shatter moments before Gunnar caught her and dove in a graceful arc through the vacant pane. Chelle tucked her knees to her chest and flipped forward. Her booted feet made contact with the ground with barely a sound. She turned to look back up at the house to find Gunnar watching her from the window.

Well, she guessed that kiss answered the question of whether or not a werewolf recognized its mate.

Things were about to get interesting. Good thing Chelle never backed down from a challenge.

Gunnar watched as the vampire turned away from the house. Her movement was nothing more than a graceful smear against the dark backdrop of night as she ran with preternatural speed to the edge of the property and disappeared. His wolf gave a forlorn howl in the back of his mind and, not for the first time, Gunnar wished he could muzzle the damn thing.

Gods. How could this have happened? Nonwerewolf pairings were seldom heard of. Those matings that did occur outside of the various packs were considered taboo. A bad omen that had to be dealt with swiftly and without mercy. It wouldn't have taken much for Aren—or any other member of the pack—to recognize the bond between Gunnar and the vampire. And if that had happened, they would have run a stake through the female's heart, right before they'd put a silver bullet through his.

He didn't know a damned thing about her. Hell, he didn't even know her name. And yet, Gunnar knew that had she died, it would have gutted him. His wolf never would have recovered from the loss and he would have gone mad. He'd seen it happen before. And the thought that he'd been so close to experiencing that madness sent a rush of adrenaline through his bloodstream.

"Gunnar!"

His head whipped around to find Aren and three other pack members scrambling up the staircase to the third-story landing. They were armed to the teeth and ready for a fight, and he knew he'd made the right decision to send his mate away. No matter what his wolf thought to the contrary.

"What in the hell is going on?" Aren came to a skidding halt a foot from the broken window. "Sensors are being tripped everywhere." He glanced out the window to the grounds and Gunnar fought to hide his relief that his mate had disappeared into the night. "Someone broke the window?"

Gunnar's jaw clenched. "I broke it."

Behind Aren, the three others stood at the ready. Sven, his mate, Jillian, and Jaeger were all battle ready, eyes glowing gold and muscles tense. Gunnar knew of no other pack in either the north or the southwest territories that rivaled the Forkbeard pack in strength. They were certainly a formidable lot. And there wasn't a single one of them who wouldn't have killed the vampire on sight.

"What in the hell is going on?"

Gunnar met Aren's concerned gaze. He scrubbed a hand over his head and flipped his straight hair to one side. "I climbed the fire escape to get to the third story. Broke the window to get in. Someone cracked the safe. I interrupted the thief before anything was stolen."

Aren's eyes went wide. "Well . . . ? Who—or what—in the hell was it?"

Gunnar's wolf issued a warning growl in his mind and he urged the beast to silence. It took a sheer act of will to force his muscles to relax. He hiked a shoulder. "Ski mask, nondescript black clothes. Could've been anyone."

Aren looked as though Gunnar had lost his mind, which probably wasn't too far from the truth. "What did the fucker *smell* like?"

It wouldn't do any good to lie. A werewolf could smell deception from miles away. Gunnar turned to look out the window. "A vampire."

"*Själlös tjuv.*"

Soulless thief. Gunnar let out a soft snort. Aren's sentiment was certainly appropriate given the circumstances.

"What do you think the bastard was after?" Jaeger asked.

Gunnar turned his attention to the male whose dark brows gathered over his deep brown eyes. The male was older than Gunnar by twenty years. Strong. Smart. But had never had any aspirations to become Alpha. Level-headed in a conflict and reasonable, Jaeger might be the only member of the pack who'd understand Gunnar's situation. That didn't mean he was ready to divulge anything.

Gunnar headed to the safe room and the others followed. Curiosity burned to discover exactly what his mate had been after, but he didn't want the others to be privy to that information just yet. As soon as he diffused the situation and everyone calmed down, he'd investigate. Until then, he had to do whatever he could to keep the pack in the dark.

"Your guess is as good as mine." The vampire hadn't really disturbed much of anything in her quest. A smart thief. Obviously not her first rodeo. Gunnar's lips twitched, threatening a smile. A crafty female. Smart. It rankled that he didn't even know her name.

"There are countless antiques and relics in the pack's possession that are priceless," Jillian chimed in. "Maybe the vampire was looking for something to fence?"

"More likely looking for something to use as leverage," Aren interjected.

So they were back to this? Gunnar let out a sigh. Aren would no doubt use the attempted break-in as leverage himself. To convince the pack to ally with the berserkers in their war against the Sortiari and vampires.

Sven, usually the quiet one, spoke up. "You're sure nothing was stolen? It might be a good idea to do a full inventory."

Gunnar intended to do just that, but he'd be doing it

alone. "I'm sure. But you're right, it's a good idea to double-check."

"Jillian and I can do it," Sven suggested.

Jillian was unofficially the pack's curator. She cataloged their priceless possessions, transferred centuries' worth of history and records to digital formats. The female was the youngest member of their pack at sixty-five years old, though she didn't look a day over twenty-five. She'd been attacked by a rogue and left for dead. The Forkbeard pack had taken her in and Sven's wolf had recognized its mate in an instant. At the time, Gunnar had found himself disdainful and mistrustful of such an instantaneous bond. No longer. His wolf had taken one look at the beautiful vampire and laid claim.

Mine.

"Gunnar? Did you hear me?"

Gunnar shook himself from his thoughts and met Aren's suspicious gaze. The male had been on edge for weeks. Tonight's break-in wasn't going to do anything to calm him. Gunnar's brow arched in question. Whatever the hell point Aren was trying to make, he wished he'd get the hell on with it.

"I said we need to increase security on the property until we know exactly what the vampire was after."

"There are military bases with less security," Gunnar remarked. Truly, it was a wonder the vampire had managed to breach their security with such ease. She was obviously agile and quick. The warrior in Gunnar appreciated that. "Besides, the vampire will be expecting it." Of that Gunnar had no doubt. Intelligence shone behind her forest-green eyes. Cunning. She was far too smart to be thwarted by a mere boost in surveillance.

She'd be back, no doubt about it. And Gunnar wasn't about to go out of his way to keep her out.

"You're suggesting we set a trap?" Aren asked.

Of course that's where he'd go. Not that Gunnar hadn't been thinking the exact same thing. Their motives might have been different, but Aren was Gunnar's second because their minds tended to work in the same way.

"Not necessarily." Gunnar wanted the pack placated with his plan, but not overly bloodthirsty. From here on out, he'd have to tread on eggshells. Wolves tended to steamroll over things. They acted on instinct and executed with brute force. Finesse wasn't exactly Gunnar's thing.

"But you do think the vampire will return?"

Of that he had no doubt. A tremor of anxiety vibrated from the top of Gunnar's head and traveled the length of his spine. Aren was ambitious, but was the male traitorous?

"I think anything is possible," Gunnar said after a moment. "And I plan to keep my guard up and my eyes and ears open until I get to the bottom of whatever the hell is going on."

A murmur of agreement spread through the small group.

Jaeger moved toward the hallway. "I'll get a hammer and some plywood to cover up the window until we can get it fixed."

"Good idea," Gunnar replied. "Jillian, if you wouldn't mind putting the safe back in order? I'll deal with the inventory in the morning. Sven, we'll need something to temporarily secure the safe since the vampire managed to destroy the tumbler."

He gave a sharp nod of his head. "I'm on it."

"Aren, reset the motion detectors and the security system. We'll need to run a test on the system as well to make sure everything is online and functioning properly."

Aren's gaze narrowed as he studied Gunnar with an intensity that made his skin crawl. How he wished he could climb into the male's mind and hear his thoughts. "Want me to do a perimeter check as well?"

Gunnar's wolf gave a warning yip but he disregarded it. "Yeah." Right now, he needed to keep up appearances even though he worried the vampire had left a trail to track. "Take backup and check in."

His answer seemed to satisfy Aren. "Will do."

The group dispersed and Gunnar returned to the broken window to stare out at the property. The vampire had damned near stilled the breath in his lungs. Sharp, precise features, high cheekbones, eyes that reflected the forests he loved to run and hunt in, and tawny hair that shone like gold.

Beautiful.

And she belonged to *him*.

CHAPTER
4

Despite only two hours' sleep, Gunnar was up with the sun. His wolf was restless, and not simply because the moon grew fuller. The wolf wanted its mate. Unfortunately, there wasn't a whole hell of a lot Gunnar could do about it.

Maddening.

He hadn't planned to kiss the vampire moments before shoving her out the door. But gods, her full lips had practically begged for the favor and Gunnar never was one to turn a lady down. Her mouth was as honey-sweet and heady as mead. The kiss had gone straight to his head. Made him drunk. And he'd barely had a sip. What would it be like to taste her fully? To savor her at his leisure? Gunnar's cock stirred at the thought and he willed the bastard down. The vampire was a variable. Dangerous. His wolf recognized her as its mate, but did vampires bond in the same way? Their kind had always been so gods-damned secretive, little was known about their ways and customs. After the Sortiari had waged war on the vampires and attempted to eradicate them in their crusade to change the course of fate, vampires had become an inconsequential piece of history. Forgotten.

Gunnar let out a soft snort. They were all fools to think any part of history could—or should—be forgotten.

Jillian had done a decent job of cleaning up the safe. Everything was in order and back in its rightful place. There was no need to inventory anything at this point. Gunnar didn't plan on leaving this room until he knew what the vampire had been after, though.

Curiosity ate at him. Worked his wolf into a damned lather. The animal didn't want to be cooped up in the tiny room and he made his wishes known with a low snarl. Last night, Aren and the others had caught the vampire's scent. They'd tracked it to a mile from the borders of the pack's property until it disappeared. Which meant she hadn't come on foot. Gunnar's wolf wanted to track its mate, but the animal refused to listen to Gunnar's reasoning. The closer they got to the full moon, the more in sync the dual parts of his nature would become. Until then, they existed as two separate entities inhabiting a single body. It frustrated the fuck out of him.

Rumors of Mikhail Aristov's ascension to power had spread quickly. Over the course of almost a year and a half, he'd managed to find his mate and replenish the vampire race. But it was also widely known that the process so far had been slow. How many vampires could there be? A handful at most, Gunnar surmised. And all of them would belong to Aristov's coven. The female would be easy to find. All Gunnar had to do was drive to L.A. and request a meeting with the vampire king. He let out a chuff of disdainful laughter. He'd as likely get an audience with the king as he would sprout a pair of tits. Besides, Gunnar wasn't interested in using political machinations to find his mate.

Gunnar was certain she'd come to him. Or more to the point, come *back* to him.

So many baubles . . . which one were you after?

The relics of the Forkbeard pack were cataloged individually in drawers contained within the safe. Some were ancient texts, others symbolic representations of the lives they'd lived centuries ago. Amulets and runes carved into bones that had been used for religious or superstitious purposes. None of which would be useful to a vampire in any way, shape, or form.

"Looking at you right now, the phrase 'heavy hangs the head that wears the crown' comes to mind."

Gunnar looked up to find Jillian standing in the doorway. She might not have been young by human standards, but to a werewolf, the female was barely a pup. The modern world could be tough to negotiate for those of them with so many centuries under their belts. Gunnar had been grateful that Sven had found a mate in Jillian. Her knowledge and expertise were invaluable to the pack. And besides that, he genuinely liked her.

"The times are wild. Contention, like a horse full of high feeding, madly hath broke loose."

Jillian laughed at his rebuttal. She settled herself on the floor near Gunnar. "How goes the inventory?"

"Everything's here. But you already know that."

"Then why do you look like you're ready to take someone's head off?"

Gunnar blew out a breath. "Tell me, Jillian. What do we have that a vampire would want?"

She studied him for a quiet moment. "You think Aren's right, then? That the vampire wasn't looking for something to fence?"

Mikhail Aristov had to have amassed a fortune. One of the benefits of being long-lived. The dhampir covens weren't hurting for money as far as Gunnar knew. And it's not like the vampire had stumbled upon his property. Pasadena was a good thirty-minute drive from L.A. and the pack's property was another fifteen minutes from the city proper. No, she'd come here for a reason.

"The covens have wealth," Gunnar replied. "And if it was a simple robbery, why come all the way out here?"

Jillian pursed her lips. "Good point." She flipped the length of her straight, auburn hair over one shoulder. She crinkled her nose in thought, scrunching up the concentration of freckles that marred the skin there, making her look all the more childlike. "So you're thinking that it wasn't necessarily something of real value the vampire was after, right?"

Exactly. Gunnar closed the drawer that held the jeweled crown of the pack's first Alpha. "Nothing of monetary value," he stressed.

"Gotcha." Jillian stared at some far-off point as she tapped her forefinger against her lips. "Hmmm."

Gunnar's wolf yipped with impatience but he willed the animal to silence. He refused to let it master him. "I can't think of any texts in our possession that even mention vampires, can you?"

After joining the pack, Jillian had devoured every ounce of information she could get her hands on. An academic, she'd been fascinated by their history, the legends. With Sven's help translating, she'd gone through their entire library of texts in a matter of weeks.

"Me, either." Jillian continued to contemplate and Gunnar resisted the urge to pace. "Okay, so what if it's not *our* knowledge the vampire was after?"

Gunnar canted his head to one side. "What do you mean?"

"Well, you said the vampires have been virtually extinct for two centuries. I can't imagine they know very much about their own kind."

"It's valid reasoning, but in truth, I have no idea what they know." It annoyed the hell out of him, too. What did the vampires know, if anything, about their history, their creation? Did Aristov know anything? And if he did, did the male impart that knowledge to his coven or did he covet it?

"We might not have anything in our books that pertain to vampires, but we have something that could lead a vampire to more books and information than a person could read in a lifetime."

Jillian still thought of time like a human did. It would be centuries before she'd fully grasp the scope of her virtual immortality. "We do?" Gunnar asked. "What?"

Jillian smiled. She pushed herself up and went to one of the drawers in the safe. She pulled it open and placed in Gunnar's hand a chunk of worn gold shaped like a medallion but with a protruding part at the top and a slot on one side. The face of the medallion had likely once been etched with symbols but time had worn its surface smooth.

Gunnar studied what might as well have been a useless hunk of gold. It had been entrusted to the pack so many centuries ago that Gunnar could barely remember its purpose. They'd been tasked with protecting it. Keeping it out of the hands of anyone who might use it for dark purposes. *Gods.* Gunnar didn't think there were any creatures still alive who would know its purpose aside from himself and a few pack members.

Rather than find answers, it seemed Gunnar had only managed to dredge up more questions. "That piece is useless," he remarked. "It's one of three."

Jillian cocked a brow. "Who says the vampire doesn't already have the other two?"

Indeed. Gunnar's mate was obviously full of surprises. He didn't even know her name and the female had managed to captivate and fascinate him in no less than five minutes. "At any rate, we have something the vampire wants."

"True," Jillian said. "So . . . what now?"

"Now? We wait."

Chelle paced the confines of the cottage, her stomach tied into an unyielding knot. She wanted to punch something, just to release some of the tension that pulled her muscles taut. The wall of Mikhail's fancy guesthouse could take the brunt of her frustration, but she doubted the vampire king would take kindly to her demolishing his property.

"Argh!"

She punched at the air but it didn't lend her the type of satisfaction that putting her fist through the drywall would offer. From the living room, Lucas gave her a scolding look and shook his head.

"You need to calm down."

Easy for him to say. Lucas had been a member of the reclusive Thomas Fairchild's sheltered coven of dhampirs. As pure as the driven snow, Lucas had been given the task of acting as Chelle's personal buffet after she'd been turned. Mikhail had thought that making Lucas Chelle's blood donor would level her out and bring him into their fold. Instead, Chelle had accidentally drained Lucas and, in her guilt, had forced her own blood down his throat and made him a vampire.

What a way to prove to everyone that she had her shit together, huh?

"I can't calm down," Chelle said in a huff. It annoyed the crap out of her that Lucas could be so chill when she was about to crawl out of her damned skin. "I'm too agitated."

Lucas continued to watch her as though she were an animal at the zoo. "This is a good thing, Chelle. Your soul is returned!"

Leave it to the wide-eyed, innocent newb to see the bright side. Stupid optimists. She supposed that having been without a soul for only several months, she could be happy she wouldn't have to endure centuries in an empty, emotionless state. Still, her tethering had really put a monkey wrench into her plans. Stupid werewolf. Stupid, arrogant, sexy, Viking *god* of a male . . .

She whipped around to face Lucas. He watched her with an amused smirk. Ugh. "Do I have the key?" He opened his mouth to reply but Chelle cut him off. "No. So this isn't a good thing, Lucas. Not by a long shot."

The male gave a disinterested shrug. "Maybe you don't need it anymore."

Chelle froze in her tracks. She leveled her best scary-vampire death stare on Lucas, but after he'd gotten to know her over the past few months, the shade she threw him had little effect. Damn it. Things were so much better when Chelle had been able to bluff him.

"I need it. *We* need it."

Chelle was an anomaly among vampires. She had powers and abilities that no other vampire—not even Mikhail Aristov—had. As her offspring, Lucas shared some of those unique traits. Until she knew more about Set's Chest—the magic coffin that had transformed her—and the magic it contained, they were both in danger.

Lucas gave a sad shake of his head. "Do you really think Mikhail, or even your own brother, would condemn you for something you had no control over?"

Esta magia limpiará la tierra. The rhythmic words spoken by the shifter right before he shoved her in that gods-forsaken box all those months ago echoed in Chelle's mind and she shuddered. The shifter had thought that the chest created demons. Mapinguari. Is that what Chelle was? A demon?

"I think that Mikhail would do anything to protect the

race," Chelle replied. "And I think that Ronan is loyal to his maker."

Lucas tsked. "Blood is thicker than water."

"Exactly." Chelle resumed pacing. She and Ronan were twins. That bonded them to an extent. But Mikhail had turned Ronan. Made him a part of the vampire collective memory. Vampires and dhampirs existed much in the same way an aspen grove lived. From a single tree, many saplings were produced. Each of them interconnected by their roots. Ronan had been bound to Mikhail, his coven, and the Collective. Chelle wasn't a part of that. She was a single tree and Lucas her only sapling. They were vulnerable. Separate. Lucas might be too naïve to understand, but Chelle knew what happened to a weed that sprouted in a garden where it didn't belong.

"I have to know, Lucas."

His lips thinned and his expression became sad. "Know what?"

"What we are. What we're capable of." She paused. "Whether or not we're a threat."

Lucas's brows drew together. "A threat to whom?"

Chelle let out an unsteady breath. "To anyone."

He shoved himself up from the couch. "Do you feel like a threat? Because I don't."

That's because Lucas could never conceive of behaving so uncivilized. Chelle knew better. They were as wild and untamed as any animal. Feral. Dangerous because of their abilities.

"I'm going back for Gunnar's third of the key," Chelle declared. It's not like she was asking permission. She needed none.

"He'll be waiting for you this time," Lucas warned. "He'll be prepared."

Of that Chelle had no doubt. She brushed her fingertips over her lips. She swore she could still feel the sparks of electricity that ignited there when the werewolf kissed her. Such a male! Virile. Wild. Bold.

"I know," she replied as though the prospect of meeting Gunnar face-to-face again bored her. "But I'll be prepared for him, too. It's still a level playing field either way."

"If you say so." Lucas didn't sound convinced and why would he be? If he dug around enough, he'd know Chelle's thoughts. "You should take me with you."

Chelle's gaze widened. "Out of the question."

Lucas's hulking form towered over Chelle's slighter one. He was certainly an intimidating vampire: tall, bulky with cords of muscle, his countenance stern. It was only when she looked into his eyes that she saw the gentleness, the innocence. His guileless sky-blue eyes were Lucas's only flaw. They gave everything away.

"I can handle Gunnar."

"I don't doubt that," Lucas replied. "But can you handle the rest of his pack?"

True, Chelle had no idea how many of the furry bastards were crawling around Gunnar's estate that rivaled a small hotel in its size and stature. Seriously, the guy could make a killing with Airbnb.

"The house is big enough to shelter several litters of werewolves." Lucas chuckled at the remark and Chelle stifled a grin. "I don't know much about mutts but if they're all as strong as Gunnar, I might run into a hiccup."

"I'm sure your mate would be thrilled to hear you refer to him as a mutt," Lucas scoffed.

Chelle's head snapped up. "Don't call him that."

"Why not?" Lucas was seriously pushing his luck. "That's what he is."

The tether was a spiritual bond. Soul-deep and unbreakable. That Chelle's soul had secured itself to Gunnar's wasn't her fault. She hadn't chosen the tether. That conniving bitch Fate had made the decision for her. How was that fair? She didn't know a damned thing about him aside from the fact that he turned into a dog once a month and that his mouth felt like heaven against hers.

"Werewolf, not dog," Lucas corrected. "And what about his mouth?"

Chelle shot Lucas a withering glare. Reading each other's minds was *off limits*. They'd made the rule to establish boundaries.

Lucas threw his hands up in surrender. "I couldn't help it. You were projecting so loud you might as well have shouted it at me."

Chelle chose not to respond.

"Ronan was tethered by a witch. I'm tethered by a werewolf. Mikhail's mate started out as a human!" Chelle threw her arms up. "Do you know how many nonvampire or dhampir tetherings there've been in our history, Lucas?"

He shook his head. "No."

"Three."

Again Lucas didn't seem fazed. "Doesn't surprise me. We're a nearly extinct race, Chelle. If Fate is responsible for whose souls ours choose, it stands to reason that in order to thrive, we'd have to find mates outside of our own species."

"It stands to reason that Fate is a fucking moron," Chelle said. "Do you know what sort of complications being tethered to a werewolf is going to create?"

"No," Lucas admitted. "Do you?"

Chelle's jaw went slack and she stared agape at Lucas. "Uh . . . well . . . I mean . . . no." She stomped her booted foot with frustration and the floorboards creaked under the stress. "But that's not the point."

Lucas let out a long-suffering sigh. He walked back into the living room and flopped down on the couch. "Then what is the point?"

"I don't know." Chelle was done arguing with Lucas.

She needed to get back to Pasadena so she could get her hands on Gunnar's third of the key. She turned and stalked down the hallway toward her room. "There is a point, though!" she shouted as she slammed the door behind her. "And when I figure it out, you'll be the first to know!"

Lucas's mocking laughter sounded from the living room.

Smart-ass. She projected the thought loud and clear. Chelle had liked him a hell of a lot better when he was nothing more than an innocent dhampir.

CHAPTER
5

Saeed Almasi cradled his head in his palms. His heart raced in his chest and his lungs burned. Thirst scorched a path up his throat despite the fact he'd recently fed. Myriad voices echoed in his mind and he moved to cover his ears as though somehow he could block out the sound.

He'd lost himself to the Collective once again. And once again, he was paying the price.

The pain, the madness, would all be worth it, though. If he found *her*. The willowy fae with eyes like starlight and hair like fire. Saeed thirsted for her blood even though he'd never tasted it. He longed to inhale her intoxicating scent though he'd never smelled it. Hungered for her satin skin though he'd yet to lay a finger to it. Since the night he'd been turned, Saeed knew only empty, unsatisfied lust.

Saeed's soul had been ripped from him and it left a raw, gaping wound. And he knew without a doubt that only the female in his visions could heal him and make him whole again. Without her, his soul would be lost to the void for eternity.

"Saeed." Sasha's gentle voice reached his ears as

though spoken from above the water. Of the members of his coven, she was one of his favorites. She was his closest confidante. He trusted no one above her.

"Saeed."

Her hand covered his shoulder and he flinched. The contact was too much, adding to the sensory overload he experienced whenever he let himself fall headlong into the memories of the countless vampires who'd come before him. Vampires who no longer walked the earth. Was the beautiful fae among the dead? If Saeed's soul were intact, the thought would have squeezed his heart like a fist. Instead, he felt nothing. Empty. Always empty.

Sasha pulled her hand away and Saeed let out a slow breath. "Mikhail has asked for you."

Upon his turning, Saeed had pledged his loyalty to the vampire king, his maker. It would do no good to deny Mikhail an audience. His mind was muddled, thick and muddy. Reality became memory and memory reality. The Collective pulled at him once again, urging him to return to its company, and Saeed swayed on his feet. How could he possibly resist its call if there was even a slight chance he'd see her again?

"Saeed!"

Sasha rarely raised her voice and the command inherent in her tone snapped him to attention. Saeed allowed his eyes to open, just a crack, and the brightness of the lights overhead made him cringe. He was a creature of darkness now . . .

"If Mikhail sees you like this, he'll put a stake through your heart. Is that what you want?"

Was it? In death, at least he'd find respite from the visions that plagued him. Saeed opened his mouth to respond, but the dryness in his throat silenced his voice. Maybe it was for the best. Part of him was still back there, with her. He wasn't sure he'd be able to form a coherent string of words.

He'd found her in the Collective so many times, though he'd yet to discover her name. Gods, how he wanted to say it. To feel the vibration of it on his lips.

"He's on his way," Sasha said. The urgency in her tone did little to motivate Saeed. "Jenner is with him."

As though the threat of Mikhail bringing his enforcer along would somehow change things. Saeed didn't fear Jenner. He didn't fear anything but the prospect of losing her. *Lose her?* Saeed chuckled. He hadn't even found her.

"Stop this," Sasha commanded.

Saeed allowed his gaze to focus on the female. Concern was etched into her soft features and wide sapphire eyes. She brought her wrist to her mouth and bit down. Blood scented the air and his eyes dropped to her outstretched arm. Two drops of crimson formed on her skin before they welled over and the blood trickled down either side of her wrist.

"Drink," she hissed. "Before Mikhail arrives and sees you in a state of madness."

What did it matter? Until he found her, Saeed was lost.

Sasha pressed her wrist to his mouth. Instinct took over and his secondary fangs elongated as he punctured the skin to reopen the wounds. She relaxed against him as the euphoria of feeding swept them up. Saeed took long pulls, swallowing greedily as her blood flowed over his tongue. His mind began to clear by small degrees and he no longer heard the voices of memory ringing in his ears. Saeed continued to drink until the fire in his throat was quenched. When he closed the punctures, Sasha let out a contented sigh. How he wished he could feel such contentment from something as simple as offering a vein.

"Thank you." His own voice sounded foreign in Saeed's ears, as though it had gone years without use.

"Saeed." Sasha gave a sad shake of her head. "You can't continue to chase ghosts and visions. Mikhail expects more from a coven master. He expects more from a vampire tasked with caring for those weaker than he is. *I* expect more of you."

He knew Sasha's words should cause him pain. That he should be ashamed of the way he'd behaved. In the weeks since his turning, he'd been unable to care for anything but the Collective and the memories that sucked him in. He might have been soulless, untethered, but Saeed was not without reason. Sasha was right. The coven needed his leadership. Mikhail needed to know that he'd made the right decision in turning him. But his fae wasn't a ghost. Saeed refused to believe it. He'd find her. He'd search for her over centuries if he had to.

"When should I expect to receive Mikhail?" His mind was clear, but a few moments of peaceful clarity would be appreciated before he faced the vampire king.

"He'll be here in about twenty minutes," Sasha replied.

"Good. I'll see him in the study. I'd appreciate it if you were there as well."

Sasha inclined her head. "Of course."

Of course. She was always ready to do whatever was asked of her. Perhaps it was Sasha who should have been turned and not Saeed. His selfishness was a detriment to their coven. He took her hand and laid a gentle kiss to her knuckles. He didn't know what he'd do without her. "I think we should prepare to receive our king, then."

Sasha gave him a gentle smile. "Yes."

At one time, Saeed had been one of the three oldest dhampirs in existence. Now, he was nothing more than a fledgling vampire, learning the world from a new perspective, much like a butterfly that had finally escaped its chrysalis. Even the history of his own people meant something different to him now. He'd been afforded the opportunity to see the passing of time through the eyes of other vampires. Within the Collective, Saeed lived many lives.

So much untapped wisdom . . .

The myriad voices called to him, threatening to pull him into their undertow once again. He cast a sidelong glance Sasha's way to find the female watching him, brows drawn together with obvious concern.

"I'm fine," he assured her. Annoyance leaked into his tone and he forced a pleasant smile onto his face. "There's no need for worry."

Sasha gave a slight nod.

Saeed cocked his head toward the sound of a car approaching. His keen ears knew the specific rumble of the engine belonging to Mikhail's town car. He went to the foyer and Sasha followed close behind. Before the vampire king could knock on the front door, Saeed pulled it open and bowed his head as the father of the vampire race entered.

"Mikhail," Saeed greeted. "I trust you're well."

"I am." The male smiled, revealing the dual points of his fangs. "And how are you?"

Saeed didn't miss the note of concern in his king's tone. "The adjustment has been . . . interesting, but I'm handling it well."

Mikhail gave a tight-lipped smile that didn't reach his eyes as he stepped fully into the foyer. "I'm glad."

Behind Mikhail stood Jenner. The hulking vampire couldn't have appeared more menacing if he tried. He had a wild, feral look about him that promised death and retribution to anyone who crossed him. If Saeed himself wasn't formidable, the brutish vampire might have made him nervous. At any rate, Jenner wasn't a male Saeed would want to make an enemy of.

"Jenner," Saeed greeted.

The male jerked his chin in response. He'd never been much for pomp and circumstance, which suited Saeed just fine. The sooner this meeting concluded, the sooner he could resume his search for the fiery-haired fae.

Saeed held out a hand. "Let's take our conversation to the study."

He led the way, with Mikhail and Jenner following close behind, and Sasha taking up the rear. Saeed rarely used the study; its stuffy formality wasn't conducive to productive thought. He waited for his king to settle into a wing chair in the corner of the room before Saeed lowered himself onto a sofa opposite Mikhail. Jenner chose to stand—no surprise there—as did Sasha, who stood at attention near the doorway. She focused her gaze on some far-off point as though she couldn't care less about the ensuing conversation, but Saeed knew better. Sasha would commit every word spoken here today to memory and analyze it all later. The female missed nothing.

"I don't see any point in beating around the bush," Mikhail began. "Trenton McAlister has asked for a meeting. I've put him off for as long as I can. Now I suppose I have no choice but to meet the bastard face-to-face."

Saeed studied Mikhail for the barest moment. What could the director of the Sortiari possibly want that didn't involve driving a stake through Mikhail's heart? "What does he want?"

Mikhail's gaze darkened. "What does the Sortiari ever want? To further their own agenda."

Cryptic, but not untrue. The guardians of fate were indeed self-serving, no matter their claim to serve the greater good. "Why indulge him at all?" Saeed would have told the bastard where he could shove his request.

"We have reason to believe the berserkers have left the Sortiari's fold and are planning a coup."

Saeed's eyes went wide. Could it be? The Highland warlords had been indentured to the Sortiari for as long as he could remember. Never outright claimed as slaves, but existing in servitude nonetheless. "And you're sure you can trust your intel?"

Mikhail's gaze slid to Jenner and he nodded.

"The implications of such a coup could be far-reaching," Saeed said. "The ripples would stretch throughout the supernatural community."

"Balance would be upset," Mikhail agreed. His brow furrowed. "I can't believe I might be forced to pick a side." He let out a rueful laugh. "Defend the beasts that nearly eradicated our race, or help to support those who gave the command."

The timing for such an uprising couldn't be worse. The new vampire race was still in its infancy, and with some of the dhampir covens—like Siobhan's—feeling threatened by the resurgence, the political landscape was volatile at best. Saeed would be expected to shoulder a certain amount of responsibility, which meant his mind would need to be clear. He'd vowed to find the fae who haunted his every waking thought. How could he possibly serve Mikhail and his own desires at the same time?

Saeed uttered a low curse under his breath.

"Exactly," Mikhail said.

It seemed Saeed would be forced to shift his focus. For the time being at least. His obsession with the female he'd seen so many times in the Collective burned like a cinder in the center of his chest. It ate away at him, slowly eroding his sanity. He'd made a pledge to Mikhail, though. The king had given Saeed the gift of transformation and without it he never would have gotten a glimpse of the fae. He owed his king nothing less than complete loyalty. His search would have to be put on hold. For now.

"It pains me to say it," Saeed began, "but I fear the Sortiari far less than I do the berserkers."

The Sortiari were a dangerous lot, no doubt about it, but their members possessed intelligence and a certain amount of good sense, no matter how misdirected it might be. The berserkers, on the other hand, were violent, rash creatures who acted on base instinct. They preferred violence over diplomacy. If they managed to overthrow the Sortiari, the consequences would be disastrous.

"It pains me even more to agree with you," Mikhail replied. "At least McAlister operates under the assumption that he's doing the wrong things for the right reasons. The berserkers know no reason. Only vengeance."

Saeed was old, but not the oldest among them. There were some vendettas older than the years he'd walked the earth. "Vengeance for what?"

Mikhail answered him with silence. If the vampire king knew the reasons for the berserkers' actions, he wasn't about to reveal it.

"When will you meet with McAlister?"

Mikhail let out a heavy sigh. "In two weeks. I've managed to put him off for the time being, but he's grown impatient and suspicious of my motives for delaying him. There's friction enough between us; I don't see any reason to make matters worse."

"What can I do?" Saeed had sworn to serve Mikhail. Payment for his transformation.

"Pick three dhampirs from your coven to turn," Mikhail replied. "Our numbers are too small for my peace of mind, and with so much turmoil on the horizon, I want us as strong as possible."

A simple enough request. Saeed's gaze slid to Sasha. She kept her attention focused away from the conversation, but he knew she'd be the first to petition him for the favor of being turned. Would he do it? Could he? She was the most levelheaded among them. The Collective scratched at the back of Saeed's mind and he fought its pull yet again. Who would save him from the grips of madness while she adjusted to the change?

"Of course," Saeed answered after a moment. Mikhail stood from his chair, indicating that business was, for now, concluded. "Please, Mikhail, if there's anything else I can do—"

Mikhail put a hand on Saeed's shoulder. "I know," he said. "I'll be in touch."

As the king departed with Jenner at his side, Saeed met Sasha's determined gaze. If he denied her the honor of being turned, she'd never forgive him.

If he turned her, though, he might lose himself to madness once and for all.

CHAPTER
6

From the top of the hill at the edge of the property, Chelle took in the expanse of Gunnar's vast estate. It might have been the most valuable property in Pasadena. A wonder of modern architecture, it was the sort of place hotshot corporate executives built as a way to prove to all of their buddies they had the biggest dick. Somehow, though, she doubted Gunnar had to prove his manhood to anyone.

A three-quarter moon hung high in the sky, casting its silvery glow over the grounds. It might've been dangerous to attempt another B and E so close to the full moon, but Chelle wasn't about to waste another second, let alone days. Her unease had grown since her tethering. She'd become astute at blocking out the thoughts of those around her, but she still picked up on bits and pieces of their memories without warning. Her vulnerability during the daylight hours still plagued her. The second the sun peeked above the horizon, she was helpless to succumb to the oblivion of daytime sleep. Just yesterday, she'd held a sterling silver spoon in her hand for over an hour. After her turning, she hadn't been able to tolerate contact at all without becoming sick and weakened from silver poisoning. But with each passing day, she became more tolerant and wondered if she'd soon be completely immune to its effects.

Her own nature and the mystery of her transformation frightened her more than anything in this world. The Alexandria Library was her last hope. If she couldn't find answers there, they wouldn't be found anywhere. And the only thing that stood between her and the second piece of the puzzle was a two-hundred-and-fifty-pound werewolf.

Heat pooled low in Chelle's belly as she recalled the toe-curling kiss he'd laid on her only a few nights ago. Fate truly was cruel. Her own creation, fear, and curiosity had led her here. As though Fate had laid a path of bread crumbs straight to the male who would tether her. Her own quest for Set's Chest had led Ronan to his mate, further proving that none of them sat in the driver's seat. Was there no aspect of her life that she had control over?

Fate could go suck a bag of dicks as far as she was concerned.

Chelle had definitely been too cavalier in her plans to storm the castle without backup. It was probably time to put her ego in check and exercise a little stealth. As she continued to watch the property, a ripple of trepidation danced down her spine. Lucas was right: if she encountered an entire pack of angry werewolves, she doubted she'd be able to fend them off. Would Gunnar allow the pack to kill her? Did it really matter? If Mikhail got wind of Chelle's increasingly volatile power, he might do the deed himself.

"Damn it." Nothing would be accomplished sitting here worrying about it all night. She stood from her crouched position, ready to put the werewolf's high-tech security system to the test once again.

"Finally. I thought you were going to sit there like a statue all night."

Chelle jumped at the sound of the deep, rumbling voice. "Son of a bitch." So much for stealth. She'd wasted too much time forming a plan of attack when she should have gotten her ass in gear. The werewolf had been stalking her. Watching. With such silence, she hadn't even noticed. He must have been standing upwind of her. Sly bastard. That's what she got for going head-to-head with an animal, she supposed.

Chelle didn't bother to turn and face him. Instead, she kept her gaze straight ahead. "I thought I smelled wet dog."

His low laughter sent a pleasant tremor through Chelle's body that settled low in her abdomen. The breeze shifted and Chelle caught wind of his scent. It reminded her of the ocean and the redwood forests. Masculine and clean. Not like a wet dog at all, damn it. Against her better judgment, she inhaled deeply. Her throat became hot and dry with thirst and Chelle stifled a moan. She knew the taste of his blood would have no equal and she yearned for just a sip.

"What took you so long?" Chelle's eyes drifted shut at the sound of his deep voice. Gods, it was like music to her ears and made her chest feel altogether too light and airy. "I expected you back the very next night. You disappointed me, vampire."

"It's Chelle." *Stupid! Gods, Chelle, don't tell him your name!* She hadn't meant to say it but somehow it bothered her to be referred to as simply "vampire."

"Chelle." The sound of her name spoken in that warm timbre, with the barest hint of his native accent, made her shiver. He made it sound sensual, a caress that she felt the entire length of her body.

"The key isn't here, Chelle." He made sure to emphasize her name as though he knew the effect it had on her. "It's gone."

Gone? Any pleasure she might have felt was immediately replaced with panic and a fair amount of annoyance. She couldn't show her hand, though. She had to play this close to the hip. "What key? I don't know what you're talking about."

He laughed. The grass didn't even stir with his movement as he came up behind her. The fine hairs on the back of Chelle's neck stood on end. His breath brushed the back of her neck and her nipples hardened. *Gods.* How could he have such an instant and visceral effect on her? It made her feel even more out of control and it drove Chelle crazy.

"You know exactly what I'm talking about." He reached up and stroked a lock of her hair that dangled from her ponytail. "I like your hair better down."

The compliment shouldn't have caused her stomach to twist in on itself. Chelle bucked her chin in the air. "Then I'll be sure to wear it up every day from here on out."

He let out a soft chuff of laughter. "My mate is defiant. I like a female with fight."

Indignant anger boiled in Chelle's chest. *Mate?* So he had sensed the bond between them that night. She whipped around to face Gunnar, their bodies so close they touched. The heat of his body permeated the thin fabric of her T-shirt and Chelle suppressed a groan. She took a step backward and squared her shoulders.

She chose not to acknowledge their bond. "You haven't begun to see defiant, buddy." She poked a finger at his chest and found it hard as stone. "And don't call me 'female' or 'vampire.' Got it?"

"Why not?" His brow puckered with genuine curiosity. Was this guy for real? "It's what you are."

Chelle took in the sight of him. Gunnar had certainly

stepped right from the pages of a history book. The low-slung jeans that rode his hips and tight T-shirt that showcased the hills and valleys of muscle that adorned his body gave him the modern hipster vibe. But without the modern clothes, he screamed Viking warrior badass. He seemed to find a perverse satisfaction in antagonizing her and she found herself wanting to encourage it. Sick. "You know, you might want to update your hair and trim that yeti beard. The whole Viking-warrior thing went out of style a thousand or so years ago."

Gunnar grinned. Gods, that expression. Wolfish. Totally cliché considering, but there was no other way to describe it. "You don't like the way I look?" He made a show of sniffing the air. "Your scent says differently."

Undermined by her own gods-damned pheromones. "I didn't say I didn't like it." There was no use denying her attraction when her body had already betrayed her. "I just said you might want to update your look."

"There's an entire generation of hipsters who'd disagree with you." Humor sparked in his bright blue gaze and Chelle found herself wanting to smile at his wit.

"You might be right." She saw countless men parading around L.A. trying to pull off what Gunnar came by naturally.

His eyes crinkled at the corners. "Might?"

Chelle refused to give him the satisfaction of an outright admission. The werewolf obviously knew he was attractive. She didn't feel the need to stroke his ego. Or anything else for that matter.

"Why do you want the key?" he asked again.

So confident he knew what she wanted. It really pissed her off that he'd read her so well. Gunnar wasn't only sexy as fuck. The male was obviously shrewd. The safe had been loaded with all sorts of relics and books. How could he have possibly deduced that the key was what she'd been after? Chelle had hoped she'd be up against a stupid animal. A mindless tough guy. Once again she'd underestimated him. She'd be damned if she let it happen again.

"I told you. I have no idea what you're talking about."

Gunnar cocked his head to one side and studied her. Chelle bristled under the scrutiny and, at the same time, it excited her. Her breath came in quick little pants and her heart raced in her chest. She could honestly say that she finally knew what prey felt like.

"Do you know what you are, *vampire*?"

He went out of his way to aggravate her. She wanted to kick him in the shin. And maybe kiss him a little, too. "No. What am I, *werewolf*?"

His teeth snapped together and he leaned in close. "You're *mine*."

Oh, hell no. It was time someone put this arrogant male in his place.

"Yours?" Chelle scoffed. Her incredulous tone only egged Gunnar on. "I'm no one's property."

Did she know his wolf had claimed her as theirs? He'd called her "mate," and though it hadn't seem to faze her, neither had she acknowledged it. Her scent, sweet with desire, drove him mad with want. Gunnar fought the urge to grab her again, pull her against him and show her exactly to whom she belonged. Instead, he kept himself in check. He liked the game they played and so did his wolf. A mating dance of sorts that made winning the prize all the sweeter. Worry scratched at the back of his mind, however. He'd been lucky enough to catch her scent while out patrolling the property tonight. If Aren, or any of the others, had been on duty, it might not have gone so well.

It was important to keep her presence here tonight a

secret. He needed her as far away from the pack as possible, which was one of the reasons he'd moved the key and thereby eliminated the temptation for her to return.

"If you tell me why you want the key, I might give it to you." He wondered if she'd smell the lie on him. Werewolves easily detected lies through scent, and minuscule tells such as an increase in body temperature, dilated pupils . . . Gunnar had no idea what a vampire was capable of detecting.

"I can detect everything you can and more."

Gunnar took a cautious step backward. She responded as though she'd plucked his thoughts right from his head. His mate was indeed dangerous. But he owed her thanks for revealing such a talent to him. He'd have to be more careful from here on out. He kept his stance relaxed as he closed the distance between them once again.

He'd tried to bluff and failed. The only option was to keep up with the pretense. If anything, to get a rise out of her. "Then you know what I say is true."

Chelle scoffed. "That you'll give me the key? Please. Even without hearing your thoughts, I know that's a lie."

She made the admission easily enough, confirming his suspicion. Perhaps it was a trait all vampires possessed. His mate was full of surprises and Gunnar couldn't wait for her to spring the next one on him. "No." Gunnar let his gaze roam over her fine features and down the length of her shapely body. "That you're *mine*."

Her scent changed almost imperceptibly. His claim made her anxious. Whether she liked it or not, his wolf had claimed her. It was a bond not easily broken.

"Tell me, wolf, what makes you so sure?"

She was playing with him. Getting him to divulge something. Gunnar wasn't about to lose the upper hand, though. "I *know*. That should be explanation enough."

Chelle's answering laughter rang out around them. The sound peppered his skin like a warm summer rain. She fascinated him. So arrogant, so defiant, his little thief.

But that defiance would surely get her killed. "Quiet," Gunnar commanded. "Mine aren't the only ears that can hear for miles."

Chelle's laughter stopped in an instant and she fixed him with a serious gaze. "Is that a threat?"

He could add mistrustful to her list of personality traits. It wouldn't be long before the breeze shifted yet again and Aren and the others caught wind of her scent. He needed to get her out of here, now, and she wasn't exactly being cooperative.

Gunnar reached out and gripped her upper arm. His first mistake. Chelle grabbed him by the forearm and twisted, the action so quick and with so much strength behind it, she'd flipped Gunnar and put him on his back before he knew what happened. His breath left his chest in a *whoof!* of air as his world flipped on its axis. Chelle bent over him, her lips pulled back into a snarl that revealed the dual points of her razor-sharp fangs.

Magnificent.

Gunnar reached out and grabbed Chelle's ankle. He gave her a swift jerk and she went down in the grass beside him. A warning growl gathered in her chest but Gunnar didn't give her time to retaliate. He wanted her on the defensive, off her game and unsure. The faster she made the decision to retreat, the better.

He'd hoped her skill lay in stealing, but Gunnar quickly discovered his mate's talents were many. Rather than tuck tail and run, she readied herself for a fight. *Foolish!* Her want of the key was such that she'd put herself in the path of danger to get it. Did she not realize it would do her no good if she was dead? He moved toward her to pin her to the ground, but Chelle was much too quick. She rolled away and was on her feet in a heartbeat, fists raised, her stance ready for impact.

"I'm not going to make it easy for you," she warned. Brilliant silver swirled in her irises like a building storm and Gunnar stared, transfixed by her beauty. "I'm not about to become kibble for your pack."

Gunnar let out an annoyed snort. "Stubborn female," he ground out from between clenched teeth. "I'm trying to protect you. Not *kill* you."

"Sure you are." She bounced on her toes, ready to dart to one side or another at a moment's notice. "I know how werewolves operate. Pack first."

It was true that loyalty to the pack was undeniable, but Chelle knew nothing of werewolves. If she did, she'd know that loyalty to one's mate trumped all else, even the pack bond. "If you knew the nature of werewolves, you'd be miles from here right now, hiding yourself away."

"From what?" Her words rang with bravado, but Gunnar saw the fear behind her eyes. "You?"

"As long as I have breath in my lungs, you've nothing to fear from me," Gunnar replied.

Chelle froze and her fists dipped to her sides. "Sure."

Gunnar pushed himself up to stand. He brushed the grass and dirt from his jeans. "I would just as soon die as allow any harm to come to my *mate*."

"I'm not your mate."

Her scent soured with the lie. Which meant she'd sensed their bond as well. Interesting. Gunnar cocked a brow. "No?"

He dared her to deny it again.

Their gazes locked and for a moment they simply stared. Gunnar's wolf let out a warning growl in the recess of his psyche and Chelle cocked her head to one side.

"What is it saying?"

She could hear his wolf? Gunnar's chest tightened and

he fought the urge to rub the sensation away. He wondered, What did the animal sound like to her?

"He's warning me," Gunnar replied.

Chelle's gaze narrowed. "Of what?"

"Danger."

"Good." Chelle's stance once again became defensive. "I'm glad one of you has a lick of sense."

"I'm not the one in danger," Gunnar ground out. *"You are."*

CHAPTER
7

"The key isn't here," Gunnar said, this time with more urgency. "Now get the hell out of here."

His scent was clean and, likewise, his thoughts didn't betray a lie. Frustration knotted Chelle's stomach. The myriad unanswered questions pinging around in her brain made her head throb.

"Where is it?" she seethed. There was no point in pretending. It was nearly impossible to deceive a supernatural creature.

"Tell me why you want it first."

This again? Chelle wasn't about to give in. "Give it to me and I'll tell you."

She could play the game as well as Gunnar could. Hell, she could play it *better*. The wolf yipped in Gunnar's mind.

"I can do this all night, werewolf."

Gunnar cast a nervous glance toward the house. He'd managed to stalk her without alerting her to his presence. Could they be surrounded by his pack at this very moment?

"Give it to me," Chelle said. "You'll never have to see me again."

His head whipped around. A deep groove cut into his brow just above his nose, as though her words caused him pain. Chelle's own heart clenched and she felt the tether between them give a gentle tug. She couldn't afford emotions right now. They'd only get in her way.

"So ready to be rid of your mate, vampire?"

Don't be so quick to discount your emotions, idiot.

Chelle did know how to play this game. She'd flirted her way out of plenty of situations in the past. What would it hurt to use the tether to her advantage? Especially if it got Chelle what she wanted.

"How can I be ready to get rid of you?" she asked. "I barely know you."

Gunnar's eyes narrowed at her honeyed tone. Okay, so maybe she was pouring it on a little thick. Might be a good idea to dial it down a bit.

"And I barely know you." His accent seemed to thicken with his agitation. Chelle couldn't help but find it charming. "That relic was entrusted to my pack for safekeeping. You'll not get your hands on it soon, I can promise you that." With every second Gunnar seemed to grow more agitated. "So do as I ask and get the hell out of here. You'll only invite disaster if you stay. Especially when they find out what you are."

"A vampire?" Chelle scoffed. "I didn't know my kind was so offensive."

"No," Gunnar stressed. "My *mate*."

His words knocked the air right out of Chelle's lungs. Only hours ago, she'd been arguing a similar point with Lucas, pointing out that until now, vampires had rarely been tethered outside of their species. Chelle wasn't afforded a glimpse into the Collective as Mikhail and the others were. Had they ever seen a nonvampire pairing in the memories of dead vampires? And if so, what had the consequences of those tetherings been?

Urgency welled up within her and Chelle turned to run. Fear fueled every step as she darted to the forest at the edge of Gunnar's property and the cover of dense foliage. Her breath sawed in and out of her chest as she vaulted a fence. A body crashed into hers mid-flight and took her to the ground in a none-too-gentle tackle.

Chelle's arms flailed as she fought to throw a punch but her wrists were caught in an iron grip and forced to the ground. She kicked, struggled against the weight of the body that held her down, snapped her jaw and hissed. The male who pinned her smelled of the forest like Gunnar but the underlying musky scent made her nose wrinkle.

"Move another inch, vampire, and I'll break your fucking neck."

Chelle stilled, but not because she was worried the werewolf would break her neck. To kill her, he'd need to put a stake through her heart or sever her head completely. Chelle allowed herself to still because he'd taken a good whiff of her and his thoughts rang out loud and clear:

The bitch smells of Gunnar.

Shit.

It shouldn't have mattered to Chelle what deduction the male would make from catching Gunnar's scent on her. But something tugged at the center of Chelle's chest that begged to differ. "Get the fuck off of me or I'll take it upon myself to neuter you, mutt."

Chelle could give as good as she got. Idle threats didn't mean a damned thing to her. Power vibrated from the werewolf, but not with the same intensity as it emanated from Gunnar, which only helped to strengthen Chelle's assumption that Gunnar was the Alpha. He'd never outright proclaimed it, but that was the thing about those with power: they never had to boast about it. Anyone who crossed their path simply *knew*.

The werewolf wrapped his right hand around Chelle's throat and squeezed. She wanted to roll her eyes but resisted. Her lungs didn't need oxygen. The only thing attempting to cut off her air supply would accomplish was to piss her off.

The male might not have been successful in choking her out, but he did manage to silence her voice. She'd had enough of playing it safe. Chelle was so over tonight and all she wanted to do was go home and lick her damned wounds: namely, her pride. The male straddled her waist, leaving Chelle's legs free. Didn't he know anything about immobilizing someone? She brought her legs up like a whip, shifting the werewolf's weight in an instant. She wrapped her ankles around his throat and, just as fast, brought her legs down, propelling him away from her body. The male rolled several feet away before a large bush stopped him. He let out a low groan that coaxed a smile to Chelle's lips, but she didn't have time to revel in smug satisfaction. She hated that she trusted the tether enough to take Gunnar's warning to heart. She needed to get the hell out of here.

"Move and I'll put a silver bullet through your heart."

The sound of metal grinding on metal met Chelle's ears as the male righted himself and pulled back the slide on a .40 caliber Ruger. Werewolves who carried silver ammo? Damn, that was cold.

While silver didn't exactly agree with vampires, it was even deadlier for a werewolf. The silver poisoning moved slowly in a vampire depending on the concentration. It weakened them considerably and in certain situations might kill them. But even a small amount of silver could easily put a two-hundred-fifty-pound werewolf down in a second flat. That Gunnar's pack used that sort of ammo made Chelle wonder just what they needed to protect themselves from. A rival pack, perhaps? Because they sure as hell weren't outfitted with silver bullets on the off chance they'd run into a vampire.

"Only if that bullet moves faster than I do," Chelle replied. Too cocky? Maybe. "And I'm willing to bet it doesn't."

The werewolf's dark eyes narrowed as he sighted in the gun. One of the benefits of supernatural senses, the dark didn't impede his eyesight. *Well, shit.* Looked like Chelle was going to have to put her money where her mouth was. She shifted her weight to her right leg, ready to propel herself out of the way of the bullet as she attempted to pull off some real Superman shit. The report of the gun rang out at the exact moment a wall of muscle steamrolled into her, taking her to the ground. Good gods, two full-body tackles in one night? Werewolves really were full-contact creatures.

Sheesh.

Chelle opened her eyes to find Gunnar's ice-blue ones trained on her face. Rage simmered below the surface of his expression and Chelle had a feeling it wasn't the guy with the gun who'd sparked his ire. His jaw flexed with agitation and golden fire flashed behind his irises, letting the wolf shine through for a brief moment. A shudder shook Chelle's body and her blood ignited in her veins. If she'd thought him handsome when annoyed with her, he was absolutely magnificent in his anger.

Without word or preamble, Gunnar flipped Chelle onto her stomach. A rush of molten heat shot through her bloodstream and she had to remind herself that this was a *hostile* situation. Thanks to the tether, her body turned traitor, anxious for whatever Gunnar would do next. He jerked her hands behind her back and bound her wrists with a length of cord. Not exactly what she'd been hoping for, but under different circumstances a little light bondage might have been fun.

If he thought a thin rope was going to keep her compliant, Gunnar had another think coming. Chelle pulled her wrists to break the bonds and met with resistance. Her brow knitted as Gunnar's deep, rumbling laughter filled her ears. Bastard. Whatever he'd bound her with wasn't so easily broken. Clever. And annoying as hell.

He straddled her ass to lean forward over one ear and Chelle was suddenly *very* aware of his body. Behind his fly, the firmness of his cock brushed the small of her back. If he didn't get himself in check, he wouldn't have to worry about Chelle spilling the beans to his pack. His own physical reaction was enough of a tell to seal both of their fates.

"Keep your mouth shut and your gaze down," Gunnar warned with a snarl. "And *maybe* you'll live to see your next sunset."

Chelle wanted to smack her forehead against the ground. So far, everything had gone according to plan. Jesus. Some burglar she'd turned out to be. Tethered and captured by a pack of werewolves, all in less than a week's time. What else could she manage to screw up?

Maybe she didn't want the answer to that question.

Stubborn female! If she'd simply done as Gunnar had asked, the *first time* he'd asked it, she wouldn't be in this mess. He couldn't help her now, not without the pack knowing exactly why, and this was dangerous enough ground to tread without attempting to fight centuries of tradition. Tradition he'd helped to uphold. His wolf let out an angry snarl in the recess of his psyche and Gunnar did his best to quiet the animal. Aggression would do them no good. From here on out, they'd need to use their wits and stealth. It wasn't easy to deceive a werewolf. Gunnar certainly had his work cut out for him.

"What did I tell you about those gods-damned silver bullets?" Gunnar rounded on Aren, more than willing to take a little of his frustration out on the other male. "You could have killed me!"

A feral light shone in Aren's dark gaze. Something dangerous and hungry that gave Gunnar's wolf pause. Aren quickly recovered and his expression once again became the unflappable one Gunnar was used to. "I had no idea you were about to pounce." The excuse held as much sincerity as a sieve did water. "And not much else is going to put down a vampire except a stake."

Thank the gods Aren hadn't thought to arm himself with one. Otherwise, Gunnar might have lost his mate tonight. Hell, Gunnar had almost taken a silver bullet tonight. In which case, they would have both died. Surely Aren had heard Gunnar approach. Scented him on the breeze. If Aren had truly meant the bullet for Chelle, wouldn't he have fired a split second sooner? A tremor of worry moved through him and his wolf let out a concerned whimper. The message was clear: Aren could no longer be trusted.

Really, could any of his pack be trusted if they found out their Alpha had taken a vampire as a mate?

"I don't want her put down." Gunnar allowed his wolf to the surface and a snarl gathered in his chest. Aren met his gaze for a beat too long before looking away and it only served to further enrage the already agitated animal. "I want *answers*."

He hauled Chelle up to stand and held her by the rope that bound her wrists. It was a useful bit of hardware to be sure, a seemingly common length of nylon rope. However, this one had been reinforced with magic. It weakened supernatural strength. Never broke no matter how much stress was exerted upon it. Gunnar had paid a mint for the enchantment and it had proven to be worth every penny.

"I'll give you an answer," Aren said. "The vampire is a thief. That's all the answer you need. Lop off her hands and send her back to the vampire king as a warning to any other ambitious bloodsuckers who think to steal from us."

Funny, Gunnar had considered doing just that the other night before his wolf had claimed her. "I'm sure that wouldn't incite a war."

Aren snickered at Gunnar's sarcastic tone. "Maybe it's time to poke the bear."

Viking diplomacy or werewolf diplomacy? Neither one could be considered very diplomatic by any stretch of the imagination. "You're restless," Gunnar remarked. "It doesn't matter who you poke as long as you get a fight."

Aren shrugged. The fine hairs stood on the back of Gunnar's neck. The noncommittal answer didn't do much to assuage his suspicions. "It's true I'm restless. But not indiscriminate. The vampire being here is proof enough that we need to pick a side in what's to come."

This again? Gunnar was quickly tiring of the berserkers and their grudges. "The vampire being here has as much to do with Ian Gregor and his vendetta as a shifting breeze has with the cycle of the moon. At least, he hoped. In truth, he had no idea what Chelle's motives were in attempting to steal his third of the Alexandria key. He'd wanted to get some real answers tonight. Instead, all he'd gotten was a damned headache.

"I already told you, we're *not* getting involved in Gregor's bullshit." Gunnar was sick and fucking tired of having his authority undermined. Aren's continued arguing would only create strife within the pack.

"Staying neutral will only make us enemies to both sides," Aren stressed. "We should ally ourselves with the berserkers now, while it can still benefit us."

Whether or not his wolf had claimed Chelle, this was not the time or the place to hash out pack business. "We'll discuss it later," Gunnar said. "When it's appropriate."

Aren glanced at Chelle and sneered. "Who cares what the vampire hears? She won't likely make it out of here alive."

Chelle leaned forward and spat at Aren's feet. "We'll see about that, asshole."

Gunnar had to admire his mate's tenacity. He let out an amused chuckle and Chelle bristled beside him. Such fire. She had the heart of a warrior. It was no surprise his wolf had claimed her. "We need to get her back to the house," Gunnar said. "See what she knows before we decide what to do with her."

Of course Gunnar knew that hell would freeze over before Chelle divulged anything. At any rate, he'd enjoy trying to get something out of her. "Move, vampire," he ordered. She glanced over her shoulder at him, eyes narrowed to hateful slits. Amusement curved Gunnar's lips as he gave her a gentle nudge forward.

Chelle brought the heel of her boot back and it connected smartly with Gunnar's shin. He let out a pained grunt and stumbled back a step, causing him to give the rope a rough jerk. Chelle recovered quickly, her every movement fluid and graceful in comparison to Gunnar's.

Aren shook his head with a soft chuckle as he moved to take up a place at Gunnar's side. "You might not want to lop off her hands now, but by the end of the night you might be tempted to."

Chelle was sure to test his patience. Gunnar let out a slow sigh. For once, Aren might be right.

The walk to the main house spanned a little over a

quarter mile, but to Gunnar it felt like ten times that. He worked to form a plan that would protect Chelle while at the same time allowing him to save face in front of his pack. If Aren had his way, they'd be chopping his mate into bits and pieces to send back to Mikhail Aristov in a box. All of this could be alleviated if Chelle would just come clean and tell him why she wanted the key. But since that wasn't going to happen, Gunnar would have to find a plan B.

"Hope you've got a cell built out of whatever this rope is made from, *mutt*." Insufferable female would no doubt go out of her way to push Gunnar's buttons. So far, she was doing a damned fine job. "Because if you don't, I won't be here for long."

"Shut your mouth, vampire." Aren couldn't help but chime in. "You're a thief and a trespasser on pack property and subject to pack law."

"You know, I haven't eaten all night," Chelle said offhand. "I think when I bust out of here, I'll drink you dry first."

Gunner stifled a smile. His wolf, however, didn't appreciate the mental image of its mate's mouth anywhere near the other male. A predatory growl built in Gunnar's chest. Chelle's step faltered and she glanced back at him, her expression curious as she studied him. She could crawl right into his head and he needed to remember that. It was too damned easy to let his guard down in her presence. The mate bond weakened Gunnar and it vexed him. Weakness wasn't tolerated in the pack and certainly not from the Alpha.

"Quiet." Gunnar hoped the sternly spoken word would have enough subtext to get his message across. His mate was in enemy territory. It would do her no good to be lippy.

"What's the matter, werewolf?" Chelle practically purred. "Jealous?"

Annoyed was more like it. Gunnar's wolf on the other hand was more than ready for a fight. Gunnar couldn't be sure if it was the mate bond, or the nearly full moon overhead that allowed his wolf so much control over Gunnar's mind. Either way, he found the encroaching imbalance disturbing. With so much unrest in the pack—not to mention throughout the area's supernatural population—Gunnar needed to have his shit straight. He couldn't afford a distraction right now. Even one as beautiful and tempting as Chelle.

"Jealous?" The wolf growled and Gunnar willed him to silence. "Hardly."

Chelle cocked her head to one side as she walked, sending the hair gathered at the top of her head over one shoulder. Her scent wafted over him, sweet and delicious, and Gunnar swallowed down a groan.

"You say no . . ." Chelle glanced over her shoulder and grinned, showing a bit of fang. Gods, what would it be like to feel the sharp point graze his skin? "But I'm thinking your thoughts might betray you, *mutt*."

Aren stopped and leveled his gaze on Gunnar. "What in the hell is she talking about?"

Good gods. The vampire was sure to be the death of him.

"Who knows what she's talking about," Gunnar said. "But if she doesn't keep quiet, I'm going to duct-tape her mouth shut."

Chelle chuckled. There was a spring in her step that hadn't been there before. His mate certainly liked to antagonize, didn't she? Yup. She was definitely going to be the death of him.

CHAPTER
8

Chelle knew better than to press her luck but she just couldn't help herself. Pushing buttons was sort of her thing. Gunnar looked like he might blow a gasket at any second and his crony was more than ready to take an axe to her hands à la eleventh-century justice. She guessed you could take the werewolf out of Scandinavia but you couldn't take the Viking out of the werewolf. Or . . . something like that.

The more agitated Gunnar got, the more it revved Chelle's engine. Totally messed up, but it didn't change the fact that she liked to see him riled and wild. On edge. Unpredictable. Chelle was a seat-of-her-pants sort of female. She was used to turning on a dime, running halfway across the world to chase a lead on this relic or that. Gunnar struck her as the sort of male who lived his life by a strict set of rules. Never put a toe out of line. Planned everything to the last detail. *Bo-ring!*

"What's the rope made of?" Chelle's pride had taken a serious hit when she couldn't break the bonds. "Silver threads braided into the nylon?" Probably not. Her tolerance to silver had grown with each passing month. She doubted a few silver threads would have weakened her that much.

Gunnar snorted but didn't respond.

Her brother Ronan's mate was a witch. Perhaps Gunnar had someone on the payroll like Naya? A white witch capable of enchantments and whatnot. She glanced over her shoulder and met Gunnar's wild blue gaze. "Witchcraft?"

Though he kept his mind remarkably void of thought, his posture stiffened. Almost imperceptibly. So, yep. Magic. Bummer. Chelle definitely would have been able to break the rope if it was infused with silver. Magic was something she didn't understand and had no desire to mess with. Especially after everything that had happened to her in Crescent City. It made her twitchy as hell and more than ready to have the damned rope free of her body.

"I hope it was a white witch." Chelle did her best to keep her tone conversational and light despite the anxiety that crept up on her. "Because I've dealt with dark magic and it's not something I'd wish on my worst enemy."

"Didn't we tell you to shut your mouth?" Gunnar's cohort totally had a stick up his ass.

Chelle allowed her mind to quiet and listened for the male's thoughts. His wolf was quieter than Gunnar's. She heard barely any sign of its presence in the male's mind. It could've been the tether that allowed her to hear Gunnar's wolf so clearly. Or maybe Chelle's abilities were starting to short-circuit. *Who knows?*

"What sort of dark magic?"

Gunnar's voice distracted Chelle from eavesdropping on the other werewolf's thoughts. The deep timbre vibrated over her and a pleasant shiver traveled from the top of Chelle's head to the tips of her toes.

She considered continuing to mess with him, but thought better of it. Dark magic wasn't something to fuck around with and Chelle wasn't about to treat it lightly. "The sort created by gods." Why mince words? Might as well hit him with the big guns.

His friend let out a derisive chuff of breath. "She's mad," he said. "It proves what sort of egos we're dealing with that a vampire would claim to know anything of the gods."

"I know more than you think." Chelle's tone grew icy. She didn't like being called a liar and she wasn't about to let the cocky male get away with it. She drew on what knowledge she had of Viking culture—in particular, their superstitions—more than ready to scare the bastard right out of his fur. "I've been touched by one."

He'd called her mad, why not feed into his paranoia? If the werewolves feared her, she'd have the upper hand right off the bat. Of course, it might just convince them to chop off her head and send it to Mikhail in a box. It was a chance she was willing to take.

"Did you hear that?" the male said to Gunnar. "She's all but admitted it! We can't trust the words of madness. We need to take care of her and be done with this."

Well, that was one vote for beheading. It only took a few seconds to scare the male. She wondered if Gunnar would spook as easily.

"Get a room ready in the basement," Gunnar barked. "And fetch Sven and Jillian."

The male's lips curled upward. Smug bastard. He obviously thought Chelle's crazy talk had won him a victory. His lack of common sense was probably why he hadn't ascended to become Alpha of the pack. Something Chelle could be grateful for at this point. He took off at a clip, throwing open the front door and disappearing into the house.

"Scare tactics?" Gunnar chided once they were alone. "Really?"

"Psychological warfare," Chelle corrected. Gunnar dropped his hold on the rope and rounded Chelle to face her. She flashed him a feral grin, showcasing her fangs. "Worried?"

Gunnar's answering grin was downright disarming. A contented purr echoed in his psyche and she sensed the animal that lived there approved of her wiles. Pleasure bloomed in her chest and spread outward. She shouldn't want Gunnar's—or his mutt's—approval. But somehow, it made her feel damn good.

"You consider me your enemy, then?" Was it concern that accented his words?

"I don't know what I consider you," Chelle replied without guile. "But your friend? Yeah, he's definitely a hostile."

"Aren is my second," Gunnar said. "He answers to me."

For someone who ranked lower than his Alpha, Chelle sensed that Aren consistently pushed his limits with Gunnar. Something the Alpha of a pack should be concerned with. "He only answers to you because he has to," Chelle said. "Give him the opportunity, and he'll turn on you."

Gunnar's gaze narrowed. She'd hit a nerve. He must have suspected the same thing. "I am a *king*." His voice dropped an octave and gold burned behind his eyes. "Descended from kings. Alpha of the Forkbeard pack. If you ever undermine my authority—my dominance—in the presence of others, there will be dire consequences. Do you understand me?"

Gunnar meant business. A surge of power leaped from him, filling the air with a static charge that made the fine hairs on Chelle's arms stand on end. The warning growl she'd heretofore only heard in his mind vibrated loud and clear in his chest. Lesson learned: never take a potshot at the ego of an Alpha. Just the suggestion that someone in his fold might question his authority was enough to set off his temper.

He painted quite the frightening picture. He towered over her by at least a foot. Every inch of him was packed with dense muscle and his large hands could easily squeeze the life out of an enemy with little effort. Chelle could only imagine what he'd looked like so many centuries ago, dressed in full battle armor, smudged with dirt and the blood of his enemies. Sweat beading his brow and a well-used sword held aloft in his hand. Her heart beat a little faster at the mental image and her breath raced.

A groove cut into Gunnar's brow. He took a step back and he brushed his hand over the hair that fell to one side of his shaved head. "I didn't mean to scare you," he said, low. "I apologize."

He'd read her physical reaction and thought he'd scared her? Chelle wanted to laugh. She was so turned on right now she was about to crawl right out of her freaking skin! "You don't scare me." The only thing she was really afraid of was her own power and what it might become.

Gunnar scented the air, the act so gods-damned animalistic that Chelle nearly swooned. The male was living, breathing sex. Realization struck and his pupils dilated as a hungry grin split his full, sensual lips. "Brave and wanton." The words reached out like a caress. "Both qualities I admire in a female."

Chelle couldn't allow herself to be seduced by the sexy werewolf. Not when she had so much to lose. They'd only occupied the same space twice and already he was becoming a temptation she didn't want to resist. A forbidden fruit begging to be plucked. The tether brought with it an instant connection. Physical as much as it was spiritual. Emotions didn't come into play, though. So the werewolf was fuckable? Chelle had sown her oats with males just like him. It didn't mean anything, though. She wasn't in love with Gunnar. She'd probably never be in love with him. They had absolutely nothing in common. Of course, that didn't mean she couldn't enjoy the scenery and try out the trails while she was visiting . . .

Snap out of it! Chelle gave herself a mental shake. Pheromones, hormones, whatever you wanted to call them, forced a connection between them. The tether bound them. But Chelle refused to give in to her base urges. She refused to let magic—in any form—continue to hold any sway over her.

"You're lucky I'm tied up," she remarked. "The last male who got cheeky with me was nursing more than just his pride when I was through with him."

Okay, so the last guy who'd gotten cheeky with her was Lucas. And only because she'd eaten the rest of the Pop-Tarts. And the only thing he'd nursed was his own disappointment in missing out on the frosted strawberry goodness. But Gunnar didn't need to know that.

"I don't doubt it," Gunnar replied, as smooth and heady as aged bourbon. "But that male wasn't me."

Chelle cocked a brow. "A challenge?"

"A promise," Gunnar said. "Don't test me, *vampire*." The derogatory emphasis didn't go unnoticed. Giving her a taste of her own medicine. "Don't think to challenge me. You'll lose."

Maybe, but that didn't mean Chelle wouldn't give it her best shot. "Don't be so sure, werewolf."

Chelle couldn't help but dance too close to the flames. She only hoped she wouldn't get burned in the process.

Gunnar's wolf vacillated between lust and worry, which only helped to wreak havoc on his body. Chelle was enough to test any male's mettle: beautiful, full of fire and fight, with a sharp wit and an even sharper tongue. As much as he wanted to play with her, this was no game. The very serious threat of how the pack would want to deal with her still loomed. Gunnar might be Alpha but that didn't always mean his word was law. He had to answer to those entrusted to his care. His responsibility was to the pack. And Chelle was a threat to everything he held dear.

Her antagonistic nature made him want to rise to the challenge. But there'd be no winner in a verbal sparring match. They could go round and round until the sun rose to put her down for the day. A finger of anxiety stroked down Gunnar's spine. She'd be vulnerable once the sun rose. Completely helpless. In a few short hours, he might be forced to choose between his mate and his pack. He didn't even know Chelle and yet his wolf would urge them to fight to the death to protect her.

And what of the twenty werewolves under his roof that also looked to him for not only leadership, but protection?

This was why a nonwerewolf mating was considered taboo. Had Chelle been one of them, the transition would have been smooth. She would have joined the pack without anyone batting so much as a lash. Every member of the pack would have accepted her with open arms. But Chelle wasn't pack. She wasn't a werewolf. She couldn't walk in the daylight. She needed blood to exist. And what of her coven? Did it operate like a pack? Would Mikhail Aristov simply allow her to leave his fold? The logistics made Gunnar's head spin. No good would come of any of this. Their fates were inescapably intertwined and inevitably headed toward disaster.

"Mind your mouth once we're inside." Gunnar reached behind Chelle and grabbed the rope that bound her. He gave her a gentle nudge and she walked in front of him, toward the open front door. "Aren doesn't usually have such a quick temper, but the full moon is only a few days

off, Chelle. It would behoove you not to anger him or anyone else. We are all volatile right now."

Once the moon was on the wane, things would settle
down. The timing couldn't be worse for Chelle to be here,
though. The pack was restless, their wolves too close to
the surface and fighting for dominance in their minds and
bodies alike.

"So you're saying I shouldn't jerk anyone's chains?"

Gunnar rolled his eyes. "Yes." Did she ever take anything seriously? "That's exactly what I'm saying."

He guided Chelle through the foyer to the staircase that
led to the basement. The area was rarely used. The space
consisted of an infirmary, two offices, a small armory, and
a sparsely furnished cell. Gunnar regretted that he had no
choice but to lock his mate up. But she'd attempted to steal
from not only him, but the pack. Twice. Where else did a
criminal belong but in a cell?

"Tell me, Chelle, does everyone find you as infuriating as I do?" Gunnar asked as they negotiated the steep
staircase.

"Depends." She threw another flirty smile his way.
Gunnar's stomach clenched as hot lust shot through him.
"How infuriated are you right now?"

"On a scale of one to ten?" Gunnar asked. "I'm hovering just below an eighty."

Chelle chuckled. "Then yes, everyone finds me as infuriating as you do."

When they hit the bottom stair Gunnar was almost
thankful for the opportunity to put a little distance between them. He knew that the more he learned about
her the more fascinating he would find her and that was
a huge problem. A female hadn't held his attention in a
good long while and Chelle's fiery spirit did more than
spark his interest.

Aren had readied the cell. The door—also infused with

magic—was left wide, the key still in the lock. Gunnar guided Chelle into the cell. Once inside, he untied the rope that bound her and gathered it up in his hands.

Chelle massaged her wrists and her mouth puckered. "I can still feel the magic tingling on my skin."

For the first time, Gunnar noticed the distress that marred her features. "It hurt you?" His wolf howled in the back of his mind as though sharing in her agony.

"It still wigs me out to hear him in your head," Chelle leveled her forest-green eyes on his. "It doesn't hurt. Not really. I'm—" She tucked her bottom lip between her teeth and her dual fangs nicked the skin. Four tiny crimson drops formed on her petal-pink lips. She licked the blood away and Gunnar found himself drawn to the simple act. "Never mind," she said after a moment. "It doesn't matter."

It mattered a great deal. Frustration welled in Gunnar's chest. So many obstacles to overcome and there seemed to be no end in sight. Too many things stood in the way of settling into a solid mate bond with her. And how did Chelle feel about being bound to a werewolf? What would her coven think if they learned of it? Would they settle into their bond or forever be fighting against it? Gunnar supposed he'd have to spend more than five minutes at a time with her in order to answer any of those questions. He let out a slow breath. Perhaps he was doomed to play this game with her forever. Cat and mouse, give and take, with nothing more than a few fleeting minutes before she ran or he set her free. Only to start over again.

With so much stress on an already tenuous bond, Gunnar worried that it might easily snap. The loss would destroy his wolf and take Gunnar down with him.

"So, this is the thief, huh?"

Gunnar started at Jillian's voice. He stepped out of the cell, slid the door closed, and turned the key to lock it. He made a show of taking the key and sliding it into his pocket. Chelle's eyes narrowed into slits right before she turned her attention to Jillian and flashed a cocky smile. He'd asked Chelle to behave and Gunnar was beginning to worry that she hadn't taken his admonition seriously.

Jillian approached the cell. Normally Gunnar could count on her to be a calming presence. Diplomatic. She studied Chelle, her expression curious. "I've never seen a vampire before. Everything I've read, though, asserts that they're alluring by nature. The texts got it right. You're very pretty."

Gunnar released the breath that had lodged near his sternum. At least he could count on one of them to keep a level head.

"It's the diet," Chelle remarked with a wily grin. "Blood does wonders for the complexion."

If Jillian was shocked, she gave no outward show. Still, Chelle watched her intently. Gauging her reaction by intruding on her thoughts? She might have been his mate, but Gunnar couldn't condone such a violation of Jillian's privacy. Especially without her knowledge.

"That's enough, vampire." It pained Gunnar not to say her name. He craved that familiarity. His aloofness was for her safety, though. He gave her a pointed look, letting her know that he was onto her. "Jillian, it's important to guard your thoughts in the presence of vampires."

She turned to face him, eyes wide with excitement. "They can read minds? That's not in any of the books."

Chelle shot a dirty look his way, no doubt cursing him a thousand different ways in her mind.

"I'm not certain," Gunnar replied. "But I have my suspicions."

"Well?" Jillian turned toward Chelle. "Can you?"

Chelle zipped her fingers across her lips and winked.

If there was a more aggravating female on the face of

the earth, Gunnar had yet to meet her. "Where are Sven and Aren?"

"On their way," Jillian said. "They're filling in everyone on what's going on."

Not ideal. But it's not like he could keep a vampire in the house without anyone finding out. Especially in as tight-knit a group as theirs.

"Aren wants to cut off her hands," Jillian remarked. "I told him that was a pretty antiquated punishment."

Ever the voice of reason. At least Gunnar knew he'd have someone in his corner. "And what is Sven's opinion on the matter?" Sven was older than Gunnar. If anyone would adhere to old ways, it was him.

Jillian shrugged. Her eyes slid to Chelle. "Sven said you should mount her head on a pike. But I reminded him that Viking justice might not jibe with the current American legal system. He agreed."

A few thousand years ago, they would have stabbed first and asked questions later. Gunnar included. The centuries had domesticated him somewhat. If only they had tamed some of his brethren.

"I'm glad one of you is the voice of reason," Gunnar remarked.

"Eh." Jillian grinned. "I do what I can. We do need to get to the bottom of what's going on, though, Gunnar. On that I agree with Aren and Sven. We have to know what she's here for and why. If the pack is threatened, we need to take action." She cast an anxious glance at Chelle. "And things might get messy in our quest for answers."

Jillian might have been the voice of reason, but she was still a werewolf. Gunnar certainly had his work cut out for him tonight.

CHAPTER
9

Chelle had hoped that she'd get the opportunity to see Gunnar's buddy again. So, when Aren walked through the door with another male who she assumed was Sven, Chelle was more than ready to poke around inside his brain to see what she could dig up. Before Gunnar had broken her concentration earlier, she'd gotten a glimpse at something that disturbed her. A glimmer of thought that could be detrimental not only to Gunnar but to Mikhail as well.

War.

The word had rung loud and clear in Aren's mind. He was obviously looking to stir up some shit and she'd gathered enough from his earlier conversation with Gunnar to know he wasn't above getting into bed with berserkers to get it done. A male with machinations like that could mean serious trouble. Chelle already had her hands full. The last thing she needed was to be dealing with an ambitious werewolf with a penchant for violence.

They were all animals, though, weren't they? Violence sort of came with the territory.

"Have you questioned her yet?" For someone who *wasn't* the Alpha, Aren sure was bossy. "If she's reluctant to give us anything, I say we send her back to Aristov in a body bag."

Chelle rolled her eyes. Did he get all that big talk from watching action movies? "I already told you, *mutt,* you can try to lay a finger on me, but it's not going to happen."

His lip curled into a sneer. *If this pack were mine, she'd be dead by now.* Aren's thoughts couldn't have been clearer if he'd spoken them out loud. *Maybe Gregor will pay a bounty for her head.*

From the sound of it, Aren wasn't simply urging Gunnar to ally himself with the berserkers. If Chelle had to guess, the male was busy making back-alley deals behind his Alpha's back. Jillian watched as Chelle studied Aren in silence, clearly suspicious, thanks to Gunnar's earlier warning. She certainly didn't need the female to rat her out the way Gunnar had. Chelle averted her gaze and stared at some far-off point on the wall.

Gunnar looked on with guarded amusement. Chelle had no idea what he was playing at but she refused to let any of them get the better of her.

He turned to Aren. "Let's see what we can get out of her before we start chopping off body parts."

Aren let out a chuff of breath.

"You're shit at diplomacy, Aren." The larger werewolf, Sven, was definitely the quiet, observant type. In Chelle's experience those were the ones you had to watch out for. Hotheads like Aren were easy to deal with, not so much the smart ones.

"This is an interrogation," Aren replied. "There's no room for diplomacy."

"An interrogation?" Gunnar cocked a brow. "By all means, question her."

Chelle shot him a dirty look. For all his ominous warnings, he sure as hell seemed to be enjoying himself.

Aren's chest puffed out as though he'd just been handed the keys to the castle. "Who sent you, bloodsucker?"

Chelle smirked. "Bloodsucker? Really? You couldn't think of a better insult than that?"

Behind Aren, Gunnar stifled a grin.

Aren leaned in close to the bars of Chelle's cell. "What does Aristov want?"

"How should I know?" Chelle asked. "Maybe you should ask him that."

"Don't try to bullshit me," Aren spat. "You reek of deceit. You're looking for leverage to use against the pack. What is it?"

Chelle fixed Aren with an accusing stare. "Tell me, mutt, just what are you up to that you'd think I—or anyone else—would need leverage against you?" Rage simmered under the surface of Aren's seemingly calm expression as Chelle attempted to goad him into revealing something in his thoughts. "You're new at this whole interrogation thing, aren't you?"

Her gaze met Gunnar's and his thoughts rang out loud and clear: *Don't press your luck, vampire.*

She cocked a challenging brow. She hadn't begun to press her luck.

"I'll ask you one more time before I take my axe blade to your wrists," Aren snarled. "What did you come here to steal?"

Chelle clucked her tongue. "Sort of brutal, don't you think?"

Aren bared his teeth. Finally she was getting a rise out of him. *Cheeky bitch. You'd be dead if I was Alpha. You won't be quite so cocky after Gunnar gets to Maywood tonight and Gregor gets his claws in him. You'll have no one but me to answer to.*

Had Aren set Gunnar up? Chelle's gaze narrowed as she stared Aren down. His eyes sparked with a gold light but his intimidation tactics didn't do a damn thing to rattle her. What was Gregor up to? And for that matter, what did Gunnar have going on that would put him in a position to be potentially ambushed? Damn it. Chelle *so* didn't have time for this. She needed to get her hands on Gunnar's third of the key so she could focus her efforts on getting the last and final piece before she jetted to Alexandria and put the key to good use. Keeping Gunnar from having his ass handed to him by the crazy berserker warlord didn't fit into her schedule even a little bit.

Chelle really hated when her plans got derailed.

She let out a dramatic sigh. Gunnar's brow furrowed with curiosity but she pretended not to notice. Truth be told, he held her attention despite the many distractions in the room. Including the damned cell that felt like it was slowly shrinking in on her.

Chelle's own memories intruded on her thoughts, stealing her focus. Chills broke out on her skin and she began to sweat as she was assaulted by the reminder of her time in that dank cellar in the middle of the forest. The silver bars of her cage had burned her palms and left angry red blisters that healed in an instant. The scent of her own blood had clung to her skin and driven her thirst to unmanageable levels. She'd been so weak in comparison to what she was now, an infant without the strength to care for itself. She needed to get the hell out of this cell before she went out of her freaking mind.

Aren brought up his right arm to show her the very axe he intended to chop her up with. How very Viking of him. Chelle squared her shoulders and knocked her chin up a notch. "That's a pretty big axe," she replied. "Sure you know how to use it?"

A menacing growl erupted in Aren's chest. Gunnar

took a lunging step forward. He opened his mouth to speak but Chelle cut him off before he could do anything to draw undue attention to himself.

"Put the axe down." Chelle infused her words with power as she held Aren's gaze. "And step back."

His eyes glazed over and his jaw went slack. He did as Chelle asked, taking several shuffling steps back. Jillian and Sven exchanged an anxious glance as Gunnar froze in apparent shock. Chelle had a few tricks up her sleeve. Too bad she had to pull this one out so soon.

"No one move but Gunnar." A tremor vibrated along Chelle's spine and through her limbs as she forced her will on the four werewolves in the tiny room. A vampire could easily compel a single individual as long as they maintained eye contact, but Chelle could perform the feat with nothing more than her words, which allowed her to compel groups as opposed to a single creature.

It was a dangerous ability. That sort of power could easily go to her head if she let it. But instead, it scared the shit out of her. She wouldn't be using it at all if she didn't need to get out of Gunnar's basement and back home— empty-handed, again—before the sun came up.

"Gunnar, let me out of this cage." Her voice quavered with the remnants of anxiety. If someone put her in a cage again it would be too damn soon. Gunnar's brow furrowed with concentration as though resisting the urge to obey. It figured that he'd be a little tougher to compel, being Alpha and all, but that wouldn't deter Chelle. "Gunnar." The command rang with authority. "Let me out of this cage. *Now.*"

He took a stumbling step forward as he reached in his pocket for the key. The others stood by, blank expressions plastered on their faces, as he slid the key into the lock and released her. Chelle stepped up to Gunnar. The urge to put her mouth to his was almost too much to resist. But doing so would rat him out to Aren and the others and Chelle wasn't about to do that. Instead, she leaned in close to his ear and said, "I'm really sorry about this. But it's for your own good." Before taking off at a sprint for the staircase.

Strike two. She might not have gotten Gunnar's piece of the key, but the night wasn't a total waste. Aren had given her something to chew on. Gregor and Aren were up to something and Gunnar was in deeper shit than he thought. Chelle just needed to figure out what it was and warn him before Aren managed to cause a whole hell of a lot of havoc.

Gunnar's wolf let out an angry snarl. The fog lifted from his mind, slowly, as though dissipated by the heat of the sun. As he regained clarity, so did the others, each of them waking from the stupor of whatever magic Chelle had used on them. Vampires had been known to compel humans. Even some shifters were susceptible. Their dual natures made werewolves nearly impervious to such mind-control tricks, but it appeared that Gunnar's mate continued to be full of surprises.

"Fuck."

The one word vibrated in his chest as a low angry growl. The others exchanged bewildered looks, still a little dazed, as they tried to grasp what had just happened.

"Holy crap. I feel like I was hit by a bus." Jillian massaged her temples and gave a shake of her head. "What in the hell was that?"

"We've been played, that's what." Aren's acidic tone echoed in the room. "Now do you understand why we need to join with Gregor, Gunnar?"

Chelle had certainly done a bang-up job of strengthening Aren's case. Her power surprised even him, revealing a vulnerability in the pack that only added to Gunnar's worry. Chelle was unlike any vampire he'd ever encountered. For centuries Mikhail Aristov had been the only one. Was this a new breed made stronger somehow through Mikhail's bite?

"I'm not joining with anyone," Gunnar snapped. "The pack has never needed to form alliances to be strong and nothing has changed. Gregor's hatred toward the Sortiari and Aristov does not concern us. I won't choose sides in another male's personal vendetta no matter what just happened here."

"She turned us into puppets!" Aren's incredulous tone bit into Gunnar's flesh like barbs. "Brought our wolves to heel like they were nothing but helpless pups. Is that not dangerous? Does that not threaten the entire pack? If we wait to choose a side, we may not have a say. The vampires could easily enslave us and we'll have no choice but to obey like the dogs they think we are."

"He's got a point," Sven said. His eyes were still a little glazed over and his complexion paler than usual. "I don't know about you, Gunnar, but I don't like having my head messed with. If all of Aristov's vampires are capable of compelling to this extent, we need to consider what we should do to protect ourselves."

Gunnar needed to talk to Chelle. To get down to the bottom of all of this once and for all. If any member of the pack kept secrets from the others, the consequences would've been dire and Gunnar himself would have carried out the punishment. Now, it was he who kept the secrets and put his pack in jeopardy in the process. He couldn't allow things to continue like this.

"I agree with Sven." It was no surprise that Jillian would side with her mate. "Not that we should fight for anyone's cause, but that we should do something to protect ourselves. I don't know about you guys, but that freaked me out. It was like I was watching from outside myself and totally helpless to do anything to fight it."

Gunnar should have been able to resist. That Chelle had so easily controlled him made his hackles rise. She might have been his mate but that didn't excuse her behavior. The bond between them was sacred and she'd soiled it by using her power to compel against him.

"I agree with everyone," Gunnar said at last. "We can't allow the pack to be vulnerable"—he leveled his gaze on Aren—"to anyone or anything."

"Then what are you going to do about it?" Aren asked.

Gunnar flew at his second in a fit of rage. He slammed the other male against the opposite wall and braced his forearm across Aren's throat. A snarl tore free from his chest as Gunnar let his wolf take control. His vision sharpened and his nose wrinkled at the tang of Aren's anxiety. But not fear. Oddly enough, Aren wasn't afraid of his Alpha's wrath and that was a *huge* problem.

"I'll handle this situation however damn well I see fit." His voice was distorted, gravelly and rough as his wolf took hold. "Do you understand me?"

Aren's gaze shone with gold as his own wolf rose to the surface. For months he'd become steadily bolder, challenging Gunnar's wisdom and decisions when he had no right to do so. Gunnar had dismissed it as Aren being simply overzealous, eager to please, and ready to prove himself. Now, though, Gunnar suspected there was more to Aren's show of defiance.

Rather than respond, Aren gave a sharp nod of his head. Gunnar increased the pressure on his windpipe before pushing himself away and allowing Aren to catch his breath.

"The fuck's the matter with you, Gunnar?" Aren massaged his throat. "We're on the same side, aren't we?"

There weren't sides within the pack dynamic. Gunnar's nostrils flared with his labored breath. "You know there are no such things as sides within the pack."

"Really?" Aren's gaze went wide. "Then maybe you should start acting like it."

Gunnar's wolf rose closer to the surface. Power vibrated through him, building in force until he felt the impact in his very marrow. Aren's knees buckled as though the floor pulled him down. Gunnar appreciated his loyalty to the pack but he wouldn't tolerate his defiant bullshit for another second.

Jillian and Sven both took a tentative step away, their eyes cast toward the floor. The tumultuous climate of the supernatural world cast ripples that had finally reached the pack. Gunnar was a fool to think they could keep themselves apart from it forever. He'd be damned if he let Gregor suck him into his vendettas, though.

"You'll put this bullshit with Gregor out of your mind," Gunnar commanded. "Stay out of that crazy bastard's business."

"He's talking to the other packs," Aren asserted. "It won't be long before they pressure you as well."

Gods damn it. Was there no end to Gregor's ambitions? Gunnar let out a forceful breath. "Who has he spoken to?"

"Marcus Allegria," Aren said. "I was on my way to tell you that Marcus called and requested a meeting with you before I caught scent of the vampire and decided to track her instead."

Shit. If Gregor was also courting the Alpha of the Maywood pack, it could only mean trouble. His was the second-largest pack in Southern California. It was time to shut this down before the situation got out of hand. "When and where does he want to meet?" Gods. He'd hoped to go after Chelle tonight. Instead he was going to have to deal with a bunch of political bullshit he didn't want to have to address.

"The industrial park," Aren replied. "You know the one, nearest the ocean with the cement riverbed."

Gunnar knew the place. Marcus considered it neutral ground and used it for meetings such as this regularly. At least he'd be in L.A. "Call him and tell him I'll be there. In the meantime, the pack is on lockdown. I don't want anyone leaving until I get back. Understand?"

Aren gave a sharp nod of his head. "Got it."

Gunnar's problems were beginning to pile up faster than he could handle them. He just hoped that Aren hadn't already gotten them in too deep with Gregor. Because Gunnar wasn't sure he'd be able to get them out in time.

CHAPTER
10

Gunnar tried to stay out of L.A. if at all possible. Hell, he tried to avoid politics if at all possible. The factions of supernatural creatures inhabiting the city were vast. Vampires, dhampirs, fae, and witches. Shifters, mages, werewolves, and the Sortiari. Berserkers. Gods, how he wished they would have stayed across the Atlantic where they belonged and as far away from the coming storm as possible.

He pulled up to the industrial park and killed the engine of his Mercedes. At the opposite end of the park was an empty concrete canal that spanned several miles and led directly to the ocean. The clean scent of the salt air carried to Gunnar on the breeze and he drew in a deep breath. Marcus owned a handful of properties in the area and several werewolf packs used the industrial park as neutral ground to conduct business. They were territorial, volatile creatures prone to beating on their chests as they sought to establish their supremacy. It was a wonder they hadn't killed each other off thousands of years ago. Despite their natures, packs continued to thrive and their numbers grew. Perhaps that's why Gregor sought to make his alliances with the various packs. They were as close to the berserkers in nature as anything in the supernatural world.

Meeting with the Alpha of the Maywood pack was a good idea. It burned that Marcus had requested the meeting before Gunnar had thought of it himself, but what benefited the pack was what mattered right now. His agitation over the night's events still burned as he got out of the car. The moment he'd slammed Aren against the wall replayed in his mind. In the countless centuries they'd been together, they'd rarely fought. Lately, though, it seemed an increasingly common occurrence. Aren was his second. His way of thinking might have been misguided lately, but he was still pack. Gunnar had to believe Aren's primary interest was still taking care of his family and advising Gunnar to the best of his ability.

After the full moon, things would settle down. For now, he'd get this meeting out of the way, and then he'd deal with locating Chelle.

"Gunnar?"

Marcus Allegria stepped out of the shadows. His eyes burned bright with gold and each step placed was wary. Typically, Gunnar would have sent Aren to meet with another Alpha in his stead. Too much tension vibrated between Alphas when they came face-to-face. A power struggle that their wolves sought to find a victor for. Supremacy was key to the order of their world. Control, a must. This business with Gregor was too important to leave to anyone else, though. Marcus obviously realized that as well.

Gunnar fought to quiet his wolf. It had been one hell of a night and the animal was already agitated. Keeping the animal calm in a hostile situation took an act of will Gunnar wasn't sure he could pull off. But if he was at all interested in avoiding a war, he had to do this. He had to know what the Maywood pack had decided. If they'd chosen wrong, Gunnar had to do his best to dissuade them.

"Marcus," he said in greeting.

"Gunnar."

The other male's voice held an undertone of hostility that made Gunnar's hackles rise. He flipped the length of his hair to the other side of his head. He scrubbed a hand over his beard and took a deep, cleansing breath. If this meeting didn't devolve into a fight, it would be a miracle.

"The situation isn't ideal but since this is a matter we both feel needs to be addressed personally, I trust we'll get through it without any issues." Tension vibrated up Gunnar's spine. He rolled his shoulders in an effort to relieve the ache in his muscles. "Aren tells me you've been contacted by Ian Gregor. That he's amassing an army to overthrow McAlister and the Sortiari."

Marcus gave a slight nod of his head. "He has." The male didn't mince words, something Gunnar could appreciate. "Sent an envoy about a month ago."

Marcus was an imposing figure. Tall, skin as dark as night, his voice deep and commanding. He was an Alpha deserving of fear and respect. The berserkers were either very brave or very foolish to have walked willingly into his lair.

Gunnar chuckled. "I can only imagine how well that meeting went."

Marcus flashed a toothy grin. "I told the son of a bitch to get his foul-smelling ass out of my sight before one of my pack decided to take a piss on him in order to improve the air."

Heh. That sort of compliment was sure to rile the berserkers. Gunnar's brow furrowed. "So you told him you weren't interested in furthering Gregor's cause?"

"I didn't tell him anything either way," Marcus said. "I'm not interested in seeing those warring bastards take over the city. But neither am I keen on Aristov gaining the upper hand and doing the same."

They all had the same concerns. It was inevitable the power dynamic would shift. "I've no love for the guardians of fate, McAlister, or Mikhail Aristov," Gunnar said. "But the Sortiari have held the balance of power for millennia and haven't managed to fuck anything up to the point it couldn't be repaired. Perhaps we should assume that they can continue to maintain that balance."

Marcus snorted. "You call nearly eradicating an entire race maintaining balance?"

"Nearly," Gunnar offered with a shrug. "They didn't succeed."

"Who's to say the next time they attempt to wipe out a species it won't be ours? The Sortiari are fickle and no one knows who they truly answer to. Fate?" Marcus gave a rueful laugh. "Who the hell is that?"

The Sortiari claimed to serve Fate. Or more to the point, claimed to intervene to keep Fate on course. It was a silly notion to be sure, one that didn't seem any more valid today than it had a thousand years ago. "I told you, I've no love for any of them." Gunnar's wolf grew agitated and he began to pace to burn off the energy that pooled in his limbs. "But one thing's certain. If we ally ourselves with either side, they'll do nothing but use us as pawns."

"Expendable," Marcus agreed.

"Yes."

"And yet . . ." Marcus's warning tone gave Gunnar pause. Whatever the male was about to say, Gunnar knew he wouldn't like it. "I wouldn't mind seeing those smug fuckers put on their asses."

Gunnar didn't need Marcus to clarify just who those

smug fuckers were. "Gregor deserves his vengeance. But that doesn't mean I want to help deliver it."

"All I know is I'm not ready to take any side but my own," Marcus said. "But you can be assured that when I do, not McAlister, Gregor, Aristov, or even *you* will sway my decision."

"Fair enough." Gunnar couldn't ask any more of the male. "For the record, I won't side with Gregor. He's too bloodthirsty for my taste, and now that he's off his leash, he's unpredictable."

"So you'll side with McAlister and possibly Aristov?"

"I'm not saying that, either." His bond with Chelle complicated the hell out of things. And not until he straightened out that tangle would Gunnar be able to make a rational decision.

"So we're both neutral," Marcus said. "For now."

"It appears that way."

"Aren wouldn't like it so." Marcus's words stopped Gunnar in his tracks. Aren wasn't in the position to share his opinion on pack matters with anyone outside of the pack.

"He told you that?" Gunnar's wolf issued a warning growl in his mind.

Marcus's posture changed, no longer relaxed. It was time to adjourn their little meeting before their wolves' patience was tested any further. "No," Marcus said. "Not outright. But I got the impression."

Giving Marcus any impression was as bad as an outright admission as far as Gunnar was concerned. "I appreciate your candor. I'll be in touch."

"Send Sven next time," Marcus remarked as he turned to leave. "I enjoy his stories."

Without another word, Marcus disappeared into the night.

The drive to L.A. to exchange a few mostly useless

words with Marcus might have been a total waste of Gunnar's time if it hadn't given him an excuse to go looking for Chelle. The scant useful bits of information he'd gleaned from his conversation with the other Alpha gave him much to ponder as he turned and headed for his car. Aren seemed hell-bent on creating strife and hadn't been too discreet in his efforts to sway Marcus to his way of thinking. Why? What did it benefit Aren to see Gregor amass power? Surely he knew the berserker couldn't be trusted.

A body slammed into Gunnar, taking him to the hard pavement. On instinct, the wolf took hold in his mind, ready to fight their attacker to the death. His eyesight sharpened and he peered through the impenetrable dark in search of whoever had knocked him down. He spun to his right and then his left, ready to defend from any direction. A foul odor hit his nostrils, causing Gunnar to exhale a chuff of breath in order to clear it from his nose. Berserker. He knew the beasts were in L.A. but what were the odds they would have known he'd be here tonight?

Had Marcus set him up?

The foul smell intensified and a warning growl sounded in Gunnar's chest. Not only in front of him, but behind him and to all sides, he was engulfed in the musky odor that caused his nose to wrinkle. The berserkers moved with silent grace. Killing machines with no remorse. Their black eyes didn't reflect in the darkness, making their sockets look empty and monstrous. There would be no battle dance to precede an attack. No words of bravado. The berserkers didn't need anything to bolster their courage. Synchronized without a word spoken between them, they rushed at Gunnar and attacked.

His last thought as Gunnar said a silent prayer and prepared for impact was of beautiful tawny hair and forest-green eyes.

* * *

Chelle shook with unspent adrenaline. It had been over an hour since she'd escaped Gunnar's cell and she'd yet to calm down. Her power to compel both shocked and frightened her. It had taken almost no effort at all to bend four powerful werewolves to her will. It shouldn't have been possible, and yet she'd done it with ease. Just like she'd plucked the thoughts from their minds, she'd planted new ones, tiny seeds that grew in an instant.

Gods. No creature should have that sort of power. Least of all, her. Chelle pulled up to an empty riverbed lined with concrete that ran parallel to the only industrial park in Maywood—at least, that she could find—and got out of the shiny red BMW X1. Gunnar had to be here. Somewhere. She couldn't be sure if what she'd heard in Aren's thoughts would lead to anything. Hell, she might not even be in the right place. This was a wild-goose chase at best. If Gunnar was smart, he'd be wary of anything the male told him. Of course, Gunnar wasn't privy to Aren's thoughts the way that Chelle was.

He could definitely use someone like her on his side. Which was why, despite her better judgment, she was here now.

A delicious scent hit Chelle's nostrils and thirst ignited in her throat. She ran toward the source, mad with want. She knew the scent. Craved it. Blood had been spilled— Gunnar's.

Chelle focused all of her senses into hyperawareness. A few hundred yards away, near some sort of mechanic's shop surrounded by a chain-link fence, Gunnar fought for his life against ten berserker warlords in the grips of full battle rage. *Shit.* Chelle's step faltered as she picked up her pace. How was he still alive?

Once consumed with battle rage, berserkers were virtually unkillable. They took very little damage in a fight, were faster than and just as strong as the average vampire, and healed impossibly fast. The only way to put one down for good was to sever its head completely from its body.

It was lucky for Gunnar that Chelle wasn't an average vampire.

"Is that all you've got?" Gunnar's voice carried over the din of the fight in an angry roar. "Why don't you put a little muscle into it?"

Chelle cringed as a booted foot came into contact with Gunnar's gut and he doubled over and fell to his knees. She swore she felt the blow in her own stomach and she vowed to make the bastards pay. Had it been one-on-one, Chelle might not have intervened. But this was nowhere close to a fair fight. Only cowards ganged up on a foe like this. Chelle hated bullies. And the berserkers fit the profile perfectly.

Myriad thoughts assaulted Chelle's mind and she stumbled. Gunnar's wolf snarled and howled. The sound in her mind hollowed out her chest and the tether gave a violent jerk at her center. She dug her feet into her boots and propelled herself across the cement so fast that her surroundings blurred out of focus. She crossed the last twenty yards in less than a second and launched herself into the fray without preamble.

Chelle wasn't as seasoned a warrior as Ronan. She wasn't ruthless like Siobhan. She couldn't intimidate like Jenner and she lacked Mikhail's strategic wit. Chelle was a clever thief with a lot of curious ambition. Not super-helpful in a fight. But that didn't mean she didn't have instinct and a little of her brother's tutelage to guide her. She was scrappy when she needed to be. And she wasn't about to let these assholes kill her werewolf.

Mine?

Focus, Chelle. One crisis at a time.

She was unarmed but not helpless. Chelle grabbed the

first berserker by the head and twisted. The bone and muscle cracked and snapped. She released her hold and the male crumpled to the ground. Disabled, but definitely *not* out of the fight. At this point, their best bet for survival would be to slow the berserkers down so they could make a retreat. If Gunnar had come here armed, he wasn't anymore, which meant they had to fight their way out of this with nothing more than brute force.

"Chelle! What are you doing? Get the hell out of here!"

She didn't have time to roll her eyes or give Gunnar a lecture on feminism. His gallantry was cute—about a century or so ago—but right now, he needed to put his concern on the back burner and work with her to deliver as much damage as possible on their attackers.

The momentum of the fight shifted. Chelle managed to provide just enough of a distraction for Gunnar to regroup.

Berserkers healed almost instantaneously, which meant any damage they sustained would be short-lived. The one whose spine she'd broken would take a bit longer to get back on his feet simply from the severity of the injury, which meant in order to immobilize any of them, she'd need to stay the course and aim for the spine.

Gods, she wished she had a sword or at least a freakin' dagger. Hell, at this point she would have settled for a rusty razor blade.

"Chelle! Behind you!"

Gunnar's warning shout came a beat too late. The burn of silver across Chelle's skin coaxed a cry from her lips as the slayer's blade sliced into her torso. Pain and anger radiated through her but the cut wasn't deep and the momentary contact with the silver did nothing to weaken her. She pulled back her right arm and let it fly, backhanding the berserker who'd cut her. He flew through the air and landed a good five or so feet away with a sickening crunch of broken bones. Not enough to slow the bastard down, though. He got right back up as though she'd given him a love tap and rushed back into the fray, his black, fathomless eyes focused on Chelle.

Gunnar shoved at the bodies that pressed in on him and rushed at the berserker. He painted a violent picture as he closed the space between them, launching himself at the berserker. In the time it took for Chelle to draw a breath, Gunnar reached out and grabbed the male's head, twisting it with a rough jerk as he gave it a quarter turn that effectively damaged the spine. The berserker fell to the ground. Once again down, but not out.

They'd never get the upper hand. Not when their opponents could heal so quickly. Chelle had thought they could turn the tide, but it became apparent that they'd continue to be on the defensive, merely keeping the slayers at bay until they became too tired to fend them off. It was only a matter of time before Chelle and Gunnar both died.

A shout of pain drew her attention and Chelle turned her head with a jerk to her left. Gunnar's hands flew to his gut where blood spread and soaked into his shirt at an alarming rate. Chelle's heart stuttered in her chest and her breath stilled. If he'd been cut by a silver blade, he'd die within minutes. A berserker rushed her and Chelle's focus shifted as she blocked the arm that swept down to stab at her chest.

She had to get Gunnar out of here. Now. Before it was too late.

"Stop!"

Power resonated through her body in a rush of electricity as she shouted the command. Ten berserkers and one injured werewolf froze in their tracks, immobile. Violent tremors shook Chelle from head to toe, the drain of power and her own fear taking its toll as she fought to impose her will on the berserkers' minds.

She didn't know how much longer she could compel them to stillness. Time to make a break for it.

Chelle had never been much of a multitasker. She had an obsessive personality that fixated on one thing at a time. Tunnel vision made it tough to even put one foot in front of the other as her mind focused on the single task of keeping the berserkers frozen in place.

"Gunnar? Can you walk?"

He gave her a sharp nod and managed two stumbling steps before going down hard on one knee. Well, guess that answered her question. Gunnar wasn't going to make it out of here on his own steam. It would sting the burly werewolf's pride, but Chelle didn't have time to worry about such trivial things. She made her way to Gunnar as quickly as she could, making sure to keep her thoughts focused on the berserkers.

She couldn't allow herself to look at Gunnar, to take in the extent of his injuries, as she sidled up next to him and bent down. The tremors that rocked her intensified to the point that Chelle's teeth chattered. She reached down and grabbed Gunnar's arm to guide it over her shoulders. Even with her immense strength, lifting him took effort, but she managed to get him on his feet and stable enough that he could shuffle beside her as they retreated.

"How . . ." Gunnar grunted with pain and Chelle swore she felt the burn of silver in her own gut. ". . . long can you hold them?"

Good question. Chelle had been so fearful of her vampiric abilities, she'd never really put them to the test. It stood to reason that she'd only be able to control the berserkers as long as she could see them, which meant they had about twenty yards before they'd be free to come after them. Chelle's knees wobbled with every step. She didn't think she'd have the energy to stop them again. If they didn't pick up their pace and get to the damn car, they'd be toast.

"We've gotta jet," she said by way of explanation. She didn't want to reveal anything about the scope of her power to Gunnar. "Can you pick up the pace?"

"How far?"

His voice went low and Gunnar stumbled again. A rush of anxiety zinged through her and the tether gave a violent tug at the center of Chelle's chest that caused her breath to catch from the force of it.

"Twenty yards," she said. "Maybe thirty."

"I'm not sure I've got twenty feet left," Gunnar replied with a laugh that ended on another pained groan. "Their daggers . . . Magic or silver. I'm not sure which."

Probably both. Did it matter, though? Either one could deliver a mortal wound.

Chelle's control slipped. The berserkers shifted, their movements slow and humanlike as they began to shake the magic that held them. Even distracted, even carrying a two-hundred-and-fifty-pound werewolf, Chelle was faster. She pushed herself as hard as she could go, covering the twenty yards in a second. Her hold on the berserkers broke like a frayed cord and she rushed for the car, dragging Gunnar in her wake.

There wasn't time for relief when they reached the BMW. Chelle pulled open the door and shoved Gunnar inside. The berserkers' battle cries echoed in the darkness and the sound of their rushing footsteps was like thunder in Chelle's ears as she rounded the car and jumped into the driver's seat.

"Hang on!" She started the engine and took off with a squeal of tires. Gunnar lurched in his seat, but she didn't have time to worry about him smacking his head or anything else. The walls of the empty concrete canals rushed by in a blur of gray as Chelle sped away.

She glanced to her right to find that Gunnar had slumped back in the seat, his eyes closed. She reached over and smacked him across the face. He came to with a start. A snarl vibrated in his chest and his eyes glowed gold as he turned to face her.

"Don't you *dare* pass out," she said through clenched teeth.

He canted his head to one side and Chelle searched his mind for coherent thought. The man had given way to the animal and all she heard was a low, territorial growl that sent a shiver down her spine.

"You keep him alive," she said to the wolf. "I know you understand me."

Gunnar's head turned away but he didn't lose consciousness.

Chelle's grip relaxed on the steering wheel as she sped toward Hollywood. If Gunnar's wolf managed to do as she asked, it would be a miracle. The wolf might have thought they were big, tough sons of bitches, but even an Alpha could succumb to death from contact with silver.

She just hoped when she got him to safety, she could do something—anything—to save him.

CHAPTER
11

The swords spun in a dizzying blur of silver. A dance so fluid and graceful that it mesmerized. The fae was an artist. Practiced. Skilled. A master of her craft. And no doubt as deadly as she was beautiful. Long, vibrant red curls of hair fanned out behind her like ribbons in the wind as she spun. The locks settled about her shoulders, wild and beautiful. Just like her.

Saeed watched, transfixed, through the eyes of a vampire long dead. The memory held him firmly in its grip and he had no desire to leave it. Not as long as she was here and he could observe her at his leisure.

"She is my most prized possession." The male who leaned in to whisper close to Saeed's ear wasn't fae. Nor was he vampire. Magic sparked the air around him. Mage.

The mage owned his beautiful fae. Anger churned in Saeed's gut and his fangs throbbed in his gums. But despite his desire to tear out the mage's throat, he was helpless. Simply a visitor in another's body observing moments that could never be recaptured, like water that had already flowed downstream, lost.

The fae continued to dance, her arms swinging, wrists turning as she maneuvered the swords in her grip. She seemed to float on the air as she moved, her feet gliding silently over the polished surface of the marble floors. The Romans were an arrogant lot, living in excess, flaunting their extravagance. This mage enjoyed showing off his possessions. Saeed wanted to gut him with a dull blade.

"Surely her talents range beyond this entertainment." Saeed's mouth moved against its will, his voice not his own as he spoke the dead vampire's words.

"She's wild," the mage declared. "If not for the bonds of slavery, she'd cut my throat as I slept. But there is not an assassin as deadly as she for thousands of miles. Why do you think I have no enemies?"

How had he bound her? With magic? Did he treat her with cruelty to keep her in check? Beat her? Saeed's bloodlust mounted. It burned through him with a heat that left him raw and shaken. His beautiful fae spun, kicking her legs up to propel her as she performed a graceful twisting maneuver. She landed on her feet with nary a sound and, as the music came to a stop, went to one knee before her master.

The revelers broke out into wild applause. Saeed's ghostly hands came together to join them though he felt no sensation, no joy in the act. All he knew was his thirst and his empty obsession. A hollow ache throbbed in his chest, the absence of his soul somehow more pronounced in this dream realm. Perhaps it was his proximity to her that affected him. Made him want to drop to his knees and howl in agony. Saeed tried to cradle his head in his hands but they refused to move. They belonged to the vampire in his memory. Saeed had no control in the Collective.

The mage gave a bored flick of his wrist. The fae straightened. Her gaze met Saeed's and he went deathly still. Hair like fire. Skin as luminous as stardust. Delicate features, high cheekbones, full lips that formed a tiny bow. Wide, expressive eyes, shaped like almonds and unlike anything Saeed had ever seen. The irises were green and gold, light as though washed out or weathered. His chest hitched at the depth of emotion he saw there. An excess of it. The complete opposite of the emptiness he felt. For the barest moment she studied him before dropping her gaze.

She'd seen him. Hadn't she? Not the vampire whose skin he wore but him.

The floor gave way beneath him and Saeed fell. Down, down, down, through the abyss, the myriad memories that reached out to snag him like clawed hands. He came back to himself with a jolt, his gasp of breath a gut reaction as his body started.

He lay on the floor. Hard, bare, as cold as his own skin. The polished hardwood rested against his cheek and Saeed let the sensation ground him to reality. His stomach heaved and Saeed swallowed down the nausea that washed over him. How long had he given himself over to the Collective as he'd chased her through the memories? Russia, Italy, Spain, England. Across Europe and Asia, over the sea to Australia. The mage had traveled the globe and she'd never been far from his side. Where were they now? Did she feel the shackles of slavery still? And if so, for what purpose did he use her?

Saeed's jaw clamped down. His fangs punctured his bottom lip and his tongue flicked out to lick the blood away. When he found her, he'd kill the mage. Rip his throat out and watch the male bleed out. He would set her free. The nameless fae with hair like fire . . .

"Diego!"

Saeed pushed himself up to sit and crossed his legs before him. He let his head drop into his palms and let out a shaky breath as he swallowed against the dry burn in his throat. How long had it been since he'd fed? So weak. So tired. So . . . *lost*.

The door to his bedroom opened, letting in a swath of light that cut through the darkness. It reminded him of the shine of the fae's blades as she'd swung them. Saeed bobbled as he fought to stand. All he wanted was to go back to the Collective. To her.

Diego entered the room, tentative. Had Saeed still possessed a soul, it might have pained him to realize that his coven had become wary of him in the weeks since his transition. They thought him unstable. Mad. Lost to the memories of dead vampires and unwilling to leave them in favor of the company of the living.

"What day is it?" Saeed's voice rasped in his throat. So dry.

"Friday," Diego said. "It's been almost a week."

Friday already? "Since what?"

Diego came closer. "Since you've fed."

Saeed listened for the sound of his own heart. Its beat was barely discernible and slow. His lungs didn't move with breath and his mouth had become so dry that his tongue stuck to the roof of his mouth.

"Mikhail?" He couldn't manage more than one or two words at a time. Gods, his throat was on fire. He'd promised Mikhail that he would begin the process of turning members of his coven. Instead, Saeed had retreated into the Collective in search of the fae.

Diego rolled up the sleeve of his shirt. "Nothing from the king," he replied. "Sasha would have come for you had he called. You need to feed."

The male bit into his wrist. The scent of blood filled the air and Saeed took a step closer.

"Sit," Diego instructed.

Two months ago, no member of his coven would have ordered Saeed to do anything. Now, they treated him as though he were a helpless child, incapable of taking care of himself. He moved to the sofa at the far end of the room and did as he was told. Diego settled down beside him and brought his wrist to Saeed's mouth.

Saeed cradled the male's wrist in his hand and sealed his lips over the punctures. His eyes drifted shut as he bit down, and he imagined as he drank that it was the fiery-haired fae who fed him, her haunting light eyes fixed on him.

Quiet moments passed as Saeed fed. He sealed the punctures when he'd had his fill, grateful he possessed the self-control to stop. His mind was a wild and unstable place. He'd never forgive himself if he inadvertently harmed a member of his coven. With a slow sigh, Saeed fell back on the couch, eyes closed.

"I want to be turned."

He cracked a lid to look at Diego. The male's expression was stern, his dark eyes focused on Saeed. "Tired of your soul?"

"Were you tired of yours?"

"Gods, yes." Saeed had craved oblivion, longed for indifference. Wanted nothing more than the bliss of apathy. Instead, he'd lost his soul and everything that he had been was replaced with endless want and unfathomable obsession.

Diego chuckled. "It's not my soul I'm worried about."

The words might have been lighthearted, but Saeed recognized the underlying worry. "You're worried Mikhail will find out that I've gone mad and put me down."

Diego looked away. "You sit in this room night after night, in the dark, lying on the gods-damned floor mumbling incoherent words, your eyes rolled back into your

head. We know where you go, Saeed. We know you're
looking for something. You'll not find whatever it is there.
Only ghosts live in the Collective."

That might be true, but what Saeed hoped to find
among the memories of dead vampires was a glimmer of
hope. Bread crumbs that would lead him to the mage and
his beautiful assassin.

"You're looking for *her*," Diego said. "We don't know
who she is, Saeed, but you speak of her when you're in
your trances. Do you not understand that she's dead?"

Had she been a vampire, then yes, she would be dead.
And it was true, mages died every day, as did fae, but
Saeed knew in his heart of hearts that they lived. And he
wouldn't stop searching until he found them and freed her.

"Speak to me of the Collective after you've been
turned." Saeed pinched the bridge of his nose. Feeding
brought him clarity but it wouldn't be long before he
joined the company of illusions once again. "And tell me
what you think of the ghosts."

Diego's expression brightened. "So you intend to turn
me?"

"Of course." As though there'd been any question.
Saeed trusted every member of his coven. Their loyalty
could never be called into question. But of the fifteen
dhampirs, he loved Diego and Sasha best. Their minds
were sharp and their protective natures and strong wills
made them the perfect choice for transition. Besides, he
needed vampires who could take over leadership while
he chased his ghosts . . .

"Say your good-byes to your soul and come to me tomorrow night," Saeed said darkly. It would be days before Diego would be stable and that meant Saeed would
have to keep his distance from the Collective long enough
to see the male through the transition. "Choose two mem-

bers of the coven to tend to your thirst. This morning's will be your last sunrise. Are you sure this is what you want?"

Diego nodded. "Yes. I'm ready."

"Then go and make your arrangements," Saeed said. "And leave me alone."

Diego didn't take offense at the command. Instead, he gave a solemn nod of his head and left Saeed to his solitude.

A weight had been lifted from him. His coven would be protected by Diego and Sasha while he searched for the mage and his beautiful slave. There couldn't be many mages walking the earth. A handful or so. They were as rare as the magic they wielded. Saeed knew of one mage who could point him in the right direction and it just so happened that Mikhail would be meeting with the male in a few short days.

Saeed reached for his cell on the end table. He swiped his finger across the screen and dialed. A rush of excitement coursed through his veins as powerful as the thrill of feeding.

"Saeed." Mikhail answered in his authoritative tone. The male was always all business. He didn't waste time on polite greetings. His stiff formality was to be admired. No one ever doubted who was in control when they spoke with the vampire king. The Sortiari were fools to have ever thought they'd managed to kill him.

"Mikhail." The king would appreciate straightforwardness. Saeed hated to play games so it suited him fine. "I want to attend your meeting with McAlister."

Silence answered him. No doubt Mikhail wondered at Saeed's motives. "We've agreed to bring only one representative each. Jenner is mine."

Saeed could play this to his advantage. "You don't

actually trust McAlister to hold to his end of the bargain, do you? The Sortiari play by their own rules. They are beholden to no one."

"True," Mikhail replied. "But I have something McAlister wants and the only way he'll get it is by playing by *my* rules."

What could Mikhail possibly have that the Sortiari would want? Curiosity burned as Saeed tried to recall anything he might have seen in the Collective to answer that question. He'd shunned almost every memory he'd encountered that didn't involve the mage and his fae, however.

"You'll be handing over this possession?"

"No," Mikhail answered so quickly it made Saeed wonder about the item's worth. "I'm not handing anything over to McAlister."

This could work to Saeed's advantage. "What if he seeks to take it by force? I don't doubt Jenner's—or your—ability to protect what belongs to you, Mikhail, but if he wants this item badly enough, who knows what lengths he'll go to possess it."

"There is unrest within the Sortiari, and within many factions of the supernatural community," Mikhail said. "I need to establish some sort of trust with McAlister if we're to weather that unrest."

Had Saeed heard him correctly? Was Mikhail actually going to try to secure an alliance with the very beings who'd ordered the execution of their entire race? "I will say that tumultuous times can make for interesting decisions to be made, but Mikhail, think about what you're considering. Who you're climbing into bed with."

"I have." Mikhail's dark tone did little to bolster Saeed's mood. True, his motives led him far from the politics and arguments of the different factions. But that didn't mean he had no concerns over what problems that sort of alliance might create. "And don't think I haven't considered the implications. But Gregor is a far more threatening enemy than McAlister is at this point."

It was true that the guardians of fate were fickle. It seemed at times they made decisions on a whim, answering to some unknown and mystical force that changed course as often as the wind. Three hundred years ago, the Sortiari had vowed to exterminate the vampire race for whatever reason they'd deigned necessary. Now, though, it seemed their position on the matter had changed. McAlister's guard dogs no longer served them, and the vampires were no longer a threat to them.

"I suppose McAlister is the lesser of two evils." Even Saeed knew to fear the berserkers. They were wild creatures whose business was dealing death and destruction. Left unchecked, they could wreak havoc across the city. Hell, the *world*. "That doesn't mean he—or any of the Sortiari—has earned my trust. Allow me to come to this meeting, Mikhail. I'll keep my distance. McAlister won't even know I'm there."

Mikhail let out a snort. "You think you can deceive a mage, Saeed? Did your turning grant you powers of invisibility?"

Had that been the case, all of this would be moot. However, getting close to McAlister would allow Saeed to learn more about him, what he was capable of, and therefore prepare him to defeat the mage who kept his fae a slave.

My fae? Yes. Saeed was certain she was his. She would tether his soul in an instant.

"I think we need to be cautious," Saeed said at last. The Collective tugged at his mind and he was eager to return to the memories. "Please consider my request, Mikhail."

"I will," he agreed. "Is there anything else?"

"Yes, I plan to turn Deigo at sundown tomorrow. Sasha, soon after that."

"I'm glad to hear it," Mikhail said. "I hope that you'll choose a third member as I've requested, soon after. If you need anything, please call."

"I will," Saeed replied. There were many viable candidates but he wanted Diego and Sasha to make the choice of who would be turned next. "And thank you, your highness, for considering my request."

Mikhail let out a snort. "Your highness," he said with a rueful laugh. "Call me that again and I'll ship you as far from McAlister as I can manage. May the rest of the night treat you well, Saeed."

"And you as well, Mikhail," he said in parting.

The vampire king ended the call without another word.

Saeed allowed his eyes to close. His hand dropped to his side and the phone fell from his grip, toppling to the floor. He paid it no mind as he allowed the memories to take him once again. Soon, he'd find the trail that would lead him to her. And once he found it, he wouldn't stop until she was his.

CHAPTER
12

The BMW's engine growled as Chelle pulled into Mikhail's driveway. She slowed to an unassuming speed as the guard let her through the gate and she continued to remain inconspicuous as she drove around to the back of the property where the cottage was located. The last thing she needed was for anyone to be alerted to the presence of a bleeding Alpha werewolf on the property. With Mikhail's mate, Claire, and their tiny son inside the house, the vampire king wouldn't tolerate any sort of security breach. And Chelle had no doubt he'd consider Gunnar a threat. Especially if he knew they had a band of slayers tracking them.

What Mikhail didn't know wouldn't hurt him.

At least, she hoped.

The wolf still had control of Gunnar's mind when she rounded the car and opened the passenger door. A wounded animal never did well when cornered and Gunnar was no exception. Mated or not, he growled at Chelle, a warning for her to keep her distance.

"Do you want help or not?" Chelle couldn't help her

snippy tone. Were all werewolves so insufferable? "I'm taking you inside and I swear to the gods if you bite me, you're going to pay for it." The growl died down to what Chelle could only assume was a purr. So, the wolf liked an assertive female, huh? She grinned despite their grim circumstances. "That's right, buddy. For the time being, I'm in charge. So you just keep quiet and play nice and we'll see what we can do about that dagger wound."

Chelle bent down and guided Gunnar's arm around her shoulders once again. The weight of his body slumped against her and she grunted as she braced her body against his. Werewolves were freakin' *dense*. Every ounce of his body was constructed with hard, unyielding muscle. She might as well have been toting a boulder around. Even with supernatural strength, werewolf dead weight was tough to lug around.

In the few minutes it had taken to get through the gate and out of the car, Gunnar's wolf had begun to quiet in his mind. The berserkers had managed to beat him half to death, and that was before they'd carved him up with their silver blades. Dirty, low-life, cheating bastards. Chelle could only hope she'd get the chance for revenge. She'd compel those assholes right off a cliff into a pit of fire.

They got to the front door and Chelle slumped against the jamb. She laid her boot into the door, nearly kicking through the knotty pine. A few seconds later the door flew open and Lucas stared, jaw a little slack. Chelle rolled her eyes and hoisted Gunnar up a little higher.

"Don't just stand there! Give me a hand with him!"

Lucas sprang to action at her exasperated command. He went to Gunnar's right side and lifted him, helping Chelle get him through the door. "Is this him?" he asked on a breath. "The werewolf?"

"No," Chelle replied drily. "I found him passed out on

the street and thought he was kinda cute." Her eyes bugged out of her head at Lucas's serious expression. "Of course he's the werewolf!"

"Did you do this to him?"

Navigating three bodies down the narrow hallway to Chelle's bedroom wasn't exactly an easy feat. She didn't know what was more shocking: tonight's turn of events with the berserkers or the utterly ridiculous questions Lucas was currently peppering her with.

"Oh yeah." Sarcasm was the only thing keeping Chelle sane right now. "The first thing I do after I've been tethered is slice my mate open with a silver dagger."

"Silver?" Lucas's step faltered. "That's deadly to werewolves, Chelle."

"No shit, Lucas!" Obvious, much? "Help me get him on the bed."

They navigated the doorway to Chelle's bedroom one at a time with Lucas leading the way. They eased Gunnar down onto the mattress and he let out a pained groan. Sweat beaded his brow and soaked his shirt to mingle with the blood that had dried from a bright crimson to a deathly black. The tether pulled at Chelle's chest and her heart picked up its pace as she contemplated the possibility that Gunnar might not make it through the night. What would happen to her if he died? Would her soul be lost to oblivion forever?

"Let's get his shirt off."

Chelle snapped to at Lucas's words. She turned to face him, brow furrowed. "Right. Okay." She didn't know anything about how werewolves healed. Had he been shot with a silver bullet, he would've died. The cut from the slayer's blade weakened him. Had obviously poisoned him. But now what?

She leaned over Gunnar and grabbed his T-shirt at the neck. The fabric ripped as easily as tearing paper as Chelle split the garment in half, revealing the muscular hills and valleys of his bare chest. Ugly bruises marred his skin, proof of the brutal beating the berserkers had given him. Her gaze roamed from his broad shoulders, over the sharp angles of his collarbone. Over the hills of his pecs and down the ridges of his abs, his narrow torso, to the deep V that cut into his hips and disappeared in the low waist of his jeans. Chelle's breath caught. Even bruised and bloodied he was magnificent. Maybe even more so in his battered state.

Gunnar was a warrior.

A nasty gash cut into the skin on the left side of his torso just above his waist. The wound oozed blood, thick and bright crimson. Chelle's thirst flared hot in her throat and the scent of Gunnar's blood called to her in way that no one else's had or ever would. She was possessed with the desire to seal her mouth over the cut and drink until she had her fill.

"Chelle?"

She whipped around to face Lucas. How could she possibly concentrate when all she wanted was to drink? "How do I close the wound?"

Lucas shrugged. His expression was pinched and his posture stiff. The scent of Gunnar's blood wouldn't call to him the way it did Chelle, but that didn't mean it wouldn't spark Lucas's thirst as well. They were vampires after all. "Shouldn't it heal on its own?"

"He was cut with a silver blade," Chelle said. "It's a wonder he isn't dead."

"Lick him. Your saliva should heal the wound."

Chelle's eyes went wide. *"Lick him?"* Did Lucas not realize how disastrous that would be?

His mouth screwed up into a pucker as he fixed Chelle with a stern gaze. "You're tethered. Don't tell me you haven't fed from him yet."

Mind reading was by far the most annoying of their little coven's special abilities. If Chelle could, she'd quash that particular parlor trick ASAP. "Feeding only solidifies the tether," she replied. "I don't even know him."

"Life-or-death situation, Chelle," Lucas chided. "Whether or not you *know* him doesn't matter compared to the bigger picture. Seems like we're wasting time here."

Shit.

Chelle turned away from Lucas to face Gunnar. The scent of blood overpowered her and, coupled with the tether, drove her instinct to feed. Could it be that simple? Drink, seal the wound with her tongue as she would any puncture. What then? What would happen once their bond was solidified?

Did she really have time to contemplate the possibilities?

Chelle bent over Gunnar. Her throat burned with a dry fire and she felt the urge to swallow more than usual. Her palm came to rest on the mattress beside him as she braced herself and prepared to seal her mouth over the cut.

Gunnar's hand shot out and encircled her wrist like a vise. She looked up to find his gaze locked on her, eyes sparking with gold fire. A low warning growl resonated in his chest as he watched her with the wariness of an injured animal. His voice grated in his throat as he said through clenched teeth, "What do you think you're doing, vampire?"

Chelle swallowed against the lump that rose in her throat. "You're cut," she said. "Deep. With a silver blade, I think. The wound isn't healing. I was going to—"

"I'll heal." Gunnar's voice was nothing more than a hoarse growl. "I'm weak." His breath came in quick pants that caused Chelle's heart to race. "Not dying."

Not dying. The words offered Chelle a hell of a lot more comfort than they should have.

Lucas came up behind her and leaned in close to Chelle's ear. "Doesn't mean you can't help the process along."

Gunnar's focus shifted at the sound of Lucas's voice. Not an ounce of blue colored his eyes as it gave way to bright gold. A low, warning growl vibrated in Gunnar's throat. Uh-oh. Not. Good.

"Lucas," Chelle said. "You might want to take a step back." Because all hell was about to break loose.

Attacked. Injured. Disoriented. In an unfamiliar place with unfamiliar smells. Enraged. Cornered. A male. Not were-wolf. Vampire. Close to her. Touching her. Not his. Theirs.

Mine, mine, mine!

The wolf dominated Gunnar's psyche, drowning out any trace of logical thought. His injuries weren't fatal, but enough of a threat to have coaxed his wolf to the surface in order to protect them. Wherever they were now, it smelled of their mate but Chelle didn't live here alone. Another scent lingered. The male who stood behind her, his hand on her shoulder. He lived here with Chelle. Who was he to her?

Doesn't matter. The bastard was as good as dead.

"Lucas." Chelle's voice vibrated in their ears, warm and sweet. "You might want to take a step back."

Too late. All of the caution in the world wouldn't save the vampire now.

The injury that weakened them became inconsequential as Gunnar launched himself from the bed. In this state, with his wolf at the forefront of his mind, there was no separation between his two halves. Man and beast were one and the same, working in tandem. Right now, they had only one goal, to separate Chelle from the male who dared to put his hands on her, and make sure that he never touched what belonged to them again.

The pain of their injuries faded to the back of their mind. Pain didn't matter. Not when, for the second time tonight, someone threatened their mate. Chelle let out a squeal of surprise as the male took a stumbling step backward. He held up his hands as though in surrender, but that would do little to deter them. Fight or die. There was no other option.

"Gunnar! Stop!"

Adrenaline coursed through their body, fueling their stiff and aching muscles, banishing the pain of the gash in their side. Chelle's arm swept out to shove the vampire behind her. She protected him? Why? A snarl erupted from their chest as a red haze of unchecked rage overtook them.

Their breath heaved. Their upper jaw ached where the canines throbbed. The full moon was still a week away. A full transition wouldn't happen. But extreme stress could trigger a partial transition no matter the moon phase. They were dangerously close to becoming something that would terrify Chelle. And yet, there was nothing they could do to stop it.

The vampire had the good sense not to let Chelle protect him. A big bastard, packed with muscle and solidly built, but that wasn't going to save him. Their fist swung out and caught the vampire in the chin. His head whipped back but it didn't put him down. The male retaliated with an uppercut that landed solidly against their ribs. All they allowed was a grunt of pain before they went after the vampire again, determined to rip his head from his shoulders.

"Lucas, are you insane?" Chelle's shout bounced around in their head, her distress adding to their rage. "Get the hell out of here! Now. I can handle him."

"Are you kidding me, Chelle? The guy's out of control. I'm not leaving you."

Gunnar landed another blow, this time to the male's gut. He was a wall of stone, a worthy opponent, but one that had no hope of standing strong for long in the face of their rage.

Their mate stepped between them and the vampire. She shoved them back and a snarl tore from their throat. Their rage didn't faze her. Their mate was brave. She turned toward the vampire and shoved him as well. "Out." Her voice brooked no argument. "Now!"

They paced the confines of the bedroom. Their skin felt too tight on their bones. Their muscles burned. Their chest ached and labored with every breath. Chelle blocked the doorway, keeping them from their prey. They'd die before they hurt her, but she should know better than to keep them caged. To keep them from the vampire. To try to thwart their violence.

Chelle held out her hands imploringly. Her scent swirled around in their head, intoxicating and sweet. "Gunnar, you have to calm down."

Calm was unattainable in this state. Nothing short of bloodshed would calm the storm that raged within them. They rushed at her, hoping to frighten her away and clear the path. Their mate was powerful, she could control their mind if she wanted to. They were wary of her strength and had to use their wits to circumvent her. She held her ground, though. Brave. They were *Alpha*. Warriors cowered in fear of them. Battlefields were stained with the blood they'd spilled. And yet their fierce mate held her ground. Undeterred by their fearsome countenance.

Her jaw squared and she rested her hands on the curve of her hips. "Stop, or I'll stop you."

A growl rose in their throat. If she thought to master them, she would fail.

"You don't scare me, Gunnar." A silver storm gathered in her entrancing green eyes and she bared her fangs.

Beautiful. Wild. *Ours.* "Lucas isn't a threat to you. Leave him alone."

They pushed a single word through clenched teeth. "Move."

"No." Their mate was stubborn. It set their blood on fire. "You're injured and not thinking clearly. Settle down or I'll settle you down."

Did she plan to use more of her magic on them? They snarled. Her imposing thoughts filled their mind with cobwebs. Took away their control. Weakened them. She was their mate, but they wouldn't allow her to control them again.

"Gunnar," she implored. "Listen to reason."

No. There was no room for reason in their rage. They wanted out of this room. Out of this house. They wanted to tear the vampire's flesh, sink their teeth into his throat. They wanted to run. To howl. To prove to their mate once and for all that she belonged to them.

Chelle threw her arms up in exasperation and closed the distance between them. They braced for an attack, for the sensation of her foreign magic to overtake them. Instead, she put her mouth to theirs in a heated kiss that banished all thoughts of violence from their mind. Chelle belonged to them. Their mate. And after tonight, she would never again think of the vampire who lived here with her. They would prove to her once and for all to whom she belonged.

Her mouth parted and her tongue darted out to brush their bottom lip. The balance of power shifted and Gunnar reclaimed that part of his mind that controlled logical thought. He might have taken back that aspect of himself but it wasn't enough to coax him to separate himself from Chelle. Instead, his arms went around her. He cupped the back of her neck and slanted his mouth across hers to deepen the kiss.

The sweetness of her mouth had no equal.

Gunnar's heart hammered against his rib cage. His cock hardened to stone behind his fly and his muscles grew taut. He pulled her tight against him, and the tips of his fingers dug into the flesh at her hip where her shirt rode up. He nipped at her bottom lip and she groaned. The sound vibrated down Gunnar's spine and settled in his sac. The wolf retreated further into his mind, allowing him complete clarity. The scent of Chelle's arousal drove him as he thrust his tongue against hers, demanding that she answer in kind.

The wound in his torso gave an uncomfortable pull and Gunnar winced. Gods-damned silver. Had the berserker broken off any part of the blade in his gut, as was his intent, Gunnar would be dead by now. Luckily, all the bastard had managed was a slash that would take its time in healing. Chelle paused as though sensing his discomfort and broke their kiss.

"I need to bandage you up."

Her lips parted on a breath, swollen and dark pink from his kisses. Passion flushed her cheeks and quicksilver swirled in her beautiful eyes. He couldn't let something as paltry as a flesh wound interrupt the moment. Not when she was so willing in his arms.

Gunnar reached out and pulled her against him once again. His mouth hovered over hers, a tantalizing distraction that nearly wiped his mind clean of thought. "Later." Gods, she smelled good. He reached behind her and pushed the door closed. Nothing mattered in this moment. Not his wounds or the unknown male and what he meant to Chelle. Now, she belonged to Gunnar and he vowed that after tonight she'd realize it without a doubt.

Chelle pulled away to look at him. A crease marred her brow but lust burned in her gaze. "Later?"

"Later." Gunnar pulled her close and he took in the

sight of her soft lips parted as though in anticipation of another kiss. "I've suffered worse wounds and survived without being stitched up."

A corner of her mouth hitched. "Really? Care to elaborate on that?"

She wouldn't deter him. Now that he had her in his arms, he wasn't letting her go. "Chelle," Gunnar said, "stop trying to distract me."

Her eyes went wide with feigned innocence. "I'm a distraction."

"A beautiful one." Gunnar moved in closer and she tilted her head back. "Now be quiet and let me kiss you."

For the first time since they'd met, she did as he asked.

CHAPTER
13

Heat swamped Chelle. Pooled in her limbs and abdomen until she felt as though she burned from the inside out. This wasn't the place or the time to give in to her lust, but the moment Gunnar's mouth met hers once again, she found the logical part of her brain didn't work anymore.

Good gods, he could kiss!

He held her with purpose, one hand pressed against the small of her back while the other wound into the length of her ponytail. He gave a gentle tug, urging her head to one side, and she complied, more than ready to taste him once again. It seemed she couldn't get close enough, couldn't kiss him deep enough, to satisfy her. Her shirt posed a serious problem, separating her from Gunnar's naked chest. Stupid clothes were a total buzzkill. Maybe they should become nudists. Burn all their clothes and cut out the middleman.

His tongue danced with hers in a sensual glide that coaxed a low moan to her throat. Gunnar's grip on her tightened and he gave a gentle thrust of his hips, brushing the length of his erection against her hip. Chelle sucked in a breath. With shaking hands she reached for the waistband of his jeans and worked the button free. Slowly, she eased his zipper down and a contented purr rumbled in his chest.

This was insane! Chelle barely knew him. Only a moment ago he'd been ready to rip Lucas's head from his shoulders. Gunnar was wild, aggressive, arrogant, and infuriating. He had something she wanted. He was a means to an end, nothing more. So why did she want him with an intensity that left her breathless and shaking?

The tether was absolute. She couldn't escape it if she tried.

Denying there was a connection between them was as futile as resisting the urge to drink blood. It was a part of who—and what—Chelle was. What would it hurt to give in to her desires and give herself to the sexy werewolf? She wasn't pledging her heart to him, just her body. Maybe that's all this needed to be. They'd both earned the right to blow off some steam. And maybe this could open the door to negotiations between them. She could convince him to give her his third of the key. Friends with benefits. Sort of.

Gunnar abandoned her lips for her throat. Chills danced over Chelle's body as the heat of his mouth met her cooler skin. She allowed herself an indulgent moan that only seemed to encourage Gunnar. He nipped at her flesh and it caused Chelle's own fangs to throb in her gums. Gods, how she wanted to return the favor. To feel the skin of Gunnar's throat give way under her fangs as his warm, sweet blood flowed over her tongue.

No. Chelle forced the thought to the back of her mind. Taking his blood would only help to solidify their tether and Chelle couldn't let that happen. Any further entanglement would only bring them both closer to ruin.

"Do you like that?" His breath brushed the sensitive

skin below her ear and she shuddered. He bit again, harder this time, and Chelle's pussy clenched with want. "You do." He answered for her. "I can tell by your scent."

There was no use trying to put anything over on another supernatural being. She could pretend she didn't want his hands on her, his mouth, teeth, or anything else. But it would be a lie he could see through as easily as a window. Chelle wanted him like she wanted blood: with an insatiable intensity. She wouldn't deny it. But neither would she voice the words to admit it.

Instead, she let her hands slip inside the waistband of his jeans. She worked them, along with his underwear, over the muscular globes of his ass. Her palms cupped the firm flesh and she squeezed, eliciting an approving growl from Gunnar.

"Use your nails," he rasped against her throat.

A zing of electric energy coursed through her and a warm, wet rush spread between Chelle's thighs. She obliged and dug her nails in as she gripped the globes of his ass. He showed his approval by thrusting his hips against her as he continued to bite, lick, and kiss a path across her collarbone to her left shoulder.

"Gods, you smell good." He ran his nose up the length of her throat and inhaled deeply. "I want to bury my face between your thighs and lap at your pussy until sunrise."

Chelle's knees nearly buckled at his heated words. They painted quite the erotic picture in her mind. One she couldn't wait to see in person. "What are you waiting for?" she asked on a breath. "An invitation?"

He answered with an appreciative growl. Chelle let out a yip as Gunnar gripped the backs of her thighs and hoisted her up in his grip. He turned and tossed her down onto the bed, the log frame more than sturdy enough for a little rough play. Without preamble, he stripped her black leggings from her body and swept her underwear down over her thighs as well. Chelle's knees fell open, revealing herself fully to him, and Gunnar's gaze settled between her thighs.

He sucked in a sharp breath. Chelle took in the sight of him, a warrior fresh from battle, rugged and wild. She studied the tattoos that ran from the shaved sides of his head, down the back of his neck, over his shoulders and chest. His ice-blue eyes sparked with flecks of gold that made him look all the more otherworldly. He was a Viking god and she was spellbound by his fierce beauty.

"I can't wait to taste you."

Chelle swore she felt the rumble of his words along her inner thighs as his gaze drank her in. Gunnar wasn't tentative or shy. Like the night of their tethering when he'd pulled her in for an impulsive kiss, he dove between her legs with gusto. His beard brushed her inner thighs and Chelle cried out as he sealed his mouth over her sex. Gods, she hoped Lucas had the good sense to leave for a while. Otherwise, his virginal ears were going to catch fire.

"Ah, Chelle, your pussy is as sweet as honey."

Forget about Lucas's ears. Chelle's were beginning to feel a little warm from the scorching heat of Gunnar's words. The male didn't beat around the bush. He said what he wanted. Took what he wanted. And made no apologies for it. It excited Chelle. Sent her blood racing through her veins.

His tongue flicked out at her clit and Chelle's fangs bit into her bottom lip. Blood welled from the punctures and she lapped it away. Her thighs trembled in his firm grip, her back arched as her hips rolled up to press tighter against his mouth. She reached back and wrapped her hands around the slats of the headboard as though she needed something to anchor her to the earth.

With each pass of his tongue, she floated higher on a cloud of bliss.

"Oh gods." The words left Chelle's lips on a gasp. "Don't stop."

He didn't show any signs of stopping—or tiring for that matter. Gunnar seemed determined to pleasure Chelle and his prowess was deserving of a standing ovation. His tongue moved over her sensitive flesh in an intricate dance. He knew her body in a way that shook Chelle to her core. A result of their bond? Or proof of just how many women Gunnar had bedded over the centuries? Did it matter? He was hers now. At least for tonight.

Chelle spread her legs further, desperate for more of the intense sensation that left her shaken and panting. Her nails dug into the lodgepole slats of the headboard and the wood creaked under the pressure. Gunnar's tongue circled her clit. The heat of his mouth was a brand, searing her and driving her mad with want. Her hips rolled with every pass of his tongue in an effort to increase the pressure. But Gunnar knew how to play the game and refused to give her even an ounce of control.

"Be still." He pulled away and met her gaze. "Or I'll stop."

Chelle's chest heaved with her breath. She let her head fall back on the pillow and she willed her body to relax. The muscles in her thighs twitched. Her abdomen tightened. Her biceps gathered into knots as she kept her grip on the headboard. But she didn't move. Not an inch.

"That's a good girl," Gunnar crooned against her inner thigh. He nuzzled her pussy, the lightest touch of his nose against her clit and she shivered. He knew how to tease her. How to drive her crazy. It only made Chelle crave more of the same.

He kept his palms braced on her thighs. He blew lightly over her wet, aching flesh and Chelle's pussy clenched. Gods, he could make her come this way. Nothing but his hot breath on her sensitive skin. She writhed beneath him and Gunnar responded by turning her to one side and giving her ass a solid slap. The slight sting excited Chelle but she also knew that Gunnar meant business. He'd told her not to move and he expected obedience. He was the Alpha and he wanted Chelle to know it.

No male had ever excited Chelle like this. Brought her to the point of combustion with nothing more than his mouth and a few teasing breaths. She stilled once again, and when Gunnar seemed satisfied she wouldn't move again, he sealed his mouth over her clit as though to reward her.

Dear gods. Chelle had no doubt that one night with the Alpha of the Forkbeard pack would ruin her.

Chelle's pussy was fucking magnificent. Gunnar had meant it when he told her he could lie between her legs and pleasure her until the sun rose. Soft, sweet, and dripping wet. For *him*. Every cry from her lips, every twitch of her muscles, every roll of her hips was for him. He hated to admit that he'd hoped she'd disobey him. He'd longed to lay his palm to the luscious curve of her ass. The light sting and her gasp of surprise had turned his cock to stone. It throbbed almost painfully, his own need for release cresting to dizzying heights.

He scraped his teeth lightly over the tight knot of nerves and Chelle whimpered. He sucked her into his mouth, rolled his tongue over the sensitive flesh, and her quiet whimpers soon became desperate sobs of pleasure that sent a rush of adrenaline through his bloodstream. She was close. Her scent changed, thickened the air, and it drove him mad with want. He swirled his tongue over her clit and her hips bucked. He didn't break the seal of his mouth, but angled her hips to deliver another swat to her ass. His hand cracked on the bare skin and in that instant Chelle broke apart.

Her body went rigid with her orgasm and she cried out. Deep, racking sobs that echoed in the confines of the bedroom. Gunnar gripped her hips and allowed her to ride out her pleasure against his mouth. In the recess of his psyche, his wolf gave an appreciative growl. Instinct tugged at the back of his mind, centuries of need, the urge to couple with his true mate overriding any shred of common sense. Gunnar wanted to take his time with Chelle. Wanted to pleasure her again and again. Wanted to feel the heat of her mouth glide over his shaft. But that base, animal part of him had other plans. Too impatient for play, all the wolf wanted was to claim what belonged to them.

To seal their bond.

Mine.

The thought rang out in Gunnar's mind, spurring him to action. He brought Chelle down from the high of orgasm with gentle passes of his tongue and light kisses against her slick, swollen flesh. When her breath no longer hitched and her body relaxed, he pushed himself off the bed and shucked his boots, jeans, and underwear.

"Your shirt." The words rumbled with a low growl. "Take it off."

Chelle propped herself up on the bed. The green of her eyes gave way to liquid silver. The color swirled like mercury, unlike anything Gunnar had ever seen. Who was this female his wolf had claimed? He'd met his share of vampires before the Sortiari had seen fit to eradicate them. But never in all of his years on the earth had he encountered one like Chelle.

Extraordinary.

And she was *his*.

Chelle stripped her long-sleeved shirt from her body and discarded it to the side of the bed. A satin and lace bra that was nothing more than a couple of scraps of fabric encased her pert, high breasts. As much as Gunnar admired the garment, he was hungry for bare flesh. "That, too." He pointed at the bra. "I want it gone."

Chelle kept her gaze locked on his and obliged without a word. Gunnar's stomach clenched at the sight of her bare breasts, the tiny nipples hardened and puckered. How he longed to draw them into his mouth. Suck and lick her until her breath came in desperate gasps. Later. After he'd satisfied the mating instinct that drove him to take her and solidify their bond.

Gunnar climbed onto the mattress. He started at Chelle's feet and let his nose wander a lazy path up her leg to her inner thigh as he crawled up the length of her body. She smelled of a sultry summer night, of sex and desire. His tongue flicked out at her flesh, the salty taste reminding him of the ocean. He committed her scent to memory. He'd be able to track her from miles away, recognize her unique signature in a crowd of hundreds of bodies. The mate bond entrusted her into his care. Aside from his pack, Gunnar had never felt that protective urge for anyone else. Fear trickled into his bloodstream as the realization struck that he might someday have to protect Chelle from his own family. If his pack discovered their bond, they might both be killed.

Which was why, for now, he needed to keep their bond a secret.

He discarded the mantle of worry that covered him and focused instead on the female lying beneath him. Gunnar kissed the flat plane of her stomach, up her torso, to the breasts he'd admired only a moment ago. He allowed himself a moment of indulgence and sucked the tight bead of her nipple into his mouth. Chelle's back arched into the contact and a sweet sigh escaped her parted lips.

The sound brushed his senses like myriad feathers.

Gunnar abandoned her breasts. He kissed a path from her collarbone to her shoulder. He bit down there and

Chelle gasped. She spread her legs in invitation and he settled himself between them. Her back came up from the mattress, and when Gunnar bit down again, he thrust home at the same time.

Their voices mingled into a single sound of relief. Chelle's pussy squeezed him tight and Gunnar's cock throbbed in time with his racing heart. His muscles trembled with the effort it took to remain still when what he wanted was to pound into her unmercifully until they both found their release.

"Gods, Chelle." The words came as a deep rasp as he lowered his mouth to her ear. He moved slowly, pulling out to the tip before diving back in to the base of his shaft. Try as he might to find the right words, there was nothing adequate to convey exactly what he felt. She squeezed him tight, so slick and wet, every thrust created a rush of sensation over his shaft that tightened his sac and tingled up his spine.

Her legs wrapped around the backs of his thighs. She tried to control the pace, thrusting her hips up to meet him. Gunnar placed his hands at her hips and pressed her down into the mattress. They'd ride this storm out together. His mate needed to learn that she would never win a battle of wills with an Alpha. Gunnar was in control.

He fucked her slowly, pulling out before plunging in as deep as he could go. Chelle let out a low moan as her head rolled back on the pillow. She reached up and gripped his shoulders, letting the nails dig in. The bite of pain only heightened Gunnar's pleasure and his wolf growled with approval.

"Faster," Chelle begged on an intake of breath. "Harder. Please."

"I'll give you what you need," Gunnar said next to her ear. "But only when I see fit to give it to you."

She answered with a frustrated whimper as her nails

dug deeper into his shoulders. *Gods, yes.* He wanted to draw out her pleasure, but Gunnar knew neither one of them would hold out for long. He'd thought of nothing but taking her since that first night he'd caught her trying to steal from him. He'd kept himself from his mate for far too long.

Gunnar's knees dug into the mattress as he thrust hard and deep. Chelle's moans grew louder, her body tensed beneath him, and her breath came in desperate pants that brushed his neck. Her back came up from the mattress and she pressed her mouth to his throat. The points of her fangs scraped his flesh and Gunnar's pace slowed. To allow her to bite him, to drink from him, was taboo. She was his mate, though. Bound to him for eternity. Everything that transpired between them was sacred. She needed blood to survive. The thought of her putting her mouth to another male's throat drove Gunnar mad with jealousy. His wolf stirred in the back of his mind, giving permission to offer their mate the sustenance she needed. His cock swelled inside of her as he bared his throat to her, a rare act of submission for an Alpha, and waited for her bite.

She sealed her mouth over his flesh and gently sucked. Wild excitement coursed through Gunnar's veins, the anticipation spurring him to new heights of pleasure as he fucked her. Her tongue flicked out and he shuddered. Her bite would no doubt send him over the edge and he hoped she toppled over alongside him.

Her mouth opened wider, the razor-sharp tips of her fangs poised to strike. But instead of feeling the skin give way, the slick glide of her tongue replaced the sharp sting he'd expected. Chelle fell back onto the pillow, her eyes shut as her hips bucked. "I'm close," she said, low. "Gunnar, I'm going to come."

He gave a sharp, deep thrust and her inner walls clenched around his shaft. Each deep pulse of her pussy brought him closer to release. The pressure built. His cock throbbed and his sac grew painfully tight. He threw his head back with a shout as he came, each disjointed jab of his hips bringing with it a pulse of pleasure.

Gods, the intensity of it . . . Gunnar had taken his share of women over the centuries. Fucked his way across Europe and North America. But not one of those encounters compared to this moment. The connection he felt to the beautiful, fierce female beneath him. The intensity of sensation ebbed and Gunnar's thrusts became shallow and lazy.

When the cloud of lust cleared from his mind, a thought nagged at Gunnar that caused his chest to hollow out. Chelle had withheld her bite from him. In the recess of his mind, his wolf let out a mournful howl. He wasn't sure what it meant, but a chill of dread stroked down his spine.

Instead of solidifying their bond tonight, Gunnar sensed that things were about to become a hell of a lot more complicated between them.

CHAPTER
14

Thirst scorched its way up Chelle's throat and her fangs throbbed in her gums. It had taken every ounce of will-power she had not to bite Gunnar. Even now, the urge was almost too strong to resist. Gunnar lay panting on top of her, his fingers threading through the hair that spilled from the top of her ponytail. Giving in to their passions had been unexpected but not unappreciated. *Gods.* No one had ever given Chelle the sort of pleasure Gunnar just had. The male truly was a god. Her orgasm had certainly been a religious experience.

"My heart is racing," Chelle said between panting breaths. If she didn't feed soon, the beat of her heart would slow and then cease completely. But the thought of feeding from anyone but Gunnar left a sour taste in her mouth. Lucas would offer his vein. After seeing Gunnar's reaction to him tonight, however, Chelle wasn't sure that was a viable option, either.

So, what? You're just going to starve yourself?

Seemed like a pretty good idea at this point.

"Are you sure that's not my heart you feel?" Gunnar

said with a laugh. He pulled out and rolled to one side of her. Chelle felt his absence in a way that left her shaken. Was this what the tether did? Weaken her to the point that she couldn't function if he wasn't at her side? Chelle didn't like to feel weak. She didn't like to be dependent. If the tether made her those things, how could she possibly accept it?

Gunnar propped himself up on an elbow. He studied her in the darkened room, his gaze fixed on her face. Chelle kept her eyes locked on the ceiling. Too afraid to look into his beautiful eyes and see any tender emotion there. "Who is the male?" His tone was all business. A dangerous rumble that only served to heat her blood. "Why does he live here with you?"

"How do you know he lives here?"

Gunnar let out an amused snort. "His scent is everywhere. Even in this room." His lips pulled back, making him look all the more menacing. "Is he your lover?"

It was Chelle's turn to snort. "No. Lucas is . . ." What? Her child? Her brother? Would anything she said to Gunnar make sense? "Mine."

Wrong choice of words. The growl that filled the silence sent a chill up Chelle's spine.

"It's not what you think." Chelle turned to her side to face Gunnar. His eyes sparked with gold, feral and bright. The last thing she needed was a repeat of tonight's earlier violence. "I made Lucas a vampire. He's my coven."

The warning growl quieted in Gunnar's chest. "I don't understand." Not surprising. Chelle barely understood it herself. "You're not a part of Aristov's coven?"

Of course he would assume that. Anyone would. Chelle tried to muster the courage to admit to Gunnar what she really was. An anomaly that probably should have been put down a long time ago. "Not exactly," she said. "Lucas and I are . . . unique."

"I know." Gunnar traced the pad of his thumb along her jaw. Chelle's eyes drifted shut for the barest moment as she reveled in the contact. "You are unlike any vampire I've ever encountered."

Chelle's thirst for knowledge almost rivaled her thirst for blood. She'd failed to consider that Gunnar might be a font of information. "Have you encountered many vampires before me?"

"You're deflecting. Tell me more about the male who lives here and what he is to you."

And Chelle thought mated vampires were temperamental. "I told you. I'm his maker." She wasn't sure how much she should divulge to Gunnar, but she had no doubt he'd smell any lies or attempts to mislead him. "Vampires are connected. Sort of like a pack, I imagine." Gods, who was she kidding? Their lives were like apples and oranges. How could he have possibly tethered her? "Like a single thread woven into a tapestry. The connection is unbreakable."

Another low growl pierced the silence. "If he thinks he has some claim on you," Gunnar warned, "he's gravely mistaken."

"No." Chelle gave a shake of her head. Why was it so hard to explain to him? "It's not like that. You live in a family group. Your pack all live in the same house. Why?"

Gunnar's brows drew together. "We're pack. It's in our nature."

"Exactly." Some things you just couldn't explain. "It's the same for vampires. Our covens are our family groups. Lucas is my coven. That's the only connection between us."

"Why is your coven so small?" The lines that marred his brow smoothed. Chelle's fingers ached to reach up and brush the long strands of hair away from his face.

"I don't know if you noticed, but there aren't many vampires around. All of our covens are small."

Gunnar contemplated her words. His piercing gaze swallowed her whole, kept her frozen in place. It would be so easy to lose herself to him again. To give in to the passion that would no doubt sweep them both up in its storm.

"Take your hair down," he said after a quiet moment. "I don't like to see it bound."

Bossy. But not altogether a turnoff. Chelle obliged and unwound the hair tie. She reached up to brush out her hair with her fingers but Gunnar beat her to it. He brushed the strands to one side so they spilled over her shoulder and onto her breast. "Better?"

His gaze grew serious. "Yes."

A simple response that packed a punch. "Why did you warn me to run tonight?" Chelle had tried to steal from Gunnar, twice, and he'd done his best to protect her from the rest of his pack. It had to have caused a fair share of internal turmoil within the ranks. Chelle didn't know how she would have reacted if she'd had to choose Gunnar—a male she barely knew—over Lucas simply because the tether trumped everything else.

"I protect what's mine," Gunnar said.

The words suffused Chelle with warmth. *Mine*. It shouldn't have affected her so deeply. The return of her soul had stirred up all sorts of emotions that Chelle hadn't had to deal with for a while. It felt good to be wanted, even if it was some weird physical and spiritual connection that caused it.

"Aren wants me dead."

Gunnar flinched as though he'd been stung. "Aren is restless and looking for a fight. He doesn't care who brings it to him."

He didn't deny that his buddy wanted her dead. Chelle

was willing to bet he wasn't the only member of the Fork-beard pack who felt that way, either. "I doubt my little parlor trick tonight is going to do anything to win me any points with him or any of the others."

Gunnar's rueful laugh filled Chelle with dread. "No. What you did tonight . . ." He let out a long sigh. "It shouldn't have been possible. It's going to breed fear in the pack. They're going to be even more wary of you."

"I wouldn't have hurt anyone," Chelle said, low. She understood the pack's fear. Hell, her powers frightened *her*. "I knew that my being there put you in a bad position. I was trying—"

"You weren't trying to protect me," Gunnar interrupted. "You were trying to save your own neck."

Looked like Gunnar was the sort of male who wasn't afraid to call her on her bullshit. Chelle liked that. "I was," she admitted.

"Not later, though." Gunnar's tone became grave. "Not when you showed up in Maywood."

"No," Chelle said. "I knew you were in trouble. I wasn't going to let those assholes ambush you."

She reached down and traced her fingertips over the gash in Gunnar's torso. The muscles there flexed and twitched beneath her touch. The wound no longer bled and had finally begun to close. She let out a relieved breath. It could have been so much worse. They'd both gotten lucky tonight.

"How did you know?"

He'd smell a lie. And besides, Chelle didn't want to deceive him. "I heard it in his mind," she whispered. "Aren's. He might not have orchestrated it, but I'm fairly certain he knew it was a possibility."

Gunnar's icy blue gaze narrowed. "What else did you hear?"

She'd anticipated doubt. Why wouldn't he question

what she'd told him? Aren was pack. Part of his family. Chelle might be Gunnar's mate, but they didn't know each other. They had no shared history to bind them. No trust between them. She felt a certain relief that he took her word. Didn't scent the air around her, didn't try to discern an ulterior motive. "Not much. You sort of put everyone on high alert after you put me in that cell and they guarded their thoughts." She flashed him a wry smile and a corner of his mouth hitched. It softened his usually stern expression and caused a twinge of tender emotion to pluck at Chelle's chest. "I think he wants to usurp your position in the pack. And he wants a war."

"War," Gunnar scoffed. He skimmed over the whole usurping of his position part. The arrogance of an Alpha, she supposed. "Aren has lived too long in peace and forgets the horrors that war begets. He's bored and too mischievous for his own good."

"He's ambitious," Chelle said. "Not mischievous. There's a difference and one of them could create a huge problem for you."

A smile that didn't quite reach Gunnar's eyes curved his full lips. "Concerned for your mate's well-being?"

Chelle wasn't ready to admit it, but yeah, she was.

Gunnar didn't doubt the truth in Chelle's words. He'd been wary of Aren's behavior for weeks and she only confirmed what he'd already suspected. Aren's motive in wanting the pack to ally with the berserkers wasn't simply a power play. Aren was deliberately trying to cause dissension within the pack. In order to discredit Gunnar as a competent leader.

It wasn't so easy to depose an Alpha, though.

Gunnar had won his position in the battle arena. A werewolf had to fight for the right to lead the pack, and in order to become an Alpha, he'd had to kill an Alpha.

The only way for Aren to take charge of the Forkbeard pack would be to kill Gunnar.

"I'm pretty sure you can take care of yourself," Chelle said after a quiet moment. "But if I obtain information that's useful to you, I don't see any point in not sharing."

Clever female. Gunnar had no doubt she was laying the groundwork to barter for his third of the Alexandria key. Not that he'd trade anything she had to offer for it, but he didn't mind letting her assume she might break him down.

"You're generous," he said in a teasing tone. "I appreciate that my mate is so selfless." She chose to ignore the sarcasm in his tone, exactly what Gunnar expected. "I will admit that Aren's ambitions might be a problem." One that Gunnar would take care of as soon as possible. "It seems my problems are beginning to pile up."

Chelle's look of chagrin caused his chest to swell with bittersweet emotion. Finding his mate should have been a joyous occasion. One that would have been celebrated for days had Chelle been pack. Instead, he battled the internal turmoil caused by centuries of prejudice and doctrine, and worried for his mate's safety. She would not easily be accepted by the pack. Already, Aren tried to convince the others to run a stake through her heart.

As they lay side by side in the quiet dark, Gunnar let his hands explore Chelle's body. Her skin was cool and as smooth as satin. A sigh slipped from between her lips and Gunnar's cock stirred. He might not have known much about this female who'd been claimed by his wolf, but he wanted her with an intensity that burned through him like wildfire.

"I'm one of your problems," she murmured.

"You are a complication," Gunnar corrected. "But not a problem."

Chelle's soft laughter rolled over him like a caress. "Complication is just a nice way of saying problem."

"Maybe," Gunnar said with a laugh. "But of all my problems you are by far the most pleasantly distracting."

Chelle looked away, but her lips curved into a sweet smile that only served to endear her to him more.

Gunnar brushed the backs of his knuckles along her cheekbone. "Tell me why you want the key."

Chelle kept her gaze focused on the ceiling. "No."

Stubborn female. "It will do you no good to possess it without the other two pieces."

She answered him with silence. Realization dawned and a dark seed of foreboding took root in Gunnar's gut. Jillian's assumptions had been correct. "You already have the other two pieces," he said. "Or you know where they are."

"One of the pieces is mine." Gunnar sensed the admission was hard for her to make but her scent was clean, showing no signs of duplicity. "The Sortiari have the other."

Gunnar's robust laughter echoed off the walls. "Then both of our pieces are useless," he remarked. "You have a snowball's chance in hell of getting your hands on their piece."

Chelle smirked. Somehow the confident expression came off as a hell of a lot more menacing than it should have. "I'll get it," she said. "Everyone's security has a flaw."

That might be true, but the Sortiari were legion. No one knew how many members filled their ranks or the true scope of their power. Their members consisted of humans and supernaturals alike and those of the highest rank were said to be mages like Trenton McAlister. Gunnar could barely stand to be in the same room with a mage. Their magic burned his nose and made his skin crawl. Too much power.

"You must have a death wish." The thought of Chelle trying to infiltrate a Sortiari stronghold made him break out into a cold sweat. "You'll be caught and killed on sight."

"They won't catch me."

Gunnar wanted to grab her shoulders and shake some sense into her. "*I* caught you. And I can guarantee my security isn't half as impressive as theirs."

"I got caught at your place because I was sloppy. I got distracted."

"By what?"

She turned her head to look at him. "You."

The admission created a warm glow in the pit of Gunnar's stomach that fanned outward. "Me?"

"The tether," Chelle said with a nod. "It threw me for a loop."

"What's a tether?" More magic for Gunnar to be wary of?

"It's the equivalent of your mate bond," she explained. "When we're turned into vampires, we forfeit our souls to oblivion. From there, my soul sought out another to tether itself to. Essentially, your soul anchored mine. And when I came in contact with you, my soul was returned, but the tether remains."

Fascinating. Gunnar knew little of the vampires' mate bond. To think that his soul had anchored hers filled him with awe. "A wolf knows its mate," he said. "Mine knew you were ours the moment I laid eyes on you."

"Crazy, right?" Chelle gave a rueful laugh. "Forever tied to someone you barely know. Arranged marriages, extreme edition."

Chelle saw their bond as a burden. It sliced through him, sharper than the berserker's silver-tipped blade. "The mate bond is a gift." Gunnar could do nothing to banish the hurt from his voice. "It makes us stronger."

"Not you," Chelle said. "You've tethered a vampire. You said it yourself, I'm a complication. Not a gift."

She turned his words against him. Gunnar clenched his teeth until he felt the enamel grind. How would they ever find synchronicity if they couldn't even find common ground? "Has anyone ever told you that you're infuriatingly stubborn?"

Chelle smiled. "Pretty much every day."

At least he wasn't the only one she behaved this way with. "Does this Lucas know you've been tethered?"

"Yeah." She snorted. "He thinks it's great."

As much as he hated to admit it, the male might prove to be an ally. "And what of Aristov and his coven? Do they know?"

"No one knows but Lucas," Chelle said. "But I doubt it would matter. As long as it wasn't a berserker or a member of the Sortiari, I doubt they'd care who I was tethered to. Mikhail's mate is unique as well. My brother, Ronan, was tethered by a witch. Lucas said it's nature's way of balancing the scales. With only a few vampires in existence, our souls had to tether themselves to other supernatural beings."

"Nature does find ways to compensate for deficiencies," Gunnar replied. "Are you close with your brother?"

"We're twins." Chelle's tone became sad. "Can't get much closer than that."

"And yet you're not a part of the same coven?"

"Nope." She focused her attention on the ceiling once again. "Nature might be trying to right some wrongs, but Fate is a fickle, sadistic bitch."

On that, Gunnar could agree. "I know what the key unlocks, Chelle." His mate had many secrets. Gunnar needed to uncover them. "And I'm sure you do, too. What do you hope to find there? What are you seeking?"

She sat upright. Gunnar's gaze was drawn to the bounce of her breasts and the way the ends of her hair flirted with the luscious nipples. She blew out a frustrated breath and gathered her knees up to her chest, blocking the beauty of her naked body from his view. "What I want the key for is my business."

He understood her lack of trust. That didn't mean it didn't frustrate the hell out of him. "The keys were kept separate for a reason. There are some mysteries in this world that are best left undiscovered."

Bitterness leached into her tone. "Those sound like words curated by someone who wants to control the ignorant."

Gunnar sat up. He gently pinched her chin between his thumb and forefinger and guided her to look at him. "Tell me what you're searching for, Chelle."

She squared her shoulders and bucked her chin, shaking his grip. "We might be tethered, but I don't answer to you, Gunnar."

His gaze narrowed. "Perhaps you should have to answer to someone." Her defiant nature would undoubtedly get Chelle into trouble. Trouble Gunnar didn't want to have to get her out of.

"Give me the key." She met his gaze and her own was open and completely guileless. "And I promise I won't be a complication anymore. I'll be out of your hair."

Because she'd be halfway across the world in Alexandria. Gunnar's wolf let out a warning growl. She planned to run. Away from them. Away from their bond. That's why she'd withheld her bite. She kept them at arm's length while offering her body in exchange for something she wanted. The depth of her manipulation was a bitter pill to swallow.

Gunnar pushed himself from the bed and stalked across the room to where his clothes lay in a pile. He shoved his legs into his jeans and threw on his socks and boots. "As long as I have breath in my lungs, you'll not have that key." He'd keep it from her out of spite.

Punishment for using him. Rather than acknowledge the hurt he felt, Gunnar chose to channel it into anger. He turned his back on her and stalked to the door. "Play your games with a lesser male, vampire."

The thought of Chelle using her beauty, moxie, and gorgeous body to get what she wanted from anyone else sent a rush of rage through Gunnar. So intense, it constricted his lungs in his chest. He threw open the door and, without so much as a look backward, left her to her wiles.

But gods, walking away from his mate hurt more than the slash of the berserker's silver blade.

CHAPTER
15

"A werewolf?" Ronan smirked as he slid a caramel macchiato across the kitchen countertop to Chelle. "A little clichéd, don't you think?"

"You're not funny." Chelle was beginning to reconsider going to her brother. But after her fight with Gunnar last night, and his warning about the Sortiari's security, she figured she needed someone on her side who was a little more cunning and a lot less innocent than Lucas. She took a sip of the sweet, caramely goodness. If she didn't get some blood into her system soon, her bodily functions would cease and there'd be no more delicious, creamy macchiatos in her future.

"I'm hilarious!" Ronan's mocking laughter was beginning to get on her nerves. "You've got that whole *Underworld* thing going on. Talk about life imitating art."

"You were tethered by a witch." What gave Ronan the right to be so smug? "That's not clichéd?"

He popped a doughnut hole into his mouth and chewed. "Nope," he said through the mouthful of doughnut. Classy. "It's badass."

An Alpha werewolf was less badass than a witch? Somehow, Chelle doubted that. This wasn't a competition to decide who'd tethered the more impressive mate, though. Leave it to Ronan to devolve everything into a sibling-rivalry situation.

"His pack wants me dead," Chelle said.

Ronan brought up his hand for a high five. "Naya's pod wanted me dead. Looks like it's us who're the badasses."

Ronan could think he was a badass all he wanted. Chelle didn't consider herself anything but dangerous. She could compel a pack of werewolves, stop a force of berserkers in full battle rage dead in their tracks. She could pluck a thought from anyone's mind with ease. Others' memories played in her mind like movies she didn't want to see. She was faster, stronger, and healed at a more rapid rate than Ronan or any of the others. She'd developed an immunity to silver. She'd been cut by the slayer's blade and it hadn't so much as tickled. Every day it seemed she discovered some new aspect to her transformation and it scared the ever-loving shit out of her.

"Yeah, we're pretty gods-damned special, all right," Chelle said after a moment. "It's definitely going to be problematic for a while." That was putting it mildly. Naya had chosen Ronan over her pod. Somehow, she didn't think the decision to leave his family for his mate would be so easy for the Alpha of the Forkbeard pack.

"You'll work it out." Ronan gave a playful knock to her shoulder before devouring a few more doughnut holes. "We've all done pretty well so far."

Chelle didn't share in Ronan's confidence. Not that she didn't love discussing the intricacies of the mate bond with her brother, but that's not why she'd invited Ronan over this morning. Her plans to get Gunnar's third of the key had to be put on the back burner since he'd moved it with no intention of telling her where it was. Not to mention his outright telling her that he'd give it to her over his dead body. Until she could decide how best to proceed with Gunnar, it was time to focus on the next piece.

"Lucas mentioned that Mikhail is planning to meet with Trenton McAlister."

Ronan's gaze narrowed suspiciously. "Where did he hear that?"

He'd heard the thought in Jenner's mind a few weeks ago, but Ronan didn't need to know that. "Bria." Chelle mentioned Jenner's mate conversationally. Lucas and Bria were friends. It wasn't too farfetched to think she'd know about it.

Ronan's brow remained furrowed but he didn't press the matter. "Yeah," he said on a sigh. "I don't think it's a good idea, but Mikhail feels like he needs to keep his enemies close."

Chelle agreed with Mikhail. "When's that whole powwow going to go down?" McAlister was the king of the Sortiari's castle. A mage, and rumored to be pretty damned powerful. Her odds of breaking through their security would be that much better with McAlister gone. His meeting with Mikhail provided the perfect opportunity for Chelle to get her hands on the third piece of the key.

"Soon," Ronan replied. *Gah!* In the words of Chandler Bing, could he *be* any more vague? "Jenner and I advised him to wait at least a couple of months, but he's hell-bent on getting the whole thing out of the way. Especially with rumors of a berserker coup circulating."

Huh. That little tidbit of info matched up with the propaganda Aren had been spreading. Join the cause! Overthrow the Sortiari *and* the vampires in one fell swoop! *Give me a break.* "I've heard a few similar rumors. Do you think it's true?"

"It's true," Ronan said gravely. "Jenner overheard a group of berserkers discussing it about a month ago."

Chelle could only imagine how Jenner had stumbled onto that conversation. As much as she didn't want to get involved, it looked like she was going to have to. "The berserkers are recruiting others to their cause."

Ronan's eyes widened. He set the doughnut hole he'd intended to eat back into the box. "How do you know?"

"A member of Gunnar's pack." Chelle shrugged. "He's trying to get Gunnar to ally with Gregor."

Ronan's lip pulled back into a snarl. "And what has *your mate* decided to do?"

Ugh. Chelle didn't need the reminder that she was inexorably tethered. She felt it in every cell that constructed her. It seemed she was even more aware of that bond in Gunnar's absence. And she sure as hell didn't appreciate Ronan's snarky tone. "Gunnar isn't interested in the Sortiari's bullshit. Or the berserkers' vendettas. He's got enough to worry about with a vampire for a mate and a pack who wants her dead."

"Mikhail needs to be told."

Of course. It's not like Chelle expected Ronan to be anything but a hundred percent loyal to his king and maker. "Fine. But just because Gunnar won't join in the berserkers' cause doesn't mean he's going to back Mikhail, either. He wants to remain neutral. So you can tell Mikhail whatever you want, but don't expect Gunnar to agree to a friendly chat."

"All right." Ronan slid the box of doughnut holes her way. "Just because Mikhail might not be able to talk to your mate doesn't mean he won't want to talk to you, though."

Chelle shook her head at the doughnuts and slid the box back across the counter. Already her ability to digest food had decreased. She needed to feed, soon. Otherwise there wouldn't be any doughnut holes or anything else in her future. A total tragedy.

"Whatever. If his royal highness summons me, I'll come."

"He said you met with him a week ago. Asked to see Siobhan."

Well, it was only a matter of time before Ronan got down to the business he wanted to discuss. "Yeah." Ronan's eyes, the exact color of her own, narrowed as he stared her down. She never could keep a secret from him. He didn't even have to question her to make her squirm. Or make her want to fess up. "I asked her for my third of the key to the Alexandria library."

"And she just gave it to you?" Ronan asked. "No strings attached?"

Chelle laughed. "With Siobhan, there are always strings attached."

Ronan scowled but didn't press the matter concerning Siobhan any further. "You wouldn't have asked for your third of the key if you didn't have the other two pieces."

"I don't have them." It still burned that Gunnar refused to give his third up. "But I know where they are."

"How did you find Gunnar?" Ronan wasn't stupid. Chelle knew he'd piece everything together.

"I broke into his house," Chelle said. "To steal his third of the key."

Ronan pinched the bridge of his nose and let out a long-suffering sigh. "Jesus, Chelle."

That pretty much summed it up.

"I know this quest of yours isn't simply blind ambition. What are you after? What do you think you'll find?"

She met Ronan's gaze. "Answers."

His brow furrowed. "To what?"

"To what I am!" Ronan had found her in that dank, moldy basement. He'd seen what the shifter had done to her. She'd been starved, enslaved. *Changed.* And that change frightened her.

Ronan rounded the kitchen island. "Chelle."

"Don't." She held out her hand to stop him. If he tried to comfort her, she'd crack. "You know everyone is afraid of me. Hell, Mikhail kept me cooped up in this house for *months* because he was afraid." Her voice cracked with emotion. "You all keep your distance. Bria is the only one who doesn't walk on eggshells around me."

Jenner's mate, Bria, had lived in the same sheltered coven as Lucas. She visited often, checking up on both of them. Sort of an ambassador between the two vampire covens. Bria was also the only member of Mikhail's inner circle who knew that she possessed unique powers.

The sadness in her brother's eyes gutted her. "What if you don't find what you're looking for?"

She couldn't consider that possibility. Not when the thought of what she might become tied her stomach into knots. "Then I keep looking," she said.

"I hope you find what you need to put you at ease," Ronan said. "But I think we both know that there are some treasures that should stay buried."

Wasn't that the truth. If Chelle could do it all over again, she would never go in search of Set's Chest. But if she hadn't, she never would have met Gunnar . . .

Gods. Fate really was a sadistic bitch.

"What in the hell happened last night?" Aren's concerned tone caused the hairs to rise on the back of Gunnar's neck. "We were about to take a scouting party to L.A. before you showed up."

Somehow, Gunnar doubted that. Aren did a good job of staying close enough to the truth that his scent didn't betray him. More than likely, Sven or one of the others suggested a scouting party, while Aren dissuaded them.

"I ran into a little trouble." Gunnar gauged Aren's response. His eyes widened with surprise but his scent soured.

"What kind of trouble?"

Aren had been stirring shit up for months. Gunnar had dismissed it as the restlessness of a warrior too long without a fight. Something that would soon pass once Aren managed to pick a fight with someone and get the urge for violence out of his system. But Chelle had shone a new light on his second's recent attitude. A handy trick, reading minds. His mate was extraordinary. And not a little frustrating.

Gunnar fixed his gaze on Aren. "Nothing I couldn't handle." Aren wouldn't get any more information than that.

"What about Marcus?"

Gunnar couldn't be certain who were friends and who were enemies at this point. His mate bond with Chelle had occupied all of his free time for the past week. While Gunnar had worried about his own problems, Aren had likely been bending the ears of the pack toward his cause. "What about him?"

Aren's cheeks flushed with anger and gold sparked in his irises, ringing the pupil. "Why are you being so damned evasive? Are you going to tell me what the fuck happened or what?"

Gunnar's wolf stirred in his mind, agitated. A low growl built in his chest and he forced the sound to quiet. Any show of aggression right now would throw up a red flag. Until Gunnar could find out exactly what Aren was planning, it was best to play this close to the hip. "I'm convening a meeting tonight with the entire pack. We have a lot to discuss."

Aren's dark gaze narrowed. "Including the vampire?"

Shit was beginning to pile up. Gunnar had more than

enough on his plate with the prospect of having to defend his position of leadership within the pack and Aren's insistence on an alliance with Ian Gregor. Add Chelle to the mix, and Gunnar felt the walls quickly closing in on him. A cornered wolf *wasn't* a picnic to deal with. And there was no doubt that life, Fate, whatever, had backed him into a corner.

"Including the vampire," he replied.

"I'll spread the word," Aren said. "We'll all be there."

Aren would make sure of it. If anything so he'd have a platform to state his case. How long would it be before Gunnar's own pack looked on him with disdain and his home became hostile territory? He had to trust in the pack. Trust in the familial bond they shared. Otherwise, he'd lose the hold he had that seemed more tenuous by the day.

Gunnar couldn't help but wonder at the differences between packs and covens as he stood at the head of the long mahogany table, looking over his family. That's what they were: family. And with every mating, their numbers grew. But Gunnar had changed that family dynamic the moment his wolf had claimed Chelle as theirs. There was a reason why nonwerewolf pairings were taboo. It disrupted the order of their lives. Shattered the uniformity.

The vampires had managed to adapt, though. With their race's resurgence had come change. They'd accepted that change. Hell, they'd welcomed it. Why couldn't the pack adapt as well? Centuries of tradition might be hard to change, but perhaps there came a time when old traditions needed to make way for new ones. Why couldn't Gunnar be the male to usher in that change?

Of course, by attempting to do so, he might be signing his own death warrant.

Twenty sets of eyes turned to him, anxious to hear what

their Alpha had to say. For centuries, Gunnar had ruled
the Forkbeard pack. Had led them through the cultural
shifts that seemed to fly by with greater speed century
by century. Could he continue to lead them through the
coming storms? Or would the end of his reign be marked
with betrayal?

"It appears the guardians of fate have lost control of
their guard dogs. And we are being forcefully drawn into
a coming war."

Gunnar's authoritative tone reverberated throughout
the room, carrying with it the power of the Alpha. A still
silence settled over the pack. All eyes lowered before their
leader and the air became charged with electricity. Gunnar's wolf gave a low growl of approval as the respect due
them was given. The moment of silence stretched out
and after a long moment, Gunnar took his seat at the head
of the table. His commanding power sparked and dissipated in the air before low murmurs broke out among the
pack.

"The Sortiari are always making war against someone." Sven's brother Bjorn was the first to speak up. The
male was low in the pack's hierarchy. A threat to no one
and one of the first to choose peace over a fight. "Why
should their agendas concern us?"

Gunnar's gaze slid to Aren. Unfortunately, his second
had managed to make it their concern. "With the berserkers no longer held by the Sortiari's leash, they'll become
a problem for the supernatural community as a whole. I
want to remain neutral in their squabbles. However, I'm
not sure how much longer we can continue to stay out of
their path."

Aren spoke up. "There's no reason to remain neutral."

Gunnar had known Aren would use this opportunity
to further his agenda. It wasn't Aren's style to operate below
the radar. He'd never subversively sway the others to his

way of thinking. He steamrolled his way through any given situation.

"Are you suggesting we should support the Sortiari?" Sven asked.

"No," Aren said. "I'm suggesting we ally ourselves with Ian Gregor and his lot."

Another low murmur spread throughout the pack.

"You're kidding, right?" Jaeger spoke up. "The berserkers are nothing more than killing machines. Any agenda they have is going to be self-serving and a disaster for anyone who supports them."

"Honestly, I'm more concerned with our vampire problem."

All eyes turned to Jillian. Gunnar knew it would only be a matter of time before someone brought it up. He just wished it hadn't been so soon.

"Is it true she reads minds?"

"Sven said she compelled him. Jillian and Aren as well. Even you, Gunnar."

"What does she want?"

"How did she circumvent our security?"

The questions rolled in, one after the other.

"Vampires can't do any of that. Is she a hybrid? A witch?"

Gunnar filled his lungs with breath and let it out slowly. "That's enough." Power rang in his tone and every werewolf in the room stilled in an instant. His gaze slid to Aren. The male watched the others around the table, a corner of his mouth hinting at a smirk. The fear that spread throughout the pack as a result of Chelle's mere existence was enough to add to the propaganda of Aren's cause.

"Our pack alone outnumbers the vampires four to one. They're no more of a threat to us than we are to them."

Aren sat up in his chair. "One vampire compelled four werewolves. One of which is an Alpha. You don't find that a threat, Gunnar? Sort of makes that whole four-to-one statistic moot."

Fear bred prejudice. Aren was doing his damnedest to spread that fear. If the pack was scared enough of the vampires, they'd vote to join with Gregor simply to quash their worry.

"You're right." It pained Gunnar to make the concession, but it was true. Last night Chelle had frozen ten berserkers in their tracks, a feat he wouldn't have thought possible. If he told the pack that Chelle was unique in her abilities, though, he'd give too much away. "The vampire was exceptionally powerful. I don't, however, believe that any of them are a threat to us."

"How can you know that?" Jaeger asked.

How indeed? "I know." His tone dared anyone present to argue. "That should be enough."

A murmur traveled through the pack. Gunnar placed his palms on the table. He'd walked the earth long enough to know that power and a short fuse weren't mutually exclusive. He'd been rash, impetuous in his youth. Gunnar had learned patience. Control. He needed to lead by example.

"The Sortiari tried to eradicate the vampires for a reason," Aren interjected. "I think we should take that into consideration."

Gunnar fixed Aren with a stern stare. "And now, the berserkers, the same creatures who did the Sortiari's killing, are turning against them. I think we should take *that* into consideration."

"Are you saying the Sortiari have amended their opinion on the vampires?" Jillian asked.

"I am," Gunnar replied. "And so rather than jumping on anyone's bandwagon I think we should be wary. We should be watchful. And we should *not* be rash."

"But why did the vampire break in?" Bjorn asked. "Why was she here?"

"We'll get to the bottom of that," Gunnar replied. "I don't think she'll be back any time soon." Especially now that his part of the key was no longer on the property. "In the meantime, we stay the course." He looked over each and every member of the pack and said with authority, "Does anyone present challenge the final word of their Alpha?"

Gunnar was answered with silence. Aren, though compliant, refused to meet Gunnar's gaze. Their troubles weren't over. In fact, Gunnar had a feeling they'd just begun.

CHAPTER
16

"I thought you were a tracker, Whalen. So far, you've been nothing but a disappointment."

Ian Gregor wasn't the first person to call Christian a disappointment and he certainly wouldn't be the last. He tipped the glass to his lips and downed what was left of the Macallan 25. He supposed he'd need to give Gregor something. If not, he sensed his meal ticket was about to hit the end of the line.

No way could he go back to drinking cheap scotch.

"I'm looking for a needle in a haystack," Christian drawled. "You can't expect me to find her overnight."

"It's been a month." Black tendrils bled into the whites of Gregor's eyes. Gods, berserkers were scary fuckers. "And there aren't that many dhampirs in the city."

Christian shrugged. He jerked his chin at the bartender and slid his empty glass across the bar. Gregor scowled as the bartender poured another thirty bucks' worth of Macallan into the glass and slid the drink back to Christian. He took a sip of the smooth scotch and reveled in the warm glow that slid down his throat and settled in his gut.

"There aren't many demons in the city, either," he remarked. "I'm sure as hell not running into one every other block."

Gregor's palm came down on the bar with a slap. Christian's wolf stirred at the inherent threat but he forced himself to stay cool. "All you've managed to do so far is waste my time and spend my gods-damned money."

Christian was getting tired of Gregor's insufferable tunnel vision. Especially now that he suspected both he and the berserker shared in the same obsession. "Don't you have bigger things to worry about than finding a single female? Last I heard, you were busy inciting a war."

"What I do is none of your fucking business," Gregor spat.

Gregor couldn't possibly think he could make waves in the supernatural world without someone noticing. Especially when he'd spent all of his free time trying to recruit the local werewolf packs to his cause.

"The local packs are talking," Christian replied. "It won't be long before word gets back to McAlister."

Gregor's lip pulled back into a sneer. "How would you know what the local packs talk about? You're a rogue. They'd just as soon kill you as talk to you."

True. Christian took another healthy swallow of the Macallan. Not for the first time, he wished his metabolism didn't burn off the effects of the alcohol so damned fast. He wanted to be good and drunk tonight. Not listening to Gregor spew a bunch of bullshit that Christian already knew.

"You've given them more to worry about than a rogue," Christian said. He kept his gaze straight ahead, his posture relaxed despite his wolf's unease. "You've brought them to the brink of war."

Gregor let out a derisive snort. "The Sortiari are powerless. The vampires' numbers are few. I don't plan on going to war. I plan to take my enemies unawares and decimate them before they have the opportunity to fight back."

All in the name of some stupid vendetta. "How does the dhampir fit into this?" So far, Gregor had been cryptic as to why he so badly wanted the female he'd hired Christian to track. "If you kill the vampires, the dhampirs will inevitably die off. There's no point in trying to find her if she'll die before you can get your hands on her."

"They won't die right away," Gregor said. His tone was cold, as void of emotion as his eyes. "If anything, killing the vampires will flush them out of their holes."

It was one way to find someone, he supposed. "What then?" Had Gregor even thought past his plans for his little coup? "What happens after you've killed the vampires once and for all? After you've deposed McAlister— which for the record, you don't have a snowball's chance in hell of achieving—what's your plan?"

Gregor leveled his gaze on Christian, one menacing brow arched. "I don't have a snowball's chance in hell?"

"Come on," Christian scoffed. "Your numbers are in the hundreds. Two hundred? Maybe three. The Sortiari are *everywhere*. Killing McAlister might lop the head off the snake, but I guarantee you, three more will sprout in its place."

Gregor shrugged, unconcerned. "Quashing what McAlister has in L.A. will weaken the Sortiari. I don't need their numbers completely eliminated. I'll take them out one cell at a time. By the time I'm done with them, they'll know what it feels like to be powerless. To have their control taken away. And once they know fear, they'll be easy to hunt and I'll pick the bastards off one by one."

Jesus. Gregor meant business. He was the sort of ruthless son of a bitch who didn't just off the guy who'd wronged him. Nope, he took out the guy, his entire family, and every single person he'd ever come in contact with.

Gregor took vengeance to the next fucking level.

Christian drained his glass once again. "Why?" Gregor wasn't interested in status or power. He didn't want to pick up the torch and continue the Sortiari's work. "You have your freedom. Why not do something productive with it?"

"I am doing something productive with it," Gregor ground out from between clenched teeth. "I don't owe you an explanation or anything else but the cash I put in your hand. Find the dhampir. As for whatever else I have going on, mind your own fucking business."

Christian hadn't expected Gregor to offer up his reasons for his obsessive plan for vengeance. But that's not why he'd pushed the male's buttons. He wanted Gregor the hell out of Onyx. The specifically supernatural club was one of Siobhan's favorite hangouts. Christian wasn't positive Siobhan was the female Gregor was searching for, but neither was he willing to take any chances. The last thing he wanted was for the deadly berserker to run into her in the middle of the crowded club.

"Understood." Christian nodded to the bartender once again.

Gregor pushed away from the bar and leaned in until his nose nearly touched Christian's face. "Find the dhampir." Black bled into the whites of his eyes and his musky stench intensified with his anger. "Find her soon or you might just meet the same end as McAlister." He pulled away and let his gaze rake Christian with disdain. "And you can buy your own gods-damned drinks for the rest of the night."

Christian didn't move a fucking inch until Gregor turned and stalked away.

His wolf let out a low growl in his psyche and Christian willed the animal to still. A good five minutes passed before Christian could take a deep breath, but it wasn't fear that elicited such a strong physical reaction. No, Christian wanted to gut the motherfucker with his bare hands. He took his fresh drink in his grip and did his best to calm the shaking of his fingers, twitchy from the adrenaline that still coursed through his veins.

"You're a little jumpy tonight, werewolf. Does the coming moon have you on edge?"

The decadent purr of Siobhan's voice unsettled Christian for an entirely different reason. He cast a furtive glance over his right shoulder. There was no sign of Gregor but that didn't mean the bastard wasn't lurking somewhere.

"You shouldn't be out tonight." Christian reached for his glass. Siobhan beat him to it though, and cradled the heavy tumbler in her delicate hand. She brought it to her mouth and Christian watched, transfixed, as her full red lips sipped from the edge. A lump rose in his throat and he swallowed it down. *Fuuuuuck.* She exuded sensuality without even trying. But as much as Christian wanted to continue the game of cat and mouse they'd started months ago, he needed to get her the hell out of here. "Shit's going down all over the city."

Siobhan's mouth turned upward with amusement. Her emerald-green eyes warmed as she looked him over from head to toe. Christian's cock perked up like a damned pup about to get a treat and his wolf grew restless. "It's cute that you think I'm so delicate."

Mine, mine, mine, mine, mine.

Not ours. His damned wolf didn't know what was good for them.

"Not delicate," Christian ground out. "But certainly foolish."

"What do I care about the petty squabbles of supernatural factions? They've warred since the beginning of time. They'll war till the end of it, no doubt."

She had a point. That still didn't make him any more comfortable with how close she'd come to running into Gregor tonight. "Are you saying you don't have a dog in the fight?"

Her smile grew, revealing the sharp points of her tiny fangs. A shiver raced down Christian's spine as he imagined what her bite might feel like. "Which fight?" she asked. "There are so many. Who do you side with, werewolf? You're a rogue; you don't belong to a pack. I doubt you'd side with your own kind in a squabble. What about the vampires? Do you support Mikhail's ridiculous desire to rebuild the race? Or perhaps you agree with the Sortiari that the berserkers should have put them all down. Would a rogue keep such . . . unsavory company as a berserker warlord?"

She was fishing for something. Too bad for her, Christian wasn't about to bite. Gregor was a piece of shit, but he was far from the most unsavory creature Christian kept company with. "There's a lot you don't know about me. Including where my allegiances lie."

"Hmmm." Gods, the warm hum of her voice rippled through him and turned his bones to ash. "I suppose you're right. So tell me, werewolf, how can I possibly trust you?"

Siobhan took another sip from Christian's glass before handing what was left of the scotch back to him. He took the glass from her hand and allowed his fingertips to graze hers. An electric charge arced between them and Christian swallowed down a groan. He rested his left hand between them on the bar, fingers splayed. The urge to reach out and haul her against his chest, taste her luscious mouth, was almost too much to resist.

"You can't trust me." The more wary he could keep her, the better. Christian didn't want to scare her off. Shit, the thought of putting even a foot's worth of distance between them made his wolf anxious as hell. Until he knew for sure whether or not she was the one Gregor was looking for, he had to do whatever it took to protect her.

Her answering laughter only served to further agitate him. Did she have to be so gods-damned cavalier about everything? "Because someone's paying you to watch me?"

Yes! The thought was as good as a shout in Christian's mind. And rather than be afraid, Siobhan took it as a challenge. Played her games with him and worked her seductive charm. "Paranoid?" He played her game in spite of himself.

Her smile grew. "Always." Siobhan glanced over her left shoulder. "But that's why I never leave home without him."

Christian followed Siobhan's gaze to where the burly dhampir stood guard. His wolf let loose a territorial growl. The scary-looking son of a bitch was never far from Siobhan's side. A fact that caused him as much jealousy as it did relief. The male could definitely protect her from a random threat, but even someone as big and imposing as that wouldn't stand a chance against a berserker in full battle rage.

Siobhan leaned in and put her mouth at Christian's ear. "You've been lying low lately. Why is that?"

For the past few weeks, he'd suspected that Gregor was having him followed. The berserker would be a fool to trust him, and in order to keep Gregor off Siobhan's trail, he'd been careful to avoid her. Christian might've been taking Gregor's money, but at the end of the day, Christian was on only one side: his own.

He finished off the Macallen and instantly wished he

could order another. Or better yet, take the whole bottle. He turned toward Siobhan and smirked. "Miss me?"

She laughed. "No."

Her deadpan response made Christian want to prove her wrong. He closed the distance between them until a hairsbreadth separated their mouths. Jasmine scented the air and he inhaled deeply, holding her floral perfume in his lungs. Gods, she drove him mad with want.

"Ah-ah, wolf," Siobhan warned in a breathy whisper. "You know the rules. Tell me what I want to know and then we can play."

Christian smiled. He was a masochistic son of a bitch to enjoy the way she teased him. He pulled away and flashed a grin. "Go home, Siobhan." He fished a twenty from his pocket and slid the tip across the counter to the bartender. No one would be buying his drinks for the rest of the night so there wasn't really any reason to be here. Besides, he'd gotten wind of a couple of private poker games in the valley that he wanted in on. Maybe if he took off, Siobhan would have no reason to stay, either. "It's past your bedtime."

It took everything he had to turn away from her and walk toward the exit. His wolf howled at the back of his mind. Clawed and fought to return to her side. Christian locked down his will and fought the animal's influence as he forced one foot in front of the other. He made sure to pass by her bodyguard and paused only long enough to say, "Get her the hell out of here and make sure she goes straight home." There was no point in waiting for a response, he simply met the male's gaze for a split second before he headed for the door. Christian stepped out into the too warm L.A. night and let out a frustrated breath. The polluted air caused his nose to wrinkle. It wasn't half as appealing as Siobhan's jasmine scent.

Walking away from her was like walking away from a part of himself. And that scared the shit out of him.

"Werewolf!"

Christian turned at Siobhan's shout and cocked a brow in question.

"Don't throw in the towel yet."

"Oh no," Christian replied. "We'll need it to clean up afterward."

A sultry smile curved her mouth and Christian forced himself to turn again and walk away.

If Siobhan truly was the dhampir Ian Gregor so desperately sought, shit was only going to get worse from here on out. And it was going to take a hell of a lot more than his sorry ass to keep her safe.

CHAPTER
17

"Lucas! Can you get the door?" Chelle stuffed a length of nylon rope into her backpack. The pounding started up on the door again and she blew out a frustrated breath. "Lucas!" He was a vampire, for shit's sake. She shouldn't have had to shout for him to hear her. She was too damn busy to deal with whoever was here. Two days had passed since Gunnar had walked out on her and Chelle knew it was only a matter of time before fate—and their tether—pulled them together once again. She needed to do some reconnaissance if she wanted to find out where Gunnar had moved his third of the Alexandria key. No way was that going to happen with him breathing down her neck.

The overanxious knock came again and Chelle tossed her backpack down on the bed. Lucas's reason for not answering the door had better be good—like he was currently pulling a stake from his heart—otherwise she was going to throttle him.

"Don't get your panties in a bunch!" Chelle called as she strolled down the hallway to the front door. She wanted to reward the persistent knocker for their effort by making them wait as long as possible for her to get to the door. "I'm coming."

Chelle pulled open the door with a huff. Her breath caught on the exhale and her jaw went slack. She recovered and hid her shock behind a smirk as she leaned against the doorjamb. "Well, knock me over with a feather."

One of the females from Gunnar's pack stood on the other side of the threshold. Her posture was relaxed but Chelle sensed her unease. Her scent soured and her wolf gave a warning growl in her mind.

"Jillian, right?"

She gave a curt nod. "Mind if I come in?"

Chelle poked her head out the door, looking for Jillian's backup. If she'd brought a hunting party to Mikhail's front door, the vampire king would blow a freaking gasket. "How many of you are there?"

"Just me," Jillian replied.

"All right." How dangerous could one werewolf be? "Come on in."

Jillian took a tentative step inside. Chelle didn't have the energy—or the desire—to do anything to make her feel at home. Instead, indignant anger crept up on her. How had the werewolf found her? This was supposed to be her safe zone. The one place where she didn't have to worry about watching her back. Mikhail's property was better protected than Fort Knox. Which begged the question . . . "How did you get past security?"

Jillian pointed a finger at herself. "Werewolf. I'm pretty stealthy."

Great. Chelle supposed she'd have to let Mikhail know about the breach. Ever since his son had been born, he'd taken security to an almost paranoid level. Chelle didn't blame him though, especially after everything she'd learned about the berserkers' plans to overthrow the

Sortiari and wreak a little havoc in the supernatural world. Things were going to get a hell of a lot worse before they got better. It wouldn't be long before Mikhail moved them all into an underground bunker.

Chelle went into the living room and slumped down on the couch. If she'd learned one thing from Siobhan, it was the power of intimidation. She needed the werewolf to think that Chelle didn't perceive her as a threat. Which, really, in a one-on-one situation, Chelle was pretty sure she could take her.

Chelle fixed Jillian with an icy stare. "You're a little out of your territory, aren't you? How'd you find me?"

Jillian squared her shoulders. She walked into the living room and took a seat opposite Chelle in an overstuffed chair. "It wasn't hard. Mikhail Aristov has gained quite a bit of notoriety in the supernatural world over the past year. I came here to talk to him but caught wind of your scent. You were easy to track once I scented you."

Chelle was almost disappointed in Jillian's response. When she thought about it, it really wouldn't have been tough to track her down. Mikhail really needed to think about investing in a Bat Cave.

"Does Gunnar know you're here?" Chelle couldn't imagine Gunnar had given Jillian permission to come. Not when he was doing his damnedest to keep their mate bond a secret.

"Are you kidding?" Jillian laughed. "If he knew I was here, he'd have my ass."

Chelle had to admit, she liked Jillian. Of course, anyone who rocked the boat was always okay in her book. "So why are you here?" There was no point beating around the bush.

Jillian leveled her gaze and her lips thinned. "Gunnar's wolf claimed you, didn't he?"

Ruh-roh. Chelle sat up a little straighter on the couch.

Maybe she'd been too quick to dismiss the possibility of a hunting party of angry werewolves showing up on her front porch. "The pack knows?"

"Honestly?" Jillian cringed. "I don't think so. They all rely on their wolves to tell them things. They've relied on their heightened senses for too long. Gunnar has hidden it well, but I haven't been a werewolf for that long. I notice things the others don't."

"Oh yeah?" Chelle asked. "Like what?"

Jillian's mouth quirked into a sly grin. "The protective glint he gets in his eyes when the conversation points to you, for starters."

A warm glow pulsed in the pit of Chelle's stomach and fanned outward. She didn't want to feel pleased over Gunnar's implied protective feelings but she couldn't deny that it had its appeal. Wariness crept over her and Chelle centered her focus. She wouldn't have any trouble compelling Jillian, but she didn't know what the werewolf had up her sleeve.

"You're here to kill me," Chelle said, no-nonsense. "Good luck with that."

"I don't want you dead," Jillian replied. "That doesn't mean the others wouldn't kill you on sight . . . but like I said, I haven't been a werewolf for long. Their traditions aren't necessarily mine."

Despite the assurance, Chelle wasn't ready to let her guard down. "So you thought you'd just come on over and we'd do a little female bonding?"

Jillian let out an amused snort. "I'm not sure what I thought I'd do. I don't think your mate bond with Gunnar is any of my business. Just like my mate bond isn't any of yours." Jillian looked away for the barest moment. "I'm more interested in what you came to steal from us and why."

Jillian really was a female after Chelle's own heart.

"You have quite the collection of relics." Chelle liked Jillian, but that didn't mean she trusted her. "Lots of valuable artifacts to choose from."

"True," Jillian said. "But you were only interested in one relic. Why?"

"How do you know that?"

Jillian smirked. "Because Gunnar removed only one relic from the collection."

Well, at least now Chelle could be certain Gunnar had told her the truth about moving the key. Jillian's visit might be the break Chelle needed. "What can I say? I have a thirst for knowledge."

"Me, too," Jillian said with a smile. "Like for starters, I'm dying to know why everyone is so worked up about what you can do. Apparently, it's not typical for a vampire to be able to compel an entire room of werewolves."

Anxious energy trickled into Chelle's bloodstream. She forced the fear away, unwilling to give Jillian the upper hand. Rather than respond, she gave the werewolf a wan smile.

"The pack is concerned," Jillian continued, "that the new breed of vampires possesses greater power than they used to, thereby making them a greater threat."

Chelle bet that Aren wasted no time in helping to propagate that *concern*. "Your pack has nothing to be worried about. Mikhail isn't breeding a race of supervamps. I'm . . ." Chelle took a deep breath. "Unique."

Jillian's gaze narrowed. "How unique?"

"No offense," Chelle said. "But I don't think we know each other well enough to be sharing secrets. Do you?"

"Maybe not," Jillian agreed. "If you want an ally in the pack, though, I'm your best bet."

"What makes you think I need the pack at all?"

"I don't think you realize what your mate bond means

for Gunnar." Jillian sat back in her seat and pinned Chelle with her stare. "What will happen to him if the pack finds out."

Oh, Chelle had a pretty good idea. Gunnar had done his damnedest to keep her as far from the pack as possible. Still, she'd never considered the consequences he would face for their bond. He'd only ever suggested that it was Chelle who was in danger. "What'll happen to him?"

"They'll kill him," Jillian replied. "As a mercy. And after that, they'll kill you."

Wow. Werewolves took their mate bonds seriously. "Seems like an antiquated punishment, don't you think?" Their tether hadn't sat well with Chelle, either, but killing both of them in order to end it hadn't been an option.

"I was a young woman in the fifties," Jillian said with a shrug. "Interracial relationships were the basis for a lot of needless violence. Gunnar's pack has been around a hell of a lot longer than the civil rights movement."

Chelle knew all about prejudices. And though Jillian's explanation made sense, it didn't mean she had to like or accept it.

"I don't plan on dying," Chelle said after a moment. "And I doubt Gunnar does, either."

Jillian flashed a feral smile. "Maybe I can help you both with that."

Chelle scooted to the edge of the couch. "What do you have in mind?"

Gunnar watched Chelle's house from the top of the high wall that enclosed Mikhail Aristov's property. He didn't detect any sign of a fight but that didn't help to put his wolf at ease. The animal grew more agitated by the moment, causing so much nervous energy to churn in Gunnar's veins that he jumped down from his perch onto Aristov's property and paced back and forth in order to burn it off. Jillian wasn't the sort to run off and go vigilante on behalf of the pack. She was an intellectual and Gunnar knew that Chelle fascinated her. *Gods.* If Chelle and Jillian managed to put their heads together, there wouldn't be anything they couldn't accomplish.

"Usually, I shoot first and ask questions later. But I'm under the impression you've tethered my sister, so I'm going to mix it up a little this time."

Fuck. Gunnar turned to find a large, imposing vampire watching him from about thirty yards away. He bore a striking resemblance to Chelle. Same bone structure, same tawny hair and forest-green eyes. Same mocking, defiant expression and the same insufferable air of confidence. Their scents baffled Gunnar's wolf, though. As siblings, there should have been some similarity. More evidence of that "uniqueness" Chelle had mentioned.

"I appreciate that," Gunnar replied. Chelle's brother continued to watch him with the wary intensity with which one predator watched another. His wolf let out a low growl but Gunnar did nothing to silence it. He wanted the vampire to know that if he wanted a fight, Gunnar wouldn't go down so easily.

"Down, boy," Chelle's brother replied. He walked with an easy, rolling gait toward Gunnar, his fangs bared menacingly. "I doubt my sister would appreciate me laying into her mate. I can call a truce. For now."

Gunnar canted his head to one side. The vampire looked like he had no problem fucking up anyone who got in his way. And he was obviously protective of Chelle. Something he and the vampire had in common. "Why for now?"

"Once I decide if Chelle is safe with you or not."

Definitely overprotective. "I'm her mate," Gunnar said. "She's safer with me than with *anyone*."

Chelle's brother shrugged a shoulder. "Maybe." He stepped up to Gunnar, chest puffed out. He held out his hand. "Ronan Daly."

Gunnar reached out and gave the vampire a firm shake. "Gunnar Falk."

"Alpha of the Forkbeard pack," Ronan proclaimed.

Ronan shared Chelle's snarky sense of humor. Something Gunnar might have appreciated in a different situation. He wasn't a fan of Ronan's mocking tone. Gunnar was descended from kings. He demanded the respect due a king.

"That's right," Gunnar said. "Tested by strength in battle. And unchallenged for centuries."

"Relax, werewolf," Ronan said. "I'm not trying to pick a fight."

"Really?" Gunnar asked. "Because it feels a hell of a lot like you're trying to pick a fight."

"Chelle says your pack wants her dead. You're lurking around outside her house like some sort of creeper. Sorry if I'm not a little more welcoming, but only stalkers or serial killers lurk around like this."

Silver flashed in Ronan's eyes. His gaze was serious, but there was a lighthearted undertone to his words. "Chelle is a resourceful female," Gunnar said. "And stubborn. She isn't exactly receptive to help."

Ronan chuckled. His wide smile showed off the dual points of his fangs, making him look even more imposing. "That's the damned truth. It probably chaps your ass to find yourself mated to someone who tried to steal from you."

"It's less disconcerting than the fact that she won't confide in me *why* she's trying to steal from me."

Ronan let out a chuff of breath. "Tell me about it. She's a total pain in the ass. If it makes you feel any better, she's not exactly forthcoming with anyone else. She likes to play things close to the hip. It's a total kick in the gut, especially when you're trying to help her."

"Who is Chelle's maker?" Gunnar asked. It was something that had been eating at him for the past few days. "It's not Aristov."

Ronan's expression darkened. "No, Mikhail isn't her maker."

"And neither are you."

Ronan studied him. "How do you know?"

"Your scents are different." Perhaps in Ronan, Gunnar would find an ally. "Lucas and Chelle share a similar scent. In fact, if not for your resemblance to her, I wouldn't know you're related. You smell *nothing* like her."

Gunnar couldn't do anything about the accusation that leaked into his tone. Secrets were being kept from him and he was getting tired of it. Fast. Nothing was more important than a mate bond. Mates never kept secrets from one another, and since their first meeting, Chelle had done her best to deceive him.

"Chelle is unique," Ronan said.

Gunnar gave a rueful shake of his head. "Honestly? That explanation is getting a little tired. You share her flare for cryptic answers."

"It's not my place to explain Chelle's situation to you."

"Situation?" Gunnar took a step closer to Ronan. "What in the hell does that mean?"

Ronan folded his arms across his wide chest. "Anybody ever tell you that you look like that guy on that A&E show. What's it called? *Vikings*?"

Gunnar's wolf snarled. He shared the animal's annoyance. Ronan must've used humor to deflect on a regular basis. Gunnar didn't find him all that entertaining. "I want to know what it is about Chelle that has your scent souring, vampire. I don't like secrets, and I don't like being made a fool of."

Ronan let out a slow breath. Tension sizzled in the air between them and Gunnar sensed a coming fight. It wouldn't earn him any points with Chelle if he managed to hurt her twin, but the wolf wouldn't back down. Any act of aggression from Ronan would be answered with equal aggression.

"I don't know you." The words grated in Ronan's throat. "And I don't have to tell you shit. The only reason I'm here is to find out why in the hell you're watching my sister's house and how in the hell one of your werewolves circumvented security to walk through her front door a half hour ago."

"How do you know it's one of my wolves?" Gunnar asked, low. He didn't want to egg Ronan on, but the insinuation that they'd come to do Chelle harm made his wolf want to tear into Ronan's throat.

Ronan tapped the side of his nose. "You're not the only one with sharp senses, *Gunter.*"

Gunnar's nostrils flared. He'd tried to keep calm but Ronan had managed to antagonize him past the point of reason. His hands balled into fists and he took a step toward the vampire at the exact moment the door to Chelle's cottage opened and Jillian stepped out onto the walkway.

"As much as I'd like to show you where you sit on the food chain, vampire, I need to see to the welfare of my *mate.*"

Ronan's lips split into a wide grin. Chelle's brother ran as hot and cold as she did. Gunnar didn't have time to play games. He had too many questions that demanded answers and he'd be damned if he left here before he got them.

"Holler if you need me," Ronan called as Gunnar took off across the grounds toward the cottage.

Gunnar rounded the side of the cottage with barely a

sound to betray his presence. He paused only long enough for Jillian to cross the pathway to the south side of the house before he loped toward the front door. Ronan's amused laughter trailed after him and Gunnar shook his head.

Vampires.

Infuriating pains in his ass, every last one of them.

CHAPTER
18

Chelle caught wind of Gunnar's delicious scent moments before he put his fist to the door. Quite the day for were-wolf guests. Her secret lair had become a hell of a lot less secret over the course of the week, making Chelle realize that it was time to pull up camp and take her coven somewhere a little more private. Mikhail didn't need the added worry of volatile werewolves hanging around with everything he already had on his plate. And since not all of Gunnar's pack could be considered friendly, the sooner she found new digs, the better.

"Door's open!" she called from her perch on the couch. She was still pissed at Gunnar for the way he'd walked out on her two nights ago. No way was she going to greet him at the door like a doting mate.

Screw him. And his fabulous hair and rugged good looks.

Gunnar walked through the door, a scowl affixed to his face. His eyebrows cut severe slashes above his mesmerizing ice-blue eyes and a crease lined his forehead just above the bridge of his nose. "Door's open?" He let out a huff of breath. "I could have been anyone, Chelle."

"True," she said, unconcerned. Her inability to exercise caution seemed to drive him crazy so Chelle made sure to play it up. "But where's the fun in playing it safe? I rolled the dice and took a chance."

Gunnar closed the door behind him. "Are all vampires as infuriating as you or is it just the members of your specific family line who like to push buttons?"

Chelle perked up at the mention of her family, but she didn't give her curiosity away. "Which family? I mean, if we're talking family by birth, then yeah, Ronan knows how to rattle chains. If we're talking family by bite, then no. Lucas is as ornery as a newborn lamb."

"Chelle." Gunnar looked like he was about to lose his cool. Heh.

She gave him a sweet smile. "Gunnar."

"This isn't a joke. You've got to protect yourself—"

"From your pack?" Chelle let her eyes go wide and innocent. "I mean, that's who wants me dead after all. But don't you think you should be taking your own security a little more seriously? Berserkers, your own second in command . . . I'd say you've got more to worry about than I do right now."

"This isn't about me," Gunnar growled.

"I suppose it isn't." Chelle's temper mounted for no good reason aside from her own hurt at being disregarded two nights ago. "I mean, if it wasn't for me showing up at your place, you'd have one less problem to worry about. If I hadn't tethered you, you'd only have Aren to deal with and not your entire pack's loyalty." Her voice escalated and her chest ached with emotion. "I'm sure you're just itching to find a way to chew through the rope of our tether, aren't you?"

"Gods, you're stubborn," Gunnar spat.

Gold flecks shone in the blue of his eyes and his lip pulled back into a snarl. He ran a hand through his hair, flipping the length to one side of his head. The tattoos marking his scalp drew Chelle's attention before she forced her gaze away. She'd never met a more primal male and the memory of him between her legs made her instantly wet.

"I'm stubborn?" The incredulous words burst from her lips. She might have wanted to climb him like a tree, but that didn't mean she'd give him the satisfaction of knowing it. "You're a pigheaded pain in the ass if you ask me." The tether tugged at her chest but Chelle ignored it. They might be tied inexorably to one another, but that's all it would ever be. A bond. They could never have any sort of relationship. They were too different. His own pack's rules, too stern. Chelle couldn't allow him to get close. It would only destroy them both. The only option was to push him away. "If you'd just give me your third of the gods-damned key you wouldn't have to worry about me at all."

Gunnar's gaze hardened. "You're not getting that key. And that's not what this is about."

"If you don't give it to me, I'll steal it anyway."

"You won't steal it." Gunnar's confidence only doused her anger with fuel. "Because you have no idea where it is."

"You don't think I won't be able to find it?" Chelle laughed. "Don't underestimate me, wolf."

"Tell me why you want it, Chelle."

She met his gaze. "No."

His jaw squared with anger. Power sparked the air with a static charge that made the hair on Chelle's arms stand up. Gunnar's power. Fear licked up her spine. He was a truly menacing sight to behold when he wanted to be.

"What are you afraid of?" The wolf made an appearance in his tone, all growly and fierce. "Why won't you confide in me?"

"Confide in you?" Chelle shot up from the couch. "I don't even know you!"

The tether bound them. It formed an attraction. But that was nature. A trick. There was nothing else between them. No affection. No shared history. Nothing. And the sooner Gunnar realized that and set Chelle aside, the better.

Gunnar took a step toward her. Chelle's body warmed and she reminded herself that it was nothing more than a chemical reaction. "You're pushing me away." Gunnar didn't have to shout to convey his anger. It simmered just under the skin. "Why."

Not a question. A demand. Chelle couldn't admit to what he wanted to hear. That she was afraid. Of their tether. Of what his pack would do when they found out about their bond. Of her own gods-damned power and origin. Of what she might become or what Mikhail might do to her if he found out what she was capable of. Of the way he made her feel and the fact that she was having a hard time buying her own bullshit.

If Chelle couldn't convey to him in words why he needed to steer clear of her, she had no choice but to show him.

She crossed the room and pulled a silver dagger from a drawer in the kitchen. The blade sang as she yanked it from the sheath and Gunnar's gaze locked on the metallic glint in the lamplight. She pulled up the right side of her shirt, exposing the unmarred flesh of her torso, and without preamble drove the blade into her flesh.

Gunnar jumped as though he were the one who'd been stabbed. Chelle swallowed down the bite of pain and pulled the blade free. She was almost completely immune to silver now. The blade might as well have been made from steel. Gunnar stared, jaw slack, at the open wound that closed before it even got a chance to bleed.

"You heal as fast as a berserker," he said on a breath.

Finally, she was getting through to him. "You're thinking that even if your pack tried to kill me, they wouldn't stand a chance." She plucked the thought from his head like ripe fruit from a tree. "You're worried that I might decimate your entire family in the process of saving my own neck."

The muscles in Gunnar's jaw clenched. He didn't bother to confirm what she said. They both knew it was the truth.

"You're wondering if Aren is right. If the vampires are a threat. If we should be put down once and for all."

"Chelle," Gunnar warned. "Stop this."

She wasn't about to stop until he understood why he needed to stay away from her. "Where's the key, Gunnar?"

His brow furrowed as though in pain. He fought the influence she exerted over him. The power of an Alpha no doubt. His mind was stronger than the other members of his pack, but that wouldn't stop Chelle from proving to him that she was a danger to him and everyone he held dear.

"I want your third of the Alexandria key, Gunnar." Chelle infused her voice with power and Gunnar swayed on his feet. "Tell me where it is."

She was dangerous. A threat. An anomaly created from magic. She was *other*. And her only hope for answers was a library halfway across the world that had been long forgotten by mankind. She couldn't be Ronan's sister, or Gunnar's mate, or even Lucas's coven until she knew exactly what she was and what she was capable of. No one understood. But how could they? Chelle had done her best to push everyone away.

Damn Gunnar for being right.

His body grew tense, every muscle, rigid. His eyes narrowed and his nostrils flared. They fought a battle of wills. One that Gunnar would lose. "Tell me where the key is, Gunnar."

His lips twitched as he fought the urge to speak. He put one foot in front of the other, almost mechanically, as he closed the distance between them. Before Chelle could react, he took her in his arms and put his mouth to hers. Effectively shutting him up while distracting her ability to compel him.

Chelle melted against him, helpless to resist his magnetic pull. He might have managed to distract her, but this was far from over between them.

The moment Gunnar's mouth met Chelle's she released her hold on his mind. Gunnar's wolf was agitated, angry at the betrayal of his mate's attempt to control them. She might have been theirs but a power struggle between them would only cause trouble. Especially with the full moon only a few days away. Gunnar gripped the back of her neck and deepened the kiss. Chelle submitted as her lips parted for him. Gunnar couldn't help but be the aggressor. His wolf demanded it.

With his free hand, Gunnar gripped her hip. He pulled her tight against him and rolled his hips, pressing the length of his hard cock against her. Chelle sighed into his mouth, the sound like a caress. She reached up and wrapped her fingers in the hem of his shirt and gave it an upward tug.

Gunnar reached for her wrists and held them secure in his grip. She thought she could use her power to control him and he planned to give her a taste of her own medicine. He'd make the untamed vampire come to heel if it killed him. He wanted to master Chelle. Pleasure her until the sun rose. Make her inexorably his so she'd once and for all give up the ridiculous notion of pushing him away.

He didn't give a shit what his pack thought or wanted. The mate bond was all that mattered. And he'd kill anyone or anything that sought to take her from him.

Gunnar broke their kiss and turned Chelle in his arms so her back molded to his chest. Her arms fell to her sides as his hands dove beneath her shirt and ventured up her torso. Gods, her skin was satin against his fingertips and cool enough to give him a chill. He didn't remember her skin being so cold the last time they'd been together. Gunnar reached for her shirt and stripped it from her before bringing his mouth to her bare shoulder and along her neck.

"Why is your skin so cold?" he asked against her throat.

Chelle shuddered. "I haven't fed," she said on a breath. "Not since the day after we met."

His answering growl was more animal than man. Jealousy burned a path from his gut and up his throat. He let his teeth graze the juncture where her neck met her shoulder. "Who fed you?"

Chelle let out a low moan.

"Who?" Gunnar demanded.

She sighed. "Lucas."

Gunnar's hand wandered over the silky fabric of her bra that barely concealed her breasts. His fingers grazed her collarbone and he gently cupped her throat to hold her still. His mouth came to rest at her ear and he infused his voice with the power of an Alpha. "You will never feed from another male save me. Do you understand?"

Chelle gave a curt nod of her head.

Gunnar nipped at her earlobe. "Say it."

She trembled against him. "I understand."

Gunnar had never witnessed a vampire taking another's vein for sustenance, but that didn't stop his imagination from running far afield. He pictured Chelle's lush mouth at Lucas's throat. Her sharp fangs piercing the skin. In his mind, she let out a low moan as Lucas cradled her head against him. The growl in Gunnar's chest turned into a snarl, wild and vicious. "I'll break the spine of any male who seeks to offer you so much as a pricked finger."

He should have been disgusted at the prospect of having Chelle feed from him. Instead, it awakened something primal in him, bringing his wolf closer to the surface of his psyche. The wolf approved of offering their vein to their mate. To offer freely what she needed to thrive. Chelle was *theirs*. To care for. To protect. To provide for. To love.

Chelle was concerned that Gunnar didn't know her? His wolf knew her soul. Recognized her as worthy. Their other half. Right now, that was all Gunnar needed to know.

He spun Chelle around once again to face him. He claimed her mouth in another searing kiss that went straight to his head. Drunk on her taste, her intoxicating scent, Gunnar's tongue thrust against hers. Desperation fueled his actions as he tore her bra free and reached between them to unfasten the skinny-legged jeans that clung to the shapely legs he wanted wrapped around his waist.

His own shirt and jeans met hers on the floor as Gunnar stripped bare. He wanted to feel her naked flesh on his. A shiver traveled the length of his body from the chill of hers. It was the chill of the grave and it made his wolf howl with despair in the back of his mind.

"Bite me."

Gunnar pushed the words through clenched teeth. Chelle stilled. Not even her breath stirred where her mouth hovered near his shoulder. Her voice was quiet, fearful, when she said, "No."

His wolf let out a mournful howl. Gunnar felt the stab of his mate's rejection in the center of his chest. He gripped Chelle by the shoulders and set her at arm's length. A crease marred her brow and her chin quivered. Unshed tears glistened in her eyes that swirled with liquid silver. Her fear was his own and Gunnar swallowed against the lump that rose in his throat.

"Why?" He could do nothing about the harshness of his tone. "I deserve to know. Damn it, Chelle, why do you refuse me the opportunity to give you this thing that you *need*?"

"Because I'm afraid!" Chelle tried to pull away but Gunnar held her fast. "And you should be, too! Haven't you figured it out yet? I have no idea what I am, Gunnar, and it scares the shit out of me. I can't let you get any closer than you already are. I don't—" Her voice hitched. "I don't want to hurt you."

"Gods, Chelle." Gunnar gave a sad shake of his head. He didn't know the secrets she kept, but one thing was certain: her own existence frightened her. "You could *never* hurt me."

A single tear trailed down her cheek. "You've seen what I can do. I'm not like the others. How do you know I couldn't hurt you? I'm sure as hell not convinced."

Gunnar pulled her against him and bowed to put his forehead to hers. He let his eyes drift shut and his wolf gave a contented purr. "This is how I know," Gunnar whispered in the quiet stillness. He put his palm to his chest, and then to hers, over her heart. "We are bound, Chelle. Forever. You—are—*mine*."

Chelle drew in a shuddering breath but she didn't pull away.

Many obstacles stood in their way. Her secrets, his pack, her coven, their very existences, and the damned Alexandria key that she coveted so fiercely. But in spite of all of that, Gunnar had never once doubted their bond. It was the only damned thing in his life that he was sure of right now.

"Put your mouth to my throat, Chelle." He kept his tone even but no less commanding. "Pierce the flesh. I am not afraid."

She cradled the back of his neck as a sound that was half relief, half defeat escaped from between her lips. Her body trembled with restraint. Even after he'd given her permission—hell, after he'd demanded she take his vein—Chelle resisted. She fought the very instinct that drove her.

"You won't hurt me," Gunnar assured her once again. "You can't."

"I've thirsted for your blood since that first night." Her voice was so quiet, Gunnar had to strain to hear. "What if I can't stop?"

"You will."

"I didn't with Lucas. I couldn't. I turned him and he never had a choice—"

"Stop." The regret in her words tore through Gunnar. "The past doesn't matter. Nothing matters but you, me, and this moment. I trust you, Chelle." He pressed her against his throat. "Drink."

She struck with the speed of a cobra, sinking her fangs deep into Gunnar's throat. Her strength astounded him as she gripped the back of his neck and took long pulls from his vein. Gunnar's thighs quaked and his legs grew weak. He trusted her. He had to.

CHAPTER
19

The euphoric bliss of breaking the flesh at Gunnar's throat had no comparison. The rightness of feeding from his vein left Chelle shaken. Power crested within her with every deep pull of suction. The tether that connected them grew taut as their bond was further strengthened. That she'd given in to her desire to take his vein didn't diminish her fear. Instead, it intensified. Rather than put distance between them, she'd only managed to get closer. She wanted to push him away, but like the tides were drawn to the moon, she was helpless to resist his pull.

His blood was as sweet as she'd imagined it would be. A delicious nectar she couldn't get enough of. Gunnar's hands gripped her hips, his fingers digging into her flesh as she continued to drink. He trusted her. Wasn't afraid. Had faith in the tether that bound them. Gunnar knew that Chelle wouldn't hurt him.

And finally, Chelle realized it, too.

Her thirst was under control. It had been since she'd met him. It was the fact that she hadn't fed from anyone but Lucas that prompted her to believe otherwise. She'd assumed Lucas was strong enough to support her raging need for blood, but the truth was, Chelle had leveled out and she hadn't even realized it. Too preoccupied with all of her other oddities, she'd failed to acknowledge the change. That didn't mean her abilities were any more in check, but maybe this was a start.

"You're warm." Gunnar's tone was filled with awe.

The crisp hair of his chest grazed her nipples, causing them to harden. His erection brushed against her hip, the skin like marble encased in satin. He let out a contented growl that vibrated through Chelle and settled in a low thrum between her legs. Her tongue flicked out to seal the punctures in his throat and she pulled away, unsteady on her feet.

Concern marred Gunnar's rugged features. "Are you all right?"

"Yeah," she said with a laugh. "Just a little buzzed. Your blood. It's . . . *wow*."

The warmth of Gunnar's chuckle caused her stomach to clench. He bent his head low to kiss her throat down to her bare shoulder. "That good?"

Chelle shivered. "You have no idea."

Gunnar's mouth met hers in a searing kiss. Their physical attraction and compatibility couldn't be denied. They were combustible. Fire and gasoline. Even if that was all they'd ever have. Even if they never felt an emotional connection. Even if the complexities of their lives divided them, Chelle knew they would come together again and again to satisfy this need that burned within them. Heat pooled in her limbs, her heart hammered in her rib cage.

"Gods, Chelle. You're like the moon to me. A power that calls to me. Holds sway over me. Commands me."

His words sent a thrill through her bloodstream. No male had ever said such wonderful things to her. Always chasing treasures, always in search of something *more,*

Chelle had never given herself over to romantic entanglements. Her affairs were nothing more than brief flashes of moments. Fleeting and unimportant. Gunnar was more than a spark, though. He was more than a distraction.

He was *everything*.

With a low growl, Gunnar abandoned Chelle's lips. He kissed a path across her collarbone to her breast. The searing heat of his mouth elicited a sharp intake of breath as he sucked her pearled nipple into his mouth. Chelle's back bowed as she gave an indulgent moan. Every touch, every kiss, every one of his breaths fired her heightened senses. Her clit throbbed as a rush of wet warmth spread between her thighs. She needed him inside of her. Ached for him. And yet he pleasured her at his leisure, as though his own need hadn't crested to the same maddening heights as hers.

"Gunnar. Oh, gods. I want you to fuck me."

Chelle didn't bother to stem the flow of her wanton words. Why should she? With Gunnar she didn't have to hide anything. The tether bound them in a way that freed her from shame. She could show her true self to him and she knew that he would accept her. For a week, she'd fought the bond. Fought what it created between them when she didn't have to. Admitting she wanted him was a small step toward trust, but it was a step all the same.

"Your scent drives me mad." Gunnar's voice grated with restraint and Chelle heard the wolf stir in his mind. "Your taste . . . I want to lick you from head to toe." He nuzzled her breast before running the flat of his tongue over the swell. "Feed from no male save me." Gunnar nipped at the flesh just above her nipple and Chelle drew in a sharp breath. "Promise me."

As if she could ever take another's vein after having a taste of Gunnar's blood. It would make their situation even more problematic, but Chelle could work around that. "I promise," she said on a breath. "No one but you."

The words resonated within her and sent an anxious rush through her veins. *No one but you.* Every moment spent with Gunnar wound the bond between them tighter. Would Chelle continue to feel comforted or would it someday become a noose?

Gunnar paused and brought his head up to look at her. It was impossible for her to hide her emotions from him. Besides the tether, his senses would do just as good a job of reading what she felt. Chelle pushed her worry, the doubt that plagued her, to the back of her mind. Tonight, she could simply enjoy Gunnar. She could revisit her problems tomorrow.

For a moment they stared at one another. Chelle marveled at the gold flecks that shone in his eyes and she knew that hers swirled with liquid silver. Were there any two creatures more opposite of each other? Did what they were and to what faction they belonged even matter compared to the perfection of being with him?

Chelle's hands slid down Gunnar's muscular arms. Her fingertips danced over the ancient tattoos that decorated his skin. Gold swallowed the blue of his eyes and he studied her with the intensity of a predator about to pounce. The thrill of his hungry gaze egged her on as she went to her knees before him, kissing a path down the ridges of his abs and down the groove that cut into the juncture of his thigh and hip.

Chelle took the hard length of his erection in her hand. Gunnar sucked in a sharp breath as she stroked from the swollen head to the thick base. Her eyes met his and a corner of her mouth hitched in a half smile as she leaned in closer. He shivered as her panting breaths met his sensitive flesh the moment before she took him into her mouth.

"Gods, Chelle," Gunnar said on a groan. "That's . . ."

The words died on his lips as her fangs scraped along

his shaft. Gunnar's fist wound into her hair. His grip was possessive, commanding, and it drove Chelle wild with want. She sensed he wanted her to take him deeper, but he restrained himself from urging her to do so. He gave her all of the control, which must have been quite a feat for an Alpha. Chelle rewarded him by allowing her lips to slide farther down the length of his cock.

Gunnar gave a shallow thrust of his hips. Chelle cupped the delicate flesh between his thighs and massaged with one hand, and gripped the back of his thigh with the other.

Good gods. They were in the middle of Chelle's living room, naked and going at it like they were starved for each other, without giving any attention to the possibility that Lucas could show back up at any second. The tether made it difficult to focus on anything else but each other.

"Take me deeper, love."

Love. The word was nothing more than an endearment, but for the briefest moment, Chelle wanted it to mean something more. It shouldn't matter how Gunnar felt about her. They'd be tethered whether they loved, hated, or were indifferent to one another.

Chelle forced her mind to clear of troubling thoughts. Instead, she focused on the sensation of Gunnar's hand in her hair. The way the muscles in his thigh bunched beneath her touch. His panting breaths and low groans. The heat of his body against hers.

Gunnar let out a grunt as she took him deeper into her mouth. His thighs quaked. She looked up and he tipped his head toward her. The straight locks of hair at the top of his head fell to one side. His blue and gold gaze devoured her. He was wild, fierce, passionate . . . the physical embodiment of Chelle's own soul.

She pulled away to the glossy head and swirled her tongue over it. Gunnar's hips bucked and his grip on her hair tightened. Chelle followed up with a downward plunge that caused him to draw in a sharp breath. Over and again she repeated the motion in an easy rhythm, all the while keeping her eyes locked on his.

She'd never experienced anything so erotic.

Gunnar's head fell back on his shoulders. Chelle continued with her unhurried pace, her cheeks hollowing as she took him as deep as she could. She pulled away again, dragging her fangs along every rock-hard inch. When she got to the swollen head, she bit down, piercing the skin. Gunnar's answering moan caused Chelle's clit to throb. Blood welled on his skin and she licked it away, closing the punctures. Gunnar released his grip on her hair and reached for her forearm, pulling her up to stand. His mouth claimed hers in a ravenous kiss that left her breathless, shaking, and mad with want.

"I need to fuck you, Chelle. Now."

Gods, her bite . . .

Gunnar would have never imagined the act could be so damned erotic. That it could give him so much pleasure. A pleasant rush came on the heels of the momentary sting. It infused his body with warmth, caused his limbs to tingle. It made him drunk. Dizzy. And it gave him a rush that rivaled the high of marching into battle. It connected Gunnar to a part of himself he'd thought the passing of time had long tamed.

The scent of her arousal drove his wolf wild. The animal surged to the surface of Gunnar's mind, precariously close to the point where their two identities merged into one. He hoisted Chelle in his arms as he kissed her. Her legs wrapped around his torso and hooked at the small of his back. A few steps put her back against the wall and Gunnar thrust home.

"Oh gods, Gunnar."

The husky timbre of her voice was all the encouragement he needed. Her want of him fueled his lust and he withdrew completely only to allow himself the pleasure of driving deep once again. Gunnar had never known he could want so desperately.

With each powerful drive of his hips Chelle let out a moan. The fancy artwork hanging on the wall rattled but Gunnar paid it no mind.

"Harder." Her command was wild, desperate, and he had no choice but to oblige. "Deeper." He couldn't go deep enough to satisfy either of them it seemed. Need crested to a fevered pitch and Gunnar welded his teeth together as his pace increased. "More! Don't stop, Gunnar. Gods, I need to come!"

Gunnar's sac drew up tight. The base of his cock pulsed and swelled inside of her. Chelle's inner walls squeezed him tight, so wet and velvet soft. Her nails bit into his shoulders as she buried her face against his throat. His gut clenched as he realized what she was about to do and he wound his fist in the length of her hair and pushed her closer. "Yes, Chelle," he growled. "Do it."

His skin gave way under the razor-sharp pressure of her fangs and Gunnar was flooded with sensation. He thrust wildly, driving deep with every buck of his hips. He threw his head back and a shout erupted from his throat as he came. Chelle's lips broke their seal on his throat as her own head came back to rest against the wall. Her mewling cries echoed in the dark as every tight contraction of her pussy only extended Gunnar's own pleasure.

His mate was perfect. Made for him and no other. He would never allow anything to ever come between them. Even if that meant going against the traditions of his pack.

Gunnar continued to give shallow thrusts of his hips long after their passions had been sated. Chelle nuzzled his throat and with slow, luxurious passes of her tongue closed the punctures she'd made. Her nails scraped along the bare skin at the side of his scalp before diving into his hair.

"My legs feel like cooked noodles," she said with a lazy laugh. "I don't think I could walk if I wanted to."

She didn't have to. Gunnar wasn't about to let the night end. Not when it felt so good to have her in his arms. He pulled out and cradled the round curves of her ass in his palms. She let her head rest against his shoulder as he carried her down the hallway to her bedroom. He kicked the door closed behind them before sitting on the edge of the bed. He simply held her, allowing the sound of her measured breaths to lull him.

Long moments passed before Chelle pulled away to look at him. Her serene expression belied her wild nature, as though sating her passions had somehow domesticated her. Gunnar had never seen this side of her. Soft. Content. Delicate. She seemed so fragile in his arms, as though the slightest mishandling would cause her to crack.

She kept her arms around him. Her fingers traced an idle pattern on the back of his neck and Gunnar shivered. His cock stirred, already hungry for her again. Would he ever get enough of her?

He didn't even have to contemplate the answer. *No.*

"Won't the others be wondering where you are?"

Even the timbre of her voice became more vulnerable. Gunnar stroked the length of her beautiful tawny hair, the strands slipping through his fingers like silk. Her worry lent a tang to her scent that caused Gunnar's nose to wrinkle. Every moment spent away from the pack was an opportunity for Aren to spread his propaganda. Gunnar knew where his place was. His responsibilities to his pack weighed on him despite his desire to stay with Chelle. So many complications. So much tradition to circumvent. The timing couldn't be worse, but Gunnar's wolf didn't care about politics and alliances. His wolf's only concern was their mate.

"Maybe." There was no point in denying his absence would be noticed. Jillian's visit today only proved that he'd failed to downplay his interest in Chelle. If she'd been smart enough to figure it out, it would only be a matter of time before the others did as well.

"They won't come looking for you?"

Gunnar let his fingertips wander down Chelle's spine. Goose bumps formed on her skin and she let out a contented sigh. "You know they won't." He couldn't do anything about the disappointment that leached into his tone. "Aren will capitalize on my absence tonight."

"He will," Chelle agreed. "Which is why you should go home."

She used her oddity, her own fear, their differences to push him away. Now, she used his pack as a way to drive a wedge between them. "Aren might talk a good game, but it'll take more than his persuasive words to topple me."

"Yes," Chelle agreed. "It will take more. Like a force of berserkers ready to ambush you. He's already proven he's not above playing dirty to get rid of you."

A true Alpha would fight for his position within the pack, not allow someone else to do the killing for him. "The pack would never accept Aren."

"How can you be sure?"

His wolf let out a warning growl in the back of his mind. The animal was insulted at their mate's lack of faith in their strength.

"The wolf isn't happy with what I'm saying," Chelle whispered into the darkness. "He's loud. It makes your thoughts difficult to hear."

His mate's abilities fascinated him. Gunnar reminded

himself that he needed to be more guarded. She had no qualms about poking around in his mind.

"I have plenty of qualms," Chelle replied. "I just don't know how to turn it off."

Despair accented her words. Gunnar wrapped his arms around her as though that alone could solve the problems that plagued her.

"I don't want to be able to do any of these things." Her vulnerability gutted him.

"Is that why you want the Alexandria key?" he asked. "Because you think you'll find something there that will allow you to turn it off?"

Chelle sucked in a breath. She eased away from Gunnar and climbed off his lap onto the bed. Whenever he thought he was gaining ground with her, she did her damnedest to put distance between them.

"You need to get back before Aren has a chance to do any more damage." Chelle was a pro at deflecting but Gunnar wasn't going to let her get away with it. "You can't let him bend anyone's ears."

"Chelle."

"The berserkers mean business." She kept her back turned to him as she hopped off the bed and crossed the room toward the dresser. She pulled open the top drawer and rifled through the clothes. "Something bad is brewing. Trenton McAlister wants to meet with Mikhail and the reasons can't be good. You need to protect your position—"

"Chelle." More forcefully this time.

"They're meeting in less than a week. It gives Aren more than enough time to orchestrate something."

"Chelle!" Gunnar shouted. "Stop shutting me out!"

Chelle's shoulders slumped but she still refused to face him. She snatched a T-shirt out of the drawer and pulled it on. "You can't be here with me. Not when he's waiting for you to slip up."

It was more than Gunnar could take. "I am descended from kings!" His voice rang out with the power of an Alpha. "I am the rightful Alpha of the Forkbeard pack. Your doubt, your lack of faith, *mate,* is not only misplaced, it is unwelcome."

Chelle turned. A deep groove cut into her brow and hurt glistened in her forest-green eyes. "I don't know what you want from me."

Gunnar's jaw hung slack. Gods, she infuriated him. "I want you to trust me!" he railed. "I want you to trust our bond."

CHAPTER
20

How could Chelle possibly trust Gunnar when she couldn't even trust herself? He asked too much of her. Wanted more than she could give. She was scared to death to trust him! She couldn't allow herself to feel any emotion, any tenderness, at all. And especially not when it came to Gunnar.

"I'm trying to protect you!" Her voice quavered on the words. "Why can't you see that?"

Gold shone in Gunnar's eyes, all the brighter in the dark room. "What in the hell makes you think I need your protection?"

Gods, he was insufferable. "Could you please check your damned ego at the door for half a second?" This had nothing to do with Chelle thinking he was incapable. But what Gunnar didn't realize was that there was a chink in his armor that had never been there before. She'd weakened him. Their tether weakened him.

His eyes narrowed and his jaw squared. "This isn't about me, Chelle."

"No." A knot of emotion clogged her throat. "This is

about me. You need to leave, Gunnar." Tears stung at her eyes and Chelle forced the words she didn't want to say past her lips. "And don't come back."

His answering laughter confused and angered her. He stood before her, proud, naked, glorious tattoos marking his flesh. Wild. Arrogant. Unapologetic. Strong. Stubborn. And so gods-damned beautiful it was almost painful to look at him.

"I'm not going anywhere."

His tone brooked no argument. "I can make you go." If he wanted to play hardball, so be it.

"You think so?" Gunnar asked. "Go ahead, then."

Chelle bucked her chin in the air. If he couldn't see why it was dangerous for him to be here, then she had no choice but to compel him to leave. She crossed the room toward him and closed the distance until less than an inch separated them. The heat of his body buffeted her and she fought the urge to reach out, let her fingers slide over the hard ridges of his abs.

"Gunnar." Chelle infused her voice with power and locked her gaze with his. "I want you to leave here and never come back."

His lips spread into a wolfish grin. "No."

Chelle's brow furrowed. His own power pushed back at hers, causing goose bumps to rise on her forearms. She dug deep and took a deep breath. "Gunnar," she said again. "Leave."

He cocked a brow. Gold blazed in his eyes. "No."

Without preamble, Gunnar reached for Chelle and hauled her against his body. His mouth met hers, crushing, slanting over her lips, demanding that she open for him. She brought her hands between them and pushed at his wide chest. Chelle was strong—stronger than the other vampires—but Gunnar managed to overpower her. She'd tried to show him why it was dangerous for him to be with her and all he'd managed to do so far was prove her wrong.

The starch left Chelle's arms as she melted against him. Why fight what she wanted? He wasn't going to let her push him away. Gunnar broke their kiss only long enough to strip the T-shirt from Chelle's body. His lips found hers again, hungry, and she answered his kisses with equal fervor.

"You're mine," Gunnar growled against her mouth. "My mate. Mine forever. The mate bond is *unbreakable*. You're not getting rid of me." He nipped at her bottom lip. "You might have caught me off guard before, but you won't compel me again. I'm not afraid of you, Chelle."

Was it too late to try one last time to dissuade him? "You should be, Gunnar." His mouth brushed hers, lip to lip. "I'm afraid of myself."

His tongue lashed out at the seam of her lips and Chelle lost herself to his fevered kisses once again. Gunnar's appetite for physical contact rivaled hers. It seemed they couldn't get close enough, couldn't kiss each other deeply enough.

Gunnar turned Chelle in his arms and bent her over the bed as he entered her. She cried out in relief, as though the joining of their bodies was the only thing she needed to make her whole. He thrust hard and deep. There was nothing tentative about the way he fucked her and that's the way Chelle wanted it.

"Harder."

He obliged.

"Deeper."

Every thrust jarred her and sent a rush of pleasure from her core, outward.

Chelle's fists wound into the coverlet as though to anchor her. The only sounds in the room were their labored breaths and the wild sounds of their bodies meeting and parting. Gunnar reached around her and slid his hand between her thighs. His fingertips slid over her flesh and Chelle shivered when he found her clit and circled the knot of nerves. The sensory overload nearly overtook her as Chelle abandoned all logical thought and simply allowed herself to *feel*.

"Come for me, Chelle."

Gunnar's heated breath in her ear drove her close to the edge. Her body seemed to curl inward, winding tighter and tighter until she didn't think she could bear another ounce of tension. He brushed her hair to one side and the moment his teeth grazed her throat, Chelle broke apart. Her desperate sobs grew hoarse as wave after wave of pleasure crashed over her. Gunnar followed her over the edge a moment later, letting out a shout as he came.

His chest rested against her back and he gave shallow thrusts of his hips as he brought them down from their highs. Gunnar murmured soft words near her ear in an ancient language that meant nothing to Chelle, but she felt the emotion behind them just the same. The urgent need she had for this male she barely knew consumed her. The residual fear she'd felt the moment she'd tried to send him away still caused her heart to beat a wild rhythm in her chest. The tether was absolute. Unbreakable. Chelle had no doubt that she would be Gunnar's undoing, and yet there was nothing she could do to stop it.

Gunnar pulled away and she missed his heat the instant his body left hers. He eased her up onto the bed and settled in behind her, tucking his knees under hers as he pressed his chest to her back once again. His beard tickled her shoulder as he angled his head toward hers and a chill danced down her spine. Gunnar reminded her of the sun that she'd never see again. Brilliant, warm, and blinding in its intensity.

"Werewolves aren't born." Gunnar's voice reached out to her in the darkness, rich and comforting. "They're made. And it's not a pleasant transition."

He wrapped one arm around her waist. Chelle reached for his hand and twined her fingers with his. She'd heard the transition was painful but knowing that Gunnar had experienced that agony clawed at her chest. She reached behind her and let her fingers trail from his temple, down his cheek, to the crisp hair of his beard. He angled his head and put his lips to her palm.

"We were fighting the Franks." Gunnar let out a chuff of laughter. "It seemed like we were always fighting the Franks then. We'd planned to ambush their camp at night. The full moon would give us enough visibility to negotiate the forest and the battle would be won before they knew what happened. Our war party was the one that was ambushed, though. Before we even made it to the Frankish army. The wolves attacked without warning and only a handful of us survived."

A knot formed in Chelle's throat as Gunnar's memories flooded her. The screams of the men in the moonlit wood as the wolves ravaged them echoed in her ears. Macabre shadows danced around her as the pack of wolves attacked. The chill of the wind touched her skin and Chelle shivered as she fought to release herself from the hold of Gunnar's memories.

She pushed the words past the lump in her throat. "When did you realize what had happened to you?"

His arm tightened around her and he held her close. "Not until the next full moon. I've never experienced pain like that first transition. My bones broke and re-formed. I felt as though my skin were being flayed from my body. My blood boiled in my veins. The agony was never-ending."

Chelle's own transition had been traumatic. Perhaps

that's what had drawn her soul to Gunnar's in the first place. She'd never considered it before, but they were both creatures created, to some extent, by magic. Words failed her. She had no idea how to comfort him as she relived the centuries-old memory alongside him. "I'm so sorry, Gunnar."

"I thought I'd gone mad. The wolf was in my mind. We understood each other. I believed Thor was unhappy with our warriors and had sent Loki to punish me. It was another time. Superstition ruled. Our gods had power then. Maybe they still do . . ." Silence descended and Chelle sensed she'd lost Gunnar to his memories. "We ran the woods that night. Wild. Unchecked. Hungry. I don't remember what happened and I thank the gods for it. I killed. I woke with the taste of blood in my mouth. Man? Beast? Maybe both. I might have turned someone. I pray not, though. Years passed before the others and I found a balance between our dual natures. But what do years matter to those of us who have the opportunity to see eternity?"

The sadness in his voice cut through Chelle with a razor-sharp edge. He'd been a man. Mortal. Chelle had been born into the supernatural world. Her strength, long life, accelerated healing, speed, had all been a part of her natural biology. What she could do now was the extreme version of what she'd already been capable of. She couldn't imagine how Gunnar had dealt with it all.

"We left our village. How could we possibly stay? Those left who were still human knew something had happened to us the night of the raid. We didn't trust ourselves not to hurt anyone. We had no choice but to go."

Chelle's heart broke for Gunnar. "Why are you telling me this?"

"Because I wanted you to know my most painful memory. I wanted you to share in my most vulnerable moment and trust me when I tell you that I was afraid. I want you to see me as I saw myself: as a mindless beast. A creature out of nightmare. A killer. Out of control. I need you to understand the impact that our bond has had on me. Your death would be a blow my wolf would not be able to recover from. The wolf would drive me mad with grief and the pack would have no choice but to put me down. I need you to believe that our bond is sacrosanct and there is nothing you could tell me, no admission you could make, that would cause me to turn my back on you."

Such a male. Gunnar Falk certainly was one of a kind.

Gunnar had felt Chelle slipping away. In that moment when she'd tried to overpower him, to make him leave her and never come back, their bond had bent to the point of breaking. He'd refused to let her have her way. His wolf refused to give her up without a fight. Together, they'd found a way to circumvent her ability to compel. It would take some time, but Gunnar was confident he'd soon be able to shut her out of his head as well. The things she feared, he welcomed. Gunnar had never been one to back down from a challenge. Chelle could give him her all. He wasn't worried anymore.

For long, peaceful moments they lay in silence. Gunnar let his eyes drift shut and simply enjoyed holding Chelle in his arms. It was true they didn't know much about one another, but he hoped to remedy that tonight and every other night after. They had years—centuries—to get to know one another. He didn't expect a declaration of love from her, just as he hadn't offered one. But love could come, in time.

Gunnar was nothing if not patient.

"Mikhail was the last true vampire." Chelle's voice pierced the quiet, small and almost childlike. So unlike the strong, assertive female Gunnar had come to admire. "When he became tethered and came into his power, he turned Ronan first. And then his mate. After that, was Jenner. And then Saeed. I'm not of Mikhail's line because an ambitious shifter took magic that wasn't his to wield and used it carelessly."

A tremor rocked her body and Gunnar held her closer. Her scent soured with fear and his wolf gave a low, menacing growl in the recess of his mind. Chelle took several deep breaths. The sound of her racing heart stirred his anger and Gunnar's muscles tensed. Someone had harmed his mate. Caused her to be afraid. And when he found the bastard responsible, Gunnar would make him pay.

"Really, it's my ambition that's to blame." Chelle gave a rueful laugh. "I can't leave a mystery unsolved. Ronan was certain that Mikhail would never come into his power. Without vampires to fortify our—their—strength, the dhampirs would have soon died out. Set's Chest was the answer to all of our problems. Ronan doubted its very existence let alone the myth of its power. But not me. I had to find it. I was consumed by it."

"Set's Chest?" Gunnar wasn't familiar with vampire mythology. The rules of the pack, their own desire to isolate themselves, put them at a disadvantage. Chelle gave him new insight into the supernatural world. Opened his mind to the cultures, origins, and powers of those who shared this world with him.

"It's the story of our creation," Chelle said. Gunnar stroked her hair as she talked, brushing the silky strands away from her face. "The Egyptian god Set built the chest to trick Osiris, who he then killed. He dismembered his body and scattered the parts. But Osiris's wife, Isis, refused to let him go. She enlisted the help of a sorcerer who charmed the coffin that Set had constructed for his brother.

The chest resurrected Osiris. But he wasn't the same. Fangs sprang from his gums, he was forced to hide from the sun, and he thirsted for blood. Osiris was the first vampire and we are all descended from him."

Gunnar listened with fascination. When he'd been a man, he'd been devoted to the gods. His faith had been unwavering. He paid tribute when it was due, minded the auguries of their seers, and believed that he would one day feast in Valhalla with his Viking brothers. Over the centuries, his faith began to dwindle. He learned to worship strength, turned his faith to his pack, and believed that he would never see Valhalla, but would walk the earth until its end.

He put his lips to Chelle's temple. "You found Set's Chest?"

"I did," she replied. "And its magic is *real*."

A tremor of fear traveled the length of Gunnar's body.

"The shifter had been tracking the chest, too. He caught me off guard and kept me in a cage in the middle of a gods-damned redwood forest." Her body tensed and Gunner held her close. "I can still smell it," she said on a breath. "The damp earth. It makes me sick. He wanted to use the chest's magic to make demons. But he needed to test its power first. He threw me inside." Her voice hitched with emotion and she spoke through the tears. "And when he pulled me out, I was changed."

Gunnar's jaw clenched. Rage burned through him, eating up any trace of reason. "I'll gut the fucker." His voice grated as his wolf rose to the surface. "Tear his throat out. Tell me where to find him, Chelle, and I will *end* him for what he did to you."

She pressed her body tight against his. "I don't think you need to worry about that," Chelle whispered. "His punishment was meted out by his own people."

Gunnar's jaw refused to unclench. "How can you be sure?"

"Ronan's mate, Naya, made sure. She's a powerful witch, and I wasn't the only one the shifter screwed over."

Gunnar would speak with Ronan's mate. He wouldn't be at ease until he knew without a doubt that the male who'd harmed Chelle had been made to pay for his offense. He forced himself to calm. There would be time enough to deal with the matter. Tonight wasn't about Gunnar's need to avenge his mate. This was about Chelle, her story, and what had happened to her. Tonight was about creating a foundation of trust they could build on.

"You are your own coven because the chest made you a vampire." Now that Gunnar was beginning to understand what had happened to her, Chelle's behavior made sense. "You are created by magic and unlike any of the others. This alone makes you unique."

"A freak is more like it," she said.

Gunnar hated that she thought of herself in that way. "I am created by magic," he replied. "Do you consider me a freak?"

"You were turned by magic, yes. But it wasn't simply a mystical transformation," Chelle said. She tucked her head deeper into the pillow. "You were turned by a bite that transferred that power to you. It might have seemed mystical, but at its core, your transformation was biological."

Gunnar laughed. Chelle turned her head to look at him, her brow furrowed. "Biological?" Chelle's brow crinkled further at his disbelieving tone. "Metaphysical at best. The explanation for what happened to me is abstract. Without reason. Chelle, I was human. A werewolf bit me and I became a creature of myth. I was a man with one spirit, one mind. And now I am dual natured. Two spirits who share one body. You see the world through the eyes of one who has known magic her entire life. Wondrous things are mundane to you. You are descended from a god, just as I am now descended from wolves. We are all of us born of magic. You simply refuse to see it."

She shook her head. "You don't understand. I'm volatile."

"And I'm not? You haven't seen volatile until you've crossed a mated werewolf."

Chelle allowed for a chuff of laughter. "I've always said mated males were temperamental."

"That's an understatement." Gunner urged her to turn in his arms until she faced him. "The simple thought of you in danger sends me into a state of such rage I can barely control myself."

"Rage is one thing . . ." Chelle said. "Everyone gets agitated, angry, feels out of control. But it doesn't change you." Her fear burned Gunnar's nostrils. "It doesn't become a part of you."

"Maybe not," Gunnar said. "But neither does it master you. It doesn't define you."

Chelle looked away, her silver and green gaze darting to one side. "If Mikhail finds out . . . I'm not sure what he'll do."

"Finds out about what?" Surely the vampire king knew how Chelle came to be a vampire.

"He doesn't know what I can do," she said, low. "He doesn't really know how powerful I am. I'm afraid"—she took a deep breath—"I'm afraid he'll lock me away or put a stake through my heart."

He'd kill her? As though she were some sort of rabid animal that needed to be dealt with? Gunnar's wolf stirred in his mind and let loose a territorial growl. He gripped Chelle's chin between his thumb and finger and guided her to look at him.

No one—not even the vampire king—would harm what belonged to him. "Over my dead body."

Chelle gave him a wan smile. "When a vampire is turned, we forfeit our souls to oblivion," Chelle said. "My soul found yours and tethered itself to you. If you were to die, my soul would be cut, sent out into nothingness once again, and I would never get it back."

"Your soul is safe with me." Gunnar was humbled that Chelle's soul sought his out and entrusted itself to his keeping. "I'm not going anywhere."

His pack might not approve of their bond. Aristov and the other vampires might not approve. Gunnar didn't care what anyone else thought. Chelle was his and he was hers. He'd breathe his last breath before *anyone* ever made him let her go.

CHAPTER
21

"His bloodlust seems to be under control. Remarkable considering it's only been a couple of days."

Saeed turned his attention to Sasha. "Hmmm. Yes." It was true, Diego was doing well despite having been turned a mere three nights ago. A good sign since Saeed expected Diego to soon step up and take temporary control of the coven.

"And the Collective?" Saeed did nothing to hide his curiosity. "Do the memories seem to plague him?"

Sasha's brow furrowed and she studied Saeed with an intensity that made him squirm. "Not that I know of. You could ask him yourself, you know. You haven't set foot in his room since the night you turned him."

Saeed might have felt a twinge of guilt had he a soul to allow him to feel much of anything. His head pounded and his thirst scalded a path up his throat. How long had it been since he'd fed? The hours, the nights bled into one another until he'd lost all concept of time. He lived in the past now. Submerged in memories that pulled him under the surface like tendrils of seaweed around his ankles.

Saeed drowned in memories and, no matter how hard he tried, he couldn't break free of their hold.

"His stability is a good sign." Saeed didn't want to get into a discussion about why he'd been too preoccupied to check in on Diego. "Are you ready to join him?"

Sasha drew in a deep breath. "I have concerns."

Saeed cocked a brow. "Such as?"

She didn't meet his gaze. "Such as the state of my mind posttransition."

He might have been one of the soulless, but Saeed sensed the intended sting of her barbed words. He leveled his gaze. He knew what Sasha and the rest of the coven thought of him. "You worry you'll fall into madness like your maker?"

Her pitying expression would have brought anyone else to their knees with shame. "Saeed, please go to Mikhail. Let him help you loosen your grip on the Collective. Your coven needs you." She paused and her voice became quiet. "I need you."

There'd been a time when Saeed had felt some measure of affection for Sasha. Not love, though. He was still fond of her. He admired her strength, her intelligence, her ability to be pragmatic when the situation called for it. He might have felt a certain sadness had he a soul. Now, though, there was only the fire-haired fae and his obsession to find her. It mattered more than anything—more than Diego, Sasha, and his entire coven. It mattered more than Mikhail and his entanglement with Trenton McAlister. More than the Sortiari's agenda and the berserkers' vengeance. It was a need that burned through him like wildfire. He was helpless to fight it.

"It's I that need you." Saeed motioned for her to come closer and she crossed the room to sit beside him on the antique sofa. "Mikhail can't help me. Only I can break the Collective's hold. You know what I have to do. Which is why I need you and Diego. The coven needs your strength."

"You expect us to take care of them while you chase a ghost," Sasha said.

Saeed refused to discuss the matter with her. He let out a slow sigh. "What are your other concerns?"

"The state of my soul, the possibility of never being tethered." Sasha's leather-brown eyes narrowed as she fixed Saeed with an icy stare. "The Sortiari and their slayers. The changing political climate. Mikhail's sense of order and the hierarchy he seeks to create. Siobhan . . . Would you care for me to continue?"

She'd made her point. He understood her misgivings, but that didn't mean he wanted to address any of them. Saeed had plans to make. "You worry about things you can't control. Matters that have no bearing on your decision to be turned. Your soul will be sent to oblivion, yes. But believe me when I tell you, it will mean little to you. The Sortiari and their slayers will always be a threat whether you are a vampire or remain a dhampir. The politics of the supernatural world have always been volatile. The addition of one more vampire won't change that any more than a single drop of rain will affect the ocean. As for Siobhan . . ." If anything gave Saeed pause, it was her. "She has her own agenda. One that might have a lasting effect on our coven as well as others. Which is why your transition is important. We need to show Siobhan that her prejudices are misplaced."

Sasha's dark brows rose in disbelief. "Are they?"

Not many knew the dhampir's reasons for her hatred of vampire-kind. Not even the members of her own coven. Saeed had learned much about her during his time in the Collective. Including the reasons for her seemingly blind hatred. "Siobhan has many secrets. Believe me when I tell you she has more to worry about than me, you, or Diego. Or who we may or may not choose to turn."

Sasha didn't press him further on the matter of Siobhan, which was for the best, because Saeed wouldn't have given her any more information. Her secrets weren't his to tell. The Collective was sacred. The memories he bore witness to didn't belong to him. He was merely an uninvited guest.

Sasha was quiet, though her expression remained wary.

"Have I managed to put you at ease?"

"No." Her simple reply had a razor-sharp edge. "You're anxious to turn me but not because you want to fortify our strength, and certainly not because of any promise you've made to Mikhail. You want to ease your guilt."

"The soulless have no guilt." Sasha flinched at his cool words. "But neither am I heartless. Once you've seen the Collective, you'll understand."

Her lips thinned. "I will never understand how you can leave your family to chase a dream."

Saeed would have rather told her after her transition, when his words wouldn't have hurt her. She gave him no choice, however. Perhaps by hurting her, he would convince her to do what had to be done. "I have to find her, Sasha. When I do, she will tether my soul."

Her eyes grew wide and glistened with emotion. "You truly believe that?"

He reached out and took her hand in his as though to comfort her. "I have no doubt."

Sasha jerked her hand from his grip. "You're a fool, Saeed. And you've lost your mind."

He would do nothing more to convince her. He'd struck a deal with Mikhail, and in order to free himself to find the fae, he had to uphold his end of the bargain. "You will be turned in two nights' time. If you refuse, I will forbid anyone from turning you. Ever. Do you understand?"

Pain cut through her fair features as Sasha stood. "I hope you find your mate," she spat as she headed for the door. "If only to see the regret in your eyes when you realize the extent of your selfishness and what it's wrought."

Without another word, she stormed from the room and slammed the door behind her.

There would be repercussions for his behavior. He wasn't so much of a fool as not to believe that Mikhail would disapprove of his actions. And Sasha was right, his selfishness might prove to be his destruction. The possibility of losing everything loomed: his coven, his soul, his very sanity, and perhaps even his life.

Saeed had made many mistakes over the centuries. Mistakes that haunted him. He had to believe that for once, he was doing the right thing.

"Christian, have a seat."

Did McAlister always have to be so gods-damned stuffy? Christian's wolf was already on edge. The musky scent of a shifter lingered in the director's office. *Bear.* Christian never forgot a scent and the shifter who owned this particular one made him twitchy as fuck. The last he'd heard, Caden Mitchell was hiding in upstate New York, as far away from the budding vampire crisis as possible. McAlister must have been hedging his bets by bringing in the burly, no-nonsense enforcer. The bastard had managed to put the smack-down on Gregor a little over a year ago. Whoever could get the upper hand on the infamous berserker was deserving of respect and not a little fear.

"You ever think about spraying a little Febreze in here between meetings?" Christian asked as he flopped back into the chair opposite McAlister's desk. He tapped the side of his nose. "The bear smell's a little off-putting."

McAlister's superior smirk made Christian want to

slap the arrogant bastard. He supposed it was easy to be smug when you had a two-hundred-and-fifty-plus-pound bear shifter watching your back. Caden might have been able to fuck up Gregor one-on-one, but it wouldn't be so easy to fend off an entire force of berserkers.

"Is it just me, or do you seem even more paranoid than usual?" Christian slung a casual arm over the back of the chair and stretched out one leg. "I mean, you must be on edge to bring Mitchell in. I thought he was staying as far from L.A. as possible. I can only imagine what you had to dangle in front of him to get him here." Being "employed" by the Sortiari was the closest thing Christian could think of to indentured servitude. There were no layoffs, no quitting. A death certificate was the only way to get your release papers from this gig.

Christian understood Gregor's need to be free. He might not have agreed with the male's tactics, but that wasn't any of his business. His only concerns were himself, and how in the hell he was going to keep Siobhan off Gregor's radar. Playing both sides against the middle seemed like the best way to look out for number one. Hell, maybe they'd both do Christian a big fucking favor and take each other out.

Then what? *You and Siobhan can live happily ever after?*

He snorted. *Right.* Like that would ever happen.

"I'm meeting with Mikhail Aristov two nights from now. We've agreed to bring one representative each. Caden kept a neutral position when Mikhail came into power so he seemed the best choice to accompany me to our meeting."

Wow. McAlister was pretty damned forthcoming with the information today. Must've been Christian's barb about him being paranoid. With muscle like Caden Mitchell at his back, McAlister would give an impression of strength. An illusion for sure since he'd lost his grip on Gregor and his brethren a long time ago.

"Why are you telling me?" Christian asked. "It's not like you need my permission to bring Mitchell in."

The fine hairs stood on the back of Christian's neck and his wolf gave a low growl. Magic sparked the air and burned his nostrils with a noxious tang. McAlister wasn't without power. He was a mage, for shit's sake. Their very existence was steeped in mystery. No one outside of their ranks even knew what they were capable of. Christian wondered why the male would even need Caden Mitchell at his back. For all he knew, the son of a bitch could probably shoot lightning from his fingertips or some shit.

That was the scary thing about mages, though. No one knew the extent of their abilities.

McAlister fixed Christian with his inscrutable stare. "Because I want you there as well."

Christian's disbelieving laughter echoed in the tiny outdated office. Jesus. McAlister couldn't help but be a subversive motherfucker. "So you struck a deal with Aristov, agreed to bring only one representative, and decided to promptly screw him over? Way to flex those diplomatic muscles, McAlister."

The director didn't seem fazed by Christian's ribbing. "You don't think Aristov will do the same? There isn't exactly any reason for either one of us to trust the other."

Wasn't that the fucking truth. If Christian were in Aristov's position, he would have told McAlister to shove his proposed meeting right up his high-and-mighty ass. Only a fool would agree to be in a room with the person responsible for the near annihilation of his entire species.

"Why are you meeting with Aristov in the first place?" Christian smirked. "Trying to kiss and make up?"

"Hardly." McAlister sat back in his seat. "Fate makes no apologies."

"Careful, McAlister," Christian said. "Your arrogance is showing."

The Sortiari took it upon themselves to steer the course of fate. Only a bunch of entitled, self-serving assholes would be stupid enough to think the job fell on them to do it. The Sortiari were older than recorded time. The granddaddy of all secret societies. The Illuminati were Boy Scouts in comparison.

"You do realize what's happening two nights from now?" Christian doubted McAlister kept a close track of the lunar cycle.

"You'll be less on Aristov's radar during the full moon." Looked like McAlister had thought of everything. Bastard. "And dare I say, more effective if a scuffle should break out."

Christian's gaze narrowed. "You're a real son of a bitch. You know that?"

McAlister shrugged. Obviously he'd been called worse. "I don't plan to engage Aristov. This is supposed to be a peaceful meeting. I simply believe that it's important to be prepared for every possible scenario."

"What's this about, anyway?" Christian couldn't imagine what would prompt either male to agree to be shut up in a room with the other.

"That's my business," McAlister said. "And *no one* else's."

The air sizzled with a static charge. Point taken. "What about Gregor?"

Silence stretched between them and Christian's wolf grew restless. He swore McAlister was trying to climb right inside his head.

"What about him?"

The director's deadpan response piqued Christian's curiosity. "Just wondering why you're not taking him instead of Mitchell to your little powwow."

He shrugged. "I told you, this is a peaceful meeting. Why would I bring the male who tried to kill Aristov's mate?"

For once, Christian believed McAlister might actually be walking the straight and narrow. It was tough to gauge the truth of a mage's words. Magic masked their scent. But Christian knew that Mitchell wanted no part of the Sortiari's beef with the vampires, and it was true that a surefire way to trip Aristov's temper would be to bring the male who'd tortured his mate. The entire thing seemed aboveboard. Except for Christian's part in all of it.

He sighed. Didn't it just figure that he'd be the one seedy element in all this?

"Why do you really want me there?" he asked. "Because it sure as fuck isn't for additional security."

McAlister looked like the last thing he wanted to do was confide in Christian. "Aristov is bringing a girl with him. I don't trust the vampire to protect her if anything untoward should happen. I want you to protect her."

What the actual fuck?

"Who is she?"

McAlister's lips thinned. "That," he said crisply, "is none of your business."

Interesting. The kid must've been a big deal for him to get his wizard tighty-whities in a bunch. Which made Christian wonder what kind of punch a little girl might be packing to make a mage quake in his boots. Maybe Aristov had more up his sleeve than anyone—including Gregor—thought. That sort of intel might be worth something to the berserker warlord. Maybe enough to keep Christian flush for the next month or so.

"I'll be there." He pushed himself out of the chair and headed for the door. He pulled it open and paused just outside. "But seriously, McAlister, you've got to do something about the smell."

McAlister's meeting with Aristov might be exactly what Christian needed to keep the heat off Siobhan for a while. At least until he could figure out why Gregor wanted her so badly.

CHAPTER
22

Chelle awoke with a start. For a moment, she was back in that cellar, surrounded by dirt and rot and the smell of mold. A ragged scream worked its way up her throat that already burned with unquenched thirst. She reached out blindly for the silver bars of her cage, but instead found her wrists encircled in a firm, yet gentle grip.

"Shhh. Chelle. It's all right. You're safe."

The warm timbre of Gunnar's voice comforted her in an instant. Chelle filled her lungs with breath and held it for a moment before letting the air out. The beat of her heart slowed until she no longer heard the rush of blood in her ears.

"What time is it?" The sun must have barely sunk below the horizon and that was the reason for her sudden awakening. She didn't recall succumbing to daytime sleep. The last thing she remembered was the sound of Gunnar's hushed voice in the darkness as he spoke to her.

"Dusk," he said, low. "Just barely."

"I bet you didn't expect me to check out at sunrise."

Chelle couldn't do anything about the bitterness that leaked into her tone. "Sort of like vampire narcolepsy."

The bed shook with Gunnar's warm laughter. The sound rippled pleasantly over Chelle's skin, like a hot stone massage on sore muscles. Amazing. She allowed for a contented stretch and her body slid against his. There wasn't an inch of him that wasn't packed with unyielding muscle. A Viking god.

And he belonged to *her*. All she had to do to completely claim him was admit to herself that she wanted him. She wished it could be that easy. That there weren't so many obstacles still between them.

"I wasn't surprised." He gathered her against his body once again and she settled in beside him. His breath was warm against her ear as he spoke. "You forget how old I am, Chelle. I've known vampires before you."

She craned her neck to look at him. "Intimately?" A wave of jealousy stole over her. A side effect of their tether no doubt. She couldn't deny she felt possessive of Gunnar. The thought of his hands on another female made her fangs throb in her gums.

He laughed. "No. Pack life might require a certain level of isolation but we weren't completely cut off from the supernatural world. In a way, vampires and werewolves are cut from the same cloth."

Chelle was pretty sure that sentiment would go over like a lead balloon in Gunnar's pack. "How'd you think?"

"We're both creatures of night, both at a disadvantage during the day."

Chelle snorted. "Falling dead asleep once the sun rises is a disadvantage. Walking around on two feet, not so much."

Gunnar chuckled. "True. You seem to be more affected by the sunlight than other vampires I've known, though.

I'm aware vampires sleep during the day, but you were basically unconscious."

It was true. Ronan had told Chelle he'd been able to stay awake in the daylight hours if he needed to be. He was considerably weaker, but not helpless. "I know. I think it must be the chest. I'm closer to what Osiris must have been than the others."

"A goddess," Gunnar said with reverence.

Chelle's chest swelled with emotion and she swallowed it down. "Hardly. But it's the only explanation I can think of."

"Werewolves have more than a few disadvantages. For instance, there is only one night per month when our strength and power reach their apex. You aren't ruled by anything so trivial."

"Except our thirst," Chelle countered. "Which rules us completely, steals our ability to reason, and shuts down our bodily functions, if we go too long without feeding."

"Is your thirst managed now?" Gunnar ventured.

Chelle didn't miss the heat in his voice. Her stomach did a pleasant flip and a warm rush spread from her lower abdomen outward. "It's both easier and harder to manage when you're near." The admission made her cheeks flush.

"Why's that?"

His fingers traced an idle pattern on her bare shoulder that coaxed chills to the surface of Chelle's skin. "My thirst is sated, but your blood . . ." she said on a breath. "It calls to me. I want it even when I don't necessarily need it."

His voice grew thick with passion. "Because I am your mate."

"Yes." Chelle swallowed against the heat in her throat. "Because of our tether."

"Perhaps you should feed."

Didn't he realize that offering up what she craved

would only obliterate her self-control? The husky tone of his words proved Gunnar wasn't above baiting her. "I think you like me at a disadvantage," she said on a breath. Her fangs throbbed in her gums and the dry fire intensified in her throat.

"I think I like knowing I have something you crave."

Dear gods, he was killing her! She'd never known a more sensual male. Sex practically oozed from his pores. He could get to her with a look, a simple touch. Hell, the scent of his blood turned her into a rabid, mindless animal.

"Don't tempt me." Already she wasn't sure she could resist.

"But I want to tempt you, *mate*." The deep rumble in his throat vibrated through her bones and settled at her sex. "You've been asleep too long and I've spent too many hours alone watching over you and admiring your fierce beauty."

Chelle couldn't believe she hadn't burst into flames by now. Gunnar sure knew how to use his words to get what he wanted. Who would have thought that beneath the hard exterior of the brusque warrior was the heart of a poet?

She brought her head up to look at him and cocked a brow. "You watched me sleep?" Nothing intense or creepy about that. At all.

"I watched over you," Gunnar corrected. "Like you said, you are at a disadvantage in the daylight hours. Vulnerable. If I'd slept as well, it would have left you unprotected."

The werewolf protecting the vampire. A romantic—not to mention tragic—cliché that had managed to survive over centuries of mythology. And yet, it made Chelle's heart beat faster and her blood quicken in her veins to think of Gunnar standing guard over her. Protecting her. Ensuring that nothing could touch her until the sun set.

Chelle averted her gaze. "You must be exhausted."

"I rested," he said. "Your presence calms my wolf unlike anything ever has. I feel an inner peace that I've never known. The mate bond is truly wondrous."

After sating their physical desires, they'd spent the remainder of the night in conversation. They'd satisfied each other's curiosities about their lives, their families, their likes and dislikes. Gunnar confided that he was a chocoholic, and Chelle admitted that she couldn't get through the day without a caramel macchiato. She confessed her love for reality TV and Gunnar admitted that he refused to watch historical dramas. Chelle had studied his tattoos and Gunnar told her the history of each and every one. They discussed politics, music, art . . . In the space of a few hours an intimacy had grown between them that hadn't been there before. Their tether grew stronger and it filled Chelle with a sense of wonder as much as dread. Keeping her distance would've been so much easier had she not liked Gunnar. But damn it, with each new story, every spoken word, he'd managed to work himself deeper under her skin.

"It's peaceful *here*," Chelle said. She didn't want to break the spell but nothing would stop reality from raining on their parade. "It's easy *here*. Everything seems to work when it's only the two of us. But it's not easy out there. It never will be."

"It's time for old traditions to die," Gunnar said. "I know how the others will see it. As hypocritical. I've stood by those traditions for centuries. Upheld the need for the pack to remain self-contained and aloof from the rest of the supernatural world. Our bond has opened my eyes to my foolishness. It's time for change."

"How many nonwerewolf pairings have there been in your pack?"

Gunnar let out a sigh. "None. And I thank the gods for

it. I'd not be able to live with myself if I'd killed one of our own needlessly. I hope that making a change within our pack will effect change in others. I will lead by example and quash the ignorant prejudices of our past."

"You think it'll be that easy?" Change wasn't easy for creatures like humans, whose life spans were nothing more than a blink. Shifting the culture of a pack of werewolves who'd subscribed to their beliefs for millennia . . . ? That would be damned near impossible.

"I think it will be like pulling teeth," Gunnar said with a rueful laugh. "But it has to happen. Whether they like it or not."

Gunnar was used to throwing down mandates that were obeyed without question. Sort of came with the territory when you were a big, bad Alpha. But with Aren spreading his poisonous rhetoric and urging the pack to rebel against Gunnar, it would only bend their pack to the breaking point if Gunnar tried to force anything on them. If he wasn't careful, he'd become a victim of his own pack's ancient justice. And if that happened, Chelle wasn't sure she'd survive the loss.

Gunnar sensed Chelle's unease even if she didn't voice her concerns. It wasn't as though he expected change to occur overnight. Especially when they'd lived their lives by the same code of conduct for thousands of years. He'd given her a glimpse into the pack dynamic but Chelle didn't understand the true power of an Alpha. Gunnar could bend the pack to his will if need be. Of course, he didn't want it to come to that. He didn't like exercising his power in that way. But if push came to shove, he'd do it. Because there was no way in hell he was giving Chelle up. And likewise, he refused to keep their mate bond a secret. The pack would come to accept her. There was no other option.

"Just be careful, Gunnar. Our tether isn't the only shit that's about to hit the fan."

Gunnar chuckled at her sarcastic tone. She tried to add levity to a serious issue and he appreciated that. "Oh, the shit'll hit the fan," he joked. "I'm just glad I'm not the one who's going to have to clean it up."

She angled her body until they faced one another. Her forest-green eyes searched his and a crease cut into her pale brow. "I'm serious, Gunnar. You've been away from home for almost thirty-six hours. There's no telling what sort of lies Aren has been spreading in that time. I know you think the pack is loyal—"

"I don't think." The Alpha's power was absolute. "I *know.*"

"Fine," Chelle said on a breath. "But Aren *isn't*. You have to at least admit that."

Gunnar would deal with Aren. His ambitions had done nothing more than stir up a hornet's nest and he wouldn't be allowed to continue on his path. "I admit that Aren serves his own agenda." He could concede that for Chelle. "He'll be dealt with."

"He wants your position in the pack," Chelle said. "You know he does."

"He can want it," Gunnar replied. "But he won't get it. You think it's so easy to depose an Alpha, *mate*?"

Chelle's eyes became hooded and her mouth twitched as though fighting a smile. He loved the way a simple word—mate—affected her. As though it pleased her. Gunnar's chest swelled with emotion. He wanted Chelle to be proud to be at his side.

"I don't think it's easy," she said. "And neither does he. Which is why Aren is going out of his way to get what he wants by playing dirty to get it."

"It wouldn't matter." They'd discussed the pack dynamic but not their hierarchy. "Having someone else kill me won't give Aren control of the pack."

"So . . . ? What does get him control?"

Her curiosity would be short-lived when she got her answer. "He has to kill me in combat. One-on-one. That's the only way Aren will become Alpha."

Chelle's scent soured in an instant and her eyes went wide. "Are you kidding me? That's barbaric!"

Her disbelief amused him. "We're animals, Chelle." He pinned her with his stare. "All of us."

The implication didn't go unnoticed. She knew the world they lived in. There was nothing civilized about it. They might blend in with humanity. They might wear a human guise, but beneath the surface, supernatural creatures were wild, violent, and slaves to their instincts.

"I know." Her voice dropped to a murmur. "That doesn't mean I have to like it."

Gunnar's wolf grew restless in his psyche. The animal perceived Chelle's worry as doubt. That she lacked faith in their strength and capability to keep control of the pack. It made Gunnar want to fight. To seek out Aren and settle this business between them once and for all to prove his strength to her. That was the animal part of him, though. The enraged animal was incapable of reason. Gunnar reined in that part of his nature and forced it to the back of his mind.

"When does Aristov meet with Trenton McAlister?" He should have remembered. Aren had been going on about it nonstop for weeks.

"Three nights from now," Chelle replied. "Why?"

Gunnar didn't want to broach the subject of the Alexandria key. It only caused arguments between them and the past twenty-four hours had been blissfully free of conflict. He wanted Chelle warm and willing in his arms.

Tender. Unguarded. But he could no more ignore this matter between them than he could Aren's machinations to take control of the pack.

With McAlister's attention elsewhere, Chelle would seize the opportunity to steal his third of the key. "Because I know what you're planning to do and I want you to reconsider."

"Gunnar—"

"Don't try to convince me that you're not planning to break into McAlister's stronghold."

Chelle's jaw took on a defiant set. "The Sortiari don't scare me."

"They should." Gunnar hoped he could make her understand the gravity of her decision. "Because they scare the hell out of me."

"Knowledge belongs to everyone," Chelle replied. "And not only to those who believe they have the right to dispense it at their discretion."

"The Sortiari don't control the Alexandria library," Gunnar pointed out. "No one does. My part of the key was entrusted to my family before I became a werewolf. Through a lineage of kings too long for me to trace. I imagine Trenton McAlister doesn't even know who gave the Sortiari their third. This isn't about keeping the ignorant in the dark, Chelle. Some things are locked away for a reason."

"I'm not interested in unleashing evil into the world." Chelle put a few inches of space between them. Her stubborn pride was sure to drive a wedge between them. "All I'm looking for is answers."

"The answers to what?"

Her eyes grew wide again. They'd been over and over it, but Gunnar still didn't understand. "To what I am," Chelle said on an emphatic breath. "Can't you understand how lost I feel? How disconnected?"

He did understand and that was the problem. "Your pain is my pain." Gunnar locked his gaze with hers. "The mate bond makes sure of it. But Chelle, there are other ways to find answers. Safer ways. Instead of carrying this burden on your own, let me help you. We'll have a better chance of finding what you're looking for if we do it together."

"You have your pack to take care of." She tried to mask the sadness in her tone but it cut through Gunnar just the same. "You don't need me to take care of as well."

"You say that as though I'd simply let you go." Chelle's eyes met his. "You are *mine,* Chelle. My mate. Mine forever. Don't think there's anywhere you could possibly go that I wouldn't follow you. Even if you sought to hide yourself from me, I'd track you to the ends of the earth. You may think you're stronger on your own, but you're wrong."

He traced the pad of his thumb over her downturned mouth.

"I'll bring you nothing but trouble," she said.

He refused to let her push him away. "I like trouble."

Long moments passed and she studied his expression as though in search of some truth hidden behind his earnest words.

The sound of the front door opening and closing drew Chelle's attention away from Gunnar. He swore he'd gut whoever had the shitty timing to barge in.

"Chelle? You home?"

Gunnar recognized Lucas's voice. He'd given little thought to where the male had been for the past day and a half. Instead, he'd simply been grateful to have Chelle all to himself. His arrival at the cottage effectively put an end to their conversation, though. Gunnar needed to know that Chelle understood. That she'd abandon this ridiculous quest to make whole a key that was broken for a reason.

"Yeah!" Her voice quavered on the word. "I'm in the bedroom. I'll be out in a sec!"

"Have you fed?" Lucas called back. Gunnar's wolf let out a low, dangerous growl. "If not, we should take care of that."

Gunnar grabbed Chelle round the waist and brought her body against his. He cupped the back of her head and guided her to the crook of his neck. "You'll feed from no one but me," he said, low. "And you'll make sure Lucas knows that."

As though she had no choice but to obey, her fangs broke the skin and a moan worked its way up Gunnar's throat. Gods, the sensation that coursed through him as a result of her bite had no equal. Her body relaxed against his with every deep pull of suction. Her arms went around him and she held him tight.

Something had changed between them during the quiet hours spent in this room. And Gunnar refused to let Chelle's own stubborn pride be the thing to undo the intimacy they'd forged. He just hoped she'd come to realize the value of their bond before she managed to destroy it.

CHAPTER
23

"Gunnar's going to shit a brick if he finds out. You realize that, right?"

Chelle met Jillian's gaze from across the table. For the past few days, she'd spent every night with Gunnar, holed up in her bedroom, talking, touching, giving in to their desires and sating their curiosity. The tether that bound them was stronger than ever and Chelle had begun to feel something intense and real for Gunnar. Guilt burned through her as she looked out the window at the traffic buzzing by on the street. Dusk was about to give way to darkness and the barista who eyeballed them with impatience was probably ready to start cleaning so she could wrap it up for the night. If only Chelle had her problems. Maybe she wanted to trade . . . ?

Starbucks might not have seemed like the best place for a secret meeting, but Chelle had seriously been jonesing for a caramel macchiato. Plus, she doubted anyone in Gunnar's pack would be scoping out the local coffee shops. Especially the ones thirty minutes from their home base.

"He's not going to find out," Jillian replied. She sipped from the straw of her iced mocha. "At least not from me."

Chelle was happy to have discovered there was at least one member of Gunnar's pack who didn't want to kill her. But if Gunnar found out Jillian was going behind his back to help Chelle, he might turn a little of that pack justice on one of his own. "Well, just so you know, he's not going to hear anything from me, either."

Jillian was a female after Chelle's own heart. Feminism for the win! It could have been because Jillian hadn't been a werewolf for as long as the others, but she was all about rocking the boat, changing the culture, mowing down old traditions to make room for new ones. If everyone in Gunnar's pack were as progressive as she was, Chelle might've felt a hell of a lot more secure in her tether. Jillian could have paved the way for change and helped the others to accept Chelle into the pack. Of course, if everything went according to plan tomorrow night, any hope of being accepted might be shot to shit.

"What's the scuttlebutt around HQ?" Chelle asked.

Jillian grinned. "The pack is restless. They're tired of the power struggle between Gunnar and Aren."

Now that they were down to business, the sense of levity deflated like a week-old balloon. "Aren's a bastard," Chelle remarked.

Jillian's mouth quirked with amusement. "He's intense. But can you imagine what it must be like to have to live for a thousand years as the number two guy?"

Chelle could imagine. "So why doesn't he leave? Strike out on his own and start his own pack?"

Jillian shook her head. "It doesn't work like that. If Aren were to leave, he'd be considered a rogue. An outcast. And even if he did manage to create a pack, there's no guarantee he'd be the Alpha. Our wolves and the natural order decide who the top dog is."

Chelle let out a chuff of laughter. Top dog. She'd have to use that one on Gunnar sometime. "So he figures since he's the number two guy, he'd naturally slide into that top spot if Gunnar's out of the picture."

"If he manages to kill him in combat, yes."

A tremor of fear vibrated through her. The thought of anything happening to Gunnar nearly made Chelle reconsider her plans. To stick to him like glue so he never had to doubt that someone had his back. Aren wasn't worthy to be Gunnar's second in command. He was a low-life, usurping piece of shit and Chelle was going to make sure the slimy bastard's ambitions were exposed.

Hopefully after she got her hands on McAlister's key tomorrow night.

She met Jillian's eyes and asked, "Do you think he could? Best Gunnar in a fight."

"He's strong." Jillian seemed reluctant to make the concession. "And he knows how to fight dirty. But he can't match Gunnar's strength. He's Alpha for a reason."

Chelle knew that strength firsthand. She'd felt the flex of his muscles beneath her fingertips, sensed his power when he'd refused to let her compel him. Gunnar was a magnificent male, worthy of his pack's respect and probably even a little fear.

Jillian's faith in Gunnar helped to put Chelle at ease. It took a hell of a lot more effort than she'd thought to maintain an indifferent façade. As though their tether were something trivial. Instead, she'd found herself warming up to Gunnar more and more every time they were together. His absence cut a deep grove into her heart that wouldn't be healed until he was by her side—or in her bed—again. It wasn't just about sex, though. She felt something for Gunnar. Something real and visceral that she couldn't escape. Something that grew every day. And that worried her more than anything.

Jillian cocked her head to one side. A wry smile curved her lips as she studied Chelle. "I don't have to be able to read minds to know that he means something to you."

Chelle sipped from her cup. "I don't know what you're talking about."

"Yes you do," Jillian teased. "You *like* him."

"Of course I like him." Chelle swept her hand as though to brush Jillian's observation aside. "We're tethered."

Jillian's brow furrowed. "Tethered?"

To-mato. To-mahto. "Mated. So yeah, I like him. It would be pretty awkward if I didn't."

"Are you saying you're worried about him?" Jillian asked.

Duh. "Aren't you?"

"I have faith in my Alpha."

Jillian's response cut through Chelle's chest. Was she faithless? Incapable of trust? Was she so selfish, so utterly focused on herself that she'd grown cold despite the return of her soul? Maybe she'd always been this way. Maybe her drive and ambition was all she had.

"Are you worried about Gunnar?" Jillian fixed Chelle with an inscrutable stare. "Or are you worried about what's going to happen when he finds out what you're up to?"

Both. Gunnar had said in so many words that he didn't want Chelle anywhere near the Sortiari's stronghold. And he'd made it loud and clear that he absolutely did not want her to continue her quest for the remaining two pieces of the Alexandria key.

"Aren't you worried about the same thing?" Chelle asked. Jillian sat back in her seat, lips pursed. "We both know Gunnar is going to blow a gasket when he finds out. What's in it for you? Why help me at all when you're risking your Alpha's wrath?"

Jillian let out a slow breath. "I want what you want more or less."

"Answers to my freakish origins?" Chelle ventured.

"No." Jillian gave a gentle laugh. "I want to know if there's a cure."

"For what?"

Jillian took another sip from her straw. "Lycanthropy."

Chelle slumped back in her chair. She wanted to know more about the magic of Set's Chest. She wanted to know more about what she could do and whether or not she might someday become a danger to her loved ones. But never once had she considered reversing any of it. She'd never *not* wanted to be a vampire. "You want to reverse what's happened to you?"

"Not me." Jillian's expression grew sad. "I've been a werewolf for decades. I have a mate that I love. A family. But there might be others out there who don't want this. If we could reverse it before their first transition, before the wolf takes hold, then there would at least be an option for those who wanted one."

"I've never been human," Chelle remarked. "Being immersed in this world has to be a shock."

"That's an understatement."

"Gunnar told me about his transition." Chelle averted her gaze and dropped her voice. "I know how hard it was for you all."

"It sucks balls," Jillian said. She gave Chelle a small smile. "But it gets easier, once we learn how to coexist with our wolves. It's not a total cakewalk, though. I've heard shifters can bounce between their human and animal forms without feeling so much as a pinch. Lucky bastards."

Chelle laughed. "We're both in search of knowledge, then. Seems like a noble quest to me."

"Noble as hell." Jillian held out her fist and Chelle bumped it with hers. "All right, then, let's get down to business." She pulled a small set of blueprints from her bag and spread them out on the table. "I got this from the city planning and zoning office. McAlister purchased the place a couple of years ago. There's been quite a bit of new construction but the main building hasn't changed. I'm assuming all of the improvements are related to security so you're going to have to be prepared to jump through some hoops. Gunnar has the best security system money can buy. Including a pack of territorial werewolves to watch over the place. We have to assume that McAlister's is better."

Chelle leaned over the table to study the blueprints. Man, she could have used someone like Jillian ages ago! Together, they would have amassed an invaluable collection of relics and esoteric knowledge. A force to be reckoned with. Too bad she had to keep their alliance a secret. If Gunnar found out what she'd gotten Jillian into, he would never forgive her.

Hell, even without Jillian involved he might not forgive her. Chelle hoped that Gunnar had a little of that trust and faith Jillian had mentioned earlier. Otherwise, Chelle might lose the one thing she couldn't live without.

"Okay," Chelle said on a breath. "Let's get this show on the road."

"Good idea," Jillian replied. "The moon's about to rise and I need to get home."

The timing couldn't be more perfect. Chelle just hoped that Gunnar could try to understand that she was doing what she had to do. If not, she might gain the knowledge she sought, but in the process, she'd lose the one thing she didn't think she could live without.

*   *   *

"Where's Jillian?" Gunnar wasn't about to waste a second in finding out what she'd been doing at Chelle's house yet again. He'd noticed her car as he'd left Chelle's cottage just after sundown. The two of them had become a little too chummy for Gunnar's peace of mind. They were up to something.

Sven gave a shrug of his shoulder. "Said she had an errand to run."

"I need to talk to her."

"Why?" Sven's gaze narrowed and his nostrils flared. "What's going on?"

Gunnar bristled as Aren walked into the room. He didn't want to have this conversation with the other male there. "We're still working on the inventory from the safe room and I want to double-check a couple of things with her."

"Are you sure that's the only reason?" Gunnar's wolf let out a low growl as Aren butted into the conversation. "You're not discussing anything else?"

Gunnar's gaze slid to his second. "What else do you think I'd have to discuss with her?"

Aren allowed a superior smirk. "The identity of our vampire thief, maybe?"

Sven's eyes went wide. His scent changed to a deep musk that put Gunnar's wolf on the defensive. It didn't matter that the male's aggression wasn't aimed at him. The full moon was tonight. Everyone was on edge.

"How the hell would she know that?" Sven took a step forward and Gunnar put his palm to the male's chest to stay his progress. "What are you implying, Aren?"

That superiority was replaced with an innocence that made Gunnar's teeth itch. "I'm not implying anything. She drove to L.A. yesterday afternoon, that's all."

Sven took a lurching step forward. "The fuck does that

have to do with anything? I drive to L.A. all the damned time. Doesn't mean I'm hanging out with vampires."

"Enough." The word resonated with power and both Aren and Sven stilled. They lowered their gaze in Gunnar's presence. He was sick and tired of the blind prejudice. He faced his second and pinned him with his stern gaze. "Tell me, Aren, what is it about vampires that has you so agitated?"

"I'm only agitated by the ones who try to steal from us."

Gunnar and Sven exchanged a look. "And yet you're hell-bent on helping the berserkers to exterminate them."

Aren's gaze narrowed. "I think you misunderstand my intentions, Gunnar."

"No." A lazy smile spread across Gunnar's lips. "I think I understand perfectly."

"I'm looking out for the pack," Aren said. "That's all."

"And suddenly interested in making new friends," Sven said with a disgusted grunt.

"Alliances," Aren said. "Nothing more. The climate is shifting and we don't want to get caught on the wrong end of a power struggle."

Those power struggles had little to do with the pack. But Aren was right to a certain extent. Now that Gunnar and Chelle were bound, it muddied the waters of their neutrality. Chelle might not be a member of Mikhail Aristov's coven, but she was a vampire. Any vengeance Ian Gregor sought to deliver upon them would affect his mate. The decision to pick a side had been made for Gunnar. For all of them. But even without the mate bond to sway his thinking, there never would have been any chance that Gunnar would ally himself with a violent berserker warlord.

"Why Gregor?" Gunnar needed to know why Aren had

such a hard-on for the berserkers' cause. "Why not side with the guardians of fate? They're the stronger ally."

Aren arched a curious brow. "Are they? If McAlister was strong enough to hold on to his power, why would he have used the berserkers for muscle in the first place? Think about it, Gunnar. Gregor and his lot were the ones keeping the Sortiari at the top of the food chain for so long."

It was a possibility not to be discounted, but Aren was a fool to think the Sortiari's power wasn't far-reaching. The berserkers' numbers were in the hundreds, but the membership of the secret society was legion. They were everywhere. Heard and saw everything. To make them an enemy would be signing their own death warrants.

"I disagree." He wouldn't entertain Aren's blind ambitions for another second. "The berserkers' plans for war will only bring about their own destruction. And anyone caught aiding them will go down right alongside them."

"Your fear of the Sortiari is what keeps them in power," Aren said with disgust. "Without that fear, they're impotent."

Fool. His lack of a strategic mind was yet another reason Aren would never be Alpha. He wanted to hack and slash at his foes without considering logistics. "The Sortiari have never turned their attention to us," Gunnar replied. "They've let us live in peace for millennia."

"Not so the vampires," Aren said.

Gunnar scowled. "And yet, if your intel is correct, the vampires would fight alongside those who wronged them. What does that tell you about how dangerous Gregor is and why he shouldn't be allowed to amass any more power than he already has?"

"It tells me that soon he'll have power to spare," Aren said with a confident smirk. "And that he'll be generous to those who helped him accumulate it."

Aren was a fool if he thought Gregor would share the spoils of war with anyone aside from his own kin.

"Hey, guys . . . What's up?"

Jillian walked through the front door and into the foyer. The door closed behind her and though she tried to keep her expression impassive, she could do nothing about the guilt that shone behind her eyes. Gunnar's jaw squared and he let out a slow sigh. Chelle's scent clung to her. Faint, masked by some sort of perfume. Jillian was foolish to think she could cover it up. Gunnar would be able to pick out his mate's scent even if Jillian had showered and then bathed in perfume before returning home.

"Aren, we'll discuss this later. In the meantime, I forbid you from entertaining any alliance with Gregor or any other berserker. Whatever Gregor's beef with the Sortiari, we will *not* get involved." No way was Gunnar going to allow him to continue on his path. If he was unhappy with the way Gunnar chose to rule the pack, he could leave. But he'd no longer ignore Aren's greed for power. "Jillian, I need to talk to you. Alone."

She cast a furtive gaze in Sven's direction before turning to Gunnar. "Sure. No problem."

"My office?" Gunnar suggested.

She forced a smile onto her face. "Right behind you."

They walked into Gunnar's office and he closed the door. He didn't bother sitting. This wasn't going to be a pleasant conversation. "I know you were with Chelle tonight and I want to know what's going on."

"Chelle?"

Jillian feigned innocence but her scent gave her away in a second. Gunnar gave her a look as to say, *Come on.* She knew better than to try to deceive him.

Jillian let out a slow breath. Her scent soured with fear and her heartbeat kicked up a notch. Her reaction did little to put Gunnar at ease and his wolf grew restless in his mind. Whatever the two of them had been up to, it wasn't good.

"Tell me everything," Gunnar said from between clenched teeth. "And pray I show you leniency."

Gunnar had reached the end of his rope. It was time to take back control.

CHAPTER
24

Chelle's nerves were shot and she hadn't even crossed the property line yet. It might have looked unassuming, but she knew the security guarding the Sortiari's L.A. stronghold would make the Pentagon's seem lax in comparison. There would be surveillance, protective wards placed throughout the property, and guard dogs . . . which worried Chelle most of all.

Because it wouldn't be a couple of Rottweilers ready to tear into her. No, whatever McAlister had watching over his treasures was guaranteed to be a hundred times worse.

Deep breath, Chelle. You've got this.

Most times, a little pep talk was all she needed to get the job done. Funny, now she was a vampire, Chelle had all of the advantages: super strength, speed, healing. The ability to read minds and compel anyone who stood in her way. She was so much stronger than she'd ever been but she lacked the reckless confidence she used to possess. Did that mean her transition had somehow made her wiser? She'd never felt her mortality in the way she did now. Why?

It didn't take a genius to figure that one out. *Gunnar.*

The tether changed *everything.* Even more than her transition from dhampir to freak-of-nature vampire. If something were to happen to her tonight, the hurt wouldn't simply be hers. Gunnar would suffer. He'd succumb to a wildness that would force his pack to put him down. He'd lose himself entirely to the animal and fall into madness.

That wasn't going to happen. Chelle wasn't going to die or anything else here tonight. In and out. Find the Sortiari's piece of the key and hightail it the hell out of there. Failure wasn't an option. She let out a slow breath. She really needed to up her positive self-talk game.

"I can do this."

The building on the outskirts of the city looked like the sort of place where a flourishing tech company would set up shop. Gorgeous modern architecture, the outer walls lined with sparkling clean windows, lush trees and bushes surrounding the property, winding concrete paths. At the far end of the property was an Asian-inspired serenity garden. Probably where McAlister pondered the fates of whatever species he was about to eradicate next. The stronghold was three stories, and Chelle assumed there was a basement. Gunnar had kept his valuables in the attic space. He'd relied on his security system and the strength of the pack to protect their treasures. McAlister wouldn't be quite so obvious. The Sortiari's strength was more subversive. He'd never dare someone to march into the place and rob him blind.

That's what was going to happen, though.

Chelle took several cleansing breaths as she skirted the edge of the property. She kept her steps feather light and used her speed to her advantage to cheat the cameras and motion detectors that no doubt looked down on the grounds. A quiet hiss echoed around her and sparks of residual magic sizzled in the air, scorching Chelle's nostrils and tingling on her skin.

Wait a sec . . . Not magic. Silver?

Chelle took a deep breath and instantly wished she hadn't. Her lungs burned and she coughed. Yep. Definitely silver. McAlister really was a devious son of a bitch, wasn't he? The particles were almost too fine for even her sharp eyes to see in the nearly pitch-black night. So much for cheating the motion detectors. Her presence had managed to trigger some sort of delivery system that diffused silver dust into the air. Chelle stumbled as she continued to cough, and she braced herself against a high concrete wall near the serenity garden as she tried to expel the silver from her lungs. Her tolerance of silver kept her from checking out, but it definitely aggravated her. Sort of like breathing in a cloud of fiberglass particles. Had she been a werewolf, or even a typical vampire, she'd be toast right now. The silver would have worked its way into her system and killed her within minutes. Thank the gods Gunnar wasn't here . . .

Chelle took a deep breath and held the silver dust in her lungs rather than try to push it out. She held in a scream as the burn intensified. Chelle dropped to her knees, refused to let the air out, and her body seized as it tried to reject the toxin. Nope. Not gonna happen. Chelle was tougher than McAlister and his underhanded, bullshit tricks.

Sweat began to bead on Chelle's forehead. Heat swamped her, her blood practically boiled in her veins, and her throat went dry. She tried to swallow and it was about as comfortable as working a mouthful of razor blades down her throat. No way was she letting McAlister get one up on her before she'd even made it through the front door. Dark spots swam in her vision and her knees threatened to buckle. She steeled herself against the effects of the silver, gritting her teeth against the pain. *Fight it, Chelle. You're stronger . . .*

A surge of power coursed through her veins and the heat began to subside by small degrees. Chelle drew in a ragged breath. And another. Her throat worked to swallow and it no longer felt as though shards of glass scraped the sides of her esophagus. The quaking in her limbs calmed and her legs could once again support the weight of her body as her strength returned.

The silver particles had effectively infiltrated every inch of her but it hadn't put her down. For the first time since her transition, Chelle saw an upside to being a freak of nature. *Strike one, McAlister. Let's see what else you've got.*

It took a few steps before she was sure on her feet again. Her boots were nearly soundless as Chelle flew from the concrete wall, toward the building three hundred yards away. Like a wraith, she crossed the distance, nothing more than a smear of black shadow against the backdrop of night. A breeze kicked up, parting the clouds to reveal a bright full moon. The particles of silver dust brushed her skin, tingling over her flesh before they were carried away on the wind. The very air shimmered as the dust absorbed the light that shone down.

Full moon. The only thing that could have distracted Gunnar from seeing her tonight.

Her thoughts inevitably wandered to her werewolf. Was he okay? In pain from the transition? Or was he running through the woods outside his house, chasing small game as he let his wolf have control. Or was he fighting for his life against Aren in some medieval-style arena while his pack bore witness to his murder?

Chelle gave herself a mental shake. She had to believe

he was okay. Otherwise, worrying about him would steal her focus and she wouldn't be worth a shit. By the time she hit the concrete sidewalk, her heart hammered a wild beat that threatened to crack a rib from its force. She needed to calm the hell down. Keep her eyes on the prize. She wasn't doing this simply for herself anymore. She thought about Gunnar's story of how his pack became werewolves. Of Jillian's own desire to find a cure for those who wanted it. The choice had been taken from them just as it had been taken from Chelle. They all deserved answers. They deserved to have control of their lives back.

In comparison to crossing the grounds, getting into the stronghold itself was a breeze. Way too easy. She'd picked locks at grocery stores that were harder to get into. Which meant that since she'd managed to get past the silver dust, someone wanted her lulled into a false sense of security so she wouldn't be ready for whatever was next.

These guys weren't amateurs. They meant business.

Chelle took a moment to appreciate the place. *Damn.* The Sortiari must've had deep pockets. Then again, when your organization had been around longer than recorded history, it sort of gave you the time to amass a fortune. McAlister could probably buy the U.S. out of debt with his pocket change. The sort of money and power he wielded was some scary-ass shit. He was completely unchecked. Had total autonomy.

A shiver passed over Chelle's skin.

She was about to piss off a very dangerous, very influential member of the supernatural community. McAlister's wrath could stir up more trouble than she could handle. Her actions tonight would affect more than just her. But damn it, knowledge belonged to everyone. Not only the gatekeepers who thought themselves the only ones worthy of it or capable of understanding it.

There could be more than a stack of books in that library, Chelle, and you know it.

Gunnar had managed to plant a seed of doubt. It wasn't too late to change her mind. To walk out the way she came in and abandon her quest for answers. She could be happy. If she'd allow herself to completely accept their tether, Gunnar could make her happy. Maybe what she was wouldn't matter as much with him at her side.

Chelle could be content if she wanted to be. But the not knowing would eat her alive. She had no choice but to continue on the path she'd started.

She only hoped that Gunnar, Ronan, Mikhail, Jillian, and anyone else she inadvertently got caught up in McAlister's crossfire, would forgive her.

Gunnar pinched the bridge of his nose. His lungs compressed on a frustrated breath that made his ribs ache from the force. He'd fought the encroaching transformation for too long and his body was beginning to pay the price. His wolf was angry and it fought for control over their body. The night of the full moon belonged to the animal and it wouldn't be denied. But the bastard was going to wait if it killed Gunnar. His only saving grace right now was the cloud cover. The second the light of the moon shone down on him, the choice would be completely taken away. He was running against the clock and shit was piling up, fast.

"You did what?"

The scent of Jillian's fear only served to agitate his wolf. It longed to mete out a severe punishment for putting their mate in danger and, for once, Gunnar was in agreement. Of all the reckless things she could have done, this was by far the worst.

"She was going to go anyway." Jillian's voice quavered.

"With or without my help. I wanted to do what I could to give her the upper hand."

"There is no such thing as the upper hand when dealing with the Sortiari!" Chelle knew that. And she'd gone off on her fool's errand anyway, hell-bent on standing by her stubborn convictions.

Jillian flinched and let out a whimper. Sweat glistened on her skin but it wasn't from nerves or fear. She'd be less likely to resist the transformation than Gunnar. Which meant he needed to get as much information out of her as possible before she succumbed to the animal's—and the moon's—pull.

"Where is this place?" Gunnar needed to get his ass in gear. L.A. was a thirty-minute drive away. If he had to go it on four legs, it would take twice as long to reach her.

"The stronghold is on the outskirts of the city," Jillian replied. She let out a grunt of discomfort and sat up straighter in her chair. She handed over a set of blueprints. "The plans don't show a basement space," Jillian said. "But we both agreed that the layout indicated there was definitely another level belowground."

Gunnar studied the images that had been shrunk down to fit on the eight-by-ten paper. Gods damn Chelle and her foolish pride! If anything happened to her, Gunnar would never recover from the loss. He needed to find her and make sure she was good and healthy, so he could throttle her himself later.

"Go find Sven," Gunnar said from between clenched teeth. "I'll deal with your betrayal later."

Jillian lowered her gaze in shame. "Gunnar," she said low. "There's something else."

His jaw flexed as he felt enamel grind. His wolf issued a low growl. "What?"

"Gunnar!" Sven came charging into the room, looking about as stable as Jillian.

Gods damn it. The timing for all of this shit to hit the fan couldn't be worse. Gunnar turned to face his cousin and ran his fingers though his hair. "What is it?"

"Aren and five others are gone." The gravity in Sven's expression hit Gunnar in the gut. "Jaeger said he overheard them discussing McAlister's meeting with Aristov and the berserkers' plans to ambush them. Whatever's going down, it's not going to be pretty."

That was a fucking understatement.

"I told him *not* to interfere in the Sortiari's—or Gregor's—business," Gunnar ground out. An Alpha's command was law. Breaking it could earn all involved a death sentence.

Sven cut Gunnar a look. "Obviously, he took your warnings to heart."

Gunnar should have known that Aren wouldn't back down. His ambition wouldn't allow him to. Gregor had dazzled him, offered him an opportunity for power, and Aren had taken the bait.

"Did Jaeger happen to hear where McAlister and Aristov are meeting?" Damn it, he did not want to get involved in McAlister's business. All it would manage to do is bring undue attention to the pack. And thanks to Aren, Gunnar found himself smack-dab in the middle of where he didn't want to be.

"Yeah." Sven's muscles tightened and his jaw flexed. "An old shut-down restaurant out on Highway 1. The area is pretty secluded and security is supposed to be lax. Both McAlister and Aristov agreed to bring only one representative. The berserkers alone could easily pick them off. I'm not sure why they'd even ask for our help."

So Gregor would have leverage over the pack, that's why. Fucking Aren and his foolishness!

Gunnar needed to get both of his considerably large problems under control so everyone could give in to the moon's pull. Resisting the transition would only make it more painful for all of them. "McAlister's a mage," Gunnar replied. "Magic wielders are tricky as fuck. There's no telling what he's capable of."

A visible shiver vibrated over Sven's skin. Werewolves and magic didn't mix. It agitated their wolves and burned their noses. "Aren's in for it," Sven replied. "I'd leave the bastard to his fate if he hadn't managed to convince so many to go with him."

On that Gunnar could agree. "Take everyone we have and see if you can get a warning to Aristov."

Sven snorted. "He'll never believe me."

Damn it, he was probably right. Gunnar drew a deep breath and held it in his lungs before letting it all out in a rush. "Tell him that the message comes from Gunnar Falk, Alpha of the Forkbeard pack, and tethered mate of Chelle Daly. He should believe you then."

"Mate?" Sven's jaw went slack. "Why would Aristov believe that? Unless . . ."

Aren's wouldn't be the only fate sealed tonight. In order to save the king of the fledgling vampire race, Gunnar had no choice but to reveal his mate bond to one of his own. Not the best circumstances to drop a bomb, but Gunnar was running out of time.

"Gunnar." Sven's tone was laced with disbelief. "Chelle? Is that her name? The vampire who stole from us." He looked to Jillian and her knowing expression was all the confirmation he needed. "She's your *mate*?"

Gunnar met Sven's wide-eyed stare. There was no point in denying it. He didn't want to. "She is," he said, proud. "We'll deal with that complication later, though. Get to that meeting and warn Aristov."

"I'm going, too."

Jillian stood from her chair and Gunnar rounded on her. "I'm not done with you, yet."

She knocked her chin up a notch. "Like you said, we'll deal with it later. Right now, we all have emergencies that need to be dealt with."

Sven watched their exchange with interest. No doubt he and Jillian would have much to talk about. He turned to Gunnar. "You're not going with us? Aren needs to see you there. He needs to be reminded of who and what you are."

True, but it wasn't going to happen. At least, not yet. "Like Jillian said, we all have emergencies that need to be dealt with. I'll get there as soon as I can. In the meantime, the others will answer to you."

"Get moving, Gunnar," Jillian said. "She left a little after sundown to case the place until she knew McAlister was gone."

"What in the hell is going on?" Sven demanded.

Jillian grabbed her mate by the arm and led him out of the room. "I'll fill you in on the way. But we need to get our butts in gear."

Gunnar rushed through the house. Any other night, he would have gone straight to the armory and outfitted himself with an arsenal before going after Chelle. Tonight was a whole different game, though. At any time, he might succumb to the transformation and leave his human form behind. The wolf had its enormous size, its sheer strength, speed, and superior senses. It had its ruthless animal instinct and quick healing. Strong jaws and claws to rip and tear. But Gunnar wasn't infallible by any stretch of the imagination. A silver bullet would put him down.

Gods damn it. He had to continue to believe that he and Chelle would be stronger as a team. Because he had a feeling that if they didn't work together, neither of them would make it out of the stronghold alive.

His breath came in desperate pants of pain by the time Gunnar made it to the garage. A breeze kicked up and the clouds parted. The silvery glow of the full moon permeated his flesh. His skin tightened on his frame and his bones creaked. His wolf gave an anxious snarl in the recess of his mind and a wave of power crashed over him, taking Gunnar down in its undertow. His jaw locked down tight and his knees smashed down onto the paved driveway. One femur snapped, and then the other. Gunnar let out a shout as the bones broke and remade themselves, turning as they made new angles. He knew that fighting the change would only make it worse, but damn it, he needed to get to Chelle a hell of a lot faster than the wolf could manage.

His wrists snapped, his arms as well. His neck grew thicker and hair sprouted coarse and thick on every inch of his body. Gunnar's shouts of pain quickly turned to snarls as his jaw elongated and his canines grew long and sharp. Gunnar and his wolf became one. Their thoughts focused on a single truth: their mate was in trouble, and they needed to get to her.

CHAPTER
25

Mikhail Aristov paced the confines of his study. Upstairs, his mate, Claire, put their weeks-old son down for a nap. He'd put this meeting off with McAlister for as long as he could. It was time to keep his word and give the director of the Sortiari what he wanted. It seemed a small price to pay to keep the tentative peace between them.

At least, that's what Mikhail hoped.

He still didn't understand McAlister's unusual interest in Vanessa. The human girl had lived in the same apartment building as Claire and she loved Vanessa as if she were her own. Vanessa's mother had been a troubled human. An addict who didn't have the good sense to take care of her child. The woman had fallen victim to Gregor's wrath in the berserker's quest to kidnap Claire and suffered a blow to the head that they feared she wouldn't recover from.

Brain damage.

Mikhail shook his head. Humans truly were fragile creatures. He'd paid for Vanessa's mother to be transferred to a rehab facility where she could fully recover from her injuries. So far her progress had been minimal and Vanessa continued to live here at the house with them. She'd become a part of their family, and even if her mother recovered, Mikhail wondered how he or Claire would possibly be willing to let her go.

Such a dramatic change from his years of isolation and despair. Claire had given him a new life. He owed her everything. The last thing he wanted to do was cause his mate worry by giving McAlister what he wanted: an introduction to the seemingly mundane Vanessa.

Mikhail had sensed something "other" about the human girl when he'd first met her. She wasn't supernatural per se, but neither was she simply human. McAlister was willing to declare peace with Mikhail after years of trying to eradicate the vampire race. They were far from allies, but it showed how curious the Sortiari's director was about Vanessa that he'd put centuries of strife aside.

None of this sat well with him. None of it.

"You know McAlister isn't going to play by the rules." Ronan lounged on a couch at the far side of the room, looking as cavalier as ever. "I don't see any reason why we should, either."

For what it was worth, Mikhail agreed with Ronan. He'd never known Trenton McAlister to play by the rules. "True, but I hate to sink to his level."

Ronan raised the glass of fifty-year-old scotch. "I hear ya. I'm not saying we should blatantly break the rules. I'll stay back a bit. You take Jenner like you said you would and I'll just make sure everything around the perimeter is on the up-and-up."

It was a good idea. And Mikhail would definitely feel a hell of a lot better knowing Ronan was out there keeping an eye out for anything that wasn't aboveboard. "What about Claire and the baby?"

"Already taken care of," Ronan replied. "Lucas said

he'd come over until we got back and Bria and Naya will be here, too."

Ronan's mate, Naya, was a formidable witch, and Jenner's mate, Bria, was a fierce fighter thanks to Jenner's tutelage. Lucas was a trained warrior as well. Claire and the baby would be well protected. "What about Chelle?" Ronan's wild twin could certainly be feisty when she wanted to be. "Is she coming over as well?"

"Nah." Ronan averted his gaze as he brushed Mikhail's question away. "She took off somewhere. Lucas isn't sure where."

Ronan's scent soured slightly. He hadn't outright lied to Mikhail, but he sensed that Ronan might at least have an idea where his sister had gone off to. Whatever she was up to, Mikhail hoped she was keeping her nose clean. She had a tendency to find trouble even when she wasn't looking for it.

"So then, it will be you, me, Jenner, and Vanessa."

"Yup," Ronan said. "I still don't like it, but I doubt anything is going to change your mind at this point."

"No," Mikhail said. "I gave McAlister my word. Besides, I'm afraid that keeping Vanessa from him will only cause his obsession with her to grow."

"Word." Ronan drained his glass. "It's fucking weird if you ask me. I mean, she's what, ten or twelve? Barely old enough to take care of herself let alone be a threat to one of the most powerful males in the world."

"Exactly," Mikhail replied. "Which is why my curiosity is piqued as well."

"Wouldn't it be cool if she had X-Men powers?" Mikhail rolled his eyes at Ronan's enthusiastic expression. "Like maybe she can control the weather or shoot fireballs out of her hands. That would kick some serious ass."

"Comic-book fantasies aside, we all know there's something otherworldly about the girl. I'd like to know what it is. If McAlister is the only one who can shed any light on what that is, then so be it."

"I guess," Ronan said with a sigh. "But I'd rather have my fangs pulled than be within ten miles of that murdering son of a bitch."

"That makes two of us," Mikhail said. "I'd rather be anywhere than sitting in a room with that unholy bastard."

Ronan held up his glass for a toast when he realized it was empty. "Damn."

"I imagine it will all be very civil," Mikhail said. "Neither of us acknowledging the wrongs of the other."

"Um, we haven't committed any wrongs. Unless you consider *existing* an offense to the Sortiari."

Mikhail inclined his head. "You're right. I guess I'll be sitting there, pretending not to remember that McAlister sent Gregor to put me in my grave."

"Claire as well."

Mikhail scowled at the unpleasant reminder. His lip curled back at the mental image of his mate stretched out on that table, helpless, as Gregor cut into her skin over and over again. "If McAlister so much as turns a caustic eye on me or mine, I'll tear out his throat. Consequences be damned."

"Hell, yeah!" Ronan set down his glass and pushed himself up from the couch. "No use hanging out here all night. Let's get this show on the road."

"Get Jenner and bring the car around," Mikhail said after a moment. "I'll fetch Vanessa and meet you out front."

Meeting McAlister would likely be smooth sailing in comparison to Claire's worry. Mikhail had considered keeping the meeting a secret from his mate for all of about five seconds. They didn't keep anything from one another. All secrets did was weaken them. Claire didn't want Vanessa to go, which was understandable. He'd promised her, though, that nothing would happen to Vanessa as long as he was with her. Mikhail kept his word. Always. As long as there was blood coursing through his veins, he'd protect Vanessa.

No matter what tonight's outcome might be.

Christian felt as though his skin had been wound in Saran wrap. Resisting the pull of the full moon was damned near impossible. Most months, he would have gladly given himself over to the animal for the opportunity to check out for a few hours. Not tonight, though. Both he and his wolf were twitchy as fuck.

This supposed peaceful meeting between McAlister and the vampire king was bound to be a total shit show. Especially if Gregor decided to make an appearance. Gods, he hoped that violent motherfucker had the good sense to stay away. Of course, Gregor and good sense went together about as well as steak à la mode.

It seemed like common sense was in a shortage lately. The location for tonight's little get-together was a security nightmare. The abandoned restaurant on Highway 1 was an obscure location, no doubt about it. Christian doubted anyone could connect it to either McAlister or Aristov. But it was also out in the middle of nowhere. An attack would go unnoticed and the structure wouldn't keep an ambitious dog out, let alone a force of berserker warlords in full battle rage.

Whatever the director wanted from Aristov tonight, it clearly had him distracted to the point of not giving a single shit about safety. Christian found himself feeling a little jealous of the vampire. The male obviously had leverage over McAlister. Christian would give his left nut for a little of that. Maybe if he could get his hands—well, tonight it would have to be paws—on whatever Aristov had, he'd steal the treasure away from both of them. He'd love to have something the Sortiari wanted. Then he could tell Gregor to fuck off once and for all.

"You look like shit, Whalen. Still gambling your life away?"

Christian rolled his eyes. As if tonight couldn't get any worse. He inclined his head toward the sound of the deep, rumbling voice. "I thought I smelled bear musk. Jesus, Caden, how can anyone stand to be around you?"

The shifter's proximity put Christian's wolf on the defensive. If he transitioned now, the wolf would jump Caden Mitchell and there wouldn't be a damned thing Christian could do about it. In a fight versus a five-hundred-pound grizzly bear, he'd have no choice but to kiss his ass good-bye. He willed his wolf to quiet and tried to explain to the cocky bastard that picking a fight wasn't in either of their best interests. They were tough, but not take-on-a-bear-shifter-tough.

"Try not to feel threatened, Whalen." Caden's tone was teasing, but a menacing light glinted in his bright blue eyes. "I promise not to piss on your territory."

Their roles within the Sortiari couldn't be more different. Christian was a tracker. He found the people that the Sortiari—with all of their endless resources—couldn't find. He gathered information. Worked the angles and played the games. Low-key and subversive. Christian's job wasn't to bash heads. That responsibility fell on the enforcers like Caden Mitchell.

Males like Caden were called in when someone needed to be convinced to play along. They meted out McAlister's punishments quickly and quietly, and took care of lesser problems before they became total catastrophes. Probably why the director had wanted Caden in L.A. the moment he'd gotten wind of Aristov's ascension to power. If Caden was the strong arm of the Sortiari, then Gregor and his brethren were the organization's rabid guard dogs. Berserkers were called in specifically for the catastrophes. To clean up the messes that no one wanted to touch. Caden might have been an insufferable bastard, but at least the male had morals. Standards. A code of fucking ethics. Gregor had none of those. His conscience had taken a hike a long damned time ago. Caden made Christian nervous, but Gregor fucking terrified him. Ruthless males were capable of anything. Including the near eradication of an entire race.

"I'm not worried about you pissing on anything," Christian remarked. He kept his gaze straight ahead, his posture, relaxed. "I heard you didn't want a part of any of the action down here. That you were perfectly happy shaking down unregistered mages for the director."

Caden shrugged. "Something like that. Besides, I hate the West Coast."

"Sunshine and perpetual bikini weather's not your thing, huh?"

Caden remained still. Christian's humor was totally wasted on him. "Too many berserkers for my taste."

He had that right. "I heard you handed Gregor's ass to him a while back. Wish I could've been there to see that."

Caden's deep laughter rumbled in his chest, stirring Christian's wolf once again. "Gregor was begging to be put in his place. I was more than happy to oblige him."

Christian chuckled. "Smug motherfucker must've been shocked to get a beat-down like that."

"He had it coming to him."

For a few minutes they stood side by side in silence. Christian's wolf bristled. He wondered if shifters had the same issue with duality in their mind. "Where's the director?"

Caden jerked his head to the left. "He's in the car. I told him I'd do a perimeter check. He's not moving an inch until Aristov gets here anyway."

"Think the vampire will show up?" To be honest, Christian doubted Aristov would be stupid enough to show his face.

"He will if he knows what's good for him," Caden replied. "McAlister has a stick up his ass over something the vampire has. The director is playing nice now, but I wouldn't be surprised if he resorted to force to get his hands on it."

Which was why Christian's curiosity was piqued. "The vampires' numbers are growing. It won't be long before the city is crawling with them."

Caden nodded. "I've heard. And I'm glad. The Sortiari might think the fate of the world is theirs to play with, but no one should have that kind of power."

At least on that they could agree. "So why work for them at all?" It was true that once you became a member of the secret society, the only way out was in a body bag, but Mitchell was *loaded*. The guy had billions. One more reason for Christian to hate him. "You've got enough money that you could probably buy your way out if you wanted."

Caden laughed. "You know as well as I do that buying your way out isn't an option. Besides, I don't think of myself as a Sortiari slave. Instead, I focus on the change I can effect from the inside."

Sure. When you were a scary motherfucker like Caden Mitchell, it was pretty easy to "effect change." Christian shivered and looked up at the sky. A light breeze stirred the air and the clouds began to part. "Not to be a dick, but you should probably get the fuck out of here. The moon's about to peek out from those clouds, and when it does, it's not going to be pretty."

Caden gave a solemn nod of his head. "You're always a dick," he remarked. "But I need to go check on McAlister anyway. See you around, Whalen."

Christian gave a tight nod of his head. His bones ached and his gut twisted as the clouds parted to reveal the moon. "Yeah," he grunted. "See ya."

Pain racked Christian's body as he fell to his knees. He'd lived with this fucking curse for so gods-damned long he couldn't remember a time when he didn't feel at odds with his mind, his body, his very nature. His fingers dug into the dirt and he threw his head back. Panting breaths raced in his chest and his jaw clenched.

While he was still in control of his faculties, Christian gave his wolf a command. Fuck McAlister and watching over his paranoid ass. They were going to find out what exactly Aristov had that the director coveted. And then, they'd figure out how they could exploit it to their benefit.

CHAPTER
26

Chelle combed the entire first story, skittish as a hare dodging a pursuing fox. She expected something to jump out and try to kill her at any time, but so far the place was still and quiet as a tomb. What the hell? Had the Sortiari been stupid enough to think that a little silver dust would deter any outsider from trying to break in?

Not a chance.

When they'd gone over the blueprints, both Chelle and Jillian had been convinced there was a basement level in the facility despite its absence in city records. So far, Chelle hadn't been able to find any sort of doorway, elevator, or visible staircase that went downward. Didn't mean it wasn't there, though. The Sortiari were crafty bastards. What she was looking for could very well be cloaked by magic.

Maybe she was going about this all wrong. Chelle had counted on her eyes to lead the way, but that obviously wasn't getting her anywhere. She let her eyes drift shut. It took a minute to find her focus. Chelle's mind raced with myriad thoughts. Gunnar, Lucas, Ronan, Mikhail and his meeting with McAlister. Jillian and their agreement, Chelle's very existence. She forced all of that out of her mind until there was nothing but quiet and darkness. A blank space to be filled. She focused her breathing, deep and even, and let the absence of sound fill her ears.

There. A faint ripple against her skin.

Chelle turned to her left. Her foot shuffled in a sidling step and the ripple faded. To her right, it grew even fainter. Her right foot stepped back and the ripple grew more intense, snaking up her ankle, around her knee, to her thigh. Chelle brought her left foot back and the sensation traveled that leg as well. *Getting warmer.* Another step back. Another. Her eyes came slowly open. No use tripping on anything and alerting anyone to her presence. Though right now, she doubted anyone was home. So far, the place seemed abandoned. Maybe McAlister had taken his entire crew to his meeting with Mikhail. Her lips curved into a smile. The vampire king was certainly intimidating enough to warrant McAlister's fear.

The sensation of magic crawling over her skin intensified. It wound up her legs, around her torso, her arms, neck, and head, until Chelle felt as though she were suffocating. Panic blossomed in her chest as the raw energy crashed over her. She reminded herself that the compression on her lungs wouldn't suffocate her. She didn't need to breathe, it was simply perfunctory. Her heartbeat began to slow and the panic that rose in a lump in her throat subsided. Rather than walk away, Chelle continued toward the source of power and didn't stop until she felt the deep, vibrating pulses that beat like a bass drum in the center of her body.

Wow. Whoever had laid down the mojo here was seriously packing. The force of magic nearly made Chelle's teeth chatter. She was on the money, though. McAlister's secret entrance had to be here somewhere . . .

Gotcha!

The door was nearly invisible even to Chelle's superior eyesight. The barest outline. White on white without even a seam to betray its presence. It was the sort of thing you might mistake for shadow or even an optical illusion. It was there, though. Chelle made her way to the door and the current of magic pushed over her, slowing her progress as though she were walking upstream. A nice little deterrent, but not enough to dissuade her from continuing on. She'd found the doorway—or at least, she hoped she'd found it—but that was only part of the challenge. How was she supposed to open a door that had no handle?

Chelle dug the thick soles of her boots into the marble floor as she pushed against the magic and reached the wall. Her hands came up slowly and her muscles ached at the effort necessary to move in the vortex of magic. She might as well be an ant fighting its way through a bowl full of Jell-O. Inch by inch, her palms narrowed the gap and finally pressed against the door. At the moment of contact, a shock wave of energy exploded and soundlessly threw Chelle into the air, depositing her a good thirty yards away.

Her head smacked down on the marble floor, jarring her. The crack of her skull made Chelle nauseous and she swallowed down the bile that rose in her throat as the wound healed almost instantaneously. For a long moment, Chelle lay on her back and stared upward. Nearly invisible waves of magic undulated on the white ceiling, like the reflection of sunlight dancing over water. Okay, so her first attempt at getting in had been a bust, but she wasn't about to give up so easily. There wasn't a structure in the world she couldn't break into. Her reputation was on the line, damn it. No way was she giving up now.

McAlister wasn't the only one with tricks up his sleeve. Gunnar had failed to mention it, but Jillian had been pretty forthcoming about the fact that the Forkbeard pack employed a white witch for the occasional ward. Jillian just happened to be the one who did most of their business with her. Chelle sat up and pulled her pack from her back. She unzipped the pocket and pulled out a clear glass ball that looked a lot like a Christmas ornament complete with a little gold loop at the top. Heh. Whatever got the job done, she supposed. Inside the ball, gold, blue, and teal lights swirled. Beautiful, like the aurora borealis had been trapped inside. According to Jillian, it was the equivalent of an EMP bomb, guaranteed to short-circuit any magic in the vicinity. Chelle was a little disappointed that she had to use it so early in the game. But if she couldn't get into the basement, it wouldn't matter anyway.

With a groan, she pushed herself up from the floor. Her muscles were stiff and ached from her jarring landing. Superhealing aside, McAlister's magic had put her on her ass. She was going to be feeling it for a second or two. The logistics of getting the ball of magic to explode where she needed it posed a bit of a problem. She couldn't throw the damned thing. The magic guarding the door would simply repel it and send it shooting back at Chelle's face. That wouldn't be good. Her only option was to fight her way back through the current and smash the glass ball against the door. She'd failed to ask Jillian what would happen to her if she was caught in the magical explosion. *Crap.* Hopefully it wouldn't blow her to bits. Otherwise, this entire night really would be a disappointment, wouldn't it?

Chelle took a deep breath and blew it all out in a rush. *You've got this.* She was really going to have to come up with some new pep-talk material. Because she didn't feel like she *had anything* at this point. She kept low to the floor for her second attempt. Sort of like how surfers ducked under the wave on their way out from the beach.

She dug her toes in, pushed forward as the press of magic increased. Her skin tingled, her chest constricted, but Chelle soldiered on and she dove beneath the pulses. She reached the door and stood slowly so as not to be pushed back by the current of magic. She held the glass ornament in her right palm and brought it up to the doorway. A trickle of anxiety entered her bloodstream. This could all blow up in her face. Literally.

Here goes nothin' . . .

Chelle smashed the ornament against the door. Shards of glass dove into her skin and she sucked in a breath. Magic bled from the shattered ornament, defying gravity as it ran in rivulets that branched out along the wall like seeking vines. She braced herself for impact but the explosion of energy never came. Instead, the current of magic ebbed, no longer pushing against Chelle. The vibrations along her skin grew weaker and her chest no longer felt like it was being squeezed in a vise. The current faded into nothing and she could stand without feeling like she was fighting a gale-force wind. Success!

Okay . . . Now what?

She put both palms against the door and pushed. A latch gave way under the pressure and the door opened a crack. A noxious scent invaded Chelle's nostrils and she stifled a gag. Holy shit. Whatever was in McAlister's basement, it smelled like the devil's asshole. Definitely not an odor she recognized. Which might not mean anything . . . Or, it could be very, *very* bad.

Chelle never expected this to be easy. But she'd hoped it wouldn't be quite so hard. She pulled the secret door wide. Another wave of that gods-awful stench hit her and she thought about turning around right then and there. Maybe the Sortiari kept the decomposing bodies of unsuccessful thieves down there? Chelle shivered. *Gross.*

Her footfalls were quiet as she headed down the unusually steep staircase. Step by step, the darkness became more impenetrable, even to her heightened eyesight. She put her hands out to either side of her. Rough, cold stone scraped her palms. Even the sound of her own breath became muted the deeper she went. Chelle's gut clenched as the fetid scent intensified, choking her. She pulled her shirt over her nose and focused on *not* breathing. Berserkers didn't even smell this freaking bad. *Gods.* She might pass out from the smell long before she got her hands on the Sortiari's piece of the Alexandria key.

Pitch-black gave way to low light as Chelle hit the bottom three stairs. Her boots echoed on the cobbled stone floor as she moved deeper into a room that could only be described as a treasure trove. Holy shit. She'd hit the freaking jackpot! Neat and tidy, obviously organized by someone with a few OCD tendencies, the room sported supernatural and mundane relics alike. Some Chelle knew on sight, thought to be lost for eternity. Others, she yearned to learn more about. From the main chamber, several tunnels shot off in different directions. Did they lead to other chambers? More treasures? Damn. Chelle really wished she had the time to find out.

She strolled throughout the room. The relics were stored in alphabetical order! Chelle pumped her fist in the air. If McAlister were here right now, she'd be pretty tempted to kiss the bastard right on the mouth. He'd done half of her work for her. He'd obviously been arrogant enough to think his booby traps would deter thieves before they made it to his perfectly organized room. Too bad he hadn't counted on Chelle: tomb raider extraordinaire. She hightailed it to the As. Her finger traced the air beside the shelves. Ab . . . Af . . . Ak . . . Al. She bent down a bit, her eyes wide with excitement. *Jackpot.*

A rustling sound to Chelle's left drew her attention. She straightened, her gaze focused on one of the tunnels. A low rumble came from her right and she spun around toward another tunnel. All around her echoed the scrape and rustle of something approaching. Her gut tightened and adrenaline dumped into her system. She was beginning to think those tunnels didn't lead to other treasure chambers. And apparently, she wasn't in here alone.

Shit, shit, *shit*.

That's what she got for counting her chickens before they hatched.

Their mate was in danger.

Wind rustled their fur, myriad scents invaded their nostrils. Creatures darted in and out of their line of vision. Rabbits, squirrels, mice, small birds that bedded down in the tall grass for the night. They wanted to chase. To hunt. To feed. They put those distractions to the back of their mind, however. Nothing was more important than their mate.

Worry cut into their chest. Clawed at the back of their mind. Adrenaline rushed through their blood and they pushed their pace harder, running faster than they ever had. So many miles to cross and time wasn't on their side.

Have . . . to get . . . to her. Protect. Ours.

The wolf gave a shake of his head. Those thoughts belonged to the man and they felt funny in their mind. Foreign. Their thoughts were instinct now. A guiding force that didn't need words to articulate it. Words slowed them down. Disrupted their focus.

They knew what they had to do. There was no point in thinking about it. Reason belonged to Gunnar and he was no longer in control. They worked in tandem, their minds as close to one as they'd ever be. The wolf knew only action and he urged Gunnar to trust. To let go. To allow them to do what had to be done.

Together.

Miles passed beneath their feet as they ran. In the distance, the lights of a city burned like stars in the sky. Fatigue pulled at their muscles, burned in their lungs with every breath. The pads of their feet stung with each step but they pushed on. They wouldn't stop until they reached her.

The breeze shifted and they slowed to put their snout to the wind. Faint, but they caught their mate's scent. They came to a stop and let out a low howl that echoed around them. With a yip, they changed course, their claws digging into the earth as they picked up speed. Not much farther. With sure steps they darted back and forth in a zigzag pattern as they ran, hoping to catch a stronger scent. They shifted course yet again, veering to the right and continued on their path, allowing their keen senses to guide their way.

A building loomed in the distance. Glass, metal, concrete. It smelled of magic, musk, and danger. They blew out a chuff of breath to clear their nostrils, but it didn't stop the tingle. Their pace slowed, legs stretched out, body hunched as they stalked closer to the structure. A low hiss surrounded them and a whimper worked its way up their throat as they took a breath that burned their lungs.

Silver. In the air.

Their thick hide would protect them but only temporarily. They didn't dare take another breath as they sprinted across the grounds for the door that sat ajar at the front of the building. Pain radiated through them, cinders of silver dust peppered their hide. They needed air but if any more of the silver worked its way into their body, they might not survive it.

Forty yards . . . thirty yards . . . ten. They pushed as hard and fast as they could. Their legs stretched as they leaped through the open doorway of the building. Claws scraped along the cold stone floor as they skidded across the slick surface. Exhaustion won out and their legs collapsed beneath them. They lay panting, dragging in desperate lungsful of breath. The scent of their mate was stronger in this room. She'd made it through the cloud of silver dust. They weren't surprised, she was an extraordinary female, but it sparked their ire that she would put herself in the path of danger yet again.

Silver was absent from the air, but magic lay thick and heavy like a fog. They let out a snort to clear it from their nostrils but still it tingled and burned and left a foul taste in their mouth. Witchcraft. Anxious energy skittered through their veins. Old superstitions died hard and magic wielders caused nothing but trouble. Rest would have to wait. They could replenish their strength later. Every minute was precious and they had none to waste.

Through the layers of magic that thickened the air, they caught their mate's scent. They padded across the vast open space to a far wall. A door that didn't look like a door sat ajar. With their muzzle, they worked it open until it swung wide enough to accommodate the bulk of their body.

The smell of rot invaded their senses, sending a wave of panic through them. Recognition tickled their instinct. The scent was familiar and yet . . . not. Something from memory or history. They weren't sure. Dangerous. Mindless. Violent. Murderous. Hungry. Urgency sent them down the steep stairway. The narrow path almost didn't accommodate them. Their body took up the entire space and the rough stone walls on either side of them rasped over their fur. Darkness permeated their vision, made it nearly impossible to see the path ahead. Their step faltered and they tumbled down several steps before they could find their footing and right themselves once again.

Wrong. Everything about this place was wrong.

The smell, the tight space. The steep descent that put

pressure on their ears and made them ring. The lack of sound. Of any visible light. They wouldn't be deterred, no matter how wrong it felt. Not until they found their mate.

They continued down the staircase for what felt like much too long. The pitch-black turned to a muted gray and they could finally make out the rough stone of the walls that brushed their body. An enraged shriek made its way to their ears. They knew that sound all too well. It would have amused them if not for the circumstances.

Time had run out. They took the last few steps five at a time. A large chamber opened up to them, with shelves lining the walls and multiple treasures stored there. At the far end of the room, their mate fought for her life. Her attackers, creatures out of nightmare.

Daugar. The again-walkers.

The modern-day word for what they were eluded them. Creatures of legend. Undead. Viking warriors resurrected as animate corpses. They rose from their graves as wisps of smoke. Untouchable. The *daugars'* appetites knew no satiation. Their strength and speed had no equal. Larger than an above-average warrior, they could crush their opponent as though he were an insect. According to legend only the most stalwart hero could defeat a *daugr.* A hero pure of heart and stout of mettle.

One *daugr* would have been impossible to defend against. Their mate had managed to stand strong against five. It was obvious her strength was flagging. She wouldn't last much longer. Could they be the hero she needed? Could they save their mate from death incarnate? If it came down to it, they'd sure as hell die trying.

CHAPTER
27

If not for the fact that she was about to be seriously pwned, Chelle would've taken a moment to laugh at the fact that she felt like an extra in *The Walking Dead*. That is, if the zombies were on steroids, the size of a Mini Cooper, with the strength and speed of Superman and the hunger of a competition eater. She'd heard the legends of souped-up zombies, but she'd never believed them. Had never even seen one until tonight. Obviously at the end of all the surrounding tunnels, McAlister had them stowed away and waiting for an intruder to show up to ring the dinner bell.

Ding! Ding! Ding!

But Chelle wasn't ready to check out yet.

You didn't grow up being Ronan Daly's sister and not learn a thing or two about how to fight. Her twin had cultivated quite the reputation as a warrior during the Sortiari's attempted eradication of the vampires. He'd passed some of those fighting skills on to her, later, after they'd fled to Ireland and joined Siobhan's coven.

She was scrappy, damn it! But scrappy didn't quite cut it when your opponents were *literally* already corpses.

Welp, you didn't think McAlister would make it easy for you, did you, Chelle?

Kudos to the director. His security was some next-level shit.

Chelle had given it her best effort to defend herself, but five against one wasn't the best odds. She'd been fighting these undead bastards for at least a year. At least, it felt that way. Her arms were lead weights at her sides. Her legs might as well have been mired in quicksand. Her strength diminished with each blow she delivered, and though she healed almost instantaneously, her many injuries were becoming tougher to rebound from. Avoiding the snapping jaws of their ravenous mouths was taking all of her concentration.

All she'd wanted was the opportunity to learn more about what she was and how she came to be. Instead, she was about to become zombie-chow.

A large silver-gray form sprang from the foot of the staircase and burst into the chamber, stealing Chelle's focus. Her step faltered and a large fist swung at her face. Bits of flesh hung from the zombie's forearm, and when its knuckles made contact with her jaw, it left behind a smear of sticky wetness that made her gag. She shook her head to clear the stars from her vision just in time to duck and roll to the left in order to miss a pair of eagerly grabby hands from zombie number two.

Through the chaos, a low menacing growl made its way to her ears. Chelle knew that sound. Had heard it echo in the back of Gunnar's mind. The wolf had come out to play, and he didn't sound very happy. *Shit.* If he'd found her, he must've shaken Jillian down for the information. Chelle hoped he hadn't been too hard on her. She'd hear about this later, she was sure . . .

The wolf pounced without preamble. Chelle was taken aback by his sheer size. The wolf was massive. She wondered how he'd managed to squeeze down the narrow staircase. His beautiful silver-gray fur quivered with every shift of sinewy muscle. Chelle didn't think she'd ever seen a fiercer or more breathtakingly beautiful creature in her entire life.

It seemed since she'd met Gunnar, they'd been fighting someone or something. Maybe they would've had a better chance of settling into their tether if they'd ever get a second of peace. Of course, this particular little bit of unrest was her own fault.

Another swipe of a rotting fist whizzed through the air toward her face. She caught the flash of motion from the corner of her eye and ducked before the zombie managed to coldcock her. *Okay, Chelle, time to get your head in the game.*

Gunnar had a way of making the world stand still for her. Those freakishly superhuman corpses weren't standing still for anyone, though. Like when they'd fought the berserkers, she had to let Gunnar fight his fight while she focused on hers. She had no idea how to kill a zombie. Her best bet was to take off their heads. Worked for every other supernatural on the planet. Why not these guys? The dagger she wielded in her right hand was deadly, but it wasn't going to decapitate anyone. And the Glock holstered at her hip wasn't going to do a damned bit of good against creatures who wouldn't take any damage. None of Chelle's enhanced abilities would help her in this fight. Funny, it was almost comforting to know the playing field had been leveled. She felt almost mundane.

Almost. But not quite.

With Gunnar at her side, a renewed burst of strength surged within her. Chelle fought for all she was worth. She stabbed, kicked, and punched at the zombies, meeting each attack with renewed vigor. The wolf snarled as it tore the head from one of them. Its rotting body dropped to the stone floor, twitching for the barest moment before it stilled completely.

Gods, her mate was magnificent.

Chelle might not have been able to take the head off a monster zombie, but the least she could do was offer up a distraction to help Gunnar get the upper hand.

"You don't want to eat him! Think about all the fur you'll get caught in your teeth!" Four zombie heads and one large wolf head turned toward Chelle at the sound of her voice.

The zombies sniffed the air. The wolf's eyes narrowed, and though Chelle couldn't hear his thoughts, she could read the exasperation in the animal's expression. The zombies converged in a blink and Chelle crouched low before propelling herself up toward the ceiling. She tucked and flipped forward before coming down to the floor at the zombies' backs. She was fast, but they were faster. In this case, only brute force was going to stop them. Thankfully, she had a three-hundred-pound wolf to take care of that.

The wolf used the momentary distraction to his benefit. He pounced on the zombie toward the rear of the pack, taking it down to the floor. The other three turned, ready to make a quick meal out of her protector, but Chelle wasn't going to let that happen.

"Over here!" Her words rang out over the din of the creatures' wet, hungry growls. "Free meal, come and get me!"

She couldn't fight them, but she could sure as hell elude them. While the wolf made short work of the second zombie, Chelle lured the other three away. Despite her disdain for the Sortiari, she was loath to destroy any of the relics stored here. The collection McAlister had amassed was invaluable.

Like a spring, she bounced from one corner of the

chamber to the other. She leaped into the air, twisted and
landed on her feet. Took flight once again before landing
at the opposite end of the room. From the corner of her
eye she noticed the wolf thrash its massive head, throwing the severed head of its prey to one side. Gods. That
couldn't have tasted good. *Blech.* Chelle bent her knees,
ready to jump again, but gave the wolf just enough time
to snag one more zombie from the pack before she continued to distract the others.

Three zombies dead. Well, dead-*er.* Two more to go.

The two remaining monsters must've been smarter
than their pals, if that were even possible. Rather than self-
ishly pursue their dinner, they teamed up to take their
opponent down. The wolf let out a low, dangerous snarl
as the two zombies circled him. He mirrored their actions,
the silver hairs on his back standing on end and his lips
pulled back in a snarl that revealed the deadly points of
his canines.

"Over here!" Chelle shouted. "He's not half as delicious as I am!"

They were obviously through playing games. *Damn it.*
Chelle had done her best to give Gunnar the upper hand,
but it was time to jump back into the fray. A wave of crip-
pling fear stole over her and Chelle buried the feeling to
the soles of her feet. She wouldn't be able to live with herself if anything happened to Gunnar. No way would she
let those rotting pieces of shit hurt her mate.

Chelle channeled every ounce of anxious energy she
felt into her attack. She leaped onto the back of one of the
zombies, stifling a gag as the stench of rot invaded her
nostrils. She brought her dagger down and stabbed into
the zombie's neck. A black, viscous liquid oozed from the
wound and the stench intensified to the point that Chelle
thought she might pass out.

She could safely say she now knew what "god-awful" smelled like.

With a jerk, she pulled the dagger free and stabbed down once again. She hacked at the creature's neck, bringing her arm down again and again until its head hung at an odd angle, only holding on by its spine and bits of sinew. Chelle swallowed down the bile that rose in her throat. She'd seen some truly disgusting things over the course of her existence, but this took the cake. The zombie's step faltered and it released its grip on the wolf and shuffled back several steps.

The wolf used the opportunity to free itself of the remaining zombie that had latched on to its back. He reached around with his massive head and locked his jaws around the creature's head. With a quick jerk, the wolf flung the zombie forward. Its body flailed like a rag doll and a sickening snap preceded its head being torn from its shoulders.

Blech. Disgusting.

Without even taking a second to rest, the wolf pounced on the remaining zombie. With its head already partially severed, it took little effort at all to finish it off. Chelle watched in awe as the wolf scooped up the zombie's lifeless, rotting corpse in its jaws. He carried it to Chelle and dropped it at her feet as though it were a prize.

How . . . sweet?

Chelle reached out and threaded her fingers through the wolf's silky fur. He let out a contented sound, almost a purr. She dropped to her knees and met his eyes.

"Holy shit," she said on a breath. "Am I ever glad you're here."

Their mate was pleased. Her lips curved into a sweet smile and their chest swelled with pride. They'd defeated the *daugar* and proved themselves worthy of her. She would never have reason to doubt them or their bond. They were strong. Capable. Powerful.

Alpha.

"Holy shit. Am I ever glad you're here."

The affection in her voice warmed them. The gratitude in her wide green eyes held them rapt. Her scent quickened their blood and her beauty stole their breath. But her recklessness sparked their ire and the fear of losing her had nearly crippled them.

They gave her outstretched arm a quick nip. Not hard enough to break the skin, but enough to let her know they weren't pleased.

Her brow furrowed. She leveled her gaze before letting it drop to one side. "I know. I fucked up. Big-time. I'm sorry."

Relief washed over them, but the night was far from over. Their mate was safe, but their pack was divided. If they managed to save the male who coveted these treasures, he might discover their mate's attempt to steal from him and forgive her rather than seek retribution. But if they didn't intervene, the vampire king and possibly other vampires would be killed. His pack would fight on both sides and the loss could be catastrophic. As Alpha, it was their job to protect those under their care. There would be no rest. No opportunity to nuzzle their head against their mate's fragrant throat. It was time to fight once again. They'd killed five deadly *daugar* tonight. A feeling of invincibility crested within them. It was time to prove their power to anyone who might doubt it.

Their mate didn't understand their thoughts. Not in the way she understood Gunnar's at least. They needed to make words. To tell her what they needed to do and where they needed to go.

She searched their eyes, her expression soft. "Gunnar? Are you in there?"

On the night of the full moon, Gunnar gave himself completely over to instinct. It was the consciousness they shared. Their duality had no barrier to separate their spirits. It had never frustrated them until now. When they so desperately needed her to understand.

"I can hear you." Her voice bore a trace of wonder. "Sort of. I know you're trying to tell me something, but . . . I can't quite grasp it. Let's get out of here. Off the property to where it's safe. Then we can try and figure this out, okay?"

Safe was good. As far away from the stench of rotting corpses, and magic, and the burn of silver, the better. They gave a sharp nod of their head before using their snout to urge their mate out ahead and up the narrow staircase. If any more *daugar* came from the dark tunnels, they'd rather take the brunt of their attack and give their mate a chance to escape.

They were once again plunged into darkness as they made their way back up the staircase. The tight space made them nervous but the presence of their mate directly ahead comforted them. After tonight, they'd keep her by their side always. And perhaps after tonight's unsuccessful mission, she'd abandon her quest for knowledge and let the relics she sought fade back into obscurity.

Their ascent seemed to take much too long. Their ears popped from the change in pressure and they gave a hard shake of their head. A hand came back to rest on their head and their mate said, "I know, I feel it, too," before continuing upward.

Minutes passed and they emerged from the doorway. The artificial light burned their eyes and the scent of magic lingered to scorch their nostrils. They longed for a breath of fresh air. For the silver light of the full moon. And for a soft breeze to cleanse any residual magic from their fur.

Their mate glanced around the vast, bright room. She turned and flashed them a grin that ended on a cringe. "Do I know how to party or what?"

So cavalier. Apparently the nip they'd given her earlier wasn't enough to express their displeasure with her reckless nature. They let out a low growl and headed toward the exit. She put a staying hand on their shoulder. "Hang on. We might get doused with silver dust."

They showed they agreed with a chuff of breath.

Her expression transformed from chagrin to concern. "You got a dose of that, huh? It's a good thing you're strong. Otherwise I would have had to follow you to Valhalla to kick your ass from coming after me tonight."

Her attempt at humor was unappreciated. They would have crossed a lake of molten silver to get to her. They let out a low growl.

"You might not think I'm funny," she remarked. "But not everyone agrees with you."

Did she take nothing seriously? When the pack was safe and the full moon passed, they would have a long talk with their mate about the way she disregarded her own safety.

"All right. So we know what to expect. I honestly have no idea if the silver disperses when a motion sensor is tripped, but I think it's a safe bet." She pointed to a garden at the far end of the property. "My car's parked over there on the other side of the fence. We run for it. Don't take a breath, don't stop for anything." She threaded her fingers through his fur and drew in a deep breath before she crouched low. "Ready? Go!"

As before, they sprinted across the grounds. They heard the low hiss of the silver dust releasing into the air and they held their breath in their lungs. Their mate ran up ahead, her own speed a blur compared to theirs. She moved like a berserker or one of the *daugar*. Awestruck by her power and speed, they followed hot on her heels, determined to show her that they were just as fast as she was. They reached the perimeter of the property seconds after her and leaped over the fence alongside her.

Breath filled their lungs and they shook out their fur to clear it of any silver dust. Leftover adrenaline coursed through their veins, masking any pain they might have felt.

"Oh gods, are you okay?" Their mate's concerned voice filled their ears. She frantically rustled their fur with her fingers as though to brush away the silver. Her palms came to rest on either side of their muzzle and she looked into their eyes. "Gunnar? Are you hurt?"

They canted their head to one side. Her concern made their chest ache with tender emotion. They couldn't resist the temptation and leaned in close to lap at her face. Laughter filled the silence as she squeezed her eyes shut and wrinkled her nose.

"I'm going to take that as an a-okay." She dug a key from her pocket and pressed a button. The car's lights flashed with a chirp and she pulled open the door. "Don't ruin the upholstery," she said with a wink.

They growled. Their mate wasn't half as funny as she thought she was.

"Yes I am," she replied. "I'm hilarious."

They both froze and exchanged a glance.

"I understood you."

She certainly had. Their mate was *extraordinary*.

CHAPTER
28

Okay, so it wasn't like she'd heard Gunnar's thoughts, per se. More like, she'd understood the sentiment behind them. The wolf still held dominion over his consciousness, but somehow, Chelle had sensed a unity between Gunnar and the animal. Beneath that oneness, she'd found him. Smug. And not amused by her attempt at humor.

The wolf climbed into the car, tail wagging, and settled down in the passenger seat. Chelle climbed in after him and got behind the wheel. "Okay, don't get too excited. I have a feeling this isn't going to be an exact science." She spoke to both of them now and hoped they understood. "I can't hear your thoughts like I can hear Gunnar's. I think I can get the gist of it. But I'm going to need your help."

His square head canted to one side as his golden eyes studied her. She could almost hear Gunnar's sigh of resignation as he waited for her to tell him what she needed.

Chelle slid the key into the ignition and pushed the button to start the engine. As much as she wanted to sit and figure out how to properly communicate with the wolf, she needed to get as far from the Sortiari's stronghold as possible before someone showed back up and realized she'd been poking around the place. She pulled out from where she'd hidden the BMW and onto the road, heading south. The wolf let out a mournful howl and grabbed her shirtsleeve in his teeth, giving her arm a jerk in the opposite direction.

"Hey, watch it! You're going to make me wreck."

The wolf growled and Chelle caught the wisps of thoughts. She was going the wrong way. There was somewhere else they needed to be. Their night wasn't over yet.

Chelle checked her rearview mirror before flipping a U-turn in the middle of the road. She headed in the opposite direction and the wolf's lips spread in what she swore was a smile. Knowing what the wolf wanted was a guessing game at best, and grasping on to the thin strings of thought would take too long for her to decipher what he was trying to tell her.

She was about five seconds from saying, "What is it, Lassie?" but she was pretty sure she'd get more than a nip on her arm if she did. "Argh!" Chelle gripped the steering wheel as she let out a groan. "We're headed north. To what?"

A red haze of violence crested in the wolf's mind. Aggression. Hate. Vengeance. So many ugly emotions that they compressed Chelle's lungs and squeezed the air from her chest. "Shit!" The realization hit her and she jerked the wheel, sending the car careening on the highway before she righted it. The wolf let out an enraged snarl. He might as well have shouted, "Jesus, Chelle, watch what the hell you're doing!"

"Mikhail." The word burst from Chelle's lips. The stress of everything they'd gone through tonight had her so rattled, she'd completely forgotten what had bought her McAlister's distraction in the first place. "Aren fucked you over, didn't he?"

His disdainful snort couldn't have confirmed it any better.

"That asshole." Chelle swore Gunnar wouldn't have to take care of that traitor because she was going to kill him herself. She hit a button on the display screen on the dash and said, "Call Bria." Chelle trusted Jenner's mate more than anyone. And if anyone knew exactly where Mikhail was tonight, it was her.

"Hey, Chelle?" Bria answered. "Where are you? Lucas said that—"

"No time, Bria!" Chelle cut her off. "Where's the meeting tonight?"

"I—what's going on?"

What part of "no time" didn't she understand? "Where, Bria? I'll fill you in later!" She hated to be a demanding bitch, but sometimes the only way to get shit done was to be a demanding bitch.

"They're meeting at an old diner off Highway 1. About twenty minutes from the city. It's abandoned or closed down or something. Called . . . Cup of Joe's, I think."

It might not be an exact location, but it was a start. "Who's with him?"

This time, Bria didn't so much as pause. "Jenner and Vanessa as far as McAlister is concerned. But he took Ronan with him as well. Mikhail didn't trust McAlister to follow the rules."

No one could ever accuse Mikhail Aristov of being foolish. Knowing Ronan was about to be ambushed by a bunch of berserkers with a pack of werewolves at their back didn't exactly fill her with confidence, though. Chelle punched her foot down on the accelerator. "See if you can get Jenner on the phone. Tell him to get everyone out of there."

"Chelle." Bria's voice rose with concern. "What's going on?"

"It might be nothing." Wrong. It was definitely something. But Chelle didn't want to get everyone on the home front riled up just yet. "We're on our way to them now. Just hold down the fort until I call."

"We're . . . ? Who are you with?"

"Gunnar. I'll explain later. Just see if you can get a hold of Jenner." Chelle ended the call and hit the voice command on the GPS. "How do I get to Cup of Joe's on Highway 1?"

Chelle said a silent prayer under her breath that the place wasn't so old it wouldn't be in Google's database. She waited as the maps function did its search and let out a sigh of relief when the computerized voice gave her directions. She turned her attention to Gunnar. "I hope you have reinforcements coming."

He let out a loud bark.

Thank the gods. "Good." The odds were definitely stacked against them but Chelle would take any help they could get. "I have a feeling that taking on five hungry superzombies is going to seem like a walk in the park compared to what we're about to go up against."

The wolf's answering half growl/half whine told Chelle exactly what he thought about her use of the word "we're."

"Sorry, buddy, but if you're fighting, I'm fighting. There's no way in hell I'm going to drop you off and wait in the car."

He growled and Chelle caught another glimpse of thought that was one hundred percent Gunnar. He absolutely wanted her to wait in the car.

"Not gonna happen." He could nip her arm, her leg, or whatever the hell else he wanted, later. After they saved Mikhail, Ronan, and the others, and took care of Aren and his treasonous bullshit once and for all. "We're better as a team and you know it. So don't even think you can growl at me and put me in my place. Aren is going to be gunning for you and someone has to have your back."

The wolf quieted. Maybe Chelle had finally managed to make her point. Not once, but twice, they'd faced impossible odds and surmounted them together. Not even Gunnar could argue with that logic.

"You don't have to worry about me," Chelle said. His concern for her made her chest swell with tender emotion. "Ronan's there, too, and he's not going to let anything happen to me." Her brother had always protected her. The fact that she was tethered wouldn't change the fact that he'd look out for her.

"The only way we're going to minimize the damage is if we work together." Chelle wasn't simply talking about her and Gunnar. "Your reinforcements need to know we're all on the same side."

The wolf gave an agreeing shake of his massive head.

"In one half mile, your destination is on the left."

At the GPS's prompt, Chelle looked up the road. The restaurant was definitely abandoned. A dim light from within the building was the only sign of anyone inside. Rather than pull up and alert everyone to their presence, she pulled off the highway and turned off the headlights. They could cover a half mile in a blink and they needed the element of surprise.

"This is our stop," she said as she killed the engine. "Have any idea whether or not your posse is here yet?"

The wolf let out a chuff of breath. Again, Chelle picked up on a gossamer tendril of thought that told her Gunnar would know if they were here once he scented the air.

Made sense. Werewolves had a pretty fantastic sense of smell.

"I think we should split up." The wolf growled and Chelle held up her hands. "Don't get all bent out of shape. It's safer if we flank the building and sniff out any potential threats. No one is going to get the jump on me. Unless the berserkers brought a bunch of zombies with them, I won't have any trouble compelling anyone. And you need to see if your backup is here. I'll head to the west, you take the east. We'll circle around and meet in the middle."

Whether or not he wanted to acknowledge it, Chelle knew both Gunnar and his wolf recognized it was a solid plan. For a moment, he simply stared at her as though trying to decide whether or not he'd give consent for them to split up. Arrogant male. But this time, Chelle figured it wouldn't hurt to let him think she was leaving the decision up to him. There would be plenty of time for power plays later.

He let out a slow sigh. Resignation. Not exactly the victory she wanted, but she'd take it. "I'll be fine. Promise."

The wolf leaned in and pressed his forehead to hers. The tether that bound them tugged at Chelle's chest as she was overcome with emotion. Gunnar Falk truly was an extraordinary male. And he belonged to *her*.

After a long moment he pulled away. Chelle drew in a deep breath and prepared herself for yet another fight. "Let's get this over with. I don't know about you, but I'm ready to call it a night."

She opened the car door and got out. The wolf climbed out behind her. He gave her one last piercing look before he took off toward the east at a trot. Chelle waited until he was out of sight before reaching into her pocket and retrieving the relic she'd managed to swipe from McAlister's stash. She tucked it into the center console of the car before locking it. If Gunnar knew she'd managed to steal it, she'd get more than a nip on the arm.

Two pieces down. One more to go . . .

In the center of the old restaurant, Mikhail sat across from Trenton McAlister at the only table in the building that wasn't a booth. Vanessa sat on his right, while Jenner stood at his left shoulder. Behind McAlister, near the entrance, stood a mountain of a male, his arms folded across his wide chest. Shifter. Bear, if Mikhail had to guess based on the male's musky scent. At any rate, he looked formidable. Not that he was worried. Jenner was worth two bear shifters. If McAlister thought to intimidate Mikhail with the muscle he'd chosen to bring along, he'd be sorely disappointed. It took more than brute strength to make him nervous.

"Vanessa, I'd like you to meet Trenton McAlister." Mikhail didn't see any reason not to get straight to business. The faster they got this nonsense over with, the faster he could get Vanessa home and put Claire at ease.

"I know who he is." Vanessa's little voice was confident and strong. "He's one of the sotori men."

Mikhail chuckled. McAlister didn't seem quite as amused by Vanessa's mispronunciation or her lack of reverence. "That's right. He's asked to meet you, and since we're being polite, that's why we're here tonight."

Vanessa turned to Mikhail. "Trenton is a mage."

Mikhail hid his surprise behind a mask of passivity. How did she know that? McAlister's interest, however, wasn't so subtle. He leaned forward in his chair, hands splayed out on the table. His eyes narrowed as he studied Vanessa and Mikhail's stomach clenched with a wave of anxious energy.

"Do you know what a mage is, Vanessa?" McAlister asked.

"Not really," she replied. "Bria says a mage is sort of like Naya. Someone who can do magic."

Mikhail bristled. The less the Sortiari knew about them, the better. Conveying that to Vanessa might be a bit of a problem, though. He chided himself for not coaching her prior to the meeting so that she would know what she was and wasn't allowed to say. In truth, Mikhail often forgot that little children sometimes had very large ears. It was something he'd have to remind himself of as his own son grew older.

McAlister offered an indulgent smile. "You don't seem surprised that I can do magic, Vanessa."

"I live with vampires," she said in a no-nonsense way. "Would you be surprised?"

Mikhail stifled his amusement. Full of sass. She reminded him so much of Claire.

"Who told you I was a mage?" McAlister asked.

Vanessa looked askance at Mikhail and she worried her little lip between her teeth. "It's all right," he said to her. "You can tell the truth."

She met McAlister's gaze head-on. "I had an awake dream about you."

The director of the Sortiari's eyes shone with fear. It was the first time Mikhail had ever seen the powerful, emotionless male truly rattled.

"Do you often have awake dreams?"

"Bria asked me that, too," Vanessa said. "Sometimes."

McAlister's posture straightened. "Your awake dreams are premonitions. Have you had more than one premonition about me?"

"I don't know," Vanessa replied. "Sometimes I don't remember them."

"I need you to remember." McAlister's tone sharpened slightly. "I need you to think very hard."

"What's this about?" Mikhail had agreed to let the

director meet Vanessa. He had *not* agreed to let the child be bullied or interrogated. "I think it's time you came clean."

"This doesn't concern you, Aristov." McAlister obviously wasn't interested in playing nice. Not much of a shock there. "Tell me, Vanessa, what else have you seen?"

"I saw a girl with red hair," Vanessa said after a moment. Her gaze didn't falter as she stared McAlister down as though he weren't one of the most powerful males in the world. "And she doesn't like you very much."

Beads of sweat gathered on McAlister's forehead. Whoever this red-haired girl was, Mikhail wanted to shake her hand because just the mention of her could cause the director of the Sortiari to quake in his boots.

"Where is she?" McAlister leaned across the table, his brows pinched.

"I don't know," Vanessa said.

"Don't lie to me." McAlister's tone became deathly serious. Magic sparked the air and Jenner took a step toward Vanessa at the same moment Mikhail put his arm around her. *"Where is she?"*

"He has her hidden." Vanessa's voice didn't even quaver. She was braver than most, standing strong in the face of McAlister's anger. "I don't know where she is."

McAlister didn't ask who "he" was, making Mikhail think the male knew exactly who Vanessa was talking about.

Mikhail had finally had enough of this dog-and-pony show. It sparked his ire that McAlister had known about Vanessa's visions and sought to use her to his benefit. Rumors had circulated for centuries that the Sortiari used seers to predict the future they sought to affect. If he thought to take Vanessa away, to use her for their benefit, then McAlister had another thing coming. Mikhail would put the bastard in the ground before he let him use the girl for his own selfish interests.

"We're done here." Mikhail pushed out his chair.

McAlister paid him no mind, his attention focused on Vanessa. "Will she come for me?"

Vanessa shrugged her little shoulders. "You're not the only one looking for her. I think it depends on who finds her first."

Mikhail braced his hands on the table and leaned down. "I said, we're *done* here."

"Who else is looking for her?" McAlister looked as though his head might blow from his shoulders at any second. "Tell me!"

Vanessa's eyes glazed over and her expression took on a dreamy quality. "The madman and the beast," she replied sleepily. "Whichever one finds her first will seal your fate."

McAlister's eyes went wide.

"Jenner." It was time to get Vanessa the hell out of here and away from McAlister. "Take Vanessa to the car. We're leaving."

Mikhail didn't know what Vanessa was talking about and he didn't think he wanted to. Everything she'd told McAlister tonight only served to further pique his interest in her rather than diminish it. It was stupid to have agreed to this meeting. Of course, it had been Mikhail's own curiosity about Vanessa that prompted him to agree to come in the first place. Without hesitation Jenner picked Vanessa up in his arms and headed for the doorway. The bear shifter took a wide step to one side, obviously not interested in any altercations. Mikhail turned to follow, ready to put this wretched night behind him.

"Oracles aren't simply fortune-tellers, Aristov." Mikhail stopped at McAlister's words. "She'll only grow more powerful. You should give her to us now. We're the only ones who can properly train her and teach her how to contain that power."

Bullshit. Mikhail whipped around to face the director of the Sortiari. "She's not a commodity to be traded. She is part of my coven. *Mine.* Under my protection. This is the last time you'll see her. If you try to seek her out again, any peace that's been forged between us will be nullified."

Mikhail turned on a heel and strode toward the doorway. An explosion blew out the left wall, sending glass over them like rain. The force blew Mikhail off his feet and he landed on his back several feet from the door. He pushed himself up to find Jenner crouched low, body curved over Vanessa's to shield her. Mikhail's ears rang. The tiny cuts that marred his skin began to heal and a broken bone in his right wrist knitted back together as he pushed himself up to stand. He should have known better than to trust McAlister.

"Jenner, to your left!" Mikhail caught the flash of motion moments before the first berserker breached the blown-out wall.

It seemed he and McAlister both had been sold out. And all hell was about to break loose.

CHAPTER
29

The explosion knocked them off their feet. They were still thirty yards from the building and their mate was nowhere in sight. Acrid smoke filled their nostrils and blurred their vision. They stood and gave a shake of their head to clear the haze away. The wind shifted, and they caught the scent of their pack. Individual signatures that indicated both Aren's group and Sven's group were present. They hated the divisiveness. Their family had been fractured due to the ambitious deceit of one male. After tonight, that rift would be fixed and the troublemaker would be banished.

First, though, they had to survive the berserkers.

Rather than run headlong into battle, they kept their course to round the perimeter of the building in order to meet their mate like they'd planned. They wouldn't be able to focus, wouldn't be worth a damn in a fight, until they knew she was safe.

"Jenner, to your left!"

A voice shouted over the din, drawing their attention. They knew the name Jenner. Their mate had spoken it.

Vampire. If she heard the warning shout, she'd change course to help. Stay on the path or rush to the vampire's aid? Indecision warred within them. Too many variables. They'd arrived too late . . .

A body crashed into them. They rolled in a tangle of limbs and snapping jaws, already fighting before they'd even come to a complete stop. The sound of their snarls rose above the commotion of the fight inside the building. Sharp teeth latched onto their neck, sinking past their hide into their skin. The scent of blood filled the air before they rolled and shook themselves loose of their opponent's hold. Not a berserker. Their eyes narrowed on the wolf that stood before them, lips curled back to reveal sharp canines stained with their blood.

The traitor let loose a menacing growl. They didn't have time for this petty bullshit. The berserkers would kill them all and leave them to rot. Nothing mattered but their vendetta. The traitor's attempt to usurp control of the pack meant nothing to the berserkers. Delivering death and destruction were the beasts' only goals. They cared not who helped them—or who stood in their way.

They circled the other wolf, wary. They were Alpha for a reason. Their strength, their character, and their cunning made it so. A sound from their right drew their attention and they flinched. The heavy musk of a beast reached their nostrils and they let out of chuff of breath to clear the offensive scent from their mind. They couldn't afford any distractions despite the chaos that erupted around them.

They had to get to their mate. Ensure her safety. Then, they'd deal with the traitor.

The other wolf refused to back down. This was a fight for dominance though a formal challenge hadn't been issued. The male thought to circumvent the tradition of the battle arena by catching them unawares. With the pack divided, he knew they'd be distracted. The male was determined as well as crafty. They would make him pay.

Their adversary attacked without warning. Their snarls were muted as the male went for their throat once again. His teeth sank past their hide, through skin and muscle. With a rough shake of his head, he tried to tear the wound open. He wanted them to bleed out. A yip of pain gathered in their chest. The wound was deep and the coppery scent of blood released into the air. The male's plan to distract them had worked, but it wouldn't again.

They fought with every ounce of strength they possessed. Bodies rolled, claws dug into fur, pulling it from the roots. Their teeth bit down, again and again. The taste of blood on their tongue only spurred their violence on. Their rival whimpered with every blow delivered. They went for his ankle, to sever the Achilles, the way they disabled their prey. Their jaw latched on but he kicked them free.

The momentum of the fight shifted as their rival's fear scented the air. He should be afraid. He should run as far from here as possible and never come back. The hackles rose on the back of their neck as they let loose a menacing growl that conveyed all of the power they possessed and then some. The male had two choices: back down now, or die.

Their warning growl was joined by several others. Eyes shone in the darkness as the large bodies of four of their pack members stepped forward. The wolves came to their side, standing a couple of steps back in order to show their respect for their leader. This battle would not be fought one-on-one as their rival had hoped. The pack would have their Alpha's back. The male who sought to usurp them would be wise to remember what it meant to be part of a pack. They were one. And they fought as one.

His injuries were many, but not severe enough to disable him. The male turned, his tail high as he retreated. The sound of his loping steps faded off into silence and disappointment burned in their chest that they hadn't had the opportunity to deliver retribution for his betrayal. Now, though, they could go to their mate. Her safety was tantamount.

They took off toward the building that had all but been destroyed in the explosion. Those members of the pack that had come to their aid followed close behind, their footfalls a welcome presence in their ears. The wound at their throat pulled and they pressed on despite the pain and blood that matted their fur. They were of one mind, one purpose. Their step faltered. The breeze carried the sweetest scent to their snout and they breathed it deep into their lungs. They veered to the left, to the back side of the building, and their pace increased to a full-out run. Their mate was in sight. No more than fifty yards away. Nothing would deter them.

Nothing except the black-eyed beast that stood in their path.

Talk about showing up the second the shit hit the fan . . .

Chelle pushed herself up from the ground, for the second time tonight feeling like she'd been leveled by a semi barreling down the highway at eighty miles per hour. The explosion had to have been a distraction, something to cause chaos in order to give the berserkers the advantage in the ensuing fight.

"Jenner, to your left!"

Mikhail's voice called out and Chelle's heart leaped up into her throat. Where was Ronan? He was here with Mikhail. Bria had said as much. But so far she hadn't heard his voice. Hadn't heard anyone call out for him. He wasn't close enough for her to even pick up on a whisper of thought.

Shit.

She'd promised Gunnar they'd check the perimeter of the building and meet in the middle. If she didn't follow through, how could she possibly expect him to trust her? Going off course certainly wouldn't prove to him they could be the fantastic team she considered them to be. But what if keeping her promise to Gunnar wasted precious time she could have used to save her twin?

Gods damn it.

Chelle rounded the building despite her worry for Ronan. He could take care of himself and she'd find him. After she met Gunnar like she'd promised. She had to prove to him that she could follow the rules. There would never be anything more than the tether between them otherwise.

Did she want there to be more between them?

Yes. Hell, she might even . . . love him. Probably not the best timing for that sort of revelation, but she never did anything the easy way.

A group of twenty or so berserkers swarmed the property along with the large, furry bodies of at least that many werewolves. Chelle was as likely to be attacked by one of Gunnar's pack as she was Gregor's lot. The entire situation was FUBAR and watching her own back suddenly became a hell of a lot more stressful than she thought it was going to be.

Fuck.

Through the blown-out east-side wall, Chelle got a glimpse inside the diner. Jenner held Vanessa in his arms, virtually useless in a fight. Trenton McAlister stood beside Mikhail, both of them postured to protect Vanessa and ready for a fight. McAlister stood, relatively useless, while Mikhail was armed with a wicked-looking sword. Smart. He knew a gun wouldn't do shit against a berserker. He'd brought what he needed for a beheading. Chelle had to give her head a shake to make sure she was seeing that correctly. Jesus. Who would have thought the two of them would be standing side by side, allies in battle?

Had hell frozen over and no one told her about it?

An enormous grizzly bear lumbered toward the small group, his lips curled back as he let out a loud mewl. Shifter, if Chelle had to guess. McAlister had brought the big guns with him tonight. Good thing the son of a bitch was just as paranoid as Mikhail. They should have known that nowhere would be safe from Gregor. Not while the vindictive asshole still had an axe to grind.

From the corner of her eye, Chelle caught a flash of motion. Ronan headed for the blown-up diner at about Mach 10, his expression as dead serious as she'd ever seen it. From the opposite direction, half of the berserkers' force flooded the building and made a beeline for the small group inside.

"Get the girl out of here!" McAlister shouted. "It's her they want!"

What the what? Chelle's step faltered. The berserkers were there to finish off Mikhail and get McAlister out of the picture. At least, that's the impression she'd gotten from the vitriol Aren had been spewing. It wasn't too far-fetched to think that Gregor would have deceived him as well. He'd do and say anything in order to get what he wanted.

Why in the gods' names would he want Vanessa?

Did it matter? Gregor was a steamroller of violence and he was about to take out everything in his path.

The bear entered the fray without preamble. Chelle had never seen berserkers shy from anything, but the grizzly gave them pause. Whoever he was, his reputation must have been as formidable as his hulking form. Ronan jumped right into the thick of things, armed with a short sword in one hand and a gun in the other. Chelle wanted to roll her eyes. *That's some real cowboy shit, brother.*

She could end this fight with little to no violence. Power radiated through Chelle as she made a beeline for the building. Was it wrong that she wanted to bump her fist against Ronan's and give a rousing "Wonder Twins, activate!" battle shout before she got down to business?

Even with her superior speed, Chelle felt as though she moved in slow motion. She'd compel those motherfuckers to walk off the nearest cliff into the ocean. If she had it her way, Gregor wouldn't terrorize anyone ever again.

A warning bark sounded from behind her and Chelle turned on a dime, twisting mid-run to see the one and only Ian Gregor headed straight toward her. Behind him, Gunnar sprinted, his legs kicking up dirt as he raced toward her, zigging and zagging in an attempt to circumvent the berserker's position.

Shit. Gunnar was going to try to take him down. Not good.

"Gunnar, no!" Chelle could compel Gregor and take him out without anyone getting hurt. His Alpha-male show of strength would only put him in harm's way.

Gregor changed his course in the space of a heartbeat. His reaction time was scary as fuck and meant that his mind worked just as quickly as his body. He'd heard the concern in Chelle's tone and shifted his focus to Gunnar because he knew it would buy him the most leverage. Chelle didn't think she'd ever met anyone as keen, calculating, or brutal as the berserker warlord. He scared the shit out of her.

Stupid, Chelle. Stupid!

Gunnar clashed with the berserker in the time it took

for Chelle to blink. All thoughts of Vanessa, Mikhail, and even Ronan fled as she turned and raced back to where Gregor had taken Gunnar to the ground. A silver blade flashed in the encroaching gray of dawn as the berserker brought his arm up. The petty son of a bitch had no beef with Gunnar whatsoever. Hell, for all he knew they'd been on the same side. Gregor simply went after him because Chelle—a vampire—had been concerned for his well-being.

If any harm came to Gunnar, Chelle would make Gregor regret it.

Gregor's arm came down with a forceful stab and Chelle stumbled at Gunnar's yip of pain. She swore she felt the burn of silver slice through her as the blade sank past the wolf's thick hide and into his body. Chelle dug her feet into her boots and pushed herself as fast as she could go, racing to her mate. Gregor's brutality stole her breath as his arm punched down at Gunnar again and again, stabbing into his big body multiple times before Chelle launched herself at them and shoved the berserker off Gunnar's still form.

A red haze of rage clouded Chelle's vision. Gregor's strength was immense and he was able to disentangle himself from her with ease. They both scrambled to their feet and squared off mere feet from where her mate lay, bleeding out in the dirt.

He's stronger as the wolf, Chelle reminded herself. More resilient. He'd heal. He could tolerate the silver. *He'll be okay. He'll be okay. He'll be okay.* The mantra was the only thing keeping Chelle from losing her shit and going to her damned knees.

The whites of Gregor's eyes were swallowed by fathomless darkness. A cruel sneer pulled at his lips as he held the dagger, dripping with Gunnar's blood, aloft. From a holster at his left hip, he drew a wooden stake carved to a wickedly sharp point. "Ready to die, vampire?"

His voice grated in his throat like gravel scraping over pavement. Chelle couldn't muster the necessary courage to be sassy. The berserker was death incarnate and not even a roomful of zombies ready to munch on her brains could rattle her the way that he did.

Since her turning, Chelle had never once doubted her power. Until now. They should all be very, *very* afraid that Ian Gregor had managed to shake free of the Sortiari's leash.

"Turn the knife on yourself." Chelle drew on every ounce of power she possessed as she attempted to plant the thought in Gregor's mind. "Run it through your neck to your spine."

Gregor's gaze narrowed and his muscles went taut. A tremor shook him from head to toe and his right arm twitched as the blade in his grip rose a fraction of an inch. Gods, he was stronger than Chelle thought he'd be. Her own arrogance hadn't allowed for her to consider anything but success. *Shit.*

"You're the one," Gregor said. "My men said you compelled them to stillness two weeks ago. I didn't believe them and I beat them bloody for their failure."

Sucked for them. Gregor should have believed his foot soldiers, but Chelle couldn't be bothered to muster up a bit of sympathy for the murdering bastards. "I should have done worse to them," she said through the tremor of fear that vibrated through her. "I should have made them kill each other."

Gregor gave an arrogant snort. "Yes," he said matter-of-factly. "You should have."

He rushed at her, putting Chelle instantly on the defensive. She had no weapons save the powers at her disposal—which turned out not to have much of an effect on Gregor—her own smart mouth, and a dagger that would do about as much damage to the fully enraged berserker as a needle would.

She turned to run but he was far quicker than her and snatched her round the waist, hauling her against his chest. "I'm going to run this stake through your heart while he watches," Gregor seethed. He jerked his chin to where he'd left Gunnar on the ground. "And then I'm going to finish off the rest of your kind and wipe you from the face of the earth once and for all."

Sounded about right. Chelle was certain that without being able to compel Gregor, they'd officially lost the upper hand. How was that for a fucked-up situation?

"How many times have you tried to kill Mikhail and failed?" Chelle wondered. If she was going to die, she was at least going to go down doing what she did best: irritating the fuck out of him. "Sorry, Gregor, but you'll have to forgive me for betting against you. I think when it comes to Mikhail you have a problem with performance anxiety."

Gregor brought the stake up, hovering above Chelle's heart. Her pulse raced, her breath caught, as she realized she was about to bite the big one. The only regret she had in her long life was the fact that she hadn't gotten to spend more of it with Gunnar.

Gods. Why couldn't she have found him sooner?

Both Chelle and Gregor were knocked to the ground as the wounded wolf pounced. A snarl tore from Gunnar's lips as his powerful jaws clamped down over the berserker's throat. He thrashed his head, tearing through muscle, and Gregor shoved at Gunnar's body, driving the silver dagger into his body one last time before pushing himself to stand. Chelle's stomach turned at the grisly sight of him. How any creature could survive that sort of damage was a mystery. His head hung at an odd angle and he cupped the wound as he turned and fled, a dark smear against the lightening sky.

Fucking coward. It didn't matter. He'd trip up again. And when he did, they'd rid the world of his evil ass once and for all.

Chelle turned in time to see Gunnar collapse to the ground once again. The moon gave way to the sun as dawn quickly approached and he let out a low and mournful howl that chilled the blood in Chelle's veins. All around them, the sounds of battle began to quiet. The bear let out a bellow and Ronan gave a victorious shout. Chelle had thought to save the day. Instead, had she only made matters worse? Mikhail and the others had seemed to fare well enough. All Chelle had managed to do was nearly get her mate killed.

He let out another howl of pain and the sound of his bones cracking made Chelle flinch. *Oh no.* He was changing. Suffering through the transition with mortal wounds that would no doubt only serve to further weaken him.

Shit had just gone from bad, to worse.

CHAPTER
30

Chelle didn't care if the sun burned her to a damned crisp. She refused to leave Gunnar's side while he was still vulnerable.

"Chelle, don't be stupid. He wouldn't want you to put yourself in jeopardy."

She dropped her head in Ronan's direction but didn't acknowledge him. Mikhail's mate, Claire, was immune to sunlight. Why couldn't she have that superpower? Instead, the very thought of daylight caused her blood to heat in her veins. Talk about unfair.

"I'm not going anywhere, Gunnar." It didn't matter if he understood her or not. "I'm going to wait this out with you."

He let out a mournful howl. Chelle could only imagine how much pain he was in. The transition was brutal. His bones broke and remade themselves, his body contorted in grisly, unnatural ways that made her stomach turn. Gods, if she could bear his pain for him she would.

All around them, the members of Gunnar's pack littered the ground in different stages of transition. She suspected

Gunnar's took longer because of his wolf's strength as well as his injuries. She doubted the Alpha would easily release his hold on their shared body. How much longer would he have to endure this?

"Chelle?" Ronan knelt down behind her and laid his hand on her shoulder.

"I can't leave him." She leaned against Ronan's shoulder. "Would you leave Naya?"

He didn't reply because they both knew what his response would be. "Can we at least move him? Get you inside the building where there's some measure of shelter?"

The entire east wall of the restaurant had been blown up. It would provide them about as much shelter from the sunrise as a greenhouse. "Look at him, Ronan. Who knows what'll happen if we move him. I'll be okay," she said.

Ronan let out a derisive snort. "If he doesn't fully transition within the next five minutes, none of us is going to be okay, Chelle."

She understood the undertone to his words. Ronan wasn't leaving Chelle's side just like she wasn't leaving Gunnar's. Once the sun made its appearance, Chelle and Ronan would be dead and Gunnar would succumb to madness without his mate. Basically, they'd all be fucked.

"Chelle, he's done this without you. Thousands of times. I'm sure even injured. Give him one less thing to worry about and get yourself to safety."

Ronan was right. And still, she couldn't force her body to move a single inch.

"Chelle?" Jillian's voice was weak as she emerged from within the building. Stark naked and still healing from multiple cuts and scrapes, she looked a little worse for the wear. "He's right. You need to get out of here. Gunnar will throttle us all if he knew we let you stay here."

"I can't leave him." The words were thick with emotion as she pushed them past her lips.

"You have to," Jillian said. "We've got this under control. Let the pack take care of him."

She still didn't know the extent of Gunnar's injuries. He'd fought Aren, battled Gregor. And though he'd come out on top of both, he'd taken some heavy damage. What if the stress of transition affected the speed at which he healed?

"Come on, Chelle," Ronan urged. "We need to get out of here."

The sky lightened on the horizon, streaks of lavender against the gray dawn. Time was running out. If they didn't leave now, they'd be caught without shelter. Doomed. And it would be Chelle's fault.

"Okay." Gods, she didn't want to leave his side. She might as well be leaving her own arm behind. Her leg. Her fucking spine or her liver. He was a vital part of her now. An organ that she needed to survive. Tears welled in her eyes and slid down her cheeks. If he didn't survive his injuries, she'd never recover from the grief.

Madness would be a walk in the park compared to what she'd suffer.

"I need a minute." The thought struck and she brought her wrist to her mouth and bit down. Blood welled from the punctures and she gathered her hand into a fist as she held her wrist above Gunnar's mouth.

"What are you doing?"

Chelle chose to ignore Jillian's shocked tone.

If her freakish vampiric blood was going to do anything positive for her, she prayed that it would help Gunnar to transition and heal with no complications. Aren was still unaccounted for. Gunnar had to be at the top of his game. He had to be strong. And ready to defend himself if need be. If Chelle could give him any advantage, she was damn well going to do it.

Still in the midst of transition, Gunnar coughed and sputtered as Chelle's blood ran down his throat. The wounds in her wrist closed and she tore them open again, biting deeper this time. When the wounds closed yet again, she worked her palm over his throat, still thick and sinewy as she urged him to swallow.

"You've done all you can do, Chelle." Ronan pulled her back despite her protests. "Now, let's get to safety and give him one less thing to worry about."

Tears trickled down Chelle's cheeks. She looked at Jillian who gave her a reassuring smile. "He'll be okay. But only if you get the hell out of here."

She swallowed against the baseball-sized knot in her throat and gave a nod of her head. "My car's parked about a half mile up the road." She allowed Ronan to help her to her feet and tossed Jillian her key. With one last glance at Gunnar, Chelle turned and followed Ronan to the safety of his car. They'd be racing against the sunrise. Good thing her brother's car could eat up the pavement.

It had taken more willpower than Chelle thought she possessed to leave Gunnar's side. And with any luck, she'd see him again soon.

Gunnar's brain buzzed and his blood rushed in his veins. In the recess of his psyche, his wolf's burst of energy matched his, causing his limbs to quake. Even to his already heightened senses, the surrounding sights, sounds, and even the texture of the grass on his naked body seemed intensified. He'd never felt this way after transitioning before. Not even during the one month a year where there were two full moons did Gunnar feel such a rush of power.

Chelle.

"Where is she?" he demanded with a shout. Jillian jumped and lowered her gaze to the ground as Gunnar pushed himself up to stand. "Chelle!" His voice boomed around them. "What happened to her?"

His memory was obscured by a gauzy cloud. The last thing he remembered, his mate was beside him, her wrist held to his mouth. Voices urged her to leave. To get as far from the sunrise as possible before it burned her to ash. Panic welled hot and thick in Gunnar's throat and he took a stumbling step as he rushed toward Jillian. "Where is she?" he roared.

"Gone." Jillian kept her gaze down, her posture as relaxed as possible in the face of an enraged Alpha. "She didn't want to go. Refused to leave your side. But her brother and I convinced her after . . ."

Gunnar's teeth gnashed. "After what?"

"After she fed you her blood."

Good gods. No wonder he was rocking a hard-core buzz. Vampire blood coursed through his body. And not just any vampire. One who'd been created in the same vein as a deity. His mate, his goddess, had given him her blood.

"Why?" Gunnar's head pounded and he cradled it in his palm. Jesus. How bad off had he been?

"You were badly injured," Jillian replied. "Your transition was . . . difficult."

No shit. Gunnar felt like he'd just exited the ass end of an elephant. The transition was uncomfortable on a good day. Injured, distressed, enraged, fearful for his mate's safety, and exhausted? It was a fucking nightmare.

If he couldn't be assured of Chelle's safety by having her at his side, at least she was with her brother, someone who took her safety almost as seriously as Gunnar did. He needed to see her for himself, though. To know without a doubt that she was all right. Until he did, he wouldn't be worth a shit to anyone, least of all his pack.

"Aren?" The last he'd seen of the cowardly bastard was his tail in the air as he headed north in retreat.

Jillian shook her head. "Sven took three others and tried to track him but they lost the scent. Everyone else is accounted for, though."

And those remaining members of Aren's hunting party would be held accountable for their actions. "He won't go far," Gunnar replied. Aren wasn't interested in running. He wanted control of the pack and he wouldn't stop until he got it or died.

"Chelle left her car," Jillian said. She held out her hand and gave the key to Gunnar. "We've got a Range Rover not far from here if you want it along with your clothes."

Gunnar answered with a nod. He'd go to Chelle bare-assed naked if he had to. But he supposed clothes might be a good idea if he ran into any of Mikhail Aristov's day-time security staff.

"There's something else," Jillian said.

Gunnar fixed her with a hard stare. She wasn't yet off the hook for what she'd done last night, either. "What?"

"I'll give it to you when we get to the car," she said. "It's what I promised Chelle I'd give to her."

So much to take care of. Gunnar wondered when his problems would stop piling up. "Gather the pack," he said as he followed Jillian toward where the Range Rover was parked. "No one goes after Aren. Have everyone assembled and waiting for me. I'll be back to the house after sundown."

Jillian gave an obedient nod. "Gunnar, for what it's worth, I'm sorry. I did what I thought was right."

He acknowledged her apology with a slight inclination of his head. "We'll talk tonight."

"I know," she said. "And I'm prepared to accept whatever punishment you deem fit to mete out."

Gunnar let out a slow breath. How could he expect the pack to forgive him for keeping his mate bond with Chelle a secret if he wasn't willing to offer his first? Maybe for once, punishment was not what the pack needed. Maybe it was time for forgiveness. For all of them.

Gunnar was surprised when the security guard managing the gate to Aristov's property let him in without a word. He was driving Chelle's car, but the vampire king himself must have given word to have Gunnar admitted if he showed up. He was honored to know the king trusted him enough not to have him strip-searched and questioned—or worse—prior to admittance. With the noon sun high in the sky, the vampires were at their weakest. With trust like that, Gunnar could easily sneak in and successfully finish what Gregor had started. Neither Gregor nor Aren had gone about their plans very thoughtfully. The difference between a leader and a brute, Gunnar supposed, had much to do with the inner workings of one's mind.

Aren should have made friends with the vampire king rather than ambush him. It's what Gunnar would have done had he been in Aren's position. The male had ambition but little else. Just like Gregor had a need for vengeance but little else. In the long run, their tunnel vision would get them nothing but ruin, though it was likely Aren would learn his lesson long before Gregor did.

Gunnar pulled up to Chelle's cottage and killed the engine. He relaxed his grip on the steering wheel and took a few cleansing breaths to help calm the nervous energy that churned in his stomach. If anything had happened to her after she left his side this morning, he would have found out about it by now. Gunnar had to believe that. And yet, he found it difficult to get out of the car and go see for himself.

His wolf would know if their mate was gone, even if Gunnar himself had doubts.

He forced himself from the car and walked down the paved pathway to the front door. His heart lodged in his throat, his hands shook, and his breath raced in his chest. The past twenty-four hours had been a test of patience, endurance, strength, power, and love. Gunnar paused, his hand resting on the doorknob. He loved Chelle. For all her stubbornness, sass, darkness, and power. He loved her for her beauty and ferocity, her strength, her daring, and clever mind. He loved her because his soul recognized hers as its own other half. He loved her because of the way he felt right now: terrified of the prospect of another day that didn't have her in it.

Gunnar's hand gripped the knob tight and he turned it, opening the door. He slipped silently inside, careful not to let in too much light. He closed the door just as soundlessly and padded down the hallway toward Chelle's bedroom. He let himself in and turned to face the door as he closed it, too afraid to turn around and see an empty bed.

Gods. He hadn't been this scared since he was a young boy on his first hunt. His father had set him loose in the forest and told him not to return without a boar. Gunnar had never known true fear until that night and he'd vowed never to let himself feel it again. Until now.

Turn around, you fucking coward.

Chelle slept peacefully on the mattress. Fully clothed, on top of the blankets as though she'd stumbled into the room and passed out on the bed's surface. No doubt she'd made it home seconds before sunrise. For a moment, Gunnar simply watched her sleep. Her vulnerability made his heart race in his chest. She thought she was a monster.

A creature of unimaginable, unchecked power. She thought if those close to her knew what she could do, that they'd turn on her. What Chelle didn't realize was that she was much more fragile than she wanted to admit. Like spun glass resting on cobwebs. So very, very breakable.

She took his breath away.

Gunnar kicked off his shoes and stripped down. He eased Chelle's boots off, then her socks, and peeled her torn and dirty pants from her body. With a gentle tug, he pulled the blankets down and repositioned Chelle on the mattress. He climbed into bed beside her and gathered her body close before pulling the blankets up on top of them.

Chelle nuzzled against him and let out a contented sigh. Gunnar could think of nowhere in the world he'd rather be in this moment than here, watching over her. Protecting her.

With Chelle in his arms, he was home.

CHAPTER
31

Chelle edged closer to the warmth of the body beside her. A sigh slipped from between her lips. If this was a dream, it was one of the best ones she'd ever had and she didn't want to wake up. What could be better than the contentment she felt right now? In the arms of her mate, where nothing and no one could touch them.

Chelle's eyes flew open and she drew in a sharp gasp of breath. *Gunnar!* She sat upright only to find that she wasn't dreaming. Her mate lay beside her on the mattress, his chest rising and falling evenly in sleep.

She eased the covers away from his body. Her breath caught and her blood heated at the sight of him, naked and magnificent. Not a single bruise marred his perfect body to betray the damage he'd sustained in last night's many battles. Her fingertips traced the tattoos that covered his neck, down over his shoulder, and across his wide collar-bone to his chest. Gods. He'd been through so much. It was a wonder he'd survived.

"Keep touching me like that, mate, and I'll be hard-pressed not to ravage you right here and now."

Chelle smiled at the rough tenor of his words. "I wouldn't say no to that," she murmured. "But I was checking you for injuries."

Gunnar cracked a lid to look at her. A corner of his mouth hitched in a crooked grin. "Are you satisfied with the results of your inspection?"

"So far," Chelle said with a smile. "But there's still more ground for me to cover."

Gunnar's icy-blue stare swallowed her whole. His cocky grin dimmed a bit. "You gave me your blood."

Chelle cringed. "You were hurt. The transition . . ." She let out a gust of breath. "Gods, Gunnar. How do you endure it?"

"It was difficult." Gunnar propped himself up on an elbow and Chelle's attention was drawn to the play of muscles in his powerful arm. "But Chelle, it's *never* easy."

After seeing it for herself, Chelle understood Jillian's reasoning for wanting to find a cure to lycanthropy. If she could have taken that pain from Gunnar, she would have. "So what you're saying is that I should have left you there. In pain and vulnerable with no help whatsoever."

Gunnar averted his gaze. The wolf stirred in his mind, agitated. Chelle listened to the tangled mass of thoughts, more in tune with that part of Gunnar's nature than she had been in the past. The wolf was an entity that transcended time and space. Change might've been difficult for someone as old as Gunnar to accept, but for the wolf, it was nearly impossible.

"You think that what I did weakened you in the eyes of your pack," Chelle said after a tense moment. "You think I've diminished your standing in the hierarchy."

"I think you should have trusted that I was strong enough."

Indignant fire burned in Chelle's chest. She let out a

snort. "What if our situations had been reversed? What if it had been me lying there, bleeding and in pain, with my enemies waiting somewhere for me to be weakened so they could pounce? Would you have left me lying there, Gunnar? Would you have trusted that I'd be okay? Or would you have done whatever was in your power to help me."

His jaw squared. Stubborn ass. "Our situations are very different."

"Are they?" Frankly, Chelle had had about enough of his Alpha-male bullshit. "You're the leader of your pack just like I'm the leader of my coven."

"A coven of two," Gunnar said.

Seriously? Any concern she might have felt for him gave way to annoyance. "It wouldn't matter if your pack was fifty strong and my coven consisted of me, Lucas, and a couple of cats. It's still my coven and I'm still its leader. Your responsibility to those under your care is no greater and no less than mine." Chelle took a deep breath. "Is this about my helping you? Or the fact that your pack saw me open my vein to give you my blood?"

She studied him. He kept up a strong mental shield that muted his thoughts but his wolf wasn't so easy to control. The animal's response in the back of Gunnar's mind sounded just as disgusted as she was. At this point, she was beginning to think she liked the wolf better than the man. At least the wolf didn't give a single fuck about anyone else's opinion of their mate bond.

Chelle wasn't about to sit around and be insulted. She flung herself off the bed, for the first time realizing she was no longer wearing her boots, socks, or pants. Her eyes went wide as she rounded on Gunnar. "Did you undress me?"

His expression transformed once again to smug male arrogance. "I did."

Chelle's eyes narrowed as she gave a disgusted shake of her head. "Did you get a good look?"

His lips puckered as though fighting a smile. "Not nearly good enough. If I'd been able to divest you of your shirt and underwear without jostling you too much, I might've been satisfied."

He loved to push her buttons, didn't he? "Ugh!" Chelle crossed the room and jerked open the door. "Get out." If he was ashamed for his pack to see the blood of his *tethered mate* on his lips, then she didn't want anything to do with him. Cocky SOB. Who in the hell did he think he was, insulting her while following it up with flirtatious banter?

Gunnar stretched out on the bed and folded his arms behind his head. Chelle's gaze dipped to where the sheet draped across his narrow hips. It was absolutely unfair that he could spark her anger and lust all at the same time.

"Your shirt's torn," he remarked. "Take it off."

Chelle thought her eyes might bug out of her head. "Are you serious?"

His cocky grin widened and his gaze bored through her. "Dead serious."

In an angry huff, Chelle peeled the shirt off and threw it at him. "Happy?"

His gaze heated. "Not yet. Get rid of the bra."

Her jaw went slack. "We're fighting. You do realize that, right?"

Gunnar shrugged one finely sculpted shoulder as though their argument meant little to him. "We can continue to argue while we fuck if that's what you want, Chelle, but personally, I could do without it."

She stared at him. Dumbfounded by his audacity.

"The bra?" He nudged a finger at her. "It's a crime to keep your breasts covered. I prefer them unrestrained."

"We're fighting!" she exclaimed.

Gunnar let out a long-suffering sigh. "Fine. If you

insist." He pushed himself up to sit and flipped the length of his hair to one side of his head. She wished he'd stop looking so gods-damned delectable. "What you did was reckless and irresponsible. You had no idea what your blood might do to me and yet you gave it to me anyway. And yes, treating me as though I were weak in front of the members of my pack did *not* make me happy." He brought up one knee and rested his elbow on it. "But," he said on a breath, "I know that you did what you did out of concern. And had I been in your position I would have done all of that and more."

A quiet moment passed as Chelle tried to process what had just happened. Had he just reasoned with her? In a calm and not high-handed manner? Like two grown-ups in an actual relationship?

That cocky grin reappeared on his gorgeous face. "Does that help to settle the matter?"

Chelle's mouth puckered. His maturity had totally taken the wind out of her sails. "I suppose."

"Good." Gunnar leaned back onto the pillow and assumed his relaxed position. "Now, the bra."

Chelle wanted to hold on to her anger but Gunnar made it impossible. He'd managed to shut down her indignation with a couple of artfully spoken sentences. Even the wolf quieted in his mind as though content that he'd swallowed his pride and acknowledged that all Chelle had done was try to protect them.

"What did it do to you?" she asked just above a whisper. "My blood?"

"One of the things I missed about my humanity was my inability to get drunk," Gunnar said with a chuckle. "My werewolf metabolism burns off the alcohol too quickly. Your blood . . ." He let out an indulgent moan that Chelle swore she felt in the center of her sex. "Like a cask of aged mead. So heady it made me drunk. And it did help to ease the pain of my transition as well as speed my recovery."

Chelle let out the breath she'd been holding. Relief crashed over her. She'd been worried sick that she'd made a mistake. That her blood would have some adverse effect on him. Thank the gods it hadn't.

"I was worried." It stung her pride to admit it.

Gunnar grinned. So wicked. "Alpha," he said by way of explanation. As though nothing, not berserkers, not souped-up zombies, not even her own crazy-powerful blood could harm him. "Now, don't make me ask you again to get rid of that bra."

Chelle's stomach did a pleasant flip. Mated males . . . so temperamental.

Gunnar couldn't be angry with Chelle for what she'd done for the very reason he'd told her: had he been in her position, he would have done the same thing. Hell, probably more. He would have moved the sun and moon if that's what it took. So how could he begrudge his mate's doing the same for him? It proved the strength of their bond and that made Gunnar's wolf purr with contentment. She truly belonged to them and he knew nothing would ever come between them.

Her coy smile showed the dainty points of her fangs and Gunnar's gut clenched. The thought of her biting him, the rush of feeling his skin break beneath the gentle pressure, made his cock hard as stone.

Chelle reached between her breasts and unhooked the clasp of the simple white cotton bra. She slowly pulled the two halves apart to reveal the beauty of her breasts before letting the garment fall to the floor. Gods, the way she teased him. It was a delicious torture he couldn't get enough of.

She cocked a brow. "Better?"

Gunnar made a show of settling deeper into the pillow. "Much. But you still have too many clothes on. And your hair is up."

Chelle pursed her lips and cocked her head to one side. She reached up, elongating her lovely arms and showcasing the muscles in her biceps. The act of letting her hair loose from the band that held it was a sensual act. Graceful. Gunnar's breath caught and an electric rush traveled through his bloodstream as he watched her tousle the long, tawny locks to rest on her bare shoulders.

"Beautiful," Gunnar said on a breath. "You're not done, though."

Chelle fiddled with the waistband of her underwear. Gunnar swore he'd never known a female who could make such simple garments appear so sensual. She could have worn the scraps of a plastic bag and it would have been the most erotic sight he'd ever seen. Anticipation coiled tight in his stomach as she eased her underwear down over one hip. She was a temptation. A rich, decadent dessert that he couldn't wait to taste. The headiest liquor.

And she was *his*.

Chelle eased the underwear down her thighs and kicked them off. By the time her body was bare to him, Gunnar's wolf practically yipped with excitement in the recess of his mind. His blood was heated to the point of boiling. His heart raced and his breath puffed in his chest. His cock was hard as stone and pulsed almost painfully. His need to be inside of her overrode everything else, including the fact he'd promised Jillian he'd be back to the house shortly after sundown. The pack would have to wait a while longer. Because there was no way Gunnar was leaving his mate's side quite yet.

"Come here, *mate*."

Gunnar loved the way Chelle mocked outrage whenever he stressed the word "mate." She knew he belonged to her every bit as much as she did to him. Truly, the notion of ownership didn't exist. They were simply a mated pair. Two pieces of a whole, their souls inexorably intertwined for eternity. Gunnar couldn't own Chelle any more than the moon could own the tide. But the fact remained that one could not exist without the other.

She walked to him slowly. The sway of her hips held him rapt. His gaze devoured every exposed inch of her from her ankles, up the shapely curve of her calves, to her lush thighs, the flare of her hips to her flat belly, and up her torso to her lovely upturned breasts and slender throat, to her beautiful face and cascade of golden hair.

She smelled like a midnight forest in the summer and it called to his wolf and his untamed soul.

Gunnar wanted to reach out and take her hand but he made himself resist. Instead he waited as she crawled up on the bed and straddled his hips. The sheet separated their bodies, a strategic move on her part he was sure.

"Is this where you want me, *mate*?" The words were a sensual purr and a snarky dare all wrapped up into one.

A corner of Gunnar's mouth hitched. "Almost." He gave a gentle buck of his hips as though to resituate himself. "There's a sheet in the way."

"Is there?" Chelle teased. "I hadn't noticed."

"Move it and I'll buy you a caramel macchiato."

A sensual smile spread across Chelle's full lips. "Now you're talking."

She shifted, brushing aside the sheet that separated their bodies. Gunnar sucked in a sharp breath as she settled back down and the wet heat of her pussy slid along his shaft. "Gods, you're a cruel tease, Chelle," he said on a groan.

If her wicked smile was any indication, she certainly enjoyed the game. She rolled her hips, rubbing her slippery, satin-smooth skin over his cock once again. "I'm sorry." Her feigned innocence drove him crazy with desire. "Did you not like that?"

He shrugged a casual shoulder. "I think you're using pleasure to pain me, *mate*." Gods, how Gunnar wanted to accept her challenge. A battle of wills to see who could hold out the longest. Despite his desperate want, Gunnar was convinced he'd win. He'd have her writhing and begging to be fucked by the time he was done with her.

That he had to rush home soon to address the issue with Aren only made Gunnar want to beat the sorry bastard to a bloody pulp. He should be spending the night in bed with his mate, making her come again and again, not dealing with the treasonous machinations of one foul traitor. His time with Chelle would have to be quick. But when everything was settled, he'd show her what it was to tease.

Chelle rolled her hips again. Her lids became hooded and she took her bottom lip between her teeth. One fang punctured the delicate skin and a drop of blood bloomed there. Gunnar thought of the amazing, drunken buzz he'd gotten from it and wiped the drop away with the pad of his thumb before licking it away.

Chelle's gaze heated. The scent of her arousal intensified. She liked to see him take her blood on his tongue. The primal part of Gunnar where his wolf held dominion sparked into hyperawareness. He sat up straight, gripping Chelle's hips as he lifted her and set her on top of his rigid cock.

She drew in a sharp breath that ended on a moan. Gunnar bowed his head and took one luscious breast into his mouth. Chelle's head fell back on her shoulders as she began to gently rock her hips against him. Her actions were far too tame and tentative for that animal part of Gunnar that wanted to ravage her. He nipped at the tender swell of her breast and Chelle moaned. As though she under-stood, she rode him faster, took him deeper.

"That's it," he murmured against her skin. He gripped her hips and pulled her down hard on his cock as he thrust up to meet her. "Don't stop, love."

Chelle's arms came around him. Her hold was firm as he continued to guide the motion of her hips to match the rhythm of his own thrusts. She bent her head to his. Her panting breaths in his ear caused goose bumps to rise on his skin. Her lips grazed the lobe before venturing lower. Gunnar's stomach clenched with lust. Her mouth found his throat but she hesitated. Another tease? Or something more? Gunnar never should have expressed displeasure for her giving him her blood. Her nature was nothing to be ashamed of.

"Do it." The command grated in his throat. "Bite me."

She sealed her mouth over his vein. Her razor-sharp fangs broke the skin and Gunner let out a low grunt. Ten-drils of heat spiraled through his body as a rush of intense pleasure crested over him. The deep suction, followed by her indulgent moan, drove Gunnar wild. His cock pulsed with every beat of his heart, his breath raced in his chest, and his sac grew tight. Every muscle in his body tensed.

"Come with me, Chelle." Gods, he wanted her to top-ple over the edge with him. He didn't know how much longer he could hold out. She gripped the back of his neck as she continued to drink. Her hips undulated wildly as her inner walls constricted. They were both so close. Gunnar was out of his fucking mind with want. "Give me your blood, Chelle." He wanted to feel that drunken rush again. Craved it. "I want it."

She released her hold on his throat and pulled back to look at him. Her eyes were alight with silver, her lips stained crimson. "Are you sure?" Her brows gathered with doubt.

"Do it." Gunnar never wanted her to doubt anything ever again.

Chelle brought her wrist to her lips and bit down. Four drops of blood welled from the punctures as she held out her arm in offering. Gunnar guided her wrist to his mouth and sealed his lips over the punctures. His eyes rolled back into his head as the euphoric rush swept him up. He swallowed and fiery heat chased down his throat. Better than a tumbler of aged whiskey. Richer than the mead they drank in the great halls. Thor himself had never tasted ambrosia like this. Gunnar had never known such utter bliss.

Their gazes locked. The mate bond seemed to strengthen in that moment, as though some sacred act had transpired between them. Chelle's hips began to move again, slow, purposeful rolls that took Gunnar deep. His hips bucked and Gunnar let out a shout as he came. Powerful waves of sensation crashed over him, each one more powerful than the last. The room swam in and out of focus. He braced his arms behind him on the mattress and drove his hips up to meet Chelle's. Her eyes went wide and her body rigid. A shudder passed over her as sobbing cries escaped her lips. A rush of wet heat spread over Gunnar's cock and her pussy squeezed him tight.

His mate's passion was exquisite.

She collapsed against him and Gunnar held her in his arms. Their heavy breaths were the only sounds in the quiet room. Minutes passed and still they didn't move. Gunnar could stay like this all night. His cock deep inside of her and his arms around her.

He was in love with Chelle. And after he dealt with the last obstacle between them he was going to tell her.

CHAPTER
32

The tether that bound them couldn't be stronger. Gunnar willingly took her blood on his tongue. Something that had shocked Chelle as much as it had pleased her. The exchange of blood was essential to solidifying their bond. He couldn't have known the impact it had on her, and yet, the reverence in his expression as he'd sealed his mouth over her wrist had caused emotion to bloom at the center of Chelle's being.

The tether was absolute. Forever.

Chelle's limbs remained twined with Gunnar's in the aftermath of their passion. Her breath came in quick bursts and she rested her head on his strong shoulder, arms wrapped tight around him. What she felt in this moment had no comparison.

"I have to leave."

Gunnar's words sucked the warmth from Chelle's chest. She'd known he wouldn't stay the night. Not with Aren still running around free. "I know. I'll come with you."

He stroked the length of her hair. "It's not safe tonight. The pack is in disarray."

What did it matter? "It's all out in the open now. I don't see how it can get any worse."

Gunnar let out a slow breath. "Believe me, love. It can always get worse."

The past few weeks had been one crazy, desperate situation after another. But Gunnar was right. They were far from done. "You're right. I'll keep my distance tonight."

"Once the dust settles, everything will be fine."

Chelle hoped so. "I'd like a little peace and quiet with you. The opportunity for some downtime would be great. Especially if I go to Egypt soon."

Gunnar's jaw went slack as he studied her. "What do you mean? You're not seriously considering going back to the Sortiari stronghold for McAlister's key."

Chelle averted her gaze. "I don't have to."

"What?" The word burst from his lips. Chelle sensed the coming storm and rolled away from Gunnar, separating their bodies. Cold settled over her skin and she shivered. "You have McAlister's third of the key?"

Chelle climbed off the bed. "I managed to snag McAlister's key before his zombies jumped me. It's in my car, actually. I only need one more piece."

His look of disappointment nearly gutted her. "And you went behind my back to make a deal with Jillian to get it."

"Yes." There was no point in denying it.

"She'll be punished for this, Chelle. Harshly. Do you understand that?"

Regret burned in Chelle's chest. She'd known Gunnar wouldn't be happy, but she'd hoped he'd be lenient. "I know."

His crystal-blue eyes narrowed. "And you don't care?"

Of course she cared. But she couldn't have changed Jillian's mind any more than Gunnar could change hers. "Jillian knew the consequences when she offered it to me."

Gunnar gave a disbelieving shake of his head. "I thought you could let this go after last night." His hand reached up and his fingers raked through his hair, flipping its length to one side of his head. "I thought . . ." He gave a disbelieving bark of laughter. "Hell, I don't know what I thought."

"I deserve answers," Chelle said. Surely he understood that?

"At the expense of potentially unlocking something that was never meant to be opened?"

"We can't know that," Chelle argued. "There are so many myths."

"And you know one of them that happened to be true," Gunnar pointed out. "So why discount this one?"

"I have to know." She couldn't put it any more plainly. "I have to know what I am."

"You're a vampire!" Gunnar shouted. "Jesus. There's *nothing* wrong with you, Chelle! You're not a monster or a freak or anything else. You're letting your own gods-damned fear master you."

She looked away. "I wish you'd at least try to understand."

"Oh, I understand perfectly," Gunnar said, disgusted. "You value your answers over your mate."

Chelle's jaw dropped. "That's not true."

Gunnar's gaze hardened. He snatched up his pants and shoved one leg in and then the other. He pulled the zipper up with an angry jerk and threw on his shirt. "Then prove it. Abandon this quest. Trust in our bond and don't leave me to travel halfway around the gods-damned world."

Their bond wouldn't protect anyone if her powers grew out of control. "Gunnar, please. Don't."

His socks went on next, followed by his boots. "That's all the answer I need. You'll throw away what we have for your ridiculous quest."

Chelle's hands balled into fists. It didn't matter that she stood in the middle of her bedroom, naked, shouting at an enraged werewolf. Gunnar had crossed the line. "Ridiculous? You're throwing away my feelings! Discounting my fears! Is that how a loving, supportive mate should behave?"

He answered her with an indignant snort. Without another word, Gunnar reached into his pocket. Chelle's brows gathered as he tossed his third of the Alexandria key onto the bed. "Take it," he growled. "It's all that truly matters to you anyway."

He turned on a heel and strode to the door, pulling it open with an angry jerk that nearly took the damn thing off the hinges. He cast one last withering look over his shoulder before letting it slam behind him.

Chelle stared blankly ahead. She flinched as the front door to the cottage slammed as well and listened to the sound of her own car starting up and peeling out of the driveway. Nice. He broke her fucking heart and stole her car all in the same five minutes.

Tears pricked behind Chelle's eyes but she willed them to stay put. She supposed she deserved everything she was getting and then some.

She stood in the middle of her bedroom for what felt like hours, staring at the door Gunnar had slammed in her face. Her chest hollowed out and she choked back a sob. Had she put her own selfish needs before their bond? Had she disregarded their tether, diminished its worth in favor of a quest that might net her nothing but more unanswered questions?

Chelle had never felt so conflicted in her life. Her legs gave out and her ass bounced down on the bed. She reflected on the past few weeks. Since her tethering, she'd definitely leveled out. She'd managed to control her thirst and the thoughts of others that she couldn't seem to block out before had quieted in her mind. Now, she had to search for them in order to hear them, they were no longer unwelcome white noise. Likewise, she wasn't assaulted by memories that weren't hers. For months her mind had felt like a swirling vortex, eating up memories and stray thoughts as quickly as she could absorb them. Since her tethering, that whirlpool had slowed to calm waters. The memories were still out there, floating like clouds, but they kept their distance and she kept hers. Her strength and healing hadn't diminished and her ability to compel was still extraordinary, but perhaps that wasn't such a bad thing. And she really couldn't complain about her immunity to silver. Had Gunnar managed to calm the storm that had raged within her since her transition? Was their tether all she'd needed to level out?

And you're about to turn your back on that for some stupid quest halfway around the world.

Chelle's cell rang and she started. Her heart raced as she leaned over and scooped her phone from the nightstand. She swiped her finger across the screen and couldn't muster the energy for a cordial greeting. "What?"

"Chelle?"

Jillian's concerned voice on the other end of the line caused Chelle to sit up straighter. "Yeah. What's up?"

"You need to tell Gunnar not to come back to the house tonight."

Shit. Chelle gnashed her teeth, pricking her bottom lip. She licked the blood away. "He's already gone. He left about fifteen or twenty minutes ago." Hell, maybe longer.

Who knew how long she'd sat here stewing in self-pity. "What's wrong?"

"Aren's here," Jillian said. "He says that Gunnar is unfit to be Alpha since he's formed a mate bond with a vampire and kept it a secret from the pack. Once Aren issues a formal challenge, Gunnar won't be able to turn it down. They'll be fighting for supremacy and control of the pack."

Chelle knew there was only one way it could end: with one of them dead.

"I'm on my way." She had no idea what she was going to do when she got there but she refused to sit around here while her mate fought for his life. She couldn't let Gunnar think that he meant nothing to her. That their tether meant nothing to her. There were things in this world more important than answers. Than being put at ease. Nothing mattered more than Gunnar. *Nothing.* And it was time to prove it to him.

Gunnar pulled into the driveway feeling a lot like his heart had been scooped out of his chest with a rusty spoon. His wolf let out a mournful howl in the recess of his mind and Gunnar wanted to do the same. Anything to relieve the hurt that felt like he was being torn in two.

After everything they'd been through, Chelle had chosen her quest over him. She didn't trust in their bond enough to let him help her through the mysteries of her unique existence. *It's not like you offered your help, you stupid bastard.* No. Instead, Gunnar had let his temper get the better of him and stormed out of her house. Chelle wasn't the sort of creature who could be dealt with using dominance and force. Instead, she needed to be finessed. She was a wild thing. He should have treated her with the care and respect due a wild creature. Gods damn it. He'd really fucked up this time.

The front door of the house swung wide. A swath of bright light cut across the darkness before a crowd of bodies poured over the threshold.

"Gunnar Falk!" Aren's deep voice rang out in the quiet night. "You are unfit to be the Alpha of the Forkbeard pack. I challenge your right to supremacy!"

Magic tingled over Gunnar's skin. Not the sort of magic he'd felt in the Sortiari's stronghold, but rather, the instinctual magic that all werewolves possessed upon their transition. It was as much a part of him as his wolf and it demanded that Gunnar obey.

A challenge had been issued. There was no backing down.

He had to give Aren credit, the bastard's ambition had no limits. It hadn't mattered that they were tracking him. That he'd be banished or worse for his treachery. Nope, the stupid son of a bitch had waltzed right through the front door, knowing that the second he issued his challenge, he became untouchable to anyone but Gunnar. He'd leveled the playing field with a few words. Banishment would have been a better alternative to death. But rogues were considered pariahs among the werewolf packs. Perhaps Aren's ego refused to let him live any kind of life as an outcast. He'd always craved power. His alliance with the berserkers had emboldened him. Now he had no choice but to kill Gunnar, or die.

Gunnar didn't know about Aren, but he had no intention of dying tonight.

The entirety of the pack gathered around them.

"Unfit how?" Gunnar strode toward Aren with all the confidence of his station. His wolf gave a low growl in the back of his mind.

"You took a vampire as your mate." Aren sneered. "You violated pack law. You kept that vampire bitch a secret from your family. But mostly, you're unfit to lead this pack because you are a coward who's lost his taste for battle."

A murmur traveled through the pack.

Aren would pay for insulting Gunnar's mate. "You saw last night who between us is the stronger warrior. You'll soon see it again."

"It doesn't matter." Aren's look of disgust bored through him. "Even if by some miracle you manage to kill me, it won't be long before you have to answer to your own pack's justice for taking a vampire as a mate."

Gunnar had had enough of this divisive bullshit. "After tonight, pack law will change." He didn't speak to Aren now, but the entire pack. "I'll not stand by and uphold archaic doctrine based on fear. My wolf *chose* a vampire as its mate. Willingly!" he shouted. "If that is taboo, then tell me why the wolf chose her? Mate bonds outside of the pack were outlawed by foolish, superstitious males who lived their lives in fear of the world they'd been thrust into and I'll no longer stand for it! Anyone present who refuses to accept that is free to leave this pack tonight and be considered a rogue from this day on."

Not a soul voiced even a murmur of dissension.

Gunnar turned to Aren, smug. "It looks as though you're singular in your opinion."

"After I kill you," Aren said, low. "I'm going to reintroduce your mate to the sun."

The threat drove Gunnar's wolf mad with rage. It scratched at the back of his mind as though trying to claw its way out. He tried to quiet the animal. All its anger managed to do was divide Gunnar's focus. He assured the wolf that Aren would not only pay for threatening their mate, he would *hurt* for it.

Gunnar had lost his taste for battle? All Aren's comments had done was intensify his need for violence.

"Daggers!" Gunnar declared. As the one being challenged, it was his right to choose the weapons. A heavy broadsword would tire him too quickly and hand-to-hand combat required no skill. The daggers were Gunnar's forte and Aren knew it. Close-quarters weapons combat. That way, Aren could look into his eyes and know what fate awaited anyone who dared to threaten Gunnar's mate.

Without a word, Gunnar headed onto the vast grass lawn that spread out beyond the house. The pack followed, ready to bear witness to their Alpha defending his position. Several minutes passed and Sven emerged from the house. He strolled slowly across the lawn to where Gunnar and Aren faced off. Bodies moved to allow him inside the circle. He held an ornately carved rosewood box aloft and lifted the lid to reveal four ancient daggers honed to razor-sharp edges. Gunnar reached into the box and chose two daggers. Aren did the same. Sven gave a slight nod of his head and retreated to the edge of the circle with the rest of the pack.

Without warning, Aren attacked. So much for fucking decorum. Gunnar blocked a left side jab and spun away to his right, narrowly missing the downward swipe of Aren's opposite arm. It only took a moment for Gunnar to regain his bearings. He spun the daggers in his hands to test their balance as Aren circled him, one foot crossing the other. Gold glinted in the male's eyes, giving Gunnar a glimpse of the animal that lived beneath his skin.

"You caught me off guard once, it's not going to happen again."

Aren's sly grin made Gunnar want to slap it off his face. He'd known Aren since they were boys. It broke his heart to see how much his friend had changed. Or perhaps he'd always harbored these secret ambitions and simply covered it well. Either way, the sense of betrayal that

Gunnar felt speared him through the chest as though Aren's dagger had already driven home.

Any fracture within the pack was a tragedy. Whichever of them fell tonight, it would be a needless death.

"We've hidden too long," Aren seethed. "Kept to ourselves when we could have risen within the hierarchy of the supernatural world. You made us hermits when we should have been kings."

"Don't you mean, you should have been a king?" Gunnar was descended from kings. Had that made him Alpha as a werewolf, though? No. Gunnar's strength, his character, his sense of honor made him Alpha. Aren would never understand that. "Isn't that why you made your back-alley deals with Gregor?"

Aren lunged at him and Gunnar jumped back, narrowly missing the cut of the blade. He rushed at Aren, determined to keep him on the defensive. He cut down with his left arm at the same moment he jabbed with his right. The blade sank into Aren's upper arm. A sharp kick connected with Gunnar's gut. He let out a whoof of air and stumbled backward.

"I made back-alley deals because you weren't willing to!" Aren shouted. "I led where you were content to hide."

He rushed at Gunnar, the quick movement of his arms nothing but a blur. Gunnar's blades clashed with his in a scrape of metal. Sparks jumped from the blades in the darkness as they stood nose to nose, locked together in a show of brute strength.

"You allied yourself with ruthless killers!" Gunnar ground out between clenched teeth. "Cold-blooded murderers!"

"I allied myself with *strength*," Aren said with a grunt.

Gunnar allowed a superior smirk. "And yet, you were both bested."

Aren lowered his arms first, breaking away. He threw back his head and let out an enraged shout as he came at Gunnar once again. There were no more insults to fling, no more posturing. Aren was out for blood and he fought with the determination of someone who had absolutely nothing to lose. Gunnar was pushed back to the edge of the circle where his pack looked on. He spun away, missing a wide sweep of Aren's left arm and came around with his elbow, catching the male in the center of his back. Aren went down to his knees and Gunnar used the opportunity to go for his throat. Aren was fast, though, and rolled out of the way before Gunnar's blade could hit its target.

He was a formidable opponent. In fact, the only one of his pack who might stand a chance of taking him in a fight. Gunnar thought of Chelle. Her beautiful forest-green eyes, summer scent, and fiery spirit. Had he nothing to live for, Aren might have gotten the upper hand. But Gunnar had something Aren didn't. And his mate bond made him stronger still.

Whether or not Chelle ever wanted to see him again, he'd win this fight. For her.

CHAPTER
33

Chelle brought Jenner's Ducati to a screeching halt in Gunnar's driveway. She'd managed to shave the thirty-minute drive to Pasadena down to seventeen but still it had felt like years. She'd pushed the bike to its limits despite Jenner's warning of bodily harm if she let anything happen to it. In the distance, she spotted a group of bodies that formed a wide circle in the middle of Gunnar's enormous yard. *Good gods!* They hadn't wasted any damn time, had they? Werewolves didn't beat around the bush. When they had beef to settle, they settled it.

She knocked the kickstand down and rushed to where the werewolves stood watching Gunnar and Aren try to kill each other. Her heart lodged in her throat as she found Jillian and wormed her way between her and a large male she recognized from her second visit here in order to get a glimpse of Gunnar.

Jillian started as Chelle nudged her out of the way. "Good Lord, Chelle, did you fly here?"

"Just about." Her eyes were glued to Gunnar, fighting with all the ferocity of the Viking warrior he was. Gods, she'd never seen a more magnificent male. If the situation hadn't been so damned dire, she might have taken a moment or two longer to admire him. "Who's winning?" Was there really a winner in this scenario? Either way, the results would damage Gunnar's pack. And even if Aren did come out on top, the male wouldn't live to enjoy his victory. Chelle would make sure of it.

"They're almost evenly matched." Jillian's voice bore all of the concern that Chelle fought to contain. "But Gunnar's stronger. Faster. He's smarter and you know that a level head makes all the difference in a fight."

Chelle did know that. Unfortunately, there was also something to say for ruthlessness and Aren had that in spades.

"Daggers?" Jesus. If the weapons choice was Gunnar's, Chelle was going to slap him. Why not fight it out with switchblades or straight razors? Did he want Aren in such close gods-damned quarters?

"Gunnar's choice," Jillian replied. *Of course it was.* "He's good with daggers though, Chelle. I've never seen anyone better."

Jillian's gaze moved above Chelle's head and past her. She turned to find Jillian looking at the tall male to Chelle's left. She turned to face him, her own expression daring him to challenge her presence here.

"Vampire." His deep voice vibrated in his chest as he offered the casual greeting.

"Wolf," Chelle said with as much disregard.

"Sven . . ." Jillian warned as though she thought he might try to pick a fight.

Sven turned his attention back to the fight. "For what it's worth, I think Gunnar is right in challenging tradition in regards to you." He nudged his chin toward the center of the circle. "But you do realize that your bond isn't what this is about."

"I do." This was about power, plain and simple. "But do you think I could simply stand by and wait for news of my mate's fate?"

Sven turned to face Chelle and cocked a brow. "Mate?"

"Yeah," she said, knowing he was goading her into voicing her own claim on Gunnar. "Gunnar is my tethered mate."

Sven's lips spread into a wide smile. "Jillian was right about you. Then again, she's an excellent judge of character."

Heh. Chelle was glad she'd passed the werewolf approval test by laying claim to Gunnar. "Yeah, well, you're not so bad either, for a mutt."

Chelle shook her head at Sven's robust laughter. You'd think Thunderdome-style death matches happened every day at the werewolf compound, as casually as he treated the whole thing.

"How much longer can they go at it like this?" Chelle had only been there for minutes but she knew, with their preternatural stamina, the fight could last hours.

"Until one of them dies," Sven said with a grunt.

Something disrupted the rhythm of the fight. Gunnar's step faltered, his attention wandered. Myriad thoughts peppered Chelle's mind and she blocked them out. The tether gave a gentle tug at the center of her chest as Gunnar's head turned and his icy gaze landed on her.

Focus, damn it!

This was why they were better as a team. The separation caused too great of a distraction. Aren used it to his benefit and swiped his arm low, catching Gunnar in the torso with the edge of his blade.

Chelle sucked in a sharp breath and held it. He'd ingested a fair amount of her blood over the past two nights. It gave him an edge. He'd heal quickly. Crimson bloomed from the cut, soaking the fabric of Gunnar's shirt. What the hell . . . ? He wasn't healing. He was bleeding like crazy. Chelle turned to Jillian, eyes wide. "They're fighting with silver blades?"

Jillian pursed her lips. "Werewolves aren't easy to kill." Her grave tone sent a chill down Chelle's spine.

"So you give them weapons that'll help them poison each other?" The words spilled from her lips in an incredulous burst.

"It's a fair fight," Sven replied. "If Aren is as strong as his challenge suggests."

She knew from Gunnar's previous altercations with the berserkers that because he was an Alpha, his body was able to withstand the silver poisoning in a way that a weaker werewolf might not. It served to reason that if Aren believed he possessed the strength of the Alpha, he'd be required to prove it in more ways than one.

Chelle had never met a stronger male than Gunnar. Not just his body, but his mind and spirit. He was every bit the Alpha he claimed to be and she had no doubt that he'd come out of this fight the victor. It didn't make watching him take a hit like that any easier, but she had faith. In him. In their tether. In her love for him. Fate would never be so cruel as to take him away from her so quickly.

If she didn't believe that, nothing would stop her from jumping right into the fray to help him.

Come on, Gunnar. End this now and save me a hell of a lot of worry.

Chelle flinched with every grunt, groan, and shout. The scrape of metal on metal as their blades clashed over and again grated on her ears and sent a trickle of anxiety into her bloodstream. Sweat ran in rivulets down Gunnar's face. The strip of hair that ran down the middle of his head stuck to one side of his scalp. His hardened expression and determination made him appear even fiercer. He kept Aren on the defensive, and finally, Chelle began to see the momentum of the fight shift.

For the first time since she'd arrived, Chelle allowed herself a deep breath of relief. She tucked her hands into her jacket pockets. Her fist gripped the third of Gunnar's Alexandria key that he'd tossed onto her bed before he'd walked out on her. In the larger scope of things, Chelle's quest for answers meant little compared to the delicate balance of life. Tonight's turn of events was proof enough of that. Hell, the turn of events over the past few weeks was more than enough proof of it. At any time one of them could have died. And what would those answers have mattered? Chelle had spent most of their tumultuous time together trying to convince Gunnar that they were stronger as a team. And instead of practicing what she preached, she'd all but told him she was planning to leave him behind while she ran off to look for answers she might not ever find. She'd gone behind his back and, instead of trusting his judgment, had let her own stubbornness override common sense.

They were a team. Period. Chelle would've never been able to leave Gunnar behind.

A shot rang out and Chelle's body jerked with a start. She looked on in horror as Gunnar went to his knees. Aren stood mere feet away, the gun he held in his hand still leveled on her mate. A scream built in her chest and Chelle swallowed it down. She lunged forward to run to Gunnar but her arm was encircled in an iron grip as Sven held her back.

"You cheating son of a bitch!" she screamed at the top of her lungs.

The tether that bound her to Gunnar slackened and Chelle's knees gave out. If she lost him tonight, madness would be a cakewalk in comparison to the violence she'd unleash. This was pack justice? To just stand by and watch as Aren blatantly broke the rules of combat. If so, every werewolf here would pay the price for her mate's death.

The searing pain of the bullet entering Gunnar's shoulder dropped him in an instant. Eyes wide, he stared at the gun still clutched in Aren's fist. An angry scream pierced the air and Gunnar's wolf let out a mournful howl in the back of his mind.

"You cheating son of a bitch!"

He couldn't help the smile that tugged at the corner of his mouth. His mate was so full of fire. "If the only way you think you can win is by cheating," Gunnar managed through the pain, "then you're not deserving of the position of Alpha."

"You've had no problem rewriting our laws," Aren remarked. "So why shouldn't I?"

It figured that he'd find some way to justify his dishonorable actions. Aren kept the gun trained on Gunnar as he waited for the silver bullet to do its job. Searing heat chased through his body until he thought he might pass out from the pain. His wolf quieted in his mind until the connection between them became as transparent and thin as a cobweb. For the first time in centuries, Gunnar truly felt his mortality. His gaze shifted to Chelle. Would their last words be ones of anger? Would he die before he got the opportunity to tell her that he loved her?

A bolt of pain shot through his chest. The hand that braced him upright gave out and he fell. A gasp of breath reached his ears. The cool, dew-damp grass was a balm to his heated cheek. He kept his fist wrapped around the hilt of the dagger in his right hand. He had strength enough to keep his hold on the weapon, and he refused to let it go.

A Viking who died without a sword in his hand would never see Valhalla. Gunnar would do everything in his power to guarantee he'd go to the afterlife as a warrior and drink in the mead halls with his long-dead brethren. By the gods, he'd at least do that.

"Nooooo!" Chelle's mournful cry pierced the quiet and his wolf gave a nearly indiscernible whimper. "Gunnar! Get up!"

Even from a distance, he sensed her attempt to poke around in his mind. His stubborn mate thought she could compel him to stand. To fight. To fend off the effects of the silver poisoning. He didn't want to be the one to disappoint her, but even her unique powers had their limits.

"Get up!" she shouted again. "Damn it, Gunnar! Don't you *dare* give up!"

His beautiful mate whose very existence defied the laws of nature demanded that he stand. That he fight. How could he possibly deny her anything? How could he leave her here alone, knowing that if he died, her soul would once again be severed from her body and sent out into oblivion? How could he ever consider leaving her to search the world for answers to her existence alone?

He couldn't. Valhalla would have to wait a bit longer to welcome him. Gunnar wasn't going anywhere. He'd ingested Chelle's blood. She'd developed a tolerance to silver poisoning. Her strength was his. Their bond was unbreakable.

Gunnar's shoulder screamed with pain as he forced his left palm onto the grass. His jaw welded shut, teeth clenched to the point that he felt the enamel grind. Sweat rolled from the top of his head, down his temples and cheeks, to drip from his bearded chin. He shook with the effort it took to push himself up. He could have let his good arm bear his weight, but he didn't want to leave himself unprotected. The dagger clenched in his fist was his only chance of beating Aren. If he was going to win this fight, he needed to suck it the fuck up and prove once and for all who the better male was.

"I am Gunnar Falk," he ground out. "Descended from Sweyn Forkbeard, king of Sweden. I am the Alpha of the Forkbeard pack," he said through his panting breaths. "Mated to a vampire who is descended from a god. And you, Aren Ragnarson, will breathe your last breath this night."

The air soured with Aren's anxiety. Gunnar's wolf, though still weak, reemerged in his mind to offer up a predatory growl of approval. They were far from beaten. Aren was about to find out what happened to traitors and usurpers.

His legs were as shaky as a newborn fawn's, but he forced himself upright. Aren's eyes went wide as the realization hit that Gunnar wasn't, in fact, about to die and he quickly brought the gun up and fired off another shot.

It went wide, missing Gunnar's right shoulder by inches. He dug his toes into the soles of his shoes and propelled himself forward, straight into Aren. Gunnar took the male to the ground in a less than graceful tackle, but it was enough to cause Aren to lose his hold on the gun. It tumbled several feet away, leaving Aren no choice but to fight fair.

Gunnar was far from a hundred percent. He hurt like a motherfucker and his strength wasn't what it should be. Still, his wolf grew stronger in his psyche, lending Gunnar some measure of its strength. He rolled with Aren in a tangle of limbs, swinging the dagger in his right fist in an attempt to catch the male in the throat. Aren managed to stop him, but it took both of his hands and all of his strength to keep Gunnar's dagger from piercing the skin.

"Fuck you, Gunnar!" Aren spat. His face grew red from the effort of keeping the dagger at bay and his arms shook. "You've run this pack into the ground! You've forgotten what you are. What *we* are. If I don't manage to kill you tonight, it's only a matter of time before someone else gets the job done."

Gunnar didn't have time for cocky posturing. Aren thought to further shake him by throwing his shortcomings in his face. All it did was fuel the fire and solidify his determination to come out on top.

Aren's knee came up between them and caught Gunnar in the gut. He grunted and buckled forward, giving Aren the opportunity to shift his weight and throw Gunnar from his body. With his balance off, Gunnar landed on his left shoulder where the bullet was still embedded in the muscle. His arm went numb. Completely useless.

In a quick scramble, Gunnar got to his feet. The numbness in his arm threw him off balance but he kept the bulk of his weight on the balls of his feet to equalize. He kept his left arm tucked as close to his body as he could. Blood oozed from the gunshot wound. The metallic scent agitated his wolf. The evidence that he'd been weakened would be a boon to Aren's wolf and it would urge him to capitalize. Of course, Gunnar expected that. Instinct was stronger than common sense.

Aren lunged. Gunnar stepped to the right, pulling back his left shoulder to protect himself. He worked the grip of the dagger in his palm, loosening his hold until the blade felt more like an extension of his arm. They circled one another until Gunnar reached the discarded gun in the grass. He kicked it away, making sure to keep their fight fair.

Gunnar feinted left and swept his right arm in an uppercut, stabbing the dagger toward Aren's throat. He dodged out of the way, but not before the edge caught him just below the jaw. Blood trickled down his neck and a surge of confidence rushed through Gunnar's bloodstream. The scent of Aren's fear intensified, souring the air. Gunnar's ability to tolerate the silver had rattled the other male and rightly so. Even Gunnar was still a little shocked. One of the benefits of having an extraordinary mate. Chelle was with him in the fight even though she wasn't by his side.

Like Chelle had said, they were better as a team. Gunnar would never doubt that again.

The numbness in his arm subsided as Gunnar began to heal. His strength returned by small degrees: his legs felt more solid beneath him, his balance was sure. The dagger no longer felt like a weight in his palm and his body seemed lighter, instead of feeling as though it dragged him to the ground.

Gunnar was through with this bullshit. It was time to end this once and for all. "You were my brother," he said to Aren. Regret sliced through him that it had come to this. "My friend. Closer to me than anyone. Your betrayal is worse than the bullet in my shoulder and your death will be a regret I carry with me for the rest of my days."

Aren's step faltered. A groove cut into the center of his forehead. Gold glinted in his gaze. His wolf wouldn't back down after the challenge had been issued. One of them was about to die. That was the only truth between them now.

Gunnar attacked. For their years of comradery and the many battles they'd fought side by side, he owed Aren a quick death. He'd go to Valhalla as a warrior and someday they would drink in the mead halls together. Everything would be forgiven. But tonight, Aren had to be held accountable for his actions. No matter how much it pained Gunnar to mete out his punishment.

Aren wasn't prepared for Gunnar's speed. He spun, bringing his arm around, the motion as fluid and effortless as water passing down a stream. Aren brought his arm up to guard his throat once again but he miscalculated Gunnar's swing. The tip of the dagger sank into his chest and Gunnar buried the blade to the hilt, piercing Aren's heart.

The silence was deafening. Aren's gaze met Gunnar's, half surprise, half admiration. His grimace of pain curved into a rueful smile for the barest moment. Gunnar released his hold on the dagger's grip and took a step back as Aren fell to his knees. The gold light dimmed in his eyes and his gaze went blank. He toppled to the ground as one last breath released from his chest and went completely still.

Aren had been his oldest, dearest friend. Never in all his days would Gunnar have believed he'd be the one to kill him. *"Tills vi ses igen,"* he murmured.

Until we meet again.

Gunnar turned as his gaze locked with Chelle's. The relief in her expression compressed his lungs until he didn't think he could take a deep breath. He'd been a fool to walk away from her tonight. And he made a silent vow that he'd never walk away from her again.

Not ever.

CHAPTER
34

Chelle's legs nearly buckled with relief when Aren went down. At the same time, sorrow welled up in her chest, so thick she could barely take a decent breath. The emotions weren't Chelle's, though. The tether that bound them was a conduit to Gunnar. Aren's death had laid him low and it nearly broke her heart.

She wanted to go to him but resisted. None of the pack broke the circle. Their silence and reverent expressions kept her glued to her spot on the grass. She supposed it didn't matter that Aren had conspired against their Alpha. They'd lost one of their own.

Memories assaulted Chelle's mind. So many of Gunnar's pack had been with him since that night in the forest when they'd been ambushed and bitten. So much history. So many trials faced and hardships overcome. Tears welled in Chelle's eyes and she could do nothing to stem the flow as they ran in rivulets down her cheeks. Beneath the memories, the mournful howls of the entire pack echoed in Chelle's ears. This wasn't a victory. It was a tragedy.

Gunnar's eyes met Chelle's. Bright gold flecks sparked in the crystal-blue depths. She could no longer stay put. Her legs acted of their own volition, propelling her forward as she rushed to Gunnar at the center of the circle. His arms went wide and Chelle threw herself against him, crying as he cradled her in his embrace.

"Oh my gods, Gunnar," she said through her tears. "I . . ." The words refused to come. She didn't know if she should say she was relieved, sad, scared. Too many emotions cycled through her for Chelle to make any sense of them. "I'm sorry," she said at last. There were so many things she was sorry for. He held her tighter and let out a jagged sigh. "I'm so sorry."

"I'm a stubborn ass," Gunnar said. His hand moved to cradle the back of her head that she rested on his shoulder. "I swear to you, I'll never walk away from you again."

Chelle let out a half laugh, half sob. "I'll never give you a reason to."

Minutes passed and they simply held one another. A sense of peace and contentment settled over Chelle, the likes of which she'd never known. She was right where she wanted to be. Where she *belonged*. Whatever their opinions, Gunnar's pack was going to have to get used to having a couple of vampires hanging around because Chelle wasn't going *anywhere*.

"I love you." The words were more of a breath than a whisper, but Chelle knew that Gunnar heard her.

"Chelle." Her name on his lips was spoken with all the reverence of a prayer. "I love you, too."

Tears continued to stream down Chelle's cheeks as Gunnar held her. She didn't ever want him to let her go. "Tell me what to do." They'd been through so much in a few short weeks. Whatever she could do to help repair the fracture in his pack was more important than any quest for answers or cures. "I'll do whatever it takes to help you mend your fences. If the pack needs me to keep my distance, I can do that, too." Leaving Gunnar again would be like leaving a limb behind, but she'd do it if she had to. "Anything you need."

"What I need is to have you at my side," Gunnar said close to her ear. "If you think to leave me, *mate*, I'll track you to the ends of the earth."

A smile curved Chelle's lips. "There's nowhere else I'd rather be," she said. "Try to get rid of me, Gunnar, and see what happens."

"I do love a stubborn female," he said with a laugh.

"Be careful what you wish for. I'm a handful."

"You are and then some," Gunnar agreed. "But I wouldn't change you for the world."

She felt the exact same way about him. "You're stuck with me, you know. Forever."

Gunnar pulled back to look into her face. The depth of emotion in his expression stole her breath. He reached up to cup her face in his hands and kissed her gently. Once. "Forever sounds just about right."

It really did, didn't it?

The members of the pack gathered around Chelle and Gunnar. He straightened and put his arm around her waist, pulling her close to his body. "Chelle is my chosen mate." Gunnar's voice rang with authority and his power rippled over Chelle's skin in a warm wave. "If anyone here wishes to challenge my authority as Alpha of this pack for this reason or any other, speak now!"

A long, silent moment passed. Chelle's muscles went rigid, her stomach twisted in on itself as she waited for someone to speak up. When no one issued a challenge, she let out a slow, shaky breath and relaxed against Gunnar's side.

"Then it's settled." Gunnar's head bowed. "Take our fallen brother and prepare his body."

Without so much as a murmur, the pack dispersed, each of them knowing their individual jobs. Chelle swallowed down the lump in her throat. How many of their own had they lost over the years? How many fallen had they mourned?

Gunnar urged Chelle forward and they walked toward the house. "We have a lot to talk about," he said close to her ear. "I need a few private moments. And I need a shower."

Chelle sensed his sorrow beneath the easy words. It would take some time before Gunnar's heart was healed from what happened tonight and Chelle vowed to help him through it in any way that she could. "I'm not going anywhere," she said. "Just tell me what you need."

"Your being here is enough," Gunnar replied. "Your very presence is a healing balm."

Another wave of tears threatened but Chelle pushed them away. She knew exactly how he felt.

"Well, the least I can do is help you wash your back."

He squeezed her tight. "Funny, I was just about to suggest that."

Chelle waved her hand between them. "See? We're totally in sync."

"That we are, love." Gunnar's voice warmed with affection.

Love. Chelle didn't think she'd ever heard a sweeter word.

Gunnar's house made the cottage at Mikhail's seem like a shack in comparison. His bedroom was an apartment in itself, at least a thousand square feet and lavish. The decorating suited Gunnar. Dark forest colors, masculine furniture, and soft, plush carpeting. The room was oddly silent. With so many of them inhabiting the same space, she expected to hear movement, conversations, the usual hustle and bustle.

"It's quiet."

Gunnar's reflection gave her a soft smile from the bathroom mirror. He refused to let anyone tend to his shoulder. Instead, he dug the bullet out himself. He'd assured her that his body had already done most of the hard work, pushing the bullet to the surface of his skin. Still, Chelle had a hard time watching from across the room as he used the pincers to extricate the silver. It let loose of the wound with a slight sucking sound that made her cringe. Gunnar let out a quiet grunt and dropped the bullet into the sink. "The entire house is soundproofed. We've got to have some privacy, you know?"

"Totally." Chelle knew exactly what it was like to cohabit when you have superhuman senses. Gunnar turned to face her and Chelle stared, rapt, at the hills and valleys of his muscular torso. His body was a work of art, soft curves and sharp angles begging to be admired and explored. "I can't even take a deep breath without Lucas hearing it."

"You won't have to worry about that anymore." Gunnar crossed the room and sat on the edge of the bed beside her. "Once you're moved in, you'll have some peace and quiet."

"Gunnar." They hadn't broached the subject of living arrangements yet. "I can't leave Lucas."

His brow furrowed. "I don't expect you to."

The knot in her chest loosened a small degree. "So, what? We'll just move in and your pack will have to accept that centuries of tradition are being changed with a snap of your fingers? That's a lot to ask, even from someone who's agreeable to change."

Gunnar reached for her hand. His hypnotic gaze held hers as he brought her hand up and put his lips to each of her knuckles. "I'm not proposing anything quite so abrupt." When he looked at her with so much intensity, Chelle swore the rest of the world melted away. "But Chelle, I won't live without you. I'm not going to drive to L.A. every night and back here every morning. I don't want a few feet to separate us, let alone miles. I can do it temporarily, but I want you to live here. I want Lucas to live here. The pack will come to accept you. Those who don't may leave."

Chelle forced herself to look away. "I don't want to be what comes between you and your family. I couldn't live with that on my conscience."

"You are my family," Gunnar stressed. "My heart. My soul. Everything. If they love me, they'll love you."

Chelle quirked a half smile. "You seem pretty confident about that."

Gunnar stood and faced her. He took Chelle's hands and urged her to stand. "Of course I am," he said with a sardonic grin that turned her bones soft. "I'm the Alpha. Now, get undressed. I believe you promised to wash my back."

When he looked at her with so much heat, how could she deny him anything? "I did," she said with a smile. "I may be a thief, but I always keep my word."

She stripped off her shirt and Gunnar's smile faded into something serious and sinful. She doubted there'd be much washing in his shower. Eh, being clean was totally overrated.

Gunnar stood under the hot spray and breathed the steam into his lungs. His body was still weak from the silver, but the wound had finally closed and was now nothing more than a puckered star of scar tissue that would soon fade as well.

Chelle grabbed a bar of soap from the tray and lathered

it between her hands. Gunnar watched as the water sluiced down her naked body, running in tiny rivers between her pert breasts, over the luscious pink tips of her nipples, down the curve of her hips and downward between her thighs.

The slide of her slick hands over his skin was heaven. She massaged every inch of him with agonizing precision, loosening the knots in his muscles as she washed him. "I said I needed help with my back." Gunnar let his eyes drift shut for an indulgent moment. "Gods, her hands felt good on his skin. "I didn't expect you to be so thorough."

"What sort of a mate would I be if I neglected the rest of you?" Gunnar peeked through one lid to find Chelle's heated gaze locked on him. His cock stirred and he swallowed down a groan. "I want you nice and clean."

"Mmmm," Gunnar replied. "I'll have to return the favor."

"Oh, yeah you are," Chelle said with a husky laugh that sent a zing of excitement through his bloodstream. "If you think I'm doing this without expecting a reward for my efforts, you're out of your mind."

He was out of his mind all right. Chelle drove him absolutely crazy with lust. Gunnar reached for her but she put her arm out to keep him at a distance. "I haven't done your back yet."

"I don't give a shit about my back." He grabbed her wrist and eased her elbow to bend, closing the space between them. Her breasts rubbed against his soap-slicked chest and Gunnar groaned. "Gods, Chelle, if I don't fuck you right now, I truly might go out of my mind."

A slow, sensual smile parted her lips. "Far be it from me to disregard your mental health."

Her mouth met his. The warm, wet glide of her tongue caused Gunnar's cock to harden. His heart raced in his chest and his breath became one with hers. Would he ever not be excited by her simplest touch?

Her arms came around his shoulders. Her fingertips teased the back of his neck, nails scraping against his bare flesh. A shiver rippled down his spine and Gunnar pressed Chelle against the marble wall of the shower, cupping her ass and hoisting her upward as he thrust inside of her.

Patience didn't exist when it came to her. He needed to take her and extinguish the damnable want that consumed him like wildfire. Chelle's head fell back against the wall of the shower. Her legs went around his waist and her ankles hooked just above his ass.

"Harder, Gunnar." Her breathy words in his ear spurred him on. She moaned louder with each drive of his hips. "Like that. Don't stop."

Her pussy clenched around his shaft. Hot. Wet. Tight. Gods, the sensation was so intense he didn't know how much longer he could hold out until he went off. But he'd be damned if he came before Chelle. His jaw clenched and Gunnar slowed his pace, pulling out slowly before driving forward with a powerful thrust that made her gasp.

"Do you like that, love?" Gunnar braced one hand on the wall and kept the other firmly on Chelle's ass.

"It's horrible," she said on a moan. "I hate it."

She flashed a wicked smile as he pulled out and thrust home once again. "And that?"

Her panting breaths betrayed her words. "Awful."

His shaft slid against the stiff, swollen bud of her clit and it was all he could do to keep from pounding mercilessly into her. But he wanted to draw out her pleasure. Feel her squeeze him when the orgasm took her.

"Oh gods, Gunnar." Chelle's voice hitched. "That's so good."

Gods yes, it was. He fucked her hard and deep. Water poured down their bodies, adding a layer of sensation he hadn't expected. Chelle's head rolled back on her shoulders and Gunnar pushed away from the shower wall to grip her neck. "Look at me, Chelle."

Her eyes came open. Liquid silver undulated in her irises, the mercurial depths swallowing Gunnar whole. She was the most beautiful creature he'd ever laid eyes on. He still couldn't believe that such an extraordinary creature had chosen his soul out of the billions in the world to secure itself to. Gunnar was the luckiest male on the face of the earth.

"Gunnar!" His name exploded from her lips.

Her muscles went rigid and then relaxed all at once. Her pussy clenched around his shaft and Gunnar thrust hard and deep and his own orgasm swept over him in an intense rush that left his legs weak and shaking. He continued to pump into her, each contraction of her body milking him dry. His breath came in ragged gasps and his fingertips dug into the yielding flesh of her ass. "I love you, Chelle," he said against her ear. "Gods, how I love you."

"I love you, too," she replied. Her eyes sparked with mischief. "And I'll love you even more when you're done washing me."

She was one hundred percent fire. And Gunnar wouldn't have her any other way.

CHAPTER
35

Saeed's foot bounced with impatience as he waited for Sasha to return. Since the night of the berserkers' attack, Mikhail had been more paranoid than ever. He left no room for chance, covered all of his bases. He, Jenner, and Jenner's mate, Bria, had arranged to meet with Connor Brody. His coven was one of the few remaining that Mikhail had yet to reach out to. The berserkers' attempted ambush had pushed up the king's timetables. Their numbers needed to be fortified. And quickly. Claire was watching after their child and Ronan had work. Which left Saeed to fetch Vanessa this evening from some school function. Mikhail had begun to guard the child as though she were some sort of messiah.

At least on that, they could agree.

Saeed had listened from a distance to the meeting that transpired between Mikhail and Trenton McAlister. He'd gone that night, hoping to persuade McAlister to help him locate the mage who had enslaved his fire-haired fae. His plan had been thwarted when he realized that not only was McAlister searching for her as well, but that Mikhail's young ward was more than she appeared to be.

An Oracle.

Saeed had never put much faith in such things. Fortune-tellers, prognosticators, those who read the auguries, were nothing more than charlatans in his opinion. Con artists with the ability to translate the reactions of others in order to tell them what they wanted to hear. The child was no charlatan, however, and it wasn't simply his foolish hopes that led him to believe so.

The car door swung open. Sasha stood behind the girl and waited for her to get in the car. Strange how something so innocent could also be so menacing. An aura of power surrounded the girl that unnerved Saeed. McAlister was right about her: Mikhail underestimated what she was capable of.

"Hello, Vanessa." Saeed kept his voice level and smooth. "I am Saeed. I'm here to accompany you home."

Her eyes narrowed and her delicate mouth formed a hard line. "I know who you are," she replied.

The madman. Saeed had heard her declare to McAlister his intentions to find the fae. Who else could she have possibly meant? Saeed had lost touch with his sanity the moment Mikhail had turned him.

"And you're not frightened of me?" Who wouldn't be scared of madness? Saeed frightened himself.

"No." Vanessa climbed into the car beside him. Sasha followed suit and closed the door. "The only person who should be afraid of you is the mage."

Saeed cocked a brow. He signaled to the driver and the car pulled out onto the street. "Trenton McAlister?"

"No," Vanessa replied. "The other one. The soul keeper."

The child spoke in riddles. The Collective pulled at

Saeed's mind and he pushed the memories away. "Soul keeper?"

Vanessa didn't offer up any more information on the mage's esoteric title and Saeed thought it best not to grill her. The last thing he needed was for Mikhail to become suspicious of what his plans were.

"Are you hungry? We can stop and get you something to eat. Ice cream, perhaps?" Though it had been centuries since Saeed had been in the company of a child, he remembered that sweets usually placated them.

From the other end of the backseat, Sasha cut him a look. She knew Saeed's mind and what his intentions were so it shouldn't have surprised her or annoyed her that he would do whatever he could to make the child comfortable.

"I'm good," Vanessa replied. "Claire's making lasagna for dinner. It's my favorite."

"Some other time, perhaps." Sasha rolled her eyes and he chose to ignore it. "Tell me, Vanessa, what do you think of Trenton McAlister?" It was important to know your enemies, and if the director of the Sortiari was searching for the fae, he was at the very least Saeed's rival.

She screwed up her face in concentration. Her little brow furrowed as she considered her answer. "I don't know yet." Saeed kept his gaze ahead, his posture relaxed. Vanessa took another moment as though considering how much of her opinion she should reveal. "He's afraid."

"Of what?" Saeed wondered.

"Of dying."

Interesting. Though supernatural creatures were far from infallible, they were long-lived and that had a tendency to make the issue of their mortality low on their list of priorities. That McAlister worried over his piqued Saeed's curiosity.

"I suppose that would be frightening." McAlister

wasn't the only one searching for the fae, however. Vanessa had told McAlister that his fate depended on who found the female first: the madman or the beast.

"What do you know of the red-haired female?" Saeed couldn't help but ask. He wanted to learn as much as he could about her.

"I don't know her at all," Vanessa said. "I only had an awake dream about her. She must be pretty popular, though," she added.

"Why is that?"

Vanessa smiled. "Because so many boys want to find her."

Saeed, McAlister, this beast . . . How many others searched for her? How many others would Saeed have to kill in his pursuit to claim her as his own?

"Who else wants her?" Saeed asked. "Me, which you already know. And Trenton McAlister."

"The man with the black eyes." Fear chased across Vanessa's expression. "The one who kidnapped me and Claire. The one who hurt her and my mom."

Gregor? After Mikhail's ascension to power, rumors had begun to circulate. One of them being that Ian Gregor, the leader of the berserker warlords, had taken Mikhail's mate and tortured her. Saeed wondered at the truth of those stories, mostly because Gregor still walked the earth. It was possible that Mikhail was biding his time, waiting for the perfect opportunity to send the bastard into the afterlife. Gregor's ambush on Mikhail two nights ago proved that the berserker had similar plans with regard to the vampire king.

"Why does the man with the black eyes want her?" An anxious rush of adrenaline dumped into Saeed's bloodstream. He was racing against the clock. He needed to get to his beautiful fae before the others.

"For the same reason Trenton is afraid of her," Vanessa replied.

"I'm not sure I understand what you mean."

Vanessa shrugged her tiny shoulders, unconcerned. "I'm not sure what I mean, either."

These visions . . . premonitions . . . whatever the hell they were . . . only served to further frustrate Saeed. The girl was too young to understand and properly interpret what she saw in her mind's eye. His fae obviously possessed power. And whatever her talents, they were enough to rattle one of the most powerful males on the planet and draw the attention of one of the most feared males in the supernatural world.

"Do you know where I can find her, Vanessa?" All of this would be for nothing, if Saeed didn't know where to start his search.

Vanessa sat quietly, her gaze straight ahead. For a moment, Saeed wondered if she'd heard him or perhaps simply chose to ignore him. He cast a sidelong glance at Sasha who looked at him with obvious disgust. She didn't approve of his obsession. But it wasn't any of her concern. He'd waited longer than the promised two days to turn her and it was time to hold up his end of the bargain. Soon, she would be a vampire and would share Diego's responsibility of taking charge of the coven until he returned. Once her soul was forfeit to oblivion, Sasha wouldn't care who Saeed searched for or why. It would be a blessing for them both.

"She's far away." Vanessa's tiny voice pierced the quiet.

How much could a child know about geography? The other end of the city could be far away to Vanessa. Was it too much to hope for that he'd find his mate as close as San Diego? Saeed swallowed a snort. Probably.

"She lives by the water," Vanessa said. "There's a tall

tower that looks like a spaceship and a big mountain with lots of snow."

Saeed racked his brain. The world was covered in water and mountains. As far as the tower went, he could think of several locations with architecture that fit the description. Perhaps, in the Collective, he could find the details Vanessa left out. Which meant more searching. More time wasted. And another piece of his mind given over to madness.

Too soon the car pulled through the elaborate gate of Mikhail's driveway that led to the main house. Saeed let out a slow breath. He wouldn't say his conversation with the child had been a total loss, but neither had it shed much light on his situation. Vanessa's knowledge had proven as misleading and hazy as the memories Saeed waded through night after night.

He wasn't back at square one, but by no means was he closer to finding her.

"Thanks for the ride," Vanessa chirped as the car came to a stop in front of the house. Her gaze focused on Saeed and he couldn't help but be a little unnerved by the raw power he sensed in her. "Don't give up," she said solemnly. "And don't be afraid."

Ominous words spoken in such a sweet tone. The child was truly frightening. "Thank you for answering my questions, Vanessa," Saeed replied. "May the rest of the night treat you well."

Vanessa giggled as she opened the car door. "You talk funny."

Without a care in the world, she ran to the front door and slipped inside of the house.

The car pulled through the circular driveway and away from Mikhail's property. The ghost of emotion prodded at Saeed, despair that would have hollowed him out had he a soul to remind him to care. The quiet that remained unnerved him. He almost wished the girl were back in the car so at least he had her sweet, melodious voice to distract him. The Collective called, and though Saeed knew he needed to wait until he was safe in his home, he felt himself becoming increasingly unable to resist its pull.

"She's in Seattle." Sasha's voice pierced the silence.

"Seattle?"

Sasha didn't look at him. "The Space Needle is a tower that looks like a flying saucer. It's a port city. And Mount Rainer is visible from the city. I can't imagine anywhere else that fits the description."

Seattle wasn't close, but neither was it as far away as Saeed had feared. The more he thought about it, the more it made sense. It was as good a place as any to begin his search. Finally a glimmer of hope.

"Thank you, Sasha." She could have chosen to keep the revelation to herself. That she didn't, proved she cared for Saeed. Or more to the point, that she cared to preserve his sanity.

"I'm ready," she said, rather than acknowledge his gratitude. "I want you to turn me. Tonight."

Her tone was grave and her countenance stern. Her profile in the dark car made her look severe and deadly. She and Diego would protect the coven well. And to keep his word to Mikhail, Saeed was certain they would choose a worthy dhampir to be the third member of their group to be turned.

"Very well." Everything was falling into place. "Thank you, Sasha."

She let out a derisive snort. "Don't thank me. Because I have a feeling you're going to live to regret your decision to chase after her."

That might be, but Saeed wouldn't know until he tried.

He gave a slight nod of acknowledgment, but otherwise remained silent. For the first time since he'd been turned, Saeed felt some small measure of hope. It was only a matter of time before he found her and the Collective released its hold.

His soul would be returned to him soon.

CHAPTER
36

Chelle stood at Gunnar's side. In the distance, Aren's body had been placed on a pyre. The only thing missing in this Viking funeral was a boat to carry his body out to sea. A memory sparked in Chelle's mind, of Gunnar doing just that: standing on a craggy cliff that overlooked the ocean while a burning ship sailed out to sea. It was a tragically romantic vision. One that tightened Chelle's chest and left her breathless.

She hooked her arm with Gunnar's and pressed her body against his. A chill traveled the length of her body. The solemnity of the moment filled her with so much sadness. She carried Gunnar's sorrow as if it were her own. She didn't have to imagine how he felt. The tether that bound them took care of that.

"I'm so sorry, Gunnar." The words seemed trite. She wished she could take his pain away. Erase everything that had happened. "What can I do?"

He looked down at her, his bright blue gaze shining with unspent emotion. "You're doing it," he said. "Letting me feel the comforting weight of your body as you rest against me."

A member of Gunnar's pack, a male Chelle hadn't yet met, approached and handed Gunnar a torch. The flame danced in the light breeze, the only bright spot in the impenetrable darkness. The orange glow illuminated his face, casting shadows in sharp angles that made him all the more menacing. He eased away from Chelle and walked slowly to the pyre.

She watched in silence as Gunnar spoke to the sky in rhythmic words she didn't understand. The poetry of it rang in her ears like mournful music and she swallowed down the lump of emotion that rose in her throat. Gunnar's chanted words faded off into silence and the rest of the pack called out in unison, "Aren!" Gunnar touched the torch to the pyre and after a moment the flames took hold, devouring the tower of dry wood that Aren's body lay upon.

The fire cracked and popped, the flames reached higher into the night sky like arms reaching out imploringly toward the heavens. Chelle's mind filled with thoughts and memories, too many to separate into anything tangible. A vision of Gunnar once again appeared. Proud. Strong. Defiant. Dressed in furs and leather with a sword in his hand. Fierce. Deadly. Viking.

Chelle eased away from the pack to the point where the manicured lawn met the edge of the woods. The air smelled of smoke, of death, and of the crisp spring air.

"Trying to run, mate?"

Chelle had been so caught up in her own thoughts, she hadn't even noticed Gunnar approach from her left. The chill of the night mingled with the heat from the fire, coaxing goose bumps to the surface of her skin.

"Just wanted to give you a private moment," she said quietly.

"I wonder how my heart can feel so heavy and so full at the same time."

Chelle knew exactly what he meant. "We still have a bumpy road ahead."

Gunnar nodded. He moved behind Chelle and wrapped his arms around her torso. She leaned back against his chest, reveling in the heat of his body that soaked through her clothes. "We do," he agreed.

"But it's nothing we can't manage."

Gunnar kissed the top of her head. "True."

Chelle reached into her pocket. She opened her fist to reveal Gunnar's third of the Alexandria key resting in her palm. "I'm not going to open the library," she said. "You're right that maybe some mysteries need to go unsolved."

"Ah, Chelle." Gunnar's warm breath brushed the outer shell of her ear and she shivered. He reached out and closed his fist over hers, folding her fingers over the key. "I was wrong to tell you that. I spoke out of fear."

"Sometimes fear is okay," Chelle said. "Ronan told me once that fear was all that stood between life and death."

"He's right," Gunnar said. "But fear can also stand between life and *living*."

Chelle wondered when the intensity of emotion she felt whenever she was near Gunnar would begin to balance out. Since the night they'd met and her soul had been returned to her, she'd lived in a constant state of hypersensitivity. Like right now, his words evoked such emotion in her that she thought she'd burst.

"I don't want you to be afraid, Chelle. Not ever."

Such a male. "How can I possibly ever be afraid if I have you at my side?" She'd given Jenner shit for being a growly, temperamental son of a bitch after he'd been tethered. She probably should have cut him some slack. Because she was feeling positively sappy right about now. Cartoon heart-eyes and all.

Gunnar squeezed her tight. In the distance, Aren's funeral pyre continued to rage into the night. "We'll find your answers," Gunnar promised her. "Together."

Together sounded perfect. "We'll see," she said. "Egypt is pretty far away. The pack needs you."

"I'd follow you to the ends of the earth." In the recess of Gunnar's mind, his wolf gave an approving growl. "Pack or no pack."

A smile spread across Chelle's lips. She loved the male who held her and was pretty fond of the wolf to boot. "I'd chase you to Valhalla." She couldn't let him get one up on her.

"You won't have to, love." Gunnar's mouth found the hollow of her throat. "I'm never leaving your side."

"We're going to be one freaky coven," she said with a laugh.

"An unusual pack," Gunnar corrected.

"Whatever we are, we'll be together."

"True." Gunnar brought his head up and stared into the distance. "Whatever happens, that's all that matters."

A companionable silence settled between them. The sorrow that weighed down Gunnar's heart lifted with the smoke that rose into the sky. His emotional wounds weren't completely healed, but in time, Chelle hoped that they would scar. The wolf quieted in his mind, as did Gunnar's thoughts. He'd become quite adept at shielding his mind from her, and likewise, the tether made it possible for Chelle to tune out his thoughts and memories. They were truly made for one another. His soul had patiently waited centuries for hers, while hers had flown to his. True to their individual personalities. Fate was indeed a strange thing. If not for her uniqueness, she never would have sought his third of the key in the first place.

"I never thought I'd say this, but I'm glad that bastard shifter shoved me into that coffin."

Gunnar stiffened. "I would spare you that hurt if I could. But had you not faced that test, we wouldn't be here now."

"Exactly."

"I love you, Chelle." Gunnar's deep voice carried so much emotion it weighed her down. "I'll make sure you know it. Every day for the rest of our lives."

"I love you, too." She never thought she'd utter those words to any male, let alone a burly, tattooed, bearded Viking of a werewolf. "Twenty-four-seven, three-sixty-five."

Gunnar chuckled. "My mate is extraordinary."

"True," Chelle said. "Good thing my mate is extraordinary as well."

Chelle didn't care about the bumps ahead. Because she knew as long as she had Gunnar, it would be okay. Love was all that mattered and as long as they had that they had *everything*.

Gunnar sat in Mikhail Aristov's richly appointed study with Chelle at his right and Sven at his left. It was an amicable meeting, but still, his wolf was on edge. Change was never comfortable, especially when you'd been living in a rut for ten or eleven centuries. On one matter Aren had been right: the pack could no longer live apart from the rest of the supernatural community. It was time to come out of hiding and accept that the pack wasn't an island.

"I owe you a debt of gratitude," Mikhail said. He sat back in his chair, his posture relaxed. "If you hadn't come to our aid, Gregor would have managed to finish what he started."

"There is no debt to be paid," Gunnar replied. "I protect my family."

Werewolves and vampires alike had fallen prey to

Gregor's machinations the night of Aristov's meeting with Trenton McAlister. There was only one enemy as far as Gunnar was concerned. The berserker—and his plans for vengeance—needed to be shut down before he did something catastrophic. Chelle reached out and twined her fingers with his. The reassurance of her touch quieted his wolf and put him at ease.

"I hold no dominion over Chelle's coven," Mikhail said. "Or any dhampirs she chooses to turn. I would, however, like to keep the lines of diplomacy open in the interest of mutual responsibility."

Beside him, Chelle let out a soft snort. "If you think I'm going to run around the city, willy-nilly turning dhampirs, you have nothing to worry about, Mikhail. Unless they want to leave their covens and come live at the vampire-werewolf commune, I doubt I'll be turning anyone anytime soon."

Mikhail quirked a brow. His gaze met Gunnar's and a smile tugged at his lips. "Vampire-werewolf commune?"

Chelle's sense of humor was certainly as unique as she was.

"Pasadena isn't far from L.A.," Gunnar said. "But I realize there are logistics involved with the proximity of dhampirs to vampires. Chelle and Lucas will live with my pack. I hope that won't have a negative impact."

"Chelle is separate from the Collective and the bloodline," Mikhail replied. "She's fortunate in that she is her own source of strength and power and doesn't need to live close to the epicenter of other vampires or dhampirs."

Chelle's grip on Gunnar's hand tightened. Her uniqueness was a source of anxiety for her and he hoped that someday they could find the answers that would put her fears to rest. Until then, he would support her in all things and do whatever he could to reassure her.

"I guess that is sort of lucky, isn't it?" Chelle flashed Mikhail a cocky smile that betrayed her anxiousness. "Plus it puts a little distance between me and Siobhan, right?"

Gunnar's brow furrowed. "Siobhan?"

"Oh, don't worry," Chelle said. "She's harmless. I'll fill you in later. I do owe her a favor, though." She spoke to Mikhail this time. "And I've never known her not to collect."

Mikhail studied Chelle for a silent moment as though trying to decipher her thoughts. "I hope that when that time comes, you'll consult with me if there's any reason to worry?"

Chelle scoffed. "You worry *too much*, Mikhail. Relax. Her bark is a lot worse than her bite."

Mikhail pursed his lips as though he didn't share in Chelle's lax opinion of the female. Gunnar would have to keep this Siobhan on his radar. Anyone who had a chit to hold as leverage over his mate would have to deal with him first. And he would not be so accommodating.

"Tell me, Gunnar, how does your pack feel about Chelle having tethered you? In my experience, werewolves are a tight-knit group who don't easily accept outsiders."

Beside Gunnar, Sven shifted in his seat. "We are tight-knit, but we aren't unaccepting." Pride swelled in Gunnar's chest that Sven had easily fallen into his role as Gunnar's second and displayed the leadership qualities he'd always known the male to possess. "Chelle and Lucas are pack. Period."

Chelle grinned at Mikhail. "Trippy, right?"

Mikhail offered a half smile. "Indeed."

Chelle slid a key across Mikhail's desk toward him. "So yeah, that's basically why we're here. I'm moving out. Lucas and I have been spending most of our time at Gunnar's for the past month and I don't see any reason to put off the move to Pasadena. It's not like we're a million miles away, and of course if you or Claire, or anyone, needs us for anything, we'll be back here in a hot second."

Mikhail's expression softened with affection. It warmed Gunnar to know that the vampire king thought kindly of his mate. His wolf huffed in the recess of his mind, clearly proud as well.

"Gregor won't simply go away," Mikhail said after a moment. "He'll want retribution for his plans being disrupted."

"No doubt," Gunnar replied. "We'll be ready for him, though. Gregor is amassing enemies at a dangerous rate. He'll regret leaving the protection of the Sortiari."

Mikhail nodded. "I hope so. McAlister will want his head for interrupting our meeting."

"I'd be more than happy to give it to him," Gunnar said.

"I hoped that I could count you as an ally," Mikhail replied.

Gunnar had suspected that their informal chat with the vampire king had really been a smoke screen. What Mikhail hoped to glean from their conversation was whether or not Gunnar could be counted on if Mikhail needed him.

"My first alliance is to my mate and my pack," Gunnar replied. The Forkbeard pack might have been on the road to changing their culture, but it wouldn't happen overnight. "But Ronan is a member of your coven and thereby family as well. If it's within my power to help you, I will."

Mikhail's knowing glance and tight smile told Gunnar he hadn't given the king the emphatic answer he'd hoped for, but it would suffice. He gave a slight nod of his head. "That's all I can ask for and I would offer you the same."

An alliance. Gunnar let out a slow breath as a twinge of regret pulled at his chest. Perhaps if he'd been more receptive to change himself, Aren wouldn't have felt the need to make his deals with Gregor. Perhaps if they'd been less closed off to the world, to the supernatural creatures around them, Gunnar could have salvaged his relationship with his oldest friend before it had crumbled into a tug-of-war for supremacy.

Chelle's hand squeezed his once again. The closeness of their bond comforted him. Words weren't necessary. She knew his mind, his thoughts, his feelings. And he gladly offered them up to her. He had nothing to hide from Chelle.

"It's time to blow this Popsicle stand," Chelle declared. She stood and urged Gunnar up beside her. Sven followed suit, quiet but vigilant.

"Chelle, if you see Siobhan, tell her I'd like to visit with her again soon." She turned to face Mikhail and quirked a curious brow. He offered up a shrug that wasn't quite as casual as Gunnar suspected he wanted it to look. "I haven't been insulted in a while and thought she'd like to do the honors."

Chelle laughed. "Since we both know she won't say no to an opportunity to sling insults your way, I'll be sure to tell her. *If* I see her."

Mikhail inclined his head. "Of course."

"Don't be a stranger," she said in parting.

Mikhail chuckled. "The same goes for you."

As they walked out of the study to the foyer, Chelle guided Gunnar's arm around her. She nestled in close and he took a deep breath of her warm, summer scent. For a month they'd been separating their time between her cottage here and his house in Pasadena. A full moon had come and gone and the pack had finally given their blessing for Chelle and Lucas to join their ranks. It was a strange dynamic, one Gunnar wasn't certain how to navigate. One day at a time, he supposed. As long as Chelle was by his side, there wasn't a problem too big to surmount.

"Tell me more about this Siobhan," Gunnar said as they left the house and headed for his car.

Chelle laughed. The sound stirred Gunnar's wolf and a surge of lust coursed through him. He didn't think there would be a time that he didn't want her. Her very presence aroused him and he couldn't wait to get her home.

Our home. Gods, he liked the sound of that.

"Siobhan and I've had some crazy times," Chelle began. "There was this one time, in Cairo, we were chased down by a band of angry cat shifters. And this other time, in Mexico, we found a relic in a Mayan temple . . . Oh man. I didn't think we were going to make it out of that one alive."

He loved Chelle's adventurous spirit and he couldn't wait to make a few crazy memories of his own with her. "I can't wait to meet her," he remarked as he opened the passenger door for her.

"Oh, she's going to *love* you." A wicked smile curved her lips and mischief sparked in her forest-green eyes. "I'm definitely going to have to lay down the law with her so she knows you're all mine."

"All yours?" Gunnar didn't know if he could wait to get home before he stripped her bare. Would it be unfair to ask Sven to walk home?

"*All mine.* I wouldn't trade you for all the relics or magic in the world."

Gunnar bent down and kissed her. "Good. Because you're not getting rid of me."

"Excellent." She looked him up and down and the heat in her gaze made him sweat. "Now, let's get the hell out of here and go home. I want to show you just how much I want to keep you around."

Gunnar couldn't think of a better way to spend the night.

Read on for an excerpt from Kate Baxter's next novel

THE LOST VAMPIRE

Coming soon from St. Martin's Paperbacks

"Aren't you eating?" she asked without making eye contact. "I don't believe for a second that a little bit of blood is enough to keep you full."

"I don't need food." Saeed drove his point home by letting his gaze wander to Cerys's throat.

"Come on." Cerys pinched a few chow mein noodles between her thumb and finger. She tilted her head back as she brought her hand up and dropped the noodles into her mouth. "Vampires eat. I've seen it."

She remained standing at the bar rather than take a seat at the dining room table. This way, she could keep the countertop between her and Saeed. No need to court disaster and close the gap between them. He mimicked her actions, dipping with his fingers into the box of chow mein. He dropped the noodles into his mouth and chewed. "I can eat. But I can't digest food unless I've ingested blood first."

Interesting. Cerys had always suspected as much but it wasn't like she'd ever asked anyone about it. "But you like food, right?" She found her curiosity getting the better of her. "It tastes good and everything."

Saeed grabbed a fork from the drawer and scooped a bite of fried rice from one of the boxes. "It does," he agreed. "But in truth, no food on the face of this earth can compare to the taste of your blood."

Cerys's stomach did a back flip and a pleasant rush of heat circulated through her limbs before settling low in her abdomen. His blatant statement shouldn't have turned her on, but her thighs were practically quivering from the implication in his words. Damn. It didn't take much for him to get under her skin.

"What does it taste like?" She blurted out the question before she could think better of it. "I mean, besides like you're sucking on a dirty penny."

Saeed's brow crinkled. "Not to me." His gaze met hers and held it. "Your blood is the sweetest ambrosia and I am drunk on it from only a sip."

Gods. Cerys's breath left her lungs in a rush. It was a wonder she hadn't burst into flames. Each word from his lips brought with it a silent challenge, daring her to deny the truth. Saeed was all dark, sultry heat. Midnight in the dead center of summer. "You had more than a sip earlier," she replied wryly. "You seem fine to me."

"You think so?" Saeed's gaze roamed slow and hungry up the length of Cerys's body. "I'm quite drunk. And eager for another taste."

Oh boy. She never should've come back here with him. She was in way over her head and so close to the point of not caring that she could easily stay here all night, Rin's curfew be damned.

"Not sure I can keep up with the demand." Cerys gave a nervous laugh. "You might have to find yourself another blood donor."

Saeed's expression grew serious. "No." The finality in

that one word was like a fist to Cerys's gut. "Yours is the only blood I thirst for. I will pierce no other's flesh but yours."

Heat pooled in Cerys's stomach and she swallowed against the lump that rose in her throat. She couldn't deny that she wanted him. In fact, she hadn't wanted anything or anyone more in centuries. Saeed watched her with the intensity of a predator. His dark eyes drank her in and she suppressed a pleasant shudder. What would it be like to belong to a male like Saeed? Not as a slave. Or a possession. Not because of her power or the influence she could gain for him. She wanted to know what it would be like to belong to someone for no other reason than she wanted it that way and gave herself freely to him. She'd felt so helpless for so long. Was she brave enough to go after something she wanted, if only this once? Gods, all she wanted was to *feel*.

"Well . . ." The words tumbled from her lips as though she had no choice but to say them. "Are you going to kiss me or what?"

Saeed rounded the kitchen island in the space of a heartbeat. The moment his arms went around her she melted against him, as though her entire body had released a sigh of relief. His mouth claimed hers and Saeed swallowed an indulgent moan. His cock hardened to stone, pressing uncomfortably against his jeans. The hot lust that coursed through him was undeniable. Only his mate could evoke such a response. He refused to believe otherwise.

Her hands reached behind him. One gripped the fabric of his shirt at his shoulder blade while the other dove into his hair. Cerys pressed her body tight against his, grinding her hips into the hard length of his erection. The urgency of her actions spurred Saeed on. His tongue thrust past her lips to taste the honeyed sweetness of her mouth and in the process, one fang nicked delicate skin.

Dear gods! The taste of her blood had no equal. Unable to resist, he took her full bottom lip between his teeth and bit down harder, opening four tiny punctures. He kissed her deeply, his tongue dancing against hers as her blood drove him into a frenzy.

"Saeed." Her voice was a breathy murmur against his mouth. He'd longed to hear her say his name, infused with passion. With longing. With want. Instead, he heard nothing but quiet desperation. Pain. Loneliness. Unfulfilled need. "Please." The plea speared into his heart like a stake. "Don't stop."

He had no intention of stopping. Of giving up his quest to make her unequivocally his. Saeed reached for the hem of her shirt and broke their kiss only long enough to pull the garment over her head. The faintest luster painted her skin, so much like the glitter of starlight he beheld in her light eyes. For a moment, Saeed could do nothing but stare. The swell of her petite breasts peeking out from the cups of her bra begged for his touch. She arched her back and pressed against him once again as though to offer her permission.

He craved her like a drug. And he feared he would never find satiation.